The Devil's Land

The Devil's Land

Sunday Ahuronyeze Abakwue

Xlibris

Copyright © 2010 by Sunday Ahuronyeze Abakwue.

First printing

Library of Congress Control Number:		2010909064
ISBN:	Hardcover	978-1-4535-2475-6
	Softcover	978-1-4535-2474-9
	Ebook	978-1-4535-2476-3

All rights reserved. No part of this book may be reproduced or transmitted in any form or by any means, electronic or mechanical, including photocopying, recording, or by any information storage and retrieval system, without permission in writing from the copyright owner.

This is a work of fiction. Names, characters, places and incidents either are the product of the author's imagination or are used fictitiously, and any resemblance to any actual persons, living or dead, events, or locales is entirely coincidental.

This book was printed in the United States of America.

To order additional copies of this book, contact:
Xlibris Corporation
1-888-795-4274
www.Xlibris.com
Orders@Xlibris.com
82649

Dedicated To

All The Native American-Indians
From Whom The Land Was Taken

A Few Thoughts Before You Read:
And, Please Set Yourself At Liberty To Form Your
Personal Opinion After Reading The Express Thoughts
And The Contents Of This Book

FOOD FOR THOUGHT:

"We pledge allegiance to the flag of the United States—and to the Republic for which it stands . . . One nation under God . . ." But, in the Bible, Exodus 20: 4-5 God said "Thou shalt not 'pledge an allegiance' to anything, in heaven above, nor on earth, below. For I am a jealous God."

Regarding numerous imperialist wars~the same God warns in Isaiah 59:3-4 "For your hands are defiled with blood, and your fingers with iniquity; your "media have spoken" lies and your "religious men have" muttered perverseness.

None of "your racist system" of justice is just. "Hence, in Matthew 5: 13b "You are now the salt which has lost its flavor. Therefore, despite your grand deception, you are now good for nothing." And in verse four of same Isaiah 59, God went ahead to accuse them "You put your trust in your deadly weapons; yet you claim yourselves as my children. Repent now, or else be damned forever more."

*****

"THE HIGHEST DUTY OF THE WRITER IS TO REMAIN TRUE TO HIMSELF AND LET THE CHIPS FALL WHERE THEY MAY"

JOHN F. KENNEDY, AN AMERICAN PRESIDENT

****

"THE BURDEN OF MY LIFE IS TO LIVE IT IN SUCH A WAY THAT I MAY BECOME A LIVING SYMBOL OF ALL THAT IS BEST IN CHRISTIANITY AND IN THE LAWS, CUSTOMS AND BELIEFS OF MY PEOPLE"

—DR. KWAME NKRUMAH, FIRST PRIME MINISTER OF GHANA

******
****

"I WRITE BECAUSE I SAW THE VISION TO WRITE."

—AUTHOR, S. A. ABAKWUE

****

"If we're wrong, God Almighty is wrong . . ." remarked Dr. Martin L. King Jr. regarding the brutal state of prejudice in the United States

—Eye On The Prize

*****

Micah 5: 13-15—"Thy graven images also will I cut off, and thy standing images out of the midst of thee; and thou shalt no more worship the work of thine hands.—verse 14, "And I will pluck up thy groves out of the midst of thee; so will I destroy thy cities. Verse, 15, "And I will execute vengeance in anger and fury upon the heathen such as they have not heard."

******

Nehum 2:1-3—"Woe to the bloody city! It is all fill of lies and robbery; the prey departed not; The noise of the whip, and the noise of the rattling of the wheels, and of the prancing horses, and of the jumping chariots. The horsemen lifted up both the bright swords and the glittering spears; and a great number of carcasses; and there is none end of their corpses; they stumble upon their corpses."

******

"IN AMERICA, RACISM IS OUT OF CONTROL; ONLY THOSE WHO LOVE IT, PRACTICE IT, AND THOSE WHO HAD NEVER LIVED IN AMERICA WILL FOREVER BELIEVE THAT AMERICA IS 'A LAND OF OPPORTUNITY' HOWEVER, THE GREATEST 'OPPORTUNITY' IN AMERICA IS THE 'OPPORTUNITY' FOR BLACKS TO SUFFER"
**—Mrs. Ala-Oma, a white,
female attorney married to a black African.**

******

"A nation that continues, year after year, to spend more money on military defense than on programs of social uplift is approaching spiritual death."
**—Martin L. King told the so called
'One Nation Under God"**

CHAPTER ONE

There were many things calling the wretched immigrants toward the American Paradise—flashy cars, sex, glamorous life styles, pretty houses, and, indeed the lady of liberty.

The new immigrants were so many. Some of them were women, and many were men. There were children among them. Many of the women were pregnant and they were looking forward to the day their offspring would become new American citizens, even before them.

Even as they walked through the tunnel to face the beautiful immigration officials, their gaze could not even evade one thing so phenomenal—the greatest idol of the civilized world. They looked up, and indeed, there it stood: a robust, female idol, the Monarch Of Freedom. Here was the thing that embodied beauty, wealth, dream, fantasy, and even glory.

Here was the idol, eternally married to the Old Glory, the triple-colored, star-spangled piece of cloth which every American would readily die for, to uphold its universal glory.

The idol of liberty was quite majestic in outlook: She held her eternal touch of liberty in her right hand, waving its pleasant light for the miserable immigrants to see the way. She needed not the rich nor royal; but, she simply asked the helpless, weak, and wretched to come over to the American shore.

Even as she waved her light, indeed, there was an aura of maternal compassion about her. This, indeed, was self-evident in the way she called them. She begged them to just come. She wanted

11

them. She needed them. And, she had no desire to ever reject them in her Freedom Of Paradise, or, the Great American Paradise Of Freedom. And, in honor to her invitation, so universally made, in thousands, even in millions, the weak, wretched, and even the helpless thronged through, to embrace the light, to embrace her liberty, to hear, up close, her sermon of liberation, to taste her freedom, and to enjoy, and to have everything the American Paradise had to offer.

Indeed, they entered America, the greatest Continental Country of a phenomenal kind. They were heading for the pictorial waves of excellence—a nation where twinkling lights of freedom dotted across the American sky. Indeed, they were heading to the glory made by human hands. Indeed, they were bound for a nation of fantasies—in there they would enjoy all kinds of sexual experimentations. They would have to enjoy or endure the glories of racial prejudice. They would enter a stage in life in which one man would be exalted on the basis of his skin pigmentation, while the other would be thrown down the pit of the American dream. They would see the unfair advantage everywhere in America; they would see it deeply rooted in American culture; and they would see how it is supported by the American prejudice.

While they saw the light, they observed something even better: The lady of liberty was upsizing the American dream; she was extending her reach, bringing those whose dreams were dead in their homes of domicile, to a land where their dreams would arise and live again. She invited the Zulus from Africa, and up to the Armenians in the old Soviet Union. She was open and limitless. Lo and behold, the Black Shakas, Imperial Sheiks, Ominous Shaitans, and even the Great Red Czars were happy to honor her invitation.

On the other side of the American shore were the deprived Mexicans, who, soon after they crossed over, would be mercilessly beaten by the element of border immigration police force. The message they received was direct and crystal clear: the American dream was not meant for them. And, it did not matter, of course, though their land was part of the American dream. And, there was no way smart Uncle Sam would allow them to re-claim the land which was taken from them by the power of the big stick.

The police people who manned the Mexican borders were armed to shoot. They ranged in ranks from Field Marshals to the Field Privates. Their weapons of border patrol were awesome and war-like. They were trained so well. And, their unique trainings were colored with variety of American ribbons: In there were so many ribbons of racism—Some were red, black, yellow and mostly white. And the ribbons of racism wore their colorful stripes. And each ribbon held its armor—a gun, a handcuff, a baton—all the symbols of the powerful stick.

They fenced the borders, and dug bathyal zones. They patrolled the borders in air, by land, and even on the high seas. They were armed with helicopter gunships. Electronic sensors were buried deep along the border lines—to detect those who would venture to dig an underground tunnel, to cross over.

Also, there were mounted, up high, many giant rotating electric search lights, switched on day and night, to control and check on their zeal to cross over.

There were millions of other people who were looking for an opportunity to breathe free—and the lady with a Freedom-Touch, in her right hand, offered them the needed respite. They too came over, and entered in. And, they too passed through into her bosom, by way of the Great Lady Of Liberty.

As they got in, they began to search for the El Dorado; but, she offered them hope . . . work . . . and an open space. She asked them, challenged them to conquer the new frontiers. She showed them land to be cultivated, wilderness to be subdued, and even natives to be killed along the American way. She raised a Moses among them, and she inspired many Joshuas to lead the bloody, and noble way.

The frontiers were many and totally varied. There arose a call to vanquish the natives, and in the process, claim their primitive inheritance. The weak and wretched were eager to answer the call, made by the blood-stained holy idol of freedom. Indeed they did. And they began to send the natives back to their ancient ancestors. The hand of the terrible idol was with them.

She was powerful, thirsty for the blood of the natives. She used the chosen Moses and the American Joshuas to inspire the weak and wretched. In turn, the weak and wretched became fighting machines, the war-lords of the American wilderness.

Again, the benevolent idol struck another challenge. From her Holy Island went forth a command to cross over. She ordered them to chain black Africans; and, to bring them over for a term of prolonged servitude. Again, the holy warriors and their war lords stood, and they crossed over, and did her a marvelous proud.

At one peak of the Atlantic was a Crown who controlled the wealth of the American Empire. He was a King of a small nation whose geographical map looked like a yawning cat, or even a smart, sitting and barking monkey. There was nothing so good about the nation. But, the way he was ruling the world was very disgusting to the Noble Idol Of Liberty.

Now, the Majestic Lady wanted this part of the Atlantic to become her own dominion. She knew the Crown Of England; also, she was aware that she would not have her way without a war of miracles, and a fight of a noble cause.

Once again there was a bell of freedom, a call to revolt against the Imperial Crown. And again, the weak and wretched souls formed their own army and surprised the most powerful army in their war of liberation.

Again, the Grand Cosmic Spirit began to guide the obedience of the weak and wretched souls on their path to total liberation.

***

The face of the devil was pretty, bright and quite inviting. With furious force, the future slave of eternal damnation inspired the abominable idol to set up his great kingdom from a bright coast to a far away shining sea.

There, surrounded by a huge body of water, was a temple built on a medium-sized piece of land. Right there was the home of the real American god. In there was the dwelling place, the magnificent symbol of the leader of the eternal damnation. His symbol, a sexy lady with a glowing touch in her hand.

The king of hell was pretty smart in the way he set up his earthly capital. The Kingdom was a paradise prepared by the fallen angel; a rebel who fell on an earthly zone. His kingdom was decorated; it was beautiful and very glamorous.

Even as the devil made some progress, the King of England became edgy. He foresaw a drastic reduction in his Empire, an Empire that did not enjoy a setting sun. He saw a holy Sampson, called Washington, a Moses who was ready to deliver. He saw fate handing over to him a blank check worth a dead pledge. He saw the Sampson edenize the Crown's Colonies with Zealful aim to usurpation.

As time passed by, the King saw his red-coated men fight one losing battle after another. He saw the French-carved idol praised as "god of liberty." He saw in her a vainful pledge of a remarkable proportion.

As he reasoned, thought about it, he got furious that an ordinary idol should be used in challenging his God given authority. He wondered why the idol should be revered as a monarch. Then, envy began to take care of his judgement.

Even as it did, his contempt grew within him.

"That bloody French idol is the symbol of all that ail in my Colonies, I will fight France after this war."

King George's wife was an intemperate woman. And her violent temper was ready to show off. To the then British, the man and his wife were odd Couple who were not even fit to rule the world, anyway. They quarreled often; fought often, and always reconciled their differences by having a prolonged sexual intercourse right after each fight. Once, before they jumped into a bed of reconciliation, the temperamental Queen asked her man.

"How do you feel?"

"Bad," he replied.

"Then, go and grab a machete and knock off my head," she jeered.

"No, I won't," he nagged back at her.

"Why not? Are you not the King?"

"Though I'm drunk dear, I won't behead you till you do something that deserves such punishment," he replied.

This time, though, a group of hooligans had done something that deserved such punishment. Of course, they knew what they were doing. As such, they pledged their lots, future, happiness or punishment in their declaration.

King George's wife was filled with rage. Her heart was burning with the fuel of great sadistic lamentation.

"How could he do that?" she complained tearfully to her husband. "We made him a Captain of a royal regiment. We knighted him, an Order of the British Empire. We did everything we could for him."

"Yes dear . . ." he interrupted her.

"Guess that lunatic is ungrateful to the core," she filled the cup of matrimonial conversation interruption.

"My dear," her husband, King George ventured to explain, "people can change. It's hard to keep the subjects loyal all the time."

"What does he want?" Mrs. George asked, angrily.

"Me thinks he wants to rule an empire."

CHAPTER TWO

The King of Hell was terribly mad at the King of England. For sure, the Englishman had offended him in a number of ways—Didn't the British Crown build many churches for all his subjects to serve the very enemy of Satan? Was the English not the earthly head of the Anglican Churches? And, were not the people's religious services making the Crown of demons uneasy every time?

All things given into consideration, the King of England had declared himself an earthly enemy of the Prince of demons. Really, the fallen angel was ready for a fight. It was not the first time the English Monarch had insulted him. He remembered how an English Monarch stamped a royal seal on a book that belonged to the arch-enemy of Satan.

"I've had enough of that British Monarch. He thinks he's too big. I'm going to trim him. I'll reduce him to the point he'd become a laughingstock. I'll put shame on him. I'll make him kneel before those he once ruled."

Now he was determined to really humiliate the British King. He planned his actions, and deployed his pointmen as some useful fronts.

He used the French gift as a decoy, He inspired the immigrants for a holy war. He armed them with zeal, and the word "freedom" as their battle cry. In the name of "freedom" the hand of the devil was against the British Empire. But, in the name of 'dignity' the British Crown kept on fighting a losing war.

The devil used the symbol and the idea. The King of England fell for the shining trap.

"Sometimes we have to learn the tricks of the criminal just to make the criminal know that crimes do not pay. A criminal can run, but he will never hide. Even if he hides, the better, there he will never escape. We'll seek him out, and dig him out," the King remarked. But, the King was fighting the Lord of Unrighteousness with an inferior hand.

He assembled a first-class navy. Then, the King was confident of victory. He sent word to His Majesty's First Admiralty, Lord Cornwallis, to expect a powerful reinforcement. He was confident that this awesome fleet would subdue the American Moses and his rebels, thus reclaim the falling part of his huge Empire.

While these men and their weapons were in the middle of the Ocean, the devil raised a tremendous tempest. The war ships were met with the furies of the demons. And the tempest did not give way for an atom of rescue transship; for the Lord of Evils took over the whole operation. At last, the awesome promise, men and weapons of British might, all perished in the Ocean.

The Devil was happy with his victory; but, the King was awfully humiliated by the fateful turn of the event.

"That kind of thing happens once in ten million years. Oh God of Mercy; oh my God of England, how could such a tempest claim my entire fleet?" the King of England cried, unwilling to be consoled by a band of his noble men. "Oh God of Mercy; oh my God of England, how I wish I died in their stead." Tears filled his face. Unusually dejected, he was sorrowful, lamenting and hysterical.

***

The King of England was unusually cool when he learned that Cornwallis had surrendered to a ragtag force led by an American rebel, George Washington. Just a few weeks earlier, he had allowed the Ocean to bury thirty-five thousand of his best naval men on one day. Of course, each of these did not even receive a ceremonial good-bye by their loved ones, nor the naval gun-salute. They perished like the Egyptian chariots at the rage of Moses' rod, swallowed up in the Ocean like a bunch of black slaves whose angry enslavers had consigned to be jettisoned.

It was a Manifest Destiny whose infamous cargo overwhelmed the king with a culpable lamentation. And just in a swing of things, a hero of a honky tank of fate was born. The rebellious Moses became a leader of a new nation. There, a British nobleman, a marquis was humiliated for the ceremony, all at the foothills of Virginia's Yorktown.

There, the once arrogant Charles, the Marquis of the New World, signed the King's properties over to the American Moses, who was so elated.

Just at the same blink of the benevolent devil, George Washington became more powerful than His Majesty.

And there, to the remaining British Empire, the one-toothed Moses became a single threat to the King's peace. To the niche made out to rebel against the King's law, the holigans who beat the British Crown, he was, indisputably, an incorruptible champion.

However, to the Queen, the English King's bride whose luxury knew no bound, America, stupid. To the future rebels of other nations, George was similar to proverbial excreta fluid, albeit admirably, which the British King was disgusted at, and unable, and even unwilling to touch.

And, to his fellow rebels, the elements of the old thirteen colonies, he was an embodiment of a new nation, a founding father, a symbol, the ultimate, the wheeler and dealer of A COLORFUL AMERICA.

***

When the one-toothed United States President, Captain George Washington, took over through rebellion, hardly did he know then that daughters of his black concubines would, one day, tell on him. In those days, however, his secret affairs were so many.

There were so many of his true love who had him looking, even enjoying, at then present, the futuristic sexual revolution. He had the fragile, rose-colored glass, all the time. And, he enjoyed every facet of America to the fullest.

All his black concubines were a pleasant purple rose; each, hanging in an hour-glass. They could not talk because they were slaves in every way. Unbeknown to him, he was setting up his future offsprings for a remarkable, futuristic prostitution. By his deeds he set the stage. In there was the origin, and even a legacy and an American dream. The tales were long and many. There were stories full of fun. There were tales of colorful romance, many a romance as colorful as America itself. And each was unique, even as unique as the leader with one tooth.

Prejudice was a hush-hush affair. It was an orphan boy, a prodigal child to be seen, used, and not allowed to talk.

It was a harnessed antelope, a celestial imprecation, even an anathema to hear him talk about his condition. White folks then were considered as the true human beings; while the slaves, even the natives, were relegated as 3/5 of normal homo sapiens.

The aging Crown heard about it; but, he was now powerless. After all, he had his own black slaves who served in several places of his remaining Empire. This time though, he consigned his thought to reminiscence.

"What can I say?" he remarked.

"Even on their stony conscience, however, their crimes of prejudice have also been written in stone," she answered him. The great woman, the wife of English Crown, was a woman so set in her iron mind. She was the real ruler of England, and her husband knew that. The sun had neither right nor might to set in the British Empire. And the sun knew it. Since the man was less tough-minded, regarding the need to recapture the colonies from Captain Washington, therefore, his wife did not buy his opinion.

And, it was just that. She believed that America was forever part of their Empire. She still held that Lord Charles Cornwallis, the Marquis of the New World, was always in charge of the British-American Colonies.

She was a woman drunk with delusion, a woman of fantasy who refused to let go. She had a mighty urge to become the warrior-woman. In her heart was the fighting fire of the female Shaka-Zulu, with the deadly soul of the Shaitan. She felt that a new God of the Empire had made her the Queen of the fading Empire. She had to take over.

It was a detailed royal decision, conceived in hatred and resentment; and, the devil was in the detail. She resented the one-toothed giant. And, she hated him.

She was very protective of her husband's Kingdom which the colorful rebel had resolved to divide. She was always dressed in thirteenth century costume hardly altering her customary uniform to fit into four centuries ahead of her attire.

His palaces were rich and lovely. Virtually one fourth of the world's wealth was greedily stored in them, all for her enjoyment. No wonder, she did not want to share them. Neither did she care.

Her husband's men-in-arms had made a world of changes, changes far reaching to the point that the sun did not set in their world. Then, the world was hers and her husband's football field—to play with as they saw fit. She had seen the good things, and the good things were not meant to be shared with the subjects.

To protect her own world, to change was unnecessary. A hell-bent, lunar-lover kind of a woman, a woman who would not hesitate to use her feminine charm to induce her king to conquer more Kingdoms, killing innocent people, shedding British blood, all to her selfish aggrandizement.

Now that things had changed, she was stubborn to change with her changed world. She began to transfer the rage she had for American Moses unto her love, the British King. She began to dislike, to hate, and even to disobey him. She refused to do-si-do with him anymore, unless he did something to reclaim the lost part of the Empire, for her.

She did not see the future, that her world would crack deeper, and crumble even more. And, she did not know that rage could not help; her desire, a lost dream.

CHAPTER THREE

Once again the One who has ninety-eight names plus I AM was gravely offended by the acts of the King of Unrighteousness. He warned him, time and again, to repent, to desist, and to permanently put a stop to the whole thing. But, the devil carefully increased his ugly reputation.

Then, the One with ninety nine names asked Christ to give Satan a new name—Christ obeyed. Again the evil one earned another badge of dishonor in heaven—a new acronym, DBG—a detestable compound term—Damned by God. The angels on high were completely made aware of the new code for the Prince of Darkness.

The Most Precious lived in heaven; but, his enemy, Satan, cunningly set up his own Kingdom and its Capital at the very footrest of God. From here the devil planned to launch a burning fire on the feet of God.

God looked down. He saw the handiworks of Satan. Then God's anger was kindled. He remembered how the evil one plotted to overthrow Him. He remembered the war in heaven and the wars the devil had staged against His weak children. He remembered the first and the second world wars, and the players who became the agents of the demon. He remembered the Jewish graves and the black slaves who were thrown into the Ocean. He remembered a war against the Church. And then, God decided to crush the works of the devil. And as God planned to fight from the place on high, the true King of this world was ready to fight from earth below.

With speed, the acts of the demon became an epic testimony to the evil that the once glorious Lucifer had developed an unrepentant heart. The stony heart of the Lucifer was purely made of insoluble materials. And not even God had the means to change the heart of the damned one.

The devil set up his tents of battle and established his deceptive points of contact. Among them were the occult mini-kingdoms, klan's groupings, a house of desires, temples of unholy dreams, halls of greed, and chambers of unrighteousness.

He opened his gate from a corner of his kingdom, and closed a border against those who would oppose him.

He named his new comers 'the new immigrants' and those who had not bowed to the magnificent sexy idol—the illegal aliens. He set up a system, and a pattern to his segregation. He established a code of human colors, and a way with eugenics. By his command there emerged an authentic euthenics, a superior breed of people who were simply the outgrowth of the mating between the daughters of men and the sons of the fallen angels.

The devil saw his children that they were beautiful and long-haired. He loved them, and he adored them. He breathed in them a desire to rule. These were trained to go to all corners of the world with a mission to conquer and rule by any means necessary. They developed their own culture, their thought pattern, and even their own attitude. They loved sex and they glorified it. Everything about them became their own way of life—a custom and tradition so impressive that the devil became very proud of them.

***

He became a prisoner of fate and a victim of ill-circumstance. He loved the stand of his own conscience, but the power against his own conscience was too much. He asked himself a million whys, all to no avail. He became very bitter, and he hated God.

THE DEVIL'S LAND

He felt disbelieving in God would convince Satan to let go of him. But, more misfortunes pursued him, daily.

Wherever he turned, he was bound to face nothing but one form of bad luck or the other. He looked around; he saw those who were less righteous, so blessed, yet, less deserving. As he saw them and their better conditions, he felt betrayed by an ungrateful destiny. He began to think. While he was thinking, he felt, and even began to believe that things would get better for him. But, he was still an unwelcomed guest in the American stream.

"I fell like something has singled me out. I don't know why and I don't know what," he complained everyday. "I think something is wrong. I know so because it's obvious." His complaints were a mirror-image of his state of mind, an angry mindset, even a psychological conscript, a clear reflection of a mind filled with upright indignation, and total uncertainties.

He saw himself a radical element, a rebel in the bliss of unrighteousness. There he felt the blood of an ancient zealot, a bloodstone of Zionic Moses, an Onyx of invincible power, running through him.

There he imagined himself face to face, in hand to hand combat with the odd elements. He transformed, and became a new Biblical Job in his spirit.

There he became a changed man with a new attitude. There he faced the plagues of Biblical Job as they relentlessly tormented him. Even as he faced his elements, he invariably became a shining chalcedony, the real Biblical Job in the midst of ignorant counselors.

Again, there was a special anger against God who'd allowed the devil to torture and humiliate him. There he recognized an unfair finger of God's hand.

"How come the righteous has to suffer just for God to show Satan that the righteous is God's faithful servant?" he asked himself time and again. "Does it make sense?" he continued to ask. "If so, what's the point? I just don't get it." His bitterness mounted with each quest for rational explanation. Here was a fine Muslim in a loose Christian nation under God. Here was an African in America. Here was a man who believed in One and only One God. And here was the man who wanted to fight a war for that same God. And, here was a man who would never change. And, as he saw it, things here had to change real fast.

Here was a man in the devil's land—a lonely dove in the mouth of fire-breathing dragon, a braveheart in the heart of incurable prejudice.

He saw racism in its total glorification. He heard his new name, nigger, and was expected to nigger with it. Right there racism began to teach him where he really belonged—that he was a rejected nigger in a calculus of insolence.

While the servants of prejudice endeavored to inscribe his new name on him, he himself endeavored to fight back. As he fought, he remembered his own God. And, as he remembered, he thought. While he thought, a new question erupted from his questioning mind: how could he wage a war against a land that belonged to God, God's enemy, and even many other powerful Gods?

He saw the picture of his own desire. He was afraid that he'd be known as a terrorist. He just could not do it. He saw the wisdom of Christ in that the weeds and the true crops should grow together till the time of harvest.

There he saw the rationale, the meaning, and the wisdom behind it.

He became a victim of collective kiss, a child of a wounded hawk. He was alone in the land, a lonely soul in a war zone.

There was fear; there was also joy watching the mood of each other in his throbbing heart, a pre-contract pre-contemplating, a raccoon dog of the heart with the speed of cougar and the power of an angry elephant. He was a young man who was going to go into romance with a red-hot rock. Beneath his smiling face was an urgent craving and a tearful plea of desperation.

THE DEVIL'S LAND

"Ewo! The land of serpents," the African immigrant cried. "Had I known, oh had I known, I wouldn't have come to the land of serpents." His bitterness registered his sorrows all over his face.

His heart was pregnant with an overwhelming state of sadness. In it was a note of omen, a rapid oculus of doom. A forlorn look of his tear-filled eyes marked him out as, and even like a withering tree planted in an impoverished island, an odd island surrounded by a rich and a mighty sea. There his petrified heart was self-evident, a starved soul swallowed in whole and drained by the waters of starvation. He was a man who had lost every hope.

***

He was heading to a country that knew how to make, but hardly observed the wedding promise.

He was to see divorce at its zenith of success, kids with pride of arrogance, guns in schools, and elderly relegated as useless antics of decadence. He was heading to the bowl of prejudice, bosom of materialism, and most crime-infested part of the world.

Nothing had prepared him for what he'd see. He'd see temples dedicated to the services of the ancient serpents. He'd see free people bow down and give worship to the serpents, and some of the snakes would turn around and bite them. He'd see crafty robbers parading themselves as agents of assistance. He'd see snow and less rain, snowflakes and less rays of sunshine.

He'd see smart robbers defend their loots with sharp guns, hired hands, and even with their own blood. He'd see the people under God who had no regard for human life. He'd notice divisive deities at work in the society.

He'd see cults of money in every segment of the society.

He'd find himself in a position to document evil deeds of the respectable men of the society. In their deeds he found falsehood.

In there he saw a world of opposites, receptive public who had been deceived for so long. He saw chains of grave injury done to the masses who had completely placed their lifelike trusts in them.

He'd look at their burdens, which the bearers hardly knew. Then, he'd feel angry, sorry, and even sad for them. He'd see menace in management, lawlessness in the promised-land, church burning and political whiplash, and even dim disclosure of the white crime. Then he'd see those who deceived them in high gear.

"For how much longer would these fools go on believing those who tell them lies?" he eventually asked himself. "It's a pity fools receive their consolation in grand illusion."

Again, he saw the deceived masses rejoice. They were hysterical in the way they were dancing, drinking, and praising in honor of the female idol with a touch of liberty. They were happy because they'd been 'accepted' as new citizens of the great society. They'd passed the tests and were to be fully and wholly absorbed in the segregative melting pot.

"The devil's land," he sneered, "It sucks out here." He looked around, and his entire world was watching him. He felt the rage of a zealot. Then, a different mood took over. The contagious mood of the masses held him and baptized him. He felt like one of them.

He felt like he was on top of the world. The air was breezing around, a tornado which had lost its temperamental rage. He angled his face and looked upward.

Even the birds flying above were in the mood they were enjoying the cool breeze. There, despite the massive number of people, the temperature seemed like a paradise—It was so moderate that even male demons and female angels could have easily fallen in love at its grand spell.

***

Snow had gone. It was spring. The early morning sunshine was twinkling its rays. Right there one could see God's smiling face at

THE DEVIL'S LAND

its best of disposition. There, one could feel God blessing America with the gifts of angels.

And, the gifts were a variety of fantastic, and celestial ecstasies. They danced. They cheered, and they waved the American flag. And their allegiance to it was unshakable.

As they waved, the young man came back to his senses. He was a Muslim who subscribed to Jehovah Witness' teachings in America. His allegiance belonged to none but Allah or Jehovah alone.

"How can I place my allegiance to an ordinary piece of cloth?" he questioned himself. "I will never do that. Even if they kill me. I'll never do that. They're going to see a new Daniel in the den of lions, if it comes to that." It was an angry vow. In him was a sense of righteous indignation.

"America is got to stop deceiving itself and the entire world. What the hell has gone into the heads of so many hypocrites?" he asked himself in an angry mood. "I think, in time like this God is got to stand up and claim their allegiance by thunder from the sky," he said.

He was indeed a very angry young man, a rebel in the midst of flat-allegiance. A pretty woman, a news reporter by profession who was carefully listening and taking notes of his comments drew nearer to him and asked him a question.

"Wouldn't it be nice for you to go to another place and live? Think many true Americans wouldn't miss you very much."

"Yeah, you're a native Indian. This land belongs to you, I know," he returned as his answer to her sarcastic question.

Without further questioning and suggestion, she turned her tail between her legs and walked away.

CHAPTER FOUR

The quest for the expansion of racism was strategized. It was a worldwide drive to spread the promise of race, with tact and vision. The devil, the Lord of the idea, set aside treasures of diamond and trophies of gold for those who would crusade for and with him and his angels in building strata of his Kingdom. It was a trophallaxis, a symbiosis that had to endure, in demonic Capital, even till the end of time.

There was no turning back. And the blood of those who would not comply would have to flow. The Lord of the universe knew the way. He knew the way of the mortals. He was tough; and, he was strict, and stubbornly against any opposition.

He enslaved the sons of disobedience till the day, if ever, their Christ would deliver them. He made it crystal clear that he was, indeed, the Lord of the universe.

He showered his servants with Satanic love—thus, prepared them for the eternal condemnation. He used the power of the spangled Octopus and the voice of the blood-stained sword to sound the charge and to spread his mission. And, he used the terrible blood of the Old Glory to glorify his status.

He made the terror of his sword felt everywhere; and, his might known in all corners of the universe.

He was prepared to receive his obedient children with the soft-hand of a maternal angel. However, those who took side with the power of disobedience, he made them pay dearly. He took charge and received them with the rage of his roughness.

He played a loving angel on his faithful followers; and, he played the hateful devil, he truly was, on those who really opposed him and his mission. As he drove down the Queens, and earthly majesties who stood on his way, an earthly heaven could not stop him.

He even made clear through his actions—Should Christ come down again from heaven to oppose him—that he would have no choice but to crucify him for the second time.

From heaven God looked down. From heaven He declared that Lucifer was full of wickedness. There, God's children were ridiculed before God. In there was the unwritten lampoon of divine brevity, even practical lampoon of human righteousness.

Even so, the earthly woes were the preludes to the evil things. And, the trickster of eternal age was up to his tricks eternal. He worked harder at each passing moment with a view to offend God. He worked on the smart ones, gave them all, and wasted them. He went to the smarter ones, gave them wealth, gave them fame, and at last, gave them death. He went to the smartest folks, and seduced their prurient interest.

As he did, he got them. He influenced them to run their brilliant blood to the prurient waters of sin. He gave them his bread; and they ate the bread that the devil baked. The bread of the devil appealed to their hearts, their base nature, and even the untouchable layers of their prudent walls. There, they sinned.

Cheerful, they were; though they were remarkably brilliant, yet, wasted. They gladly followed the devil; and, with same, they went down the pits dug by the devil too.

He was bound to face a ripe racist in full moon. The racist was female and a true one. He had met her before, but not in this kind of situation. She had just made an innocent black man pay the supreme price. And what she did was a price in her initiation.

She wore her hood and stood guard while her men did the dirty job. Now she was ready to wear her colorful hood, three stripes attached to it. With pride. She had waited for the day. At last she

THE DEVIL'S LAND

got the guy, the 'nigger' whose blood gave her the promotion. She would not have gotten the rank any other way—For the blood of her own kind, a white fellow, would have been too sacred. And that alone would have been a sacrilege.

The right blood for her initiation was the blood of a black man; and, nothing more. And, the blood of an Indian, or some of the Godless commies who migrated from Asia Minor, would have served the same purpose.

Now she was very happy. Her childhood friends had done it several times. Some of them had made it to the ranks of a Grand-Dragon. For some time it seemed she was a failure, left out, an outcast who could not even secure the head of one of the foolish niggers roaming around, the hopeless niggers who were not even protected by the law.

In those days, the shameful days prior to this day, she felt like a total failure, a lazy lioness in the den of fattened cows.

The bells of liberty were ringing around the world, and devil, the owner of the land was hearing them. He knew what it was all about, and he wanted to define it in his own term.

He came up, dedicated to the proposition that freedom demanded a concept of ownership. That one's belongings could range from non-living to even living things. That one should be free to exploit his belongings to his better advantage—That such issue as ownership of slaves was fine and normal. That just as a cattle rancher could own and use his livestock. So would a slave owner over his slaves—That he was free to even kill them at his own volition.

With tact and vision he carefully injected this definition into the minds of Grand Dragons. The woman had learnt it, but she lacked the innate motivation.

"Please any inconvenience is regrettably yours," she mockingly received with the man she had just betrayed. She had carefully

33

lured him to his doom. First, she invited him for dinner, in her house. At first, he was quite suspicious, being a black man. But, she carefully calmed him down.

"Isn't there any way blacks and whites could get along?" she posed a mind-twisting question. And the guy fell for it like a bear at the thought of a bee's honey—not minding that the bee could sting to defend its precious stuff.

Ala-Ọma, the African, hardly knew he was now in a dangerous land. He was just driving his car, F.O.R.D, found on the road dead, when, indeed, the car died on him. He checked the fuel tank, his fuel tank was half-full. The engine oil was filled to its tank's brim. 'What then was wrong?' he wondered. His white American wife was in the car.

He married her in the North, two sweethearts at Harvard Law School; and the first job she got, after passing her bar examination, was down here in the deep South. They had driven for two days, taking turns, in their six week old, spanking new Ford Taurus when, without warning, the car died on the road.

He pushed it off the road, his wife still inside, adjacent to the curb. "Honey, I will walk and look for help," he told her. It was 9:00 pm. on an interstate highway.

"Are you gonna leave me alone here?" she replied in protest. She got angry at him.

"If I stay with you, how can I get help?" he cajoled her. His voice was more of rebuke than consolation. She knew him to be a serious fellow, a man made in Africa whose decision in an emergency was final.

"I can't stop you," she ventured him with a humorous voice.

"Even if you could, I won't allow you," he returned. Then he began to drill her with a set of instructions

"Make sure you stay in the car till I'm back. Wind up the windows and lock them. Stay awake and do not doze off. Otherwise I would not like to pick up your bones when I come back."

THE DEVIL'S LAND

"Go honey, go. Nobody is gonna kill me," she replied in reassurance, knowing that her man cared, loved, and was deadly concerned about her.

Then, the man walked away to look for help.

****

Ala-Ọma walked for about ten yards when he heard a chorus of a loud scream. It was the voice of more than one man.

They were in pain of death. He turned toward his right, lo and behold four men were screaming for their lives, all swaying from the same tree.

He ran toward the scene with the full force of a deliverance instinct. And, as he ran, every step of his being refused to admit, contrary to his name's meaning, Ala-Ọma, that he was indeed on a deadly ground.

His deliverance instinct had already taken over his being and was powerfully pushing him to the rescue. It was an overcall which came from God, the greater enemy of the white dragons.

When he got there, it was indeed too late. The hooded dragons had already poured copious gallons of gasoline on the hanging men, and set them on fire. The agonizing chorus of scream he heard was their last pleas for mercy and even for deliverance.

He stopped running; and he stood speechless. He saw the woman who betrayed one of the four black men. He recognized her. She was the same woman he met at the great idol's Island, years before he left New York to Cambridge to study law. Now there was nothing gentle, womanly about her any more. She was now initiated, and was able and ready to kill, just like all the other hooded dragons.

He cast a chilling look at her face, and, her eyes radiated like the eyes of a lioness which had just taken her first blood. And, his brash presence alone equally cast a cold aura over those who had just taken blood.

"What do you want?" a hooded dragon removed his hood, exposed his face in the process, asked him.

"I have problem with my car on the highway. I need help. It looks like you've just killed your fellow human beings. Why?" he asked back.

"We can't help you. Take a hike nigger," came as a response.

"I won't. I want to know why you killed those four men. I must get the answer before I go away from here," Ala-Ọma resolved and replied.

"Look nigger, if you don't run now we will hang you too," another dragon added, walking toward him with a horse rope in his hand.

"Wait guys, I know him. He's not an American," this time the woman came to the rescue.

"Hey! Wo! Wo! Wo! That's my husband. Don't even think about it." The dragons turned and saw a white woman with a drawn pistol running, in full speed, toward them. "Just go back, now." She ordered the man with rope who was now half-way toward her husband.

"Move backward; any move forward I'll shoot."

Bam-bam!

She fired a couple of warning shots—and the bullets went through the space between the two legs of the man who was a few steps away from her husband.

"Ma'am, we won't hurt him; please don't shoot again."

The dragon raised his hands over his head, surrendered.

She embraced her husband "Honey, are—"

"I am fine, none of them touched me." He looked at her, lovingly. And she kissed him.

"That's gross. How dare you disgrace the white race?" One of the hooded dragons, a tall man, asked her.

"How?" she replied to the dragon.

THE DEVIL'S LAND

"How dare you kiss a damn nigger?'

"Wait a minute," Ala-Ọma's wife, the white woman, recocked her pistol, and walked to the deadly dragon who mocked her. "Remove your hood now, or I'll shoot you," she ordered him.

"Wo!" the man protested.

"Yes, do it. Or you will pay the price for what you did before you go to jail," she was deadly serious. Right there the man removed his hood. As he did, Ala-Ọma recognized him.

"Reverend Jingle!" Ala-Ọma called out to the white man. Amazed, and rather surprised. But the man he called cast his glance downward like a guilty, condemned man. "Why in the name of God did you do this? Answer me. Good God, I can't believe this. Have you thought about the thousands of my people who became Christians just because of you? Oh Reverend, Oh Reverend, why, why in the name of God? Why?"

***

The power of the Fornicatress was ominous. She charged forward toward the wife of Ala-Ọma. But, Mrs. Ala-Ọma saw the danger and raised up her pistol in self-defense.

"Are you gonna shoot me? Go ahead; fuck, you'll see," said the Judress who betrayed one of the four black men.

"Stop right there; or else—" the woman with pistol ordered the dragoness.

"Go ahead; shoot me. I don't give a damn," the betrayress was defiant.

"I'm warning you, last call; one more step and you're dead meat."

"I'm gonna die anyway. I'll better die fighting for what I believe in than die defending it in your court," said the dragoness.

"So you know you're guilty?" Mrs. Ala-Ọma asked her angrily.

"Who really cares?"

"When people like you don't give a damn about what you do, the law has no choice but to put you behind bars," Mrs. Ala-Ọma said.

"I'll kill you," responded the woman who had taken her first blood. She stretched her hands to grab the woman. But her target fired her pistol at her.

"Bam bam!"

Ala-Ọma's wife shot her.And, the dragoness felled on her feet; she wiggled for her last gasp for life-giving air. Then, she gave up the ghost.

Then, the other dragons, her male companions, began to cast an evil eye on the woman who just killed their partner.

"You, big bully; you know that?" A male dragon began to approach her. His face was red with rage.

"No. I'm a woman who fights injustice." She held her pistol ready, mindful of another eventuality. "I don't want to kill you too. But if you push it, I'll send you to your ancestors."

After a while, the Reverend looked up and said to Ala-Ọma "Son, I shall pray for you for this desire to sin." Then he added "Africa is always in my prayers because of all the corruption I witnessed while I was serving the Lord there"

"Reverend," Ala-Ọma replied "You must not pray for him who helped Christ carry Christ's cross to the cross." He paused for a few seconds. "Rather you must pray for those who crucified him." He looked at the Reverend, hoping that his words would reach the soft part of his mission mind. "I must confess, dear Reverend, Africa does no longer need your prayers regarding your corruption. I don't want to be insolent; but, with all due respect, a City alone in America will always be more corrupt than the entire continent of Africa."

CHAPTER FIVE

He was a man who had a pact with prejudice, and he was in love with it. He loved to hate blacks, the niggers who were less refined.

Oftentimes, he led his band of pure race to torch the black churches, Jewish Temples, and Ashrams of Asian-American heritage. These, as he viewed them, were the things that put nothing but blemish on the American order of righteousness.

He was on fire to stamp out the whole things, He paid no heed to the splendid places where white, female prostitutes ritualized their brand of worship. And, when he was challenged, by black preachers, to tear them down, he flatly refused to do so.

To him the issue was not necessarily the moral corruption, but the corruption of skin color. There was no doubt, in his mind, that blacks in Africa should be saved, and blacks in America had to be wiped out—That the salvation of blacks was a burden on the white race, and this had to be through American cultural refinement. And, there was no other way to black deliverance, but through the way of American Christianity.

Set in his way, he had completed part of his mission. Now, he was back in America to fulfil the second half.

America, to him, meant freest expression of pure race. Native Indians, he believed and preached, had to be wiped out. Africans he believed, were meant to remain in Africa; Asians, in Asia; and, the Godless commies, contained forever. Everything, to him, had an order; every race, its place.

SUNDAY AHURONYEZE ABAKWUE

"Our God is God of segregation. He put Africans in the dark continent. He made Asians to remain where they belong. He gave the white race the promised land so that we would live free," said the man, Reverend 'Grand Dragon' Jingle. "I think all non-whites in America have no business in being here. They are trespassing. They should leave. If they don't leave on their own, we shall take care of them.

I think they have to. But, if they refuse to leave, I swear, they deserve to die." Really, these were his angry words before he and his klan-band took away the lives of the four unfortunate men. He was very angry; and, he meant business.

A few moment earlier, he was the prosecutor, the judge and the executioner of his four victims. Now, however, he stood before a different man. A man who stood as his own judge, with a white wife as a bodyguard; here, he saw the wife of his judge, a true wife. A member of his own race, yet, a remarkably different woman. A sharp shooter—who was ready to shoot to protect the black judge.

Again, he lifted up his face. As he lifted up his face to behold his black judge, he felt something anew deep inside. It was a spiritual awakening and some tremors of spiritual bombardment. But, repentance was out of the question. There was no point in a missionary, an ordained Reverend for that matter, to confess shedding some niggers' blood as sin, to an offspring of some heathen converts. To him, the niggers were niggers, and their lives were not worth much.

He had just witnessed the Grand Dragons of Ku Klux Klan lynch four black men. The four blacks were hanged, dangling, suspended by strong ropes tied to four different branches of a mighty tree. The hooded people who killed them did not even show any sign of remorse about it.

Actually, they talked, referring their victims as if those hanging on a tree were less important than useless beasts. "Damn monkeys from African jungles," the Grand Dragon mocked those hanging on a tree.

Before he ordered his group to hang them, he sent some dragons to torch their houses. And, their houses were reduced to ashes. It was all part of Southern hospitality, a subset of Southern way of life. In Mississippi, the home of Ole Miss, Arkansas—the Kingdom of the Ozarks, and here in Alabama, the paradise of prejudice, such a Southern way of life died hard.

The rope of American way petered in and flourished throughout the States of the Bible-belt.

The temple of racism found its better home in Arkansas.

And, the State of the Ozarks saw to it that the 'niggers' and 'damn monkeys from African jungles' had their place as slaves of the superior race.

Here was a man who had been to Asia Minor and Africa on a mission work, now on a new mission. Here was a man who had converted millions of brown and black people for the cross, now on a crusade to crucify them in his own land.

When he was in Asia Minor and Africa, he played the role of an actor, Hollywood type, a maximum pretender, for God's show. Soon after his return to America, he took off his mask, and put on the hood of the devil; then, he began to pursue those who differed from him, all in their mere skin color.

Now the new immigrant, Ala-Oma, saw Dr. Jingle fresh back from mission work; all the trust he had in him suddenly vanished away. He had seen an angel in a pack-meal with the devil. To his sense of decency, a crucible of cross, such act of disloyalty was horrible. The four dead men the man of God and his dragons killed did not close the door of death. It was a fact, first, unbeknown to those who hanged and killed them. Rather, they left it the way it had always been—wide open for the living, to someday, come in.

While they lynched and burnt down, the two huge eyes of nemesis were set upon them. And, by sheer luck and circumstance, Ala-Ọma and his wife, Lucy, became the agents of a higher element.

When Reverend Jingle was a doctoral student at the Southern Theological Institute, his lectures were carefully and tacitly filled with Southern philosophies and idealism: Superiority of whites to any other human race; duty of the whites to save or judge the world; and the Manifest Destiny of the real whites to give the world a sense of direction. There was no way for anyone to change it. It was God who had ordained it from the beginning of holy time.

He was the sign of the coming doom. He was a rebel, a threat to the Southern ways. He had already crossed the line, married a white woman, and seemed hell-bent to the dangerous zone.

Here was an unknown breed from a jungle zone determined to impose integration upon the pure race. Right there the rage of the white race was ready to bum him. He could not be allowed to turn the Southern ways into a house of madness. The Governor of Mississippi was there to organize and close in against him.

The leader of Alabama would never allow that. And, the Lord of the Ozarks would close in, not just with the rage of a bison, but with the sharp jaws of a wild boar. And, if the clash at the Arkansas high did not make him fear the strength of the lake of blood, indeed lynching of him would do it.

He was now in the South, not in the corrupt North—the Northern States where the impure beasts were allowed to roam and rape at random. As they saw him, his thought pattern was illegal. And, the way he behaved was unacceptable. The fact that he was not born in America was not a genuine excuse to spare him. He was a nigger—Being a nigger, he would always be a nigger. And, he would not be accorded the luxury of a different distinction.

THE DEVIL'S LAND

There, in the Great South, segregation was the rule of the law, and the rule to live by. And, the people were quite consistent with it, with their way, and with themselves, with their churches, the dens of their God, where the symbols of eternal segregation of human race, dwelt forever. And, they enforced it with all the piquets of sanctimoniousities.

CHAPTER SIX

The King of England was still holding on to his ancient book, filled with stories of many bloody wars. Defeated Indians remembered it, and could remember their lost ones, warriors beaten at the battle of Fallen Timbers, and their leader, Tecumseh, who was born a Shawandasi, and the sign of the troubled moon.

They came, swiftly, like the speed of wind. They came with big guns, long guns and long knives. The long knives of the white men were eager to take blood.

They shot; they stabbed; and, they desecrated the graves of the Indian dead. The defeat at the Fallen Timber was the last straw of Indian humiliation.

The King of England was thousands of miles away from the natives. He broke his pact with Shawandasi and dishonoured his words before the natives.

Now, the natives believed, the King of England at Windsor Castle spoke the devil's truth. Their aging minds could see further than their doubting eyes. Indeed, all the King's belfries, and men in red-coats, were nothing but the elements of the devil's truth. His beardless men were so weak, even weaker than the native women.

The Puritans, who once served him, could now thumb down their noses before him. "What kind of king could he be that he could be so easily defeated?" wondered the defeated Indians. Now, their will to fight was broken, and their warriors' top-dog, gone.

Resigned and defeated, they were there, in camps and poor caves, chosen by those who defeated them.

They were there, like hopeless kids, abandoned in battle, who had lost track of their consciousness.

Again, the King of England at the Windsor Palace spoke the evil truth. And, his former Puritan subjects in America, once again, were enraged. They organized, twice in the year, to express their views and disapproval.

It was neither the first nor the second time his now ex-subjects had resented him. Beside, it was not in their blood to have a faraway King, a King who lived thousands of miles across the Atlantic, to tell them what to do, even with sheer elements of profound arrogance.

And, it was a matter of pathetic endurance, a resentful one so, that the English Crown had been able to lord over them. They had seen the mask of the Crown. And, they hated it.

"That King doesn't deserve to live," preached Captain Washington at Christ the King Church in Cambridge. His voice was firm, heard thousands of miles across the Ocean. And the King and his Queen mortally disliked him. However, the rebel-preacher was defiant.

They had seen in him a man capable of rebellion. And they had advised the Crown's lord of New England to watch the radical Captain with open eyes.

*****

There was a radar of love in there—love thyself; to hell with others—the American way. The Puritans had used it to their better advantage. But, the Indians were communal people who hunted for food, held land as sacred, and believed that wild-wolf was the everlasting messenger of the Great Spirit.

Their warriors went out and fought their wars, danced their war dances, and won the hearts of the young female Indians, even for marriage. Somehow their struggle against the white man was completely different. They were fighting new enemy: who really scorned them, their war dance, and viewed them as nothing but inferiors. They were fighting the people whose peace on paper was a ploy to deceive, and wipe them out.

Somehow, they had found that their enemy had another enemy; and, they had decided to take side with their enemy's enemy—so as to defeat their enemy.

Somehow, the British warriors and their king in England had made them an unfaithful promise. Now, the Indians were heartbroken, and, were at a loss to trust another white man.

"We told them not to trust the British; but, Tecumseh was bent on a warpath. Now that the British red-coats had deceived them, let's see if their friends would deliver them," said Captain Washington during his initiation as the first ruler of the United Colonies of the Americas.

"Mr. Washington, our great ruler," observed Mr. Jefferson, "every native, I reckon, has body odor."

"Yes, Mr. Jefferson, I've always noticed that," the new leader returned the joke with an equal measure of sarcasm.

"Have you too, Mr. Washington, our most noble leader?" This was from Mr. William Penn, the famous writer of the United Colonies.

"Who wouldn't, Mr. Bill Penn?" answered the new leader.

"Yes, Mr. Washington, our most able leader, everyone of them has his peculiar body odor, except one of them, though, who is odor free. Even so, Most noble leader, once a week he exudes his own peculiar odor which smells like the odor of death." said Mr. Penn.

"Primitive Tecumseh; is that not he?" asked Mr. Washington.

"The primitive warrior; that's he," William Penn responded.

****

It was a nation on the vanishing end, the land of the great Mohigans, Sioux, the tribe of Dakota, the land of warriors and scorpions. It was a land denied of their Sioux City, Sioux Falls, and even their Sioux State. The land of the people who fought the Sioux War.

It was a land its leaders were forced to do jailhouse walking for those who conquered them. Here was a land with new leaders—the men of the devil who conquered them.

The mother of Sodomy was formed as a result of the conquest. It's victory gave birth to a new nation in the hands of the demon. By quest and expansion, wars and bloodshed simply did corrupt the minds of the Puritans. Hatred and prejudice took over the ways of righteousness.

"Put a scorpion in a bottle, all things all the same, the scorpion will remain a scorpion," said a Union soldier, a rough rider of the first calvary infantry. "Kill the scorpion, and its kind, God knows, our new land will be safe for our unborn children, safe for our young women to farm on it; it would be safe for our children to roam and play free. Leave the scorpions, there will be this feeling, a sense of constant danger, due to, alone, the ill-repute of their presence; I reckon, friends, we cannot do otherwise on this score." The 'scorpions' the soldier had in mind were his fellow human beings, the victims of the land-grab. The very victims his Holy God asked him to love, not hate, anyhow, even in the holy book.

The new elements had found their new land; like the Canaanites or Palestinians, their land had to be taken, systematically, by sheer power of bloodshed.

Soon, after the battles and conquests, the vanquished natives found their legs in a new hot soup; the vanquished natives, their remnants, and even the black slaves, had their original names which were too hard for the conquerors and their God to pronounce. So, to help themselves and their own God, the Puritans forced the natives and black slaves to change their native names to the English ones. And, those who refused to comply were forced to do so.

It was the year Kunta Kunte lost his own name. Also, he lost, his language, and even his black African identity. It was the tale of the leaders of the infamy—They came from Europe to Africa, and to the New World.

There, right there was the age in time of the historical approval—the age the African Kings, Queens, and venerable Ashantehene, gave nod to the infamy of slave days.

It was the age in time the American Moses and the African leaders endorsed the infamy—the agreement for the enslavement of more black war-criminals, war-captives, and even the innocents. It was the unfortunate moment when the unfortunate ones passed through the dungeons built for the chained, unfortunate slaves.

The dungeons were many, and were built by Masons and Freemasons with dangerous minds. They were the mansions of doom, laced with chains, for those who were so unfortunate to enter in. The dwellers were the black slaves who went through for the abyss of the darker days. They slept in the dungeons, then, over to the Ocean of uncertainties that led to caves of the New World.

*****
****

The attorney, Mr. Ala-Ọma, saw it all in the New World. He saw the raid of the devil and the anguish of the Indian gods. He was a witness, that the God of the white man was superior—That though the Indians could fight, the gods of war of the Indians were always afraid of the better God of the Puritans.

He was a learner in a foreign land. He learnt new ideas, new legal philosophies, and even new ways of the new culture. He learnt how to approach the system, how to use it, and even how to beat it.

The philosophies of the new land amazed him—When they gave or took bribes, they called that lobbying; when they swindled, they named that con-artistry. A prosecutor, he learnt, was one who could make an innocent fellow look like a condemned criminal.

And a defense attorney, a learned crook who could make a guilty criminal shine like an innocent angel.

He met the people, heard their views and studied their laws, and, he was amazed by it all.

He saw some laddy-dads, and some mellow dudes. He saw some dappy darn kinds of grandpas, too. He enjoyed the triple combo experience.

He heard the mumbo-jumbos copied from Nazism and racial prejudice. He heard some blacks call their fellow blacks, Uncle Toms. He heard whites call blacks, niggers. And, he heard blacks call whites, hunks; and some of those were hunky-dory, indeed.

He heard whites call Asians, 'Godless commies'. He heard Japanese people called 'the Japs'. He heard the Chinese people called a name different from their individual real names.

And, he heard the Jews called 'kikes' and 'swines.' Also, he heard some Europeans and some whites call each other 'pigs'.

He heard the people of Islamic faith being known as 'terrorists'. And, those with free-will to enterprise, he heard them being named 'rogues and imperialists'. And, again, he was so amazed by it all.

Then, he turned to the way Americans saw Africans; and, he was troubled in his heart. He saw no hope but disaster in their consciousness; he saw wars and famines in the realm of the dark continent. Then, he heard American leaders and a lone black American general call Nigeria, 'a land of 419'.

He heard some white women and some black American women show profound interest in the lost continent. There he saw a reason to hope, a hope for the dead bones.

In came the people who were surrounded by nice things. Blessed, they were in every way. Yet, they decided to come. There was a surreal of beauty and elegance about them.

Soon, after their entrance, their names became nothing but a black book. These were the very people whose culture was rooted

THE DEVIL'S LAND

in wishing others, including those they did not even know, nothing but more money, all the time.

Again, the name-calling continued, the New World way. It did not stop. There, the latest arrivals, with their advanced refinement were known as the Taiwanese. Even so, the new culture called them the offsprings of 'pretty demons' and 'saintly monkeys'.

Then, the Russians were hated as deadly blood. And, they were simply called, red.

The sons of 'pretty demons' were too smart for the great insolence. Lost in their gentle innocence, they began to adapt, adopt, and even to fight back. They paid the tabs, and the tabs really tabbed their pride—A double-think in the making; and, like a storm that sought and found thunder, they became a violent tribe of the American thunderstorm.

The squaws dreaded the dragonets. The squaws, oh the dead squaws, the deeds and their desecrated bones. They formed the portraits of the lost wars, the wars that claimed them. They were once a nation. A nation so rich and so diverse; a nation conquered by some stronger wanderers. And the wanderers formed a new nation.

The new nation whose comfort was evidenced in comfort zone. The land of the forgotten race. A land taken by the offsprings of a terrible God. An offshoot which became an offsider, though an offside.

A nation always on the immediate. The people who called the Indian women nothing but 'squaws,' and raped them after killing their husbands. A land where Mongolites had no homes.

****

******

The sons of Old Puritans were people who had no respect for the elegant breed. And, they had a way with their insolence. And, by dint of offended pride, the "Saintly monkeys" could not help but endure great wave of shocking insolence.

Tabbed by the scents of arrogance, the wounds of some healing insolence, the pretty saints began to pay the pippers and to play their games, the old American way. As they played, they noticed, even so, in there was the pride of self-pity, all in the pit of self-arrogance.

As the fumes of the new tradition clapped harder and harder on their pretty faces, they faced a new wave. They felt transported back to the primitive age—the ancient time when barbarians fought with beasts—the ancient moment when powerful men put men of conviction in the dens of lions.

There was no healing balm, nor topical for the troubles of the snow-clad nation. There, they were: some, like demonic monkeys; some, like pretty saints, lost, and no turning back.

There was neither consolation, nor kraals for the wandering ones, wanderers in a violent place.

There was neither acceptance, nor salvation for them. Safe by their own destruction. And the ghosts of their departed loves wept, forever . . . all for their forsaken deliverance. As they wept, they pleaded with the shrines of their great ancestors.

Their righteous voice was a voice of true comfort. They were united voice of action, spelt out real loud. There was an aura of dual role, an air of eerie hope, a comfort too close for comfort; and, a terror too close to call hope.

Beloved, in the great land. The Spirited. And, the pretty ones. The beloved, the offsprings in a hot zone: the prayed-for, and the beloved in tears; beloved, who belied and believed in America, the dream, and in the last hope of the holy terror.

Beloved, who were in the boat of a new land; beloved, who were the Asian generation of a new land; beloved, who saw the temple of God as lamp-post of segregation; the moment of worship as the peak moment of segregation; sermon, the lampoon of holy shrine; a church, a deluxe of prejudice; the church, the center of racial wall; priests, the rapists; altar-boys, the ultimate-victims of religious sexual revolutions.

Beloved, among them who were deceived with promises, confused with empty promises, and even misled with imaginary heaven built with lofty hands of 'sweet-racism'.

Beloved, in a hostile place where smaller gods were more active than the true God. Beloved, living in a God's land where prayers were less useful than the psychic.

Beloved, living in the tent of prejudice, a tent where karma of stereotype held sway.

CHAPTER SEVEN

He was a man gazing at a white fire in a black hell, a guest in a house of madness. He saw. He studied. And, he refused to be seduced. There, he witnessed, was an elbow of prejudice and the lever of hate. Right from that moment, for sure, he began to miss the magical sound of the African rain, even the blooming rays of the tropical flowers. He saw the random logic of prejudice, and even the star-like wave of rejection.

There was a new wave of different music in the air, a second wind on a mission of rescue. The glare of hate, and the power of prejudice were evident. They held one gist in common: that America had no place for a black man.

Africa was told to return home in the lyric. There, in the music, was the tenor of hope, the manifesto of vision. There was the hope for those who would dare cross over to the last, but forgotten hope.

The racist arrogance of the bland dragons were foretold to be no more. Even the unity of the future would be bound in unity of sacrifice. There, and right there Mr. Ala-Oma remembered home. Mr. Ala-Oma came from that great African nation where presidential winners were declared some wanted men—a nation where women would permanently lose their identities and claim their husbands' as their permanent names.

As he remembered these things, he remembered, though home was always home, but his own home was not even perfect. And, as he remembered, he began to cry.

"Honey why are you sobbing?" his wife asked him.

"Home," he replied unto her. His mind rushed to the state of the vast waste of the forgotten continent. And, as he remembered, he remembered that remembering would not resolve the remembered. There he remembered effluvia of prurience, the toxic pollution on the black shores.

He remembered slaves and slave trade. He remembered the cronyism of historical dark fortune, a prelude to the shameful slave politics, and the evil of the omenic innuendo.

The element of blood, of voodoo or 'juju politics,' endorsed by the ancients, and, by the evil agents of the devil—there was erogenous, a slavogenesis and the red-carpet of the slave trade.

There, the black Africa gave the world the rope for his own undoing. The sheep was thrown to the wolf. And the west was ready to lynch him.

There, the crybabies among the braves were used in feeding the beasts of the Ocean. The songs of slaves, coming from their graves in the Atlantic, rose and went home. In there was the blueprint of the devil for racial division: The grave and terrible age when so many blacks were wronged, and the oppressed being told to shut up—the ghosts of the dead being forced to drown again.

Even as the message rang home, the offended immigrants began to get ready to return home. And, as they got ready to go, the dragons saw that those they would pick on would leave them; that they would have no one to pick on anymore. So, they had no choice but to use the media to influence the would-have-returned-homers to feel bad about their homes.

Africa was, as ever, depicted the land of the jungles—land filled with beasts, wild animals, dictators, human flesh-eating semi-human beings, and subhumans who sucked human blood.

The Indians of Asian heritage were exposed as a nation of poverty. They were shown on the television screens as beggars on the highways, the Indian Streets everywhere.

THE DEVIL'S LAND

A nation that worshipped cows, adorers of the snakes which turned around and bit them; their lots were graced with portraits of foolish-worshippers of rats, monkeys, cows, idols, and nothing but primitive tradition.

Like Indian rats, which found a permanent position in the heart of the Indian god, their ancestral goddess of luck adored the rats as its traveling companions. Though the friends of god, the rat-catchers of New Delhi caught them and used them in feeding their captive crocs.

Often, the clever rats threw sands on the faces of those who were out to catch them. Thus, rats, the food; rats, the friends of gods; rats, the fugitives; rats, the enemies of Indian farmers; rats, the friends of Indian farmers; rats, the friends of religious folks; and rats, food of the crocodile farms.

Rats, despised by some, and sacred to the others.

There, the earth of the New World could be a terrifying place when it released its deadly powers. The Japanese women began to despise the way their eyes looked—slanted. And, their looking to the West, onward, did not put a capital stop half-way.

They began to modify their eyes, glued them inward, just to fit well with God-given, Western specification.

Then, the trend shifted, but not for good. The age of "spare a dime" grew to an age of 'could you spare a quarter, brother?' A nation where beggars were contemptuously despised, despite many a healthy protest to the contrary, yet, crafty enough not to show the world the red ink in her national ledger.

It was embedded in the essence of Americanism, a powerful custom of hypocrisy—judging others without willingness to be judged by those judged by the judge. Indeed, living of the most cunning.

The nation's beggars lived in the sea of joy and tangible scent of fear. So too were they, constantly, at odds with the terrors of their perpetual place in the tough society. There was the tale of a society with no rooted culture, but imported tradition.

57

There, the jumbo-loads of baloneys, the comfort zones of the foolish ones, the free loaders—the white trash and hopeless niggers with no hope nor second winds.

The effluvia of living, the red-carpets of contempts for the lazy niggers and the white trash. There, just like some African women in Africa who tried to become nothing but white women, they bleached their bodies with acid bleach, called 'pomade'. Likewise some whites who desired dark skin in action, they spent their days, naked, to be tarred by sunlight.

There, some black women in America held a different philosophy, a radical view to the contrary. They became more African than ever.

And talk about some white women—they became more African than black women—they dressed like Africans, talked like Africans, danced no other kind of dance but African, and ate some food even made the African way,. And, their first lady loved it, and asked them to train the American children the African way—to team up like a village and raise up the new generation.

Talk about the Masais of Africa, all Cows everywhere forever belonged to them. And, talk about their dress code, they've got their admirers in the heartland of the New-World: Young men and women, blacks and whites, yellow people and brown beings, they wore their earrings, nose-rings, bellybutton rings; as they copied the eternal owners of Cows everywhere; often, they over did the way their masters dressed. There was even something in addition; the men of Masai shared their wives without violence. A Masai would simply peg his walking stick in front of his neighbor's house, if the man is not in; he would enter and enjoy his neighbor's wife. And, should his neighbor return and see the walking stick in front of his house, he'd turn around and walk away.

CHAPTER EIGHT

"My dear, why are there so many illegitimate children in America?" asked the ignoramus, the man from Africa, named
Mr. Ala-Ọma, to his smart American wife.

"Because we're a nation of bastards, honey," she informed him. She was outspoken, and an activist. She was a woman who hated the system, and was ready, anytime, to defy it.

For example, she married a black man, against her father's wish. Her father was a man who cherished the Dixiecrats. He delighted in their views and desired their ways.

He had wanted her to marry a waspy yuppie of an ivy-league. But, she was tough, and a stubborn daddy's girl. She was very free and her father was aware of his own limits in her life. And, her life was her's; not his. Her father had no right to force her to marry a man she did not want. Neither did he have a right to prevent her from marrying the very man she really loved. As things stood, America was not Africa where parents could arrange some brides for their potential sons, and ship them over to their sons—no matter where their sons might be.

And love in Africa was different from the way Americans would view it. 'You love those you're married to, not necessarily marrying those you love' . . . Mr. Ala-Ọma had tried to explain to her. But, she was still baffled by it—in that a man would even have many wives, all under his powerful control.

"Is that possible? How did they do it? Don't the women get to each other's throat?" She had asked her husband, time and again, whenever her man was up to explaining the marriage thing.

"When we go home, you'll see. You'll see them. You'll see how they live," he told her how really some young men could be stuck with some parentally chosen wives—And, should business go wrong, for the rest of their miserable lives. It all baffled her. "It's African way," he hinted. For sure, that for damn sure. There she was, proud to be an American. At least, she was free to divorce her husband. Even husbands, if cases arose, without limits.

She looked at her husband; then she began to pity him, his home Africa. As she did, a profound contempt took over.

She subconsciously lampooned the unimaginable—that primitive people could have so much power over their sons and daughters as to decide, arrange, and impose a life commitment on them, for them to lead through.

There she noticed something deep down her memory bank. There she found a predator of genetic memory, a scare-face of doom. There she felt like becoming a benevolent racist who would go to Africa and give them freedom, an American outlook, even a new lease on life. While she dwelt on these, it dawned on her that racism was a deadly beast; that to kill it, one is got to study it, know where it lived, how it behaved, what made it tick, irritated it, and what made it relax.

"Hope you won't do that to me."

"If you want me to—" replied he.

"Hell no," she replied.

"Why not?" he posed, seemingly serious.

"No way, honey. I'm one wife, one husband. I can't stand—"

"Well, I believe in polygamy, but my preference is monogamy."

"Good. Otherwise, I'd have killed you."

"Wives don't kill their husbands," he said.

"That isn't true. May be in Africa. Here, if a man takes his woman for a ride, she can take him to the cleaners, and pull a few slugs in him," she taught him.

THE DEVIL'S LAND

"I think, first, my apologies—" he was hesitant to voice out what was in his mind.

"I don't think you should apologize for anything—" she gave him the greenlight, the go-ahead.

"I think, many foreigners are, sometimes, very reluctant to marry American women, despite green card, because no man would like to lose his life because of marriage."

"Are you afraid of me, honest honey?" she looked at him, single-mindedly, searching for nothing but one and one answer only.

"Sometimes. You know me that I can't hide the truth from you," he confessed to her.

"I don't think I'd kill you, even if you cheat on me," she reassured, "Hey, don't run off and cheat on me just because I'd promise. If you do, I'll kill the woman. It's a promise," she gave him an alternative promise.

"I don't think those things are nice. For a man to mistreat his wife is wrong. For a woman to take everything a man has and kill him too is nothing but an abomination," he paused, momentarily—"I'll tell you a story."

"You know I love stories. Go ahead. Tell me."

"I'm gonna talk like an African, you go catcham?" he began.

"I'm good at pigeon English. Go on," she replied.

"Na him now. O.K. Wetin I de talk?"

"The story. Tell it," she replied. Reminding him that she could understand him.

"Na him. One Lagos bobo came to dis una country to catcham for good education."

"Yeah, what?" she was attentive.

"When de bobo finish, him marry one pretty akata lady. The thing be say, the bobo na prince shaa . . ."

"I can live with that," she pointed.

"No be all now, jari."

"What next?"

61

SUNDAY AHURONYEZE ABAKWUE

"Dem return to Lagos."

"To enjoy the riches, palace, lucky girl, all that good stuff."

"Good. Na true you de follow me well well. Are yu are; when the bobo's father wantam to become the next king, him people tell the bobo say, 'make you marry a second wife. You sabi say the King go have two or more wives before him sitam on the throne . . . ' You sabi the thing wey happen?"

"No. What happened?" she asked him.

"De American woman wey him marry took a rope go killam for imself. Na true talk. The people, when dem see am, dem shout shout say, 'na im be abomination'. The wey she behaved, sha, ino dey good-oh."

"Honey, we're talking about respect. This sister here cannot take any bull from any man."

"Hey, don't talk too much like that lest you get me offended," he cautioned her.

"I thought we're—"

"You are talking to an African, to a man who is your husband. You don't talk like a street woman when you are talking to me."

"I'm sorry," she became remorseful.

"That's fine," he accepted her apology.

"I'm glad you're very understanding," she added.

"That's ok," he answered; thereupon she radiated with joy.

"Thanks, honey" she thanked him.

"My people have a saying to that effect. We say, 'Talking without thinking.'"

"' . . . Brings dying without sickness.' I've heard that before," she completed his statement. She knew him very well; and she could read him, his trend of thoughts, like an open book.

"You see, many people have died in Africa and elsewhere because." he said.

"They did not think—" she took on.

"Yes, before they talked."

THE DEVIL'S LAND

"I know, that's why you've told me to remain calm if I didn't know the right thing to say in a fight—"

"Not 'a fight' but argument," he corrected her.

"What's the difference?" she was ready to find out from him.

"Well, a fight demands physical display of brute force, an outgrowth of brute instinct. However, an argument demands verbal display of wit, wisdom, intellect, and even foolishness," he gave her as the answer.

"Oh boy, we use fight and argument interchangeably; no big deal," she brushed it all off.

"Well, as an educated person, you're not at liberty to speak the way . . ."

"I know; I know. You understood what I meant; didn't you?"

"Of course."

"Honey, we can't be purist all the time. Here is America. Even our president wouldn't mind blowing the wrong grammar on the screen now and then; American people will forgive him."

"Yes I know; but people outside America will notice it and talk and write about it. Some of them might even make fun of him—"

"I know; I, know; I know there are many Rush Limbaughs all over the world. Of Course, these things could happen. We're privileged enough to have good education. Of course we just can't take it for granted."

"Yes; yes."

"We have all these things. However, I mean, however honey." She softened her voice, "There are many out there who don't have the privileges you and I enjoy."

"I know that for sure. Even in Africa, millions of people lead their lives with little or no education. The little education they'd got are what their illiterate fathers and mothers taught them while they're growing up. Of Course, we must not forget the influence of the entire village and the local churches. They all come together and exact an abiding influence on the African children."

63

"My apologies too, honey," she said, grinning.

"Don't give me that devil smile," he protested, amicably. There she grinned even more. "Yes, what's it?"

"Some of your African ways are funny," she said, not letting up her grinning mood.

"Give me a specific example," he challenged her.

"Yes, I will," she took him at his request, ready to deliver. But, she continued to laugh.

"Go ahead; don't stand there and smile at me like a nutty child."

"Yes, I will. Where do I begin? For example, how come your people don't bury your dead in a foreign land?"

"Because we're the Jews of Africa."

"So?"

"Our dead ones are sacred. Just like the then Jews of ancient times saw the need to carry the bones of blessed Joseph, the son of Jacob; so do my people see the need not to bury our loved ones in a foreign land. The spirit of an Igbo will have a perfect rest when the body is buried in a soil in Igboland."

How did you know these things?"

"Because I am a product of a griot; so, such I am. And, such is my heritage."

"So, if you die now—"

"You must make sure my body goes home. If you can't, tell the Igbo people around, they'll carry out their responsibility."

"That wouldn't be their responsibility, would it?"

"Yes, indeed. An Igbo belongs to all the Igbos. If I die now, you will be surprised how all the Igbos around will respond. Soon after they learnt that their brother has passed to the home of every living soul."

"No. I don't want to see that. I want you to stay alive with me, you're mine; mine only."

"O.K. But death, is certain," he reassured her.

THE DEVIL'S LAND

"Please honey, change that topic," she became nervous, "I don't feel comfortable when you talk about dying, death, and all that scary stuff," she began to sweat, nervously, "Why not talk about love, romance?" she persuaded him.

"No. Let's talk about church," he yielded; but, halfway.

"Yes, as you know, I'm Catholic—"

"Yes, what has that got to do with our conversation?" he smiled as he asked her.

"Sure, honey, quite a lot. Remember what we're talking about before you brought in the scary stuff?"

"No, What was it?" He forgot.

"Sure you do."

"No."

"Sure, I think, you should remember. Those African kids; now do you remember?"

"Fine, go on."

"I guess you didn't. Anyway, those African kids we talked about and I have a lot in common. We'll had Sunday schools Bible studies when we're growing up."

"I see. I see. You made your point. A nice one, though."

"Thank you."

CHAPTER NINE

"One thing I've noticed about those people—?" said Mrs. Ala-Oma.

"Who?" Mr. Ala-Oma plied her.

"The Klansmen."

"Knights of the Ku Klux Klan?"

"Yeah."

"You said 'Klansmen' as if its only men that made up the evil group." he said

"I know, just a few women; no big deal." she responded

"Those women are human beings too."

"You want me to call them Klanswomen? Will that make you happy?"

"No."

"What?"

"Nothing about them will make a wise person happy."

"That's right," said she.

"I wish they will repent."

"They'll never admit that what they're doing is wrong."

"I don't understand why they think like that," said Mr. Ala-Oma.

"It's all indoctrination; it's their ideal; it turns men into fanatics. Look at Muslims in Middle East. They think if they kill, they'll go to heaven," said she.

"Honey, when you cheat someone too much, too long, the person may resent, hate, or even fight you. You talked about

Middle-East, how would you feel if I sold you a common battery worth sixty-five cents for sixty-five dollars?"

"I'll kill you if I find out."

"Good. Smart response."

"Yeah, I would."

"Do you know what happened during the gulf war?" he asked her; since she was his wife, he was less timid to open up.

"We beat Saddam, the sad man; we beat back the Iraqis," she answered his question.

"Yes, Saddam was a very sad man after the allied forces counter-invaded; now dear, what else did you do?"

"We defended Saudi Arabia; we defeated Saddam's aggression."

"'Yes, that was not all; what else did you do?"

"We brought back the King of Kuwait to the throne."

"Yes; that was a very good job, restoring the poor man to his throne; now, love,what else did you do?" he asked her; waiting for her answer. This time she seemed to have run out of it.

"Honey, I don't know."

"Think, honey; you know what happened."

"Know what?" she stopped scratching her head; and, she began to gaze at him, like a smart little girl who'd ran out of answers, even before her favorite teacher.

"Yes, yes,tell me," he asked her to tell him.

"Please, tell you what?"

"Yes, you know what you did over there," he hinted.

"Yes, we helped them." She seemed self-righteous.

"True, every champion would do it."

"Of course we're the only superpower in the world who could have done it."

"But, you cheated them too."

"No way."

"Yes, you did. Listen to me before you become defensive. Just after Mr. Saddam surrendered, the Pentagon sold them billions of armaments; so much so that Saudi reserve is now in red ink."

THE DEVIL'S LAND

"Really?" She was excited.

"Not only that. The price was so inflated; the profit was nothing but an overkill."

"Well. That's free enterprise; one feeds off on the other," she defended the enterprise.

"Yes, if I had done it, you would have killed me; when the Pentagon did it to the Arabs, you said it's fine and free enterprise," he mocked her.

"Oh, common brother, when will you grow up?" she said quite sarcastically.

"I will when Osama takes up his weapons and begins to fight back."

"Oh come on."

"Yes, if I had done it, you would have killed me; when the Pentagon did it to the terrorist-Arabs, you said it's free enterprise, honey; but, remember, cheating is stealing, it does not matter who did it. It is a great sin in the sight of a righteous God. When Arabs hate America, why don't we ask ourselves 'why?' By so doing, we'd begin to do the things that are pure in the sight of the Divine Law. But, when we let our arrogant pride to becloud our better sense of righteousness, then, we begin to call them terrorists and even blow them away like a hunter who shoots a helpless egret in an open sky."

"Let's talk about the original topic, the Klans, men or women, whichever," tactfully, she changed the topic

"Yes, such people are helpless," he admitted.

"Yeah, I know you would say that."

"Honey, wait a minute, wasn't that true?" he asked her.

"What do you mean?

The Klans, right?" she asked him.

"I wonder whether you would defend them."

"God forbid," she was furious. "Such people? Hell, not even on your life."

"Oh, even if my life is involved in it?" he asked, rather sarcastically.

"Hey, you think I'm joking? Those jerks are bad; bad, bad, bad, bad is not the right word, they are so self-righteous that they declared and uphold racism, prejudice with a touch of conviction. I hate them," she replied to him, angrily.

"They're pretty fanatical. I don't know how they got such an evil ideal. I don't think their view is worth," he managed to say.

"It ain't worth anything, honey."

"Honey, what do you think will happen in Court today?" he asked her, curious in the way he posed the question. Even as he gazed at her face, hoping for an answer, there was a touch of worry written all over his face.

"Guilty, No doubt. The evidence is overhelming," she supplied the answer.

"Your case is strong. That's self-evident." He paused momentarily. "But, have you thought about how the defense attorney presented his defense, the way the judge turned around when you demonstrated how they lynched the four men, how he refused to admit the ropes used in hanging the four men as some inconclusive evidence, how the press and the jury cheered and were more attentive to the defense presentation?" he laid down his sequence of questions before her.

"To be honest, I've not thought about them. But, I've a strong case. Those beasts are murderers."

"Yes, we know that. But, if the judge threw away all the clinching evidence you have, to hook them to the murder, you have no case; then, the accused will be acquitted."

"No way," she shouted "No, honey, they can't get out. Even a blind judge can see."

"Yes, the system is blind to the core, blind to the torturing of the weak, weaker, and even the weakest ones in the system of prejudice. The whole show is a domination by the most powerful; a racial thing, you know. I read a few of the judge's handwritings on the Court's wall; therefore, I've formed an opinion. I'll bet you, with the way the case is going, the jurors, I'm black, if I may borrow the American phrase, 'I'm not prejudiced'; all the jurors are white. Their verdict will definitely be 'not guilty,' Believe me."

"I'll kill that judge if he gets those beasts off the hook," she vowed.

"I hope you won't do such a foolish thing; I'd not like to see my wife in jail. You can always appeal to the Superior Court; When a verdict is not to your liking. I'm sure you can do that. And, that's more preferable to killing a judge of the United States' Court house."

"Thanks for the advice. I shall take it if," she was receptive.

"I'm sure they're not guilty, though we saw them kill the four black men."

"That's contradiction in terms," she pointed out.

"Yeah; you're right; but, what can I say? That's the way the system works."

"How did you know all these things?" she asked him, as if she did not know.

"Is here not the South? South United States is not North of the nation."

"I don't believe you," she said.

"May be you shouldn't," he paused for a brief moment. "But what if the jury sets the people free at last, would you still not believe me, honey my dear?"

"I guess I'll make myself more legal enemies—"

"It's all political racism. They see things in terms of black and white, them versus us, two enemy groups fighting in a battle front. And, they use the books of law and courthouse as camouflage to fulfill all measure of righteousness. Believe me, there is a camouflage of racism beneath every inch of the Southern soil," said Mr. Ala-Oma with a subdued voice.

"Good grief; that's horrible," right there she was horrified by the Southern ways.

"Welcome to the South, honey my dear. Welcome to the home of the dixiecrats," her husband welcomed her to her new home.

CHAPTER TEN

"We've got to fight them—" she said to him.

"Fight what?" he pretended, unaware of what she had in mind.

"Southern ways, philosophies of Dixiecrats".

"Oh, yeah?"

"Yeah."

"I'm not sure your father will approve."

"To hell with him," she rebuked phooeyically.

"Please, never again curse your father; no matter your disagreement, you must honor him the way Divine Law asked you to do."

"I'm so sorry."

"That's alright; we'll learn."

"Thanks."

"Well, as you would say, I may add, you are cordially welcome."

"Great. I like the word 'cordially.' It sounds cute."

"Does it?"

"Yeah, it really does."

"Honey, if you want to fight the South, the odds are too great. Racism is a way of life of the South. They will fight anyone who tries to take away this baby from them. You see, judges here are predilects, their predilections show in all the cases they handle."

"Why did they hire them? They don't know what they're doing," she asked.

"Honey, on the contrary, they're smart; and, they are aware of what they are doing."

"What?"

"Yes, it's an open book. The people support it. You'll see. We're going to Court; aren't we? You'll see it all in the verdict. There, whether privy verdict or sealed one, the judge would show the direction the jurors would go."

"That's very wrong," she said, again quite phooeyically.

"Wrong in the Bible-belt, yes honey," said he.

"You bet your guts it is."

"Yeah, Bible-belt in the belt of racism."

"Yes, it is."

"This South is so bad, right?" asked he.

"This South, I hate it; their way, I mean," she corrected herself, and the reason for, and even the targets of her hate.

"Old system, you know, die hard."

"I can see why South is so backward. They're pulling America backwards to the Barbaric age," said she; her voice, a note of righteous rage. "It's all in the old Southern belt, big belt for whites, small belt for the others, I hate it."

"It's their freedom—" he noted.

"Bull!" she called their freedom. "Bull."

"You can't deprive them that; this is America," he said.

"I don't buy that. Freedom has its checks and balances. A free man is not free to lynch his fellow freeman. If we're free at the expense of others, I don't think such freedom is the right one," she lectured him.

"Don't get too philosophical about it. Let's face it. We're now in the South. Here is home of Bible-belt. Alabama is here. Mississippi is here. Arkansas is here. Some of the best Bible schools are here. Here too, you get the people who'll use the Bible to ruin the lives of those they see as their inferiors. Let's face it. That's the reality," he lectured back.

THE DEVIL'S LAND

****

The Courthouse where Mr. and Mrs. Ala-Oma arrived was nothing but a haunted house. In there dwelt the angry spirits of the innocently condemned black men, black women, and many black children, who stationed themselves in the Court, in quest of greater justice.

God had given them a choice:—either to return to paradise where their souls would rest forever, or, to retain themselves in the Court of injustice, and daily remind those who condemned them of their crimes and iniquities. God was amazed when the redeemed spirits chose the latter, all for the sake of their honor, and pride in true justice.

Mr. and Mrs. Ala-Oma saw, soon after they arrived in the Court, that some unearthly beings were the lords of the Courthouse. It was amazing, and baffling to the odd couple.

When the Court-orderly announced the entrance of the judge, however, ten different unearthly voices came out of his mouth. Among them were three distinct voices of crying children—a shouting voice of a black woman

—a nagging voice of another black woman—and five different voices of angry black men—some of which deafening—some quite commanding and even demanding baritones—a blend of viola, tuba, bastarda, and althorn. The combination produced an eerie aura. The orderly's real voice was easily drowned, swallowed up in the process.

The whole many a drama was not only haunting, but eerily funny in a living story—the entire white-colored, Court officials refused to recognize the unearthly presence.

They refused to admit that anything abnormal was present in the Courtroom. Once, though, a new female Court clerk opened her mouth too wide about the Court being a haunted place; upon order of an angry judge, she was arrested and taken to a psychiatric hospital for detailed observation. While in this confinement, she was discharged of her duties on the ground of mental derangement. Later, she was pronounced insane; eventually, she was sent to mental institution; then, transfered to a criminally insane home, via, the Isle of Alienation. Of course she died, shamefully, a horrible death, like Jesus, in a chain of common criminals.

With her, the fine judge was able to set a remarkable precedence—in that no one ever again mentioned that mere spirits of some dead niggers were harassing their living white superiors.

But now, though, the inferior spirits were again willing to make their invisible presence known.

"Say nigger, you're not the only black nigger here, boy," a voice said.

"Dah dah uncle, hi," a child's voice greeted Mr. Ala-Ọma, "What's your name?"

"Oh, me?" Mr. Ala-Ọma replied to the child's voice.

"Yeah, you sure. Daddy say you my uncle. You from Africa?" the child's voice talked back.

"Yes. But I can't see you."

"We know you can't see us because we're dead, boy; living men don't see dead ones; do they? You hear our voices; don't you boy? Those damn white folks know we're here. They can't do you no harm," a man's voice said.

"Just ignore those things, boy; they're mere hallucinations," the judge addressed Mr. Ala-Ọma, thus interrupting a man versus ghost conversation.

"Damn you," same invisible voice was quick to curse the judge.

"Who gives a damn what you say?" the white judge derided the hostile ghost in response.

"Honey, go and slap that damn fool," the invisible one gave an order to another invisible one.

Hardly had the order been given when a book from the judge's exalted desk lifted itself up. The book began to smack itself

THE DEVIL'S LAND

on the judge's face. As it did the people in the Court looked in bewilderment.

"Stop it," protested the judge, as he tried to fight off the incessant smacks coming from the big, law book.

"Slap him again," the invisible one commanded. True to its obedience, the smacking went on harder, rougher and even faster. The judge began to bleed all over, and his face was filled with bruises, and even dripping with blood. In vain the judge fought hard to fight off the book which was roughly, and violently smacking him. In vain he bled; and, in vain he began to weep like a mere baby.

"Please, friends, have mercy on him," Mr. Ala-Ọma pleaded on his behalf.

"Thank you for calling us friends. That's the first time anyone has called us friends in this dreaded court," a female voice responded.

"Why did you stop slapping him?" the male commanding voice roared.

"Are you crazy? Didn't you hear that brother who called us friends?" a familiar female voice responded.

"Thank you friends for considering my humble request. Your kind gesture will always be an eternal treasure." Mr. Ala-Ọma was quick to thank them, humoring, and flattering the invisible ones.

"Yea, them white folks deserve no mercy. They killed me and my family, me, my wife and two kids. Look at us. We didn't do them no wrong. We ain't criminals. They just killed us because we're their niggers," the invisible man, ghost in the Court, explained to it's new friend.

"I understand. Please who are the other people with you?" Mr. Ala-Ọma asked the invisible being.

"My pal and his wife, Lisa, three boys in the 'hood.'" said the Spirit.

"Yes, that's nice. But, I hear ten different voices."

"Boy, you don't wanna know the tenth fellow," said the spirit with an air of warning.

"I would like to," Mr. Ala-Ọma insisted.

"He's too powerful to be mentioned."

"Is he God?" asked Mr. Ala-Ọma.

"No, Close enough."

"Who is he, then?" the persistent man, Mr. Ala-Ọma wanted to know.

"Tell him who I am," the tenth voice said, so gentle, yet authoritatively calm.

"He's an angel."

"Wow!" Mr.Ala-Ọma's wife remarked.

"Who's that white woman standing beside you?" the man's voice asked.

"Are you crazy? Don't you know that's his wife? Them folks come from up North. Here in South, them white folks don't allow blacks marry whites," the female voice told her invisible male husband.

"Yes. She's my wife," Mr. Ala-Ọma confirmed.

"Where did you meet?" the male invisible voice asked him.

"Harvard Law School," both Mr. and Mrs. Ala-Ọma answered the invisible voice quite simultaneously.

"Hey son, and you young white lady, you're meant for each other, kids. You take good care of each other. And don't give a damn what those ignorant racists would say about it," the invisible man counseled them.

"We shall," said Mr. Ala-Ọma.

"Thank you," replied Mrs. Ala-Ọma.

"Mr. and Mrs. Ala-Ọma," the voice of the angel addressed them.

"Sir," Mrs. Ala-Ọma responded faster.

"Yes, Lord," Mr. Ala-Ọma answered too.

"Our Lord and Christ crucified prejudice on the cross. In our God there is no discrimination. So, when God joined you together,

THE DEVIL'S LAND

let nothing put you asunder," the angel quoted the scriptures for the couple as some words of wisdom regarding the bond in marriage.

"Thank you; we shall always keep that in mind," Mr. & Mrs. Ala-Ọma answered simultaneously.

CHAPTER ELEVEN

"Ladies and gentlemen of the jury, can we begin with first case of the day?" the judge began, seemingly quite settled, ready to judge those who were not beaten by the ghost.

"Shut up, fool. We ain't finished yet; da da say, 'I'm, he's the judge today," the little child's voice easily interrupted the judge.

"Hello kid," Mr. Ala-Oma was equally ready to control the little, spirit-kid.

"Ya uncle, did ya bring me balloon?"

"Yes, I have it in my car. But, you've got to keep calm, very quiet kid, till the judge finishes his job today," replied Mr. Ala-Oma to the little spirit-child.

The dead-living child listened. The child was not the only person who listened, the parents did too. The angel listened. So did the others who were once condemned, by the same judge, to mortal darkness—a lethal love of the time, a passionate file of an unjustifiable crime. Indeed, the ultimate act of control, done in-toto, without the wisdom of the eternal conscience. In there was the wisdom of the superior race, the shining path of an intellect, a grand dragon of the Knight of the Ku Klux Klan. So deeply rooted in their philosophy.

"Honey," a voice interrupted, "the golden substance made by bees takes a damn lot of work to make," the spirit paused.

"Oh yeah, baby," a voice of a male spirit, the husband of the female-spirit, agreed. Then, the female voice continued.

"Do you know that the bees can sting intruders just to protect their damn honey?" She waited again for her man's response.

"Oh yeah, baby," were his words, again.

"Their nectar-gathering takes them to damn great length, to exotic flowers, stinking dungs, shit, the damn magnetic shit."

"You mean magnetic field, baby?"

"You crazy? You betcha, I am."

"Damn, I'm a smart chump, baby."

"You betcha," there was a hysterical laughter, an unearthly terrifying female voice.

"Go on baby, your man is here. I'm not gonna leave you. I'm forever listening."

"Shoo. The bee thing and shit?"

"Yeah."

"Yeah, their pollen-baskets would store their treasure honey."

"Say, you said honey, you mean honey, or you mean them bees' honey, dear?"

"Oh, cut it off. I'm talking to you, talking about them bees' honey, honey."

"That's right, honey."

"And they'd trade pollinating of flowers for the flowers' shit, sweet juice, the sweet shit, honey."

"Yeah."

"Yeah, nigger, when they did that, they paid the damn price."

"Price of what?"

"Are you dumb-crazy? You don't understand there is no free lunch in this world, crazy?"

"Yeah. Yeah. Free lunch. Them bees pay flowers before they take away the sweet juice and shit?"

"Yeah, crazy-shit; that's what I've been saying; you acted as if you didn't hear, crazy."

"I heard you quite alright."

"Good, crazy-love; now, crazy, we're talking sweet-shit."

"Talking what? Shoo, you're the one talking, baby."

THE DEVIL'S LAND

"Crazy-love, you so crazy? I talked, you talked. Anyway, they'd load themselves with that shit, nectarine pollen and shit, whizz, they flew back to their nest, cells and chamber shit."

"I missed what you're saying."

"Crazy? Get it together, nigger."

"Oh baby, when are you gonna grow up?" the man's voice rebuked the female voice. "The way you women talk to thinking men, it sounds like an android from a faraway planet, Saturn, talking to another being from the sun or something."

"Oh damn, you hurt my feeling," the female voice protested; then, the voice's mood turned into an unearthly weeping.

"Yea, you damn right. Cry baby," the male voice mocked the weeping spirit.

"I'm not gonna cry no more."

"Fine, if you can't cry you might as well finish off your bee story."

"That black dude yonder knew those things. Them lucky folks went to college," the pal of the invisible man replied to the second invisible woman.

"Friends, I need your help. The judge needs your help. And, I am asking on his behalf, please," said Mr. Ala-Ọma.

"Shit. That's bull nigger. You don't help damn white judge."

"Oh please," Mrs. Ala-Ọma entered the conversation, pleading with the invisible ones.

"Seal your mouth woman, or else I'll take a whip to you."

"Hey, she's my wife. Respect her now. If you can't respect her because she's white, respect her simply because she's married to me, your fellow black man," cautioned the husband, Mr.Ala-Ọma.

"Yeah, Yeah," all the other living white folks, the judge, lawyers, Court Clerks, and all the people who came to do or have court services, agreed in unison.

"I've got something better to do than to listen to the agreement of damn white folks. Honey, our son is ready to take a bath, took forever in a day; give 'm paraphernalia for shower, products of giggles and guffaw and laughter. The rights to same, and rights to have relationships and the rights to be decent."

"Friend I didn't understand what you're talking about," Mr. Ala-Oma told the black spirit in the haunted Courthouse.

"I ain't talking to you no more."

"Why not?" Mr. Ala-Oma asked the complaining spirit.

"I was talking to my wife. Ain't you perjured and ambivalent?"

"No. I'm not. And I'll never be," Mr. Ala-Oma answered the spirit.

"Good for you."

"We need your co-operation so that judge would do his job."

"I ain't holding him son. If you want me to, I'll be glad to do it." True to his voice, something began to happen to the judge; he began to notice some squeezing around his neck. Followed by some breathing difficulties; then, the judge began to choke.

"I'm gonna squeeze you hard, so hard bastard," a voice of the invisible one said near the neck of the struggling judge.

"Hey, let go of him now," Mrs. Ala-Oma protested.

"No way," the invisible one refused.

"Hey, my friend, leave him alone, please," Mr. Ala-Oma commanded, with a note of pleading.

"I won't, he's the one who condemned me to where I am. Shit, when I was on the other side of immortality he had power over me. Now I have power over him. I don't want to bring him over here, because God wouldn't want us to do that. But I've enough power to torture him while he's living," said the spirit.

"You've tortured him enough," Mrs. Ala-Oma protested.

"Oh no, young woman. Consider what he did. He shed the blood of innocent people, all by the testimonies of his own mouth; with his pen he penned down their death sentence. None of us whom he killed have taken him to that length."

"At least the best you can do for him is to forgive him," Mrs. Ala-Oma appealed to the forgiving nature of the black spirit.

THE DEVIL'S LAND

"Oh please, if God would not forgive him, how would I forgive him?" asked the Spirit to the white woman.

"God is forgiveness," Mrs. Ala-Ọma lectured in her response to the black Spirit.

"You sound like a fine preacher, lady. God can forgive a sin which was not premeditated. God will forgive a sinner who would not take God's forgiveness for granted," said the voice of the underworld.

"Mrs. Ala-Ọma, beloved made a point; There's a limit to forgiveness," so said the very voice of the ministering angel.

****

When all were settled, the judge called on the prosecutor to present her case. She was to present nothing but a set of convincing facts, damning evidence far beyond the reasonable doubt.

"There we go again," a male-Spirit voice began to interrupt the Court proceeding. "White folks have a way with deception. Nigger you remember that devil called missionary who went to Africa to teach to the village people?"

"Yeah nigger. I remember quite alright," another male-Spirit voice responded.

"You remember how he prayed for them?"

"Sure nigger; he prayed and cheated them," replied the second Spirit present in the Court of the living.

"Yeah, he asked them to close their eyes," said the first spirit.

"Sure nigger; you damn right, again," the invisible second Spirit said.

"When them villagers closed their eyes, the damn devil prayed 'bow your head so we may cheat you for Christ's sake, Amen,' aint that so nigger?" said the first voice.

"White man cannot help you unless he's cheating you. Them villagers never knew that, nigger," the Spirit said.

85

"We've heard enough; Court-Clerk call on the prosecutor to present her case," the judge ventured to take over, to take control of the situation. Thus, he ventured to overrule the invisible spirits who were talking about another white man who went to Africa on a mission work.

"Your honor," Mrs. Ala-Ọma began to present her case, her evidence against 'Reverend' Jingle and his company, the members of the white supremacists who lynched the four black men.

She showed the ropes; she showed their hoods, attires, and even the pictures of the scene.

She told the learned personnel of jury everything she knew, heard, and observed while she was there, as one of the eye-witnesses. Right there she challenged the suspects to refute any, or, all of her allegations; but, none of them did.

Then, in closing remarks, she observed to the judge, and even to the listening people-of-jury. The very learned members of the jury, her deepest desire for justice. "Reverend Jingle is creating divine terrorism without God's approval. For example, he travelled to Africa to preach the word; he came back to lynch the blacks. Since he came back from Africa he'd unleashed a reign of terror, terrorizing all the people of color, his fellow American citizens."

"Blacks are not true Americans; how can niggers be American citizens?" 'Rev'. Jingle interrupted her in her closing argument.

"The evidence of this prosecution proved beyond reasonable doubt, your honor."

"Hold on," the judge ordered Mrs. Ala-Ọma. His voice, a clear indication that she was not in the North but South, a place which was so different in its views, and a place that was a man's world and a world of the supremacists. And, she held her peace. She did not want to arouse any issue which would earn her a contempt of the court.

As she held her peace, the judge began to cast away, through the judicial window, every damning and clinching evidence which

THE DEVIL'S LAND

she carefully and dutifully presented against the supremacists who lynched the four black men.

After doing that, he cast a deadly glare at the young female lawyer.

"Where are you from?" the judge asked her.

"Hoboken, New Jersey."

"Hobowhat? Do hoboes live there?"

"No, your honor; its a small city in New Jersey."

"I'm from Kansas, the bleeding State you know," he told her. Having said that, a flood of imageries rushed through her wave of understanding, and wave of comprehension. 'Yea, Kansas the bleeding State; yea the State of racism is ready to bleed more because of ignorance, prejudice and lack of open-mind; yea, Kansas will bleed again because of its love to enslave those who'd always desired to be free from bondage.' She stood there cogitating on the flood of comprehension.

"What are you thinking, Counsel?" the judge asked her.

"Nothing, your honor."

"Counsel," the judge called her the second time from his exalted seat.

"Yes, your honor," replied Mrs. Ala-Ọma. The deadly, rebuking look which was coming from his face disappeared.

In its place was a look of a father who desired to bribe his daughter into obedience.

"You are a very smart young woman." He keyed in the initial scent of a psychological bribery to recruit her to the old-boy network. She became more attentive, like a female Abraham who was waiting to follow a Divine call. He sensed it and he opened wide his bag of racial bribery "have you heard the phrase 'Survival of the most cunning?'" the judge asked her.

'No, your honor. Why, your honor?"

"Nothing. Have a look at yourself," the judge instructed her. She did. "Look at the suspects too," he added.

She did too.

87

"Why, your honor?" she asked him because she did not get the idea. She seemed confused, and lost in the wood. She was not a Southerner, as such she was clueless regarding unNorthern clues.

"I guess you don't understand. I'll put it this way: I don't see any difference between you and the suspects. You can't talk me into condemning your own people. The dead niggers you're trying to defend are gone. They were useless, evil and slaves. As far as I'm concerned this case is dismissed," he banged his stick of authority, on his exalted table. With the third bang, on his exalted table, he rendered her case impotent.

"Court stand," the Court's orderly stood and shouted. All the people in the court heard it and stood up. As they stood, the judge walked away to his chamber.

CHAPTER TWELVE

"This is ridiculous," Mrs. Ala-Oma said. She was boiling with a passionate displeasure.

"I told you it would happen," her husband reminded her.

"Should." Her anger was ready to overtake the better angel of her reasoning potential.

"No, you can only make an appeal. I won't allow you to do a foolish thing which you would only live to regret. Yes."

"No, I can play their game of fire." She was very mad.

"I think, you should not dance the music of the ignorant people. If you do, they would get you the way they had always desired. Show them, through your wise approach, that you can rise above their prejudice, above their blindness, and above their culture of color," he advised her.

"Thanks honey. I married you because you're the wisest man I'd ever met," she remarked.

"Love, you know how to flatter the ego of a proud man," said he.

"No. I mean it," she became serious.

"OK dear, I'll accept that as a compliment," finally, he acknowledged her compliment.

"And you deserve it," she reassured him.

When they came out from the Courthouse, they walked straight to the Court's parking lot, where they parked their car. There were many other cars in the parking lot—some were expensive cars;

some, moderately priced; and, some were nothing but road-worthy junks.

"Are you Arabic?" a white fellow in a sedentary Range Rover asked the black man who was walking with his woman towards a Jaguar Car.

"It doesn't matter who he is," an Arab-looking fellow, standing by, replied to the man who asked the seemingly foolish, and even stupid question, obviously putting the questioner on the notice that a person should be known as a person, and should not be known by the virtue of his ethnicity.

"I can guess," pursued the white man.

"Guess your head off; who really cares?" the Arab fellow countered the questioner; then, he asked the white man, "Why are you here, anyway?" the Arab man became irritated at his presence.

"I need a job," he answered.

"I hired you two years ago; I fired you because you couldn't hold the job

-You came back to me and begged me to give you second chance. I did; for the first one month you were late to work everyday. You slept on the job, and this business lost a lot of money because of you."

"I don't think so Moamed, those illegal Mexicans are taking away our jobs."

"I don't think so—My brother in Saudi sent me money to buy this parking lot. I did. He expects me to run it profitably. How do you think my brother will feel if I told him that his business went under because I hired only American citizens?" the Arab man asked the American man.

"I will report you to the immigration if you do not rehire me," the young man issued a threat.

"You can report me to your president, if you like. I can't rehire a lazy bum for the third time when there are millions of Mexicans who can do the job. You know, you white folks have a

THE DEVIL'S LAND

problem—you work too much with your mouth, you know. You talk too much, but you just cannot cut through the mustard. See, you're there in that van listening to music when you should be looking for a job. You came here to make trouble for me, and for those you think have taken away your job from you. It's a shame you white brats take too many things for granted."

"Oh yeah? What about you? You're an Arab terrorist. I wonder if you're planning to blow down the white-house."

"Get the hell out of here, or I'll call the cop."

"If you do, I'll tell them that you made a death threat on the life of the President of the United States."

"You're a big-time liar. Get the hell out from here, stupid."

"No. I'll leave here when I want. I'm an American. You can't force me."

While the two men were arguing, Mr. and Mrs. Ala-Ọma entered their car and drove away.

****

Some days within reach from hence, the Ala-Ọmas received many death threats. Their new residence, in Alabama, was wire-tapped by the Court's security agents, all for safety reasons.

Mr. Ala-Ọma was considered a security risk, because he had violated many laws of the land. For example, he refused to ignore, upon judge's order, the voices of aberration. He made the spirits of the inferior niggers, feel recognized in a Court where a white judge was its president. He spoke with them, as if they were equal to the white race; and, his actions gave them impetus to slap a white judge. The lawyers who were in the Court on that day knew these things. And, the man from the African jungle was guilty of it all.

Two of the white lawyers who were witnesses to what the 'jungle man' did, indeed, were ready, never to forgive him. The man of jungle was indeed an unpardonable threat to a way of life.

And, as such, he would never be allowed to get away with it all. For one thing, really, he was free to behave anyhow in his home, Africa, where witches rode the nights on the sloping hyennas' backs. He was free to eat his plague-bearing rats which wiped away more than ten million whites in Europe. Here, in America, he had no right to behave anyhow in a land of the braves.

America could not keep a miniature snake in a tournament of real dragons. 'The bushman' could claim his place as a 'bushmaster' in one of his 'African forests'. However, here, in America, he was just as powerful as a grasshopper in the den of soaring puffadders; and, like winged puffadders, or, even flying vipers, Americans would fight back whenever threatened in their own territory.

The two lawyers were so ready for him. In another respect, they were equally educated, equally aware that knowledge was power in process, even power in cold blood—that a powerful knowledge could exact an awful spell over people, including the bushman. They would fight him, with their arsenals, including, but not limited to, with blackmailing, and other poisons of prejudice.

They did not pass the touch, rather the flame of racism. Thus, to keep it burning, in the hearts of the people, with constant radiation of its deadly sun, they set a special example, with the bushman of the jungle. They did not lose hope, because they had nothing but cool heads and their outgrowths of steel nerves. They knew that winning this buck was nothing but getting the racial glory.

Their enemy, integration, had to be defeated and destroyed so that it would never again interfere with the Southern way of life. The bushman, Mr. Ala-Oma, was indeed a symbol of danger in the Great Southern County, Alabama. He and his rebel wife had already turned a sacrilege into a holy thing. And, their act, alone, was terribly unpardonable.

For example, all the other blacks in the Great County were obedient slaves, and were causing no harm, in the process. They knew their station; they behaved; like bats of Texas, they were nothing but harmless. They knew that they should not be

THE DEVIL'S LAND

educated—that education was nothing but a grand station of the white race. And, when they were forced to stay in the farm, like mulls of a cotton plantation, they obeyed with a cool head, and there was no fuss nor trouble about it. And their white superiors fed them, and, they liked it that way. But, here came this fellow, from an African jungle, a replica of a blood-sucking vampire, ready to give all the other gentle bats a bad name. Indeed, the South of the Confederate would not have him. The Great County would not keep him, not even with the unforgivable attitude of having his superior, a white lady, as a helpful wife. He had done a terrible thing. And, really, he was even out on his way to do more.

When trouble was sleeping, in the land of the white man, a troublesome pride, from an African jungle, came over and woke him up. Trouble would not take the act of the insolent pride lightly. Really, the two men who witnessed the Court's drama—the acts of Mr. Ala-Oma's insolence, and even the shocking presentation of his wife, to indict whites, for getting rid of mere niggers, were ready to stand up to the odd-couple, and show them, to show the man of the jungle that America was not Africa for him to behave anyhow.

Indeed, they hired four different contract killers to blow his brain away. Three of the hired men were hopeless blacks, homeless, unemployed and unemployable drug addicts. The fourth fellow was a white junkie who had spent a good number of his useless lifetime in jail. They had done similar job, several times, for the two men. And, they would not resist the temptation to grab fifteen hundred dollars, after doing something less than a minute's job.

"Just waste him," the older attorney told the homeless drug addict, "the money is yours." Nodding his head in blessed assurance, as he gave the homeless fellow two hundred dollars, advance payment, for the life of his fellow-lawyer from the African jungle. And, he promised the drug-addict that the balance, thirteen cool hundred dollars, would soon be in his dirty hands, right after the fine job was done.

As an American thing, however, the addict had a girl friend. And, he told her about his fortune to make some quick bucks. Displeased, she asked him to return the blood money, right away. She threatened to dump him, if he did not comply with her raving decision. Having no choice, no other woman to turn to, he listened, but, not without a measure of intense hesitation.

"Go and tell this guy what them white folks wanted to do to him," she ordered her boyfriend.

"No baby, that'd be crazy. Ain't gonna do such thing," reasoned the drug-addict, under the influence of some intoxicating blood-money.

"Yeah, you've got to, love; them white folks set one black man against another. It's a shame, love; you gotta tell him," she insisted.

"How am I gonna tell him?" he yielded, knowing that his girl-friend was an unyielding, and even a stubborn obstacle.

"I'll go with ya. Bring that goddam money with ya; shit, them white folks are something," she said.

"Baby, I ain't think is a good idea. It's an easy job. I'll just take my gun and whack him boom, the money is ours. Shoo, that money, think what we can do with it baby; lots of buzz, drugs and shit, yo, lets keep the money—I can do the job. Nobody is gonna find out," said he, tempting to reason with her.

"Shit; that's shit talk baby; them white folks, are gonna kill you, if you don't think smart," she hung in to her own gun.

"Be reasonable, baby."

"No, yu be reasonable shit; them white folks asked you to do their dirty job because they thought you're up to no good," she remarked.

"Hey, whoa whoa—" he got a rise at that.

"Yeah, I ain't telling you lie. If you're a doctor or a damn lawyer, you think they're gonna ask you to do their damn dirty-job for them? No way. Them white folks are devils, honey."

THE DEVIL'S LAND

"That's it. I've had it. Lawyers and doctors and shit, I don't give a damn, baby. They do their own dirty job," he was offended.

"But, honey, not murder for hire, or, that kind of shit. A white lawyer is not gonna defend you when you get your ass in shit. Say, that black dude is a lawyer and shit, huh?" she asked him.

"Yeah, baby; yeah, who cares?"

"Damn. Them white folks wanna kill him, huh?" she asked him, as if he were in complete agreement with her.

"Yeah, who really cares? I've got the money; see, two hundred bucks. More coming baby. I'll do this shit, and have the whole money, baby." He radiated with the voice of reassurance.

"No way. It's fucking blood money. I ain't gonna allow you do such thing; not for the damn white folks who'd put us through hell."

"Baby, be reasonable gal," he noted, yet again.

"You are the one who ain't being reasonable and shit. I'm gonna leave you if I hear you insult me anymore."

"I'm sorry, babe. You know I love you. I ain't gonna do anything that's gonna hurt your feeling, babe."

"Yeah, insult me for damn whites."

"No, babe. You, my black queen. You, my girl—you know I love you pretty much," he drew nearer to her and tried to kiss her.

"Don't kiss me," she protested; and she pushed him away.

"Yo, baby, you're my girl. I ain't gonna hurt you. You know me by now, yo, I'm gonna return the money; I'm gonna tell the guy," he promised. And, she knew that she'd got him on her side.

"When?" she asked him, ready to get him to act on his promise.

"Right now," he stood up, ready to go.

"Good. Let's go now," she smiled.

"We're gonna tell him secrecy of the deal, plot and shit."

"Yeah baby, let's go," he was ready to follow the lead of the reasonable addict.

"We'll see, them white folks are gonna deny it, shoo. When they do, at least we'd let the black dude know them white folks are out to get him," she remarked.

"Yeah, they're gonna."

"Gimme a kiss; will ya?" she commanded him.

"Shoo, baby, I'll." He radiated with jubilation.

They kissed before they left.

CHAPTER THIRTEEN

Mrs. Ala-Qma was terribly alarmed when she learnt that her dear husband was on a danger list. She shouted. She screamed. And, she became hysterical.

"Shit, honey, I ain't lying, take it easy dear; welcome to the Kingdom of Racism my fellow woman," the female drug addict tried to console the hysterical lawyer, hysterical by the mere fact that her black husband was marked to be eliminated.

"What am I gonna do?"

"Shoo, be glad my gal asked me to tell you about it; otherwise, yo'man ain't stand no chance," said the repented murder-for-hire hand.

"Thank you so much; you are a savior, and my angels; I don't know how to thank you," said the woman whose husband was the target.

She had witnessed many a black man being shot at a close range. She had seen the white cops shoot blacks the way the buffalo soldiers shot the buffaloes. She, had seen cops shoot black youths the way the Cowboys shot the Indians.

She had seen the white cops shoot and disorganize the proactive blacks called the Panthers. She had seen the toothed Panthers decimated with machine-guns, never to rise again to challenge the white race.

Her man, though black, was too precious to be allowed to perish that way. She loved him. And she had defended him before; for example, when the angry elements of Knights of the

Ku Klux Klan wanted to lynch him on the fateful day, she drew her pretty loaded pistol and was determined to use it without hesitation.

This time though, some evil men had been hired to claim the life of her beloved. Luckily, one of them had a change of heart, and was here before her. But what about the other men who she did not even know? What if the deadly men who hired the hitmen resolved to hire even more hitmen? And her husband was not home. And what if any of the other hired men met him on the way? She was worried, deeply worried now more than ever.

"I still don't know how to thank you," she said again to the black bum and his equally hopeless girlfriend.

"Yo, yu'welcome," replied the drug addict.

"Can you do me a favor?" she added.

"Shoo, what's it?" the male drug addict asked the blond lawyer.

"I'd like you to testify in Court."

"Fuck that, ain't they gonna kill me if . . . ?" the hopeless nigger disagreed.

"I'll make sure you get all the necessary protections."

"Shit that, man."

"I'm a lawyer. My husband is a lawyer," said Mrs. Ala-Ọma, to calm his fear.

"So? Shit talk nigger."

"No, It's not. Trust me," said the female lawyer to the fearful drug addict.

"You sure them cops ain't gonna whack me?" he asked, partly unconvinced.

"Yes, I'm pretty sure; I'll arrange to keep you in a safe place. Nobody is gonna hurt you." Then, she shifted the line, "I'm scared for the sake of my husband. He went to the grocery store a couple of hours ago. He's never this late when he went there. I wonder whether to call the grocery store right now."

THE DEVIL'S LAND

"Which store did he go to?" This was the voice of the female addict; her attire, a complete contrast of the lawyer's fashionable debonair.

"Super Whopper."

"There ain't nothing to worry yet."

"Give him one more hour before you alarm the grocery store. If anything bad had happened, they'd broadcast it on the television, and them goddam cops would come here and tell you. They don't waste time and shit."

"Thank you. Now I feel better."

"You shouldn't be worried. There ain't nothing to worry about," said the unkempt black woman.

"What?" Mrs. Ala-Oma screamed, as if she were senseless, "If your husband is?"

"Wait a minute dear; you're a woman like me. I understand what you wanna say. Shoo, you should be worried if you didn't know that somebody hired hitmen to whack your man and shit; shoo, what you should do now is to call the goddam judge and shitty cop to report what we just told you, dear; I ain't lying, dear; when them folks hear you know about that crap, and shit, they're gonna turn around and tell their hitmen to call it off, dear. Shoo, if you don't, betcha it'd be too late, dear. So call them right now, dear."

"Thank you. I'd do it right away."

"Yes, do it, dear."

Mrs. Ala-Oma rushed to the telephone. She picked up the telephone directory which was on a table beside the telephone. She flipped through the book's pages till she reached just a page to the middle of the book.

Right there, she saw the name, 'Lavrenzo,' the surname of the judge, 'Tillmano'. The entire address were there: ' Lavrenzo, Tillmano, judge, 225 Lovers Road.' She memorized the phone number printed besides the judge's name so fast, and she called up the judge, right away.

"Hi, Tillmano speaking, how can I help you?" a man's voice boomed from the other end. It was a happy voice. He was now at her service, ready to serve a woman he refused to even serve in his Court.

"Your honor, this is me." The lovely voice of a woman, the middle-aged smart judge heard from his own end of the telephone line.

"Oh, is that you, Mrs. Ala-Ọma? I saw your husband, the black fellow at Supper Whopper a couple of hours ago. I was leaving when he was coming in."

"Yes, Your Honor, I know he went to the store. Listen, somebody is trying to kill him."

"That's bull!" the racist judge overruled. His voice alone and the tone of it were nothing but a clockwork of racism at its best. And, she sensed it. He was a judge, and he knew it all. He was a JD: a doctor of judge-it-all and know-it-all. He knew the minds of those who were determined to kill the black man, that their hearts were clean, and as white as snow. "How could some genuine gentlemen, white folks for that matter, kill a man from an interior African jungle?" the brilliant judge wondered. Indeed, he did not hesitate to confront the woman with the same question. 'The woman was only speculating. Or, at best retelling some lies, as she retold in the Court before. Is the presumed target no longer a product of a dark continent, a continent presumed raped by those who came and helped her?' In essence, blacks were just good at telling lies. And her man must have told her lies. There was a pause, a prolonged pause. During that pause she read his mind that he did not believe her.

"Judge, I'm telling you what I know, not what you presumed. I'm . . ." she told him; and, there was a clear note of arrogance, so clearly spelt out in the way she called him 'judge' rather than 'your honor'; and, the Paramount Judge of the Kingdom of Racism did not like it.

THE DEVIL'S LAND

"Mrs. Ala-Oma," the judge interrupted her before she could do an unpardonable damage. Damage? She was rather ready to do more to defend and protect her black husband.

"Can you wait till I finish?" she returned his interruption without hesitation. She knew the no-nonsense approach of the New Englanders; and, she was not ready to take a 'bull' from a man of a slave State.

Right there, she pressed home, for the benefit of the ignorant judge. "One of the men who were hired to kill my husband is here with me. There's nothing 'bull' about it. The men who hired him are the prosecuting attorneys on that case."

"Oh bull," the all-wise doctor of judgements 'bulled' her again.

"You just don't care. Why can't you understand a thing, a fact, a deadly plot before it's too late?"

"I don't think I'll believe that kind of unsubstantiated speculation," the judge ruled and hung up the telephone.

"Damn; what a foolish judge," she shouted; then she hung up the phone.

"He didn't believe you did he, dear?" asked the dirty, female drug-addict.

"Not at all," she answered the dirty-clad woman who came to save her husband from the hands of some evil men.

However, as the judge saw it, even with all-powerful lens of racism, he knew that he'd dug some holes in the silly allegations of the foolish lady who was so foolish as to even date, make love to, and even marry a 'nigger from the jungle.' There, in his assessment, was a touch of brilliance—a divergent marplot to the interest in question; indeed, a legal doyen with a brilliant touch of attrition. Indeed, to himself in particular, a legal genius made in America.

"What can I do now?" she asked her guests; and, she needed a prudent approach now.

"Call the cops, dear," her fellow woman told her as the answer to her question.

"Yeah, do it," the male drug addict, the female's partner, added.

She picked up the phone. And as she was about to dial 911, the door opened, and her husband stepped in with two bags filled with groceries in his two hands. When she saw him, she left the telephone and ran to him and hugged him.

"Boy, am I glad you're alive," she said.

"What? Is anything wrong?"

"Yes, as a matter of fact, that's why these fine folks are here," she responded. She looked at her guests as she endeavored to measure every other word which would come out from her mouth. Though she weighed her words, she had already understood the brilliance of the powerful judge, his mind frame, and the conscript of his character. That the man had his way, by, and, for a special piece. A way of prejudice, and racism. A way supported by masses of supporters who shared and upheld his heavenly philosophy of racism. Indeed the man was a rocky legal stud, even as powerful and deeply rooted as an African Iroko tree; yet, made in America.

"What's it?" Mr. Ala-Ọma asked her.

"Ask these friends, better you hear it from the horse's mouth," she replied. In her voice was a subdued rage. A rage she copied from her husband, after she also found out that some missionaries were giving the mission work a bad name.

Mr. Ala-Ọma looked at the guests, a black man and a black woman in tattered clads, so dirty attires, unkempt, both in homeless condition. So dirty that one could feel the terrible stink oozing from their dirty clads, even some twenty, or thirty foot-steps away. He was amused; yet, he sensed there was an element of urgency about their visitation.

"Have you given them some kola?" he asked his wife.

"I forgot," she answered him.

THE DEVIL'S LAND

"That's the first thing you do when you have a guest. I don't know how many times I'd remind you of it," he admonished her. Then, he turned to the guests "I'm sorry she hadn't given you some kola; I'd bring it by myself." And, the dirty couple smiled and nodded their heads in approval. He rushed to the refrigerator; and, he brought out some sliced bread. Then, he went to the cupboard and got some bags of tea.

He turned the electric stove on. And he put the bags of tea in the teakettle. He poured some Brita-Clean water in the tea-kettle, and he placed the tea-kettle over the electric stove. Then, he put some pre-buttered aunt Jamaima sliced bread in a toaster. And he got out some sugar, powdered coffee mate, milk, and Phillie Spreadable Cheese.

When the toasts were ready, he used the Spreadable Cheese over the hot slices of bread. And the whole thing looked delicious. He poured the tea in four different tea cups, transferred the whole things in a main tray, and carried the tray to a dining-table.

"Come on over, folks," he told both his guests and his wife. They obeyed. "Here is kola. It's improvised kola. Kolanut trees don't grow in America," he quipped. They laughed. "Since there is no kolanut-tree in America, we'll make do with what we have. ".

"Shoo. This ain't bad," the female guest remarked as she took a cup of hot tea and tasted its content.

"Damn, I like it too," the male guest added his own approval.

"My husband is a fine cook; I wonder what I'd do without him," Mrs. Ala-Ọma commented.

"She's a nice woman, though she forgets at times," returned her husband.

"She's alright," the male guest noted.

"Yes, she's a fine woman. I'm teaching her a lot of African customs, and our traditions. She remembers some and she forgets the others," said the host.

"Shoo, we all forget. Ain't nobody perfect," said the guest in defense of her fellow woman.

103

"Yes, she should remember that the first thing a wife does when her husband has a guest is to bring out some kola," the man gave a divergent opinion.

"I'll I try to remember next time. I promise."

"Yes, you've promised me a million times," he teased her.

"Honey, today was different," she pleaded.

"How? Is one day different from another day?"

"Why not wait till you hear the news?" she measured her words, yet, again.

"We'll talk when we finish the kola," Mr. Ala-Ọma ruled.

"Fine with me," said the other man.

"Me too," added his girl-friend.

CHAPTER FOURTEEN

Mr. Ala-Ọma was shaken to the bones when he heard that his fellow lawyers had hired some men to take, or 'whack' his life away. As he stood there, shaking in his own hut, he saw the whole trends that led to this special deal. A spit of cobra in defense of its own invaded territory. There, more than ever, he came to despise those religious hypocrites who played the racist cards at will and at any moment. He remembered Rev. Jingle, the man who took over Africa with the power of his 'mission work'.

While he shook, a stream of ideas continued to go through the layers of his mind: 'Private racism and public ones, in them dwelt the revenge of the white dragon. Yes. That racism hurts more those who harbored the racist sentiment was a fact hidden from those who embodied the venom of the demon.'

"Let's call the police," he said in a terrible rage.

"Wise idea," the man who was to shoot him replied. Then, he pointed at the telephone, as if his host did not know where the telephone was. So ably prompted, Mr. Ala-Ọma ran to the telephone and dialled the number, '911'.

"Officer Kelly Chase, what's your emergency?" a cop replied from the station.

"Yes officer, send your people to my residence right away," Mr. Ala-Ọma ordered.

"You got it," Officer Chase replied from her end of the line.

"Good God; what type of place is this?" Mr. Ala-Ọma shouted when he hung up the phone.

"Land of opportunity," the female black, drug addict remarked; her tone was indeed very sarcastic.

"Shoo, welcome to the Kingdom of Racism, bro," said the man who was to 'whack' him.

"Yes sir, you're right. You are absolutely right," Mrs. Ala-Ọma, the lone white lady in the room, remarked in her response. She looked at her husband, his rage was equally assuming an alarming proportion. His face had turned deep black, and his eyes, red.

"Are we in a jungle war, or what?" said the African lawyer, whose life was in danger.

"In America, dear," his wife answered, with, at least, a desire for a comical compromise "racism is out of control; only those who love it, practice it, and those who had never lived in America, will forever believe that America is a land of opportunity."

"Yeah, right," added the homeless comic.

"Yeah, what can I say? The greatest 'opportunity' in America is the 'opportunity' for blacks to suffer," said Mrs. Ala-Ọma, a white, female attorney married to a black African.

"They stole us from Africa. Shit, they brought us here as slaves. They want us be slaves forever. They wanna kill us. Damn, they won't allow us go back to Africa," the black addict added.

"Yeah, Marcus Garvey tried it, 'back to land.' They didn't let the movement last," Mrs. Ala-Ọma agreed.

****
******
****

Less than five minutes, after Mr. Ala-Ọma made the call, three police cruisers arrived at Mr. and Mrs Ala-Ọma's residence. Five of the men, all whites, rushed into the apartment, with loaded drawn

THE DEVIL'S LAND

guns, pointing in different directions, intent on preemptive shooting to surprisation of the presumed intruders, as they entered.

The guests were even scared to death, by the very display of force, all by the way the armed policemen were pointing their loaded guns, here and there, mostly in their direction. Yes, only in the direction of the three black people.

"Did they rob you?" an officer asked Mrs. Ala-Ọma, as he specifically pointed his gun, swaying it towards the three black people in the room. "Don't move. Or I'll shoot."

"No," Mrs. Ala-Ọma shouted at the police officer.

"Why not? They broke into your home; didn't they?" the officer analyzed the situation, and told her why her husband called him and other police officers. She sensed his prejudice, saw his gun ready to shoot; therefore, she seized the moment to carefully walk on a tight rope.

"Actually," she continued "the man in the middle is my husband. The other two are our friends," she told the armed officer.

"So you married a nigger? Why then did you call us?" the officer remarked, nonchalantly. He began to inspect the apartment, with some air of admiration.

"This place looks like a nigger heaven" he remarked. "Guess you're happy with your company," he added quite sarcastically. Then, he bared his mind with an open box of arrogance. "I won't allow you to waste our time, ever again." His insensitive remarks got a rise out of those who called him.

"Officer, I called you because my life is in danger," Mr. Ala-Ọma told the arrogant cop.

"Yes, who'd desire to hurt a nigger?" the insensitive cop doubted him.

"Hey, I'd appreciate it if you'd be a bit careful with your choice of words," Mrs. Ala-Ọma threw her caution to the wind, and soundly rebuked the insolent police officer.

"Excuse me?" the officer disapproved her stunning rebuke "I'm not here to take away your nigger's sweet dick, honey."

"Eh, hold it there," Mr. Ala-Ọma shouted at the police officer. "I wonder where my tax money goes to when a police officer will not show respect."

"Oh yeah?" the great cop was now terribly mad. He could not take a rebuttal from a person of an inferior race.

"Hey, cut it off, all of you," a junior officer sensed danger, and charged against the hostile exchange of verbal insolence. "We're here to do our job. You, you, and you, shut up," she rebuked pointing her rageful finger, first at the host, then at the wife, and then at her superior, the insolent police officer. There was indeed a surrendering hush, a dramatic turn of event in that all the people who were exchanging verbal blows turned and became temporally friendly.

"My name is Ala-Ọma," Mr. Ala-Ọma stretched his hand, quite professionally, toward the man who had just called him 'nigger,' repeatedly.

"Mine is Peter. These gang are mine. I'm their boss." He seemed elated as he called himself a 'boss' and his crew 'these gang'

"I'm an attorney; so is my wife," Mr. Ala-Ọma stretched out his hand toward his wife, acknowledging her in the process.

"Attorney," the officer swallowed hard as he tried to vomit out that word.

Right there, Mr. Ala-Ọma sensed a tinge of jealousy, an admixture of true rage, surprise and self-deprecation. He sensed him feel like a North American rodent, called jerboa, standing before a bull-like African elephant. The pompous cop, who was a moment elated, appeared belittled, even flushed, when he heard that the man who received his flood of insolence was indeed an attorney. He didn't like it. Frankly, he hated it. He swallowed hard his arrogance. Together, even those who were his gun-happy subordinates, felt it.

And, true to their ugly reputation, the cops and their leader insisted that the two black informers be handcuffed before being taken to the police station for questioning.

THE DEVIL'S LAND

"Officer, my wife and I will drive them in our car." Mr. Ala-Oma tried to save the odd couple the unnecessary embarrassing humiliation.

"That wouldn't be necessary. We're taking them in our cruiser," the 'ugly boss' ruled, alive and powerful to his bad repute, once again.

"But, why handcuff them? They're only helping. They're not criminals," Mrs. Ala-Oma said, ventured to reason with the adamant, evil police lord.

"You don't know these colored people, ma'am, animals; they can pull the fast one, in a moment's notice. We just can't take that kind of risk. It's precaution."

"I don't like this; they're our friends, our true friends." Mr. Ala-Oma remarked when he saw the lord among the police 'gang' motion to his gang to handcuff the two black informers.

"You don't have to like many things in my line of profession, mister; if they killed any of my men, you may appear in Court in their defense; but now that we're taking a preemptive measure, I'm not surprised that a damn lawyer will complain his half-ass about it," the police 'boss' replied. And, he did not listen to the voice of reason.

The two drug addicts were handcuffed and dumped into the caged back of one of the police cruisers. Fast as they entered the apartment, off they drove, with their two black prey. And from the back of the police cruisers, the black couple cast a very understanding look at the man whose life they saved. In reciprocity, Mr. Ala-Oma fixed his own on them till the car they were in was driven off.

When they took off, Mr. and Mrs. Ala-Oma followed the police gang in their own car.

The first three vehicles, now on the road, did something quite spectacular; they sped as if they were transporting some dangerous criminals, with their sirens blaring the highway. The red, white and blue rotating bulbs, atop the cruisers, were turned on, thus, warning the public, the traffic, to clear the way for the road lords.

While they were on the main road, on their way to the Alabama Police Station, lo and behold, an elderly white gentleman, who was driving in his 1922 Ford Mustang, was on the road, having a good time. The old fellow was hard of hearing; and, his eyesight was failing him. He did not hear the police sirens; neither did he see the red, blue and white rotating lights atop the triple police cruisers. Nonetheless, the old fellow was young at heart. And he turned on his car radio, fully, to a rock-and-roll F.M. radio station. Yes, he was listening to, and even nodding his head to the American 'maximum-motion-style' music phenomenon. And, in rock music, the music was in full blast.

Slowly, and in leisurely stride, the old papa drove his car, all with hell-be-damned kind of carefreeness. He sang along the song booming from his radio.

As he drove, he carelessly blocked the road, like the real road lord.

While he took over, the police cruisers just found their better competitor—and they just could not pass by. Yes, the lead cruiser blew its horn; but, that was in vain. Frustrated at every turn, time and time again, all in every turn to overtake him, a police officer took out his gun and slugged a few bullets into the rear tire of the old man's car. Slowly and skiddingly, the car came to a complete stop.

The angry old man jumped out from his car, before those who ruined his pleasure could reach there. Scared, yet offended, he raised his two hands up. The cop who shot at his car's tire caught him.

"Please don't kill me. I've a family," the old man begged his captor.

"Shut up, dirty old man," the cop, young enough to be his son shouted, and rudely insulted the old man. He shoved him; and then, he dragged the old man along. He dragged him to one of the cruisers, the one with a galvanized metal cage, at its back.

And, professionally violent too, he dumped him at the back where the handcuffed black informants were kept for safety reasons.

THE DEVIL'S LAND

Baffled, and humiliated, but not handcuffed. Because he was not black, as such, less dangerous, the old man waited for his captors to settle down, even comfortably, in their cruiser's front seats.

Soon after the cop-cruiser was pulled out from the curb, into the main road, the old man reached into his jacket and drew his loaded .45 pistol. Before the two road lords at the front seats could even see him, their armed competitor had already started to send them to their eternal ancestors.

He blasted the brain of the driver, with three rapid shots. Then, he blew the life of the second cop, in the front seat, to the land of his ancestors, too. Then, he struggled to open the door of the running car. The car, now out of control, on the main road, swayed from one side of the multi-lane road, to the other end of the great American multi-lane road.

When, at last, the cruiser hitched to a stop, after colliding with a school bus filled with school children, the other policemen, from the other police cruisers, rushed to the scene. By this time, however, the rear door of the damaged cruiser yanked open, through the forces of multiple impacts. The old man, though wounded, still angry at it all, managed to come out from the ruined cruiser. His pistol, however, had fallen from his hand, into the car, upon the last impact of the great collision. He bled as he staggered to regain consciousness.

"Why did you shoot cops?" the lord of the police crew shouted at the handcuffed couple in the cage, at the back of the police cruiser. The couple, wounded and bleeding, were speechless at this round of brutal accusation.

"Talk or I'll shoot," the top cop ordered.

"Can you shoot a cop when your hands are handcuffed behind your back?" the handcuffed black man mustered enough courage to confront the officer who accused him and his girlfriend.

"Damn you. You niggers are terrible . . ."

"Oh ya? I know you white folks will never see anything good in the black race. I ain't even surprised," added the black woman.

"Shut up and tell me how you did it; or, I'll shoot you if you don't confess," he pointed his gun at them, with intent to shoot.

"Hey officer," a voice with an accent, addressed him. It came from behind.

He turned, "What?" the enraged officer turned, to see the black lawyer, now he loved to hate, and to know why he called him.

"Look."

"Yeah, what's it?" He faced Mr. Ala-Ọma, squarely, as if in a parade, and even a cop salute to a hated superior. Indeed, his new superior was the black attorney, he now loved to hate, a growing hatred which emerged within him was no less than it was an hour earlier.

"The man you're looking for is there on the floor beside your feet."

The officer, who was so full of hate, looked beside himself; and, right beside his own feet was the old white man who killed his two men, now bleeding to death, in his own wounds.

"So he's the one?" he asked Mr. Ala-Ọma, in a tone, full of shame and sadness.

"You too are a witness," Mr. Ala-Ọma responded to his question.

"I'm so sorry," he murmured, all to himself.

CHAPTER FIFTEEN

The public exposure of the abortive plot of the lawyers turned the enraged Knights of the Ku Klux Klan into a nationwide campaign to eradicate blacks. It was a hysterical phenomena, a racial cleansing that became a mob-call to black elimination. It was a wave of the day. And, the days ahead were fulled with it. The national hysteria was phenomenal.

Blacks, the endangered species of the American dream, were fastly becoming a done deal. There was no turning back, as the blood-thirsty Knights were out to get them. They faced the vapors of rage and eternal prejudice. They fought, though helpless, with unquestionable fortitude.

In the midst of their struggle for survival, they remembered Africa, their mama and papa's land. A land of diamonds raped by those who ravaged the continent. They fought like angels, unyielding, though overwhelmingly surrounded by menacing troops of demons.

While they fought, they cast every fear to the wind, pledging every breath, of their being to the fighting before them. They pledged their lives to their cause, and they held their lives belonged to their cause, a pledge firmly rooted in the rock of their struggle with nothing but an unquestionable exactitude.

They fought with the indomitable souls of the great kings of the forests. Like lions, they fought with nothing but their teeth, claws, and with strength of their courage. They fought those with guns, touches, and crosses for lynchings, with nothing, but bare hands and bare claws, and even with bare teeth.

They faced bullets with their right hands and their heads held high. Their men died in glory, and even their women died with their courageous heads held even higher. Their children, who had endured it all because of racism, were quick to copy the courageous ways of their parents.

It was a campaign of terror, a systematic burning, at night, even in some broad day light, of the facilities owned by the blacks. A couple of black universities, both in Southern States, were burnt down by the fire-breathing dragons.

As they plundered, and burnt down the black enterprise, they placed their symbol of hatred, a wooden cross, made by klans, in front of the burnt, and burnt their own cross too.

And, before they left each scene of vandalism, they wrote some hateful graffiti on some wooden planks, to remind the owners of the burnt-down structures that hatred was in progress.

In the time past, the noble minority of the black population had cried in vain. Now the panthers who had resolved to show strength were apt to fight back. They were the roaring lions, the vanguards and defenders of the endangered blacks.

The word of each graffito reminded them that their American dream was nothing but a war zone—That the prostitutes of imperialism could not survive without raping them time and again. They could not forever host the obligate parasites without perishing in the process. That then, there had to be a way to rid themselves of the nuisance.

But the powers of those who oppressed them were too much. It was a quest to lord over with nothing but a deadly obsession; a wake-up call similar to a deadly dose of alcohol in a punctured lung. It was a white elephant in a living-room; an exploitation for an unmerited patronage, an unpredictable show of the unwieldy system. And in there dwelt the eternal quest to obtain the unobtainable—a quest to lord over and enslave for eternal servitude.

THE DEVIL'S LAND

Indeed, the old pen of the American revolution would not have approved, perhaps and paradoxically, maybe. But here was the news of the New American Spirit in vogue and in progress—a case of clear expression in total opposition to the words of the constitution. Here was the alignment of the monument of the human element and the questionable high tide of racial divide. And Church being the embodiment of the whole troublesome show—an exobiology of the unknown, all in the world beyond new.

America was bleeding because of hatred. It was due to racism all the way; a legacy which had endorsed itself on the negative end of the broken American story. In waves of cowboy calvaries, the men in hoods fought and burnt, even black people and their belongings. And, in proportional waves of determination, the owners of the burnt and destroyed properties fought back.

They fought with the brave souls of the dead slaves in the enchanted land. Their living nightmares became sources of inspiration. Each band of fighters fought hard, facing all the devils in their opponents' ranks.

Every moment in the struggle was filled with hyperventilation.

Each moment of tempo was heightened by a terrible moment of expectation. A hope and trepidation; a hope to snatch an eternal victory from the jaws of a terrible defeat; and they were afraid lest lack of victory save the day for the wicked oppressors of the helpless blacks in the Kingdom of Racism.

Terrible things happened at every turn. Some captured slaves were slaughtered like cows, and used as meals for the youths and newly initiated. The heads of the beheaded blacks were given to the youths for Satanic Cults, and their awesome Satanic rituals. When some of the teenagers tasted the flesh of some black men, they went around and told their fellow teens that the flesh of blacks was delicious.

Some dragons killed some captured slaves and stuffed their body parts in their refrigerators, as preserved meals. They ate the human flesh, daily, as their source of protein.

They behaved like floor maggots, even like the African mosquitoes, in the way they sucked the slaves' blood. Each dragon stood up to his reputation as a blood-sucker and a flesh-eater of the black race. The dragons, the terrible Knights, were the horrible vampires of the New World.

CHAPTER SIXTEEN

There was a rapid call from the executive for racial harmony, racial understanding, and racial integration. The call for fusion of races was received with blows of rejection.

Most Southern whites were religiously adamant in their perfect opposition to the whole thing. There were some who expressed their opposition in diverse ways and diverse manners. Some of them did by killing more blacks and eating them.

There were those who sacrificed more blacks for their Satanic Cults. Scores of white men, even women jumped through the windows, some from tall bridges, and sent their souls to the land of eternal separation. Even some blacks, out of sheer pride, did the same, and became symbols of eternal hate.

America was burning with no one to quench it. And Mr. and Mrs. Ala-Oma were caught in the middle of the deadly conflagration. It was a conflagration with far-reaching and deadly consequences.

They became the new lightening rod of the old racial divide—a drop of peroxide at the root of the unhealable wound. Judges in the South would only enact 'consent decrees,' even contrary to the edict of the executive. The southern Governors, proud of being 'segregationists,' proclaimed segregation now, and segregation forever more.

The events, as they developed, and unfolded, gave credence to the notion that people could become beasts when they had tasted blood. They were wild; their youths became wild with black blood.

Killing caravans rode on their horses, riding deeper into the sunset. And, all the hells of hatred were let loose. America which was once on the verge of disintegration revamped the old pipe once again.

Arkansas, the 'Natural land of opportunity' was in the forefront, a slave State and the major basket of the Cotton world. A great refusal for integration was alive in the State of Arkansas. And, as a State law, they refused to accept blacks as human beings. Their dragons were everywhere. And their dragons were on the onslaught. The helpless survivors felt a special longing to remain alive in the natural forest of racism; they cried for mercy; yet, they were willing to fight till death for their honor, and even for the great cause. The great hate of the natural Arkansas was mutual. And, their heads did fall, and even rolled. And, they were so taxed to the extreme proportion.

They were taxed, at each passing moment, to the utmost. And, though the South was forced back into the Union, the southern States saw themselves as a separate nation from the United States. They found no ground for the North to keep on forcing them to accept blacks, contrary to the dictates of their own views.

While the executive fought to restore trust, the dragons burnt more black churches. A nation without conscience, many foreigners in the land wondered where then was the conscience of the nation under God.

Many schools were closed, indefinitely, to discourage integration. Churches which opted for integration were threatened with the cross of the dragons. Ministers of the gospel, copied the Governors, stood in fronts of their churches to discourage integration.

The nuns of churches went out to the nooks and crannies telling people, "Children repent; children repent, for Christ is coming soon." But, the very priests who sent them out grabbed the altar boys and turned them into male prostitutes.

THE DEVIL'S LAND

To be fair, the morals of the society were on a table of scrutiny. The entire world saw, and were repulsed. Hitler, the racist lord of Germany, could not step his feet on the Porcupine Empire. Though so, his dragons controlled the Empire.

The devil was near; but, the people could not think twice and call God. Some blacks of the 'Freedom Riders' found themselves hated even by the God of the white man.

They looked. They saw the demon in its own mirror. They saw the shattered image of the blessed society in its terrible shape. Young blacks who showed interest in the girls of the superior race were murdered without mercy. And, some white girls who preferred the black boys were terrified to put the boys they loved in harm's way. It was an atmosphere of fear and great prejudice.

While the executive and his cabinet were doing its image laundry in some foreign lands, however, America was burning and the blooming smoke of the burning land was in the air for the global observation.

America was terrified to come out of its racist shell. The man was a good man. He had the power to change things, and he was determined to change things. Blacks saw and loved him.

He joined hands with the blacks and sang songs of deliverance. When the dragons saw what he was doing, they booed him and ridiculed him. They hated their leader. They even plotted to kill him. And, their leader became a true prophet without a great honor even in his own home. And, they regarded his swinging honor with disdain and with vehement contempt. True, they hated and despised him, the old Southern way.

True, even as they did, there was no turning back. America was now marching forward. America was marching to redeem its past, erase itself as a devil's land, to a true land of a pure God.

CHAPTER SEVENTEEN

He came to America in a perfect disguise, a child of a German Nazi. His father was a master of terror, a Nazi Colonel of the Third Reich. His father was a structural engineer, an architect of the 'Chambers of Holocaust,' during the war, when the Nazis wanted to create a New Germanic Roman Empire.

His father, a ferocious Nazi, who found joy in killing Jews, called the most powerful of the American armed forces nothing but a "small fish." He was the man who led the ferocious Nazis at the battle of Normandy, a man of war who could turn a military dragon into nothing but a dog-tired, terrified, war-whoop coward. But, to his supreme surprise, he was humbled to the point of being unable to see action again. But, in the beginning of the German war, to take over the whole world, the great German warlord was a master of air-raids, interrogations, death-camps, torture, gas-chambers, vandalism, and fanatical allegiance to nothing but a demonic cause. The terrible monster, the German warlord, was defeated by the 'small fish,' He met his doom in Normandy; but, his son was true to his father's mission.

Like his father, he chewed his English pronunciation like a true German. And he set his base in Arkansas. Here was a man who revamped the mission of hate to a new high. Here was a second Hitler on American Throne. He was a top dragon, a Grand Master of the Knights of the Ku Klux Klan. He formed new chapter after another in the Southern States. He recruited the impressionable youths, the blue-blooded young, the able, and the hateful souls of the Aryan race. He taught them how to live a pure and superior race.

A dream of his father, he was the man who led the campaign against the executive, when he learnt that the executive had formed an alliance and sang the song of deliverance. From his headquarters, Searcy Arkansas, the son of Nazi Colonel sent out a gang of tough dragons to kill his new enemies—Mr. and Mrs. Ala-Ọma. He personally instructed them on how to do it. He asked them to mutilate them beyond recognition.

He asked them to offer their heads and blood for cult rituals. He told them to eat the flesh of the black man and burn the flesh of the white woman. Then, his plot leaked. One of his men was an element of the C.I.A. The planted informant heard him and caught all his instructions on a tape and on a pocket-book-sized hidden camera.

The ingenious weed in the midst was smart and professional too. He sent out the news to the C. I. A. head office and even to the executive. The leader of the great nation was enraged once again. He learnt about the plot against him and the war against the blacks, and others in the minority.

The terrible dragons were up to their scare-tactics. They initiated some elements of surprise with materialization of bomb-scare. State of fear became the order of the day. People, blacks and whites, could no longer venture out without fearing for their lives. And they knew the reason for it all: The drive to worship the God of the white man was a tool to make them equal to the white race. And the dragons were quick to discourage it. They burnt down, rapidly, as many black churches as ventured to worship the God of the superior race.

The executive lamented over the state of the nation. He invited some black preachers whose church buildings were burnt down by the dragons. There, in the Oval office, with the black men standing behind him, he made a desperate plea to the nation.

"In times like this," began the executive in a somber tone, "we need friends who'd understand, friends who wouldn't laugh but

THE DEVIL'S LAND

console us, friends whose friendship is humane, friends who are not fiends but friends indeed." He appealed to the better angels of the American conscience to prevail over the onslaught of the dragons.

He appealed, somewhat supplicating, to the son of Nazi Colonel in Searcy, Arkansas, to give up and surrender. He pleaded with those who were on the same warpath to repent and return to the voice of the enlightened reason.

******

****

*****

"When are you coming back?" Mrs. Ala-Oma asked Mr. Ala-Oma. "Soon," he responded.

"I hope it wouldn't be like the second coming of Christ which we've waited for more than a thousand years," she remarked.

"I'd be back next year," he said to her. He was ready to go to the Governor's office, because the executive had invited the two men plus Mrs. Ala-Oma to his office in Washington, D.C. He was going to meet the Governor, to size him up, to talk as men, before he and his wife would take off with him on the great trip.

"I was expecting you back less than half an hour," she observed.

"Well, you'll have your wish," he said.

In his quest to live in peace, he secured a roommate from hell. The Governor of Alabama was a man who believed in the superiority of his own race, and preached segregation forever more. There was no way he could share the same transport facility with a man of an inferior race on their way to the White House.

"You can find your way to Washington boy; no negro will be allowed into the Governor's plane," said the Governor of Alabama.

"I'm sorry you see it that way, Governor," replied Mr. Ala-Oma.

"You know how it is, boy. That's the way it has always been. I wasn't God who created negroes and put them in the African jungles; was I boy? If you have anything against that, I guess you might as well complain to God Almighty," the Governor jeered. His negrophobic exactitude was self-evident.

Then, Mr. Ala-Ọma looked at him. And, as he looked, he remembered home. A flood of ideas, an imminent tide of longing overwhelmed him. Here was a man who was ready to hear the call.

Here again was he who obeyed the voice of the African Patriarch, Dr. Nnamdi Azikiwe. The Patriarch had told him, "Go over there. Get the golden fleece. Return home and serve your country." He listened to his first advice to go, and he went.

He obeyed the second instruction, and he got the golden fleece. But, when he went and got the golden fleece, he refused to return home.

His people who yearned and needed his services, he doubly deprived and disappointed. They missed his presence and they lost his services. They wrote him and called him, spending their meagre resources, but he refused to return home. He preferred the pleasures and prejudice and Sodoms of Babylon to the services and longings of the people who loved him.

To those who longed to see him, who adored him at a distance, he turned a deaf ear. And his people wondered what type of charm and 'ọkpọ' the white woman had used in charming his soul away from his own people.

Some of his people, after waiting for so long, went to some native doctors in quest of a solution to the whole enigma. Some of the doctors cheated them and duped them. Some genuine ones among them told them the truth and charged them nothing. These were those who told them that patience was the answer to the great question—that 'agaracha must return home.'

The patience and twisted delay in return were nice and easy, but stupid to those who needed him. They saw him as a prodigal

THE DEVIL'S LAND

child who had forsaken his home for the sake of a foreign woman. They cried for him and doubted all the promises he made to them in what seemed like a good faith. They saw in each day of delay, a deadly day. And throughout the devil's day, they believed, the devil was in the detail.

They feared he would never ever return home. But, their hearts did not understand the yearning of their son in a foreign land.

CHAPTER EIGHTEEN

They arrived. The first lady of the great nation was the first person to welcome them to the 'White House'. The Great Governor of Alabama was seemingly on his way. And, there was no way he could bring down himself to the level of boarding the same plane with a black man. Mr. and Mrs. Ala-Ọma had no other choice but to rush to the airport and charter the earliest speed-plane to Washington, D.C. the nation's Capital

"Everybody is a rebel, huh?" the president remarked when Mrs. Ala-Ọma finished telling him what her husband went through at Alabama State House.

"Yeah, including the Governor," Mrs. Ala-Ọma replied to the Chief Executive of the Great American Empire.

"Yeah, not all the Governors are rebels, though," added the first lady who welcomed her and her husband.

"Yeah, you said it right," her husband agreed to his wife's observation.

Soon after their arrival, in came a tall white man, woman, a boy, a girl and a black man. The young black man was a good friend of the arriving American family. Before they came back to America, they were missionaries in Africa, doing all the good jobs, saving the African people from idol worship and showing them the light. The president had heard about them. Therefore, he invited them to show Mr. Ala-Ọma, despite all things, that Americans were still the best people under the sun.

Prior to the trip to Washington, D. C. the missionary family really invited the young black man to their home in Texas. He arrived. It was a lovely plane ride to a very small village in Texas. The missionary man had paid for his flight. That alone was the first sign of how generous a man of God he would be. He had lived in Africa. A truly poor African nation, known as Lamunta.

And, when he was in Lamunta, he fell in love with a young female tourist from Europe. He taught her the way of God and married her. There was no way he could marry one of the primitive black converts, from the primitive land. Rather, his job, as a man of God, was to convert them and show them the light. There was no way he would degrade his holy place by taking as a bride a woman of an inferior skin color.

Anyway, with a wife at hand, he was blessed by his God. He and his wife had twin babies—a boy and a girl. And, he loved Lamunta so much that he immortalized the poor African nation in the names he gave his two children.

Lamun, he named the boy born in Lamunta. And Lamuntana was the feminine derivative for his daughter born in Africa. He loved his children the way most men did. And, he added to the love an American touch. Lavishing toys on them, kissing them, hugging them, and helping his wife change their diapers, the nappies of the babies.

So soon after Lamuntana turned three, he broke her virginity. The little girl cried so much not knowing why the man she viewed as her earthly god was pushing his stick of manhood through her.

The little girl's mother was not home. She trusted her husband—and it did not, in her worst of dream, occur to her that her husband would do such a thing. Surely, he was a brilliant pediatrician. He doctored her very well before his wife returned from work. That was seven years ago—Seven years before the African, now a university student in U. S. came to visit him, his wife and the lovely twin.

THE DEVIL'S LAND

It was seven years since the girl, who was born in the poor nation of Lamunta, had been having fun with the man who partly brought her into the world. Seven years, he'd ably and so effectively covered his track, sealed off his daughter's mouth with paternal attention and numerous gifts of toys.

The man arrived at the airport, Dallas-Forth Worth, by Metropolitan Air. It was a pretty lovely flight with all the gorgeous American girls, blonds, at his service, all the way from the boarding port till the port of exit.

****
******

Soon after the Metro-Air made a touchdown, jetted to a stop, the African man came out from the plane. Dr. Jules and his family were already waiting for him at the terminal.

The man walked fast soon after he saw Dr. Jules and his family; he walked fast to embrace them because it has been a while. Embrace, they did. They shook hands, snapped their fingers while shaking hands, the African way.

Mrs. Jules hugged him and kissed him as well. She was a good woman; and, she loved black men to death. She would have prolonged the hugging, and even extended the on-the-cheek kissing, if her husband were not around. At times she had to bite her tongue to preserve her marriage.

"Uh, black!" the young Lamun grumbled contemptuously. Now he was behind his mother. "Hey, why are you so black? Why can't you take a bath?" he asked the visiting guest so rudely. Obviously, he was not happy with the visit. He looked at the black man quite contemptuously. And his contemptuous look turned into an outright rage. "Did you hear me? Or, are you dumb?" But the young man, to whom he addressed, simply ignored him.

And, in the spacious lobby of the Air-Port were many passengers, and some people with placards to identify and welcome them. And, in the same lobby were snack-bars, vend-machines for soft-drinks, snack-bars, and all. And, there were a variety of clean seats in the lobby of the airport: love seats, comfort ones, wooden chairs, many a couch, roundish futons, long, oblong, triangular and square ones all neatly placed in different corners, neatly and so strategic, of the airport lobby—all for the comfort of the wary travellers.

"Why not sit down? My wife and I will help with your luggages," Dr. Jules said. Then, as if he'd just remembered something, "Oh, my wife brought you some snacks," he added. "Honey," Now he turned toward his wife, "please give the snacks to him."

The African student, their guest, sat down. He began to eat the snacks potato chips, peanuts and crackers. The thoughtful woman brought, added, in good measure, a couple of soda, Pepsi. The man began to eat and to drink.

While he was eating and drinking, the young Lamun sneaked behind him with a mischievous intent. In his pant's pocket was a synthetic chicken feather. He stood there, right behind the man who was enjoying the snacks provided by his own mother. He waited, like an angry African crocodile, for the right moment to strike at the unsuspecting prey. He watched the black man dig his hand into the potato bag bought with his own mother's money.

As he watched him do it, his rage and desire for pay back increased in their magnitude. He saw the guest as a common thief. And, he hated 'the thief' with passion.

He waited. Again the black man dipped his hand into the potato bag. Out his hand came with crispy slices of the crunchy potato chips. He munched five or six times before he swallowed. And as he munched, the boy behind him made some be-speakable faces at him. But, his parents had no parental reason to rebuke him, all because he was an American son; therefore, there was no reason to rebuke him to please a black student.

Then, he popped open the second can of soda. He tipped his head backward and began to pour the delicious drink into his black mouth. Right there the boy could not take it anymore. Right there, the moment he poured, Lamun saw a perfect opportunity to apprehend the thief, to play his special, and to reveal himself to the unwelcome intruder.

He took out his feather. Closer and closer to the black man he came, holding his synthetic feather the way his father, the pediatrician, held a medical device when he doctored up his twin sister. With the moment he waited for at hand, speedily he dipped the feather right inside the black man's ear.

Irritated and annoyed, his reflex charge took over. With an equal speed his left hand knocked off the boy's intrusive hand and his synthetic feather from his right ear.

"I hate you," Lamun reacted, tears of rage falling down from his eyes. "I won't allow you to come to my house. You hit me. I hate you. You're a bad man."

"Why did you hit my son, Prute?" Dr. Jules asked, quite enraged.

"Sir, I was just drinking when, he put something into my ear."

"So, you beat him?" Dr. Jules drew a sharp conclusion.

"No," Mr. Prute Datumbuku contradicted his conclusion "I didn't. I didn't expect him to tease my ear; it was just a quick reflex."

"What do you know about reflex?" Dr. Jules murmured "Are primitive people smart enough to understand how it works?"

"Come, Lamun, I'm sorry. Come you're my friend," Mr. Pante Prute Datumbuku stretched out his hands towards the offended boy, wanting to make peace with him.

"No. You're a nigger. You're bad. I won't come to you; don't come to my house, ever. I hate you forever.

I don't need you," the boy said to Pante Prute Datumbuku.

"Honey, don't say such things. You shouldn't have done that. Don't you know he's our guest?" Mrs. Jules tried to reconcile her ten year old son with the black African student.

But, her success was to be a transient experience.

CHAPTER NINETEEN

He was born Pante Prute in a small African Kingdom called Lamunta. He was married at the age of fifteen through a process of connubial arrangement. And, as a custom and a living tradition, his father and his mother made the right choice in marriage, and gave him the right wife.

His wife, then, was fourteen, a year younger than he, when he took the great step to manhood. He was a real virgin when he got married. And, that was the green-light of the village tradition.

On the night he entered her, two nights and two good days after his wife came home, he did not know what to do with her. It was his wife who initiated it, while both were in bed, a couple of innocents who were so ignorant, all in the rich Garden Of Great Ignorance.

She took off her clothes. She giggled, she touched him. And, she prodded him. And he did the same. She began to rub him until his stick of manhood was erect. She opened up, and led him to enter her. She prompted, gestured, and taught him how to do it.

When he began to do it, she opened up wider, and his stick of manhood penetrated deeper inside. The young man was surprised, even alarmed. He sensed that there was something accidental, a tragedy in the making that needed to be corrected. She began to make the lovely sound a woman makes when she'd reached the peak of love-making called, 'orgasm.' But, to her virgin husband, it was a terrible situation.

"Chai chai chai!" he shouted. "Mother please come. My thing has punctured a hole through other peoples' daughter, oh!" shouted he, even louder.

But, his mother, who was more experienced, was happy with her son's height of new experience; and, indeed, she was ready to encourage him, in the process. She sensed her son was learning how to make love to a woman. Now, he was doing it, first time ever, to his own bride, she felt it was the way it was supposed to be—that a man should learn how to do it from his own wife.

"It's alright, son. Don't be alarmed or afraid, son, keep pumping your stick of manhood through that hole. You're doing it right. Keep going," the elderly woman replied from her room which was next to her son's room of a big hut.

At the end of the encounter, the young man came out, sweating, still fearful that the hole he punched through his wife would do her a great harm—drain her blood away, or even lead to a total exsanguination.

"Son, you're now a man. I know your seeds will fertilize her. She'll give me my first grandchild," she said. Her son had just enjoyed the divine scam called sex, the first step in the reproduction of a human life.

A young man, he had set in motion the great scramble of the competing swamps of the male gametes, in clusters of sperms, all in chase of a virgin egg. And just one of them, in perfect copulation with the female gamete, will create a piece, thereby, a unit with life's ups and downs. It's here he'd ebbed the rock of existence, opened up, for a crest the fault-line of an active, and eruptible mountain.

He'd set a pace of new existence. Above all, he was still fearful of the hole he'd punctured through 'other peoples' daughter'

Here he was in America without his true love. Every day, while in America, he remembered the young woman who taught him

THE DEVIL'S LAND

how to make love. Daily, he recalled the woman and his only son who he left behind in Lamunta.

The memory of the hole he punctured through his wife was ever his constant companion, even in a foreign land. But, here he was, in America, being used as a tool in punching holes through the tough walls of racism.

CHAPTER TWENTY

It was a thing of political blow when the man the Great, and 'All-Powerful Chief Executive' invited, for a true racial reconciliation, did not show up. To the Chief Executive, his action, a no-show, was, indeed, not a tender blow.

Mr. and Mrs. Ala-Ọma were not even surprised that the man of racism was a no show. But, the Chief Executive, and his bride, were enraged that the Governor of Alabama shunned his invitation. Now, as they saw it, his behavior was a token of demonstration of the south, its leadership, their way, hell-bent on permanent structure of prejudice.

During the meeting the executive asked Mr. and Mrs. Ala-Ọma a variety of questions. He learnt from them all they knew about racial harassment. They told him about what they had been through.

He asked them for their opinions. And they supplied him some answers to the racial question.

Then, he turned toward the man of God and asked him about all the good works he did in Africa. Dr. Jules and his wife were quick to tell him.

They told him how they converted millions of Africans from the bondage of sin. Then, they depicted themselves as the 'saviors' of the third world. They glorified America before the executive, without any atom of true desire to tell him the hard truth.

They depicted Africa and all the other third world continents as places in need of spiritual awakening and perfect deliverance. They outlined the high points of the mission doctor's achievements.

Mrs. Jules in particular praised the works of her husband before the executive. She told him how he taught them the word of God and showed them the true light.

She praised her husband. She praised him much more than God had praised Christ at the point of his glorification.

She praised him even more. She praised like someone who loved to talk. And the opportunity to talk was hers. And, as she praised, the executive received her with rapt attention. She was encouraged and she went ahead and added more salt and honey to her sermon of praise.

And, as she talked and praised, her husband nodded his head all in total agreement and approval of her words of praise.

Then, she talked more about Africa as she praised. And as she praised, she explained, in greater details, how Africans worshipped some primitive gods before his arrival.

Then, she went ahead and talked about how ruined Africa was, how needy the Africans were, how pathetic their future was, and how urgent the Africans needed some financial assistance.

She used her own mouth to turn him into a saint; and he was impressed. And, even as she talked, her husband measuredly looked at Mr. Pante Prute Datumbuku, to prevent him from voicing anything which would contradict purity of her version of his mission works in Africa. At the end, the propaganda was a ritual success.

After the meeting, they took a walk, with the first lady, to the Rose Garden; they walked further even to the Lincoln Memorial Monument. These places were good, and the flowers at the Rose Garden were in bloom.

Some sparkling water were oozing out from complex devices around the oblong structure, even on top of the monumental edifice. It was cool, and the cooling effect was a monumental blessing in itself.

THE DEVIL'S LAND

And, beside the Lincoln Monument were several benches for those who were visiting to relax on, at their chosen pleasure. The place was regularly kept clean by some Park employees of the beautiful Capital of the Great nation.

As the two black men, the first lady, Mr. and Mrs Ala-Ọma, the missionary household, and a couple of security service men approached a corner of the Monument, they saw a young, bearded white man sitting on one of the benches. Also, they saw a young professional prostitute approach him.

She was black but personable, proficient in conduct. She greeted him to draw his attention from all his thoughtful worries and cares of the entire world. Then, she rapidly increased her level of friendliness. She touched his shirt admiringly. And, she looked at him admiringly; she placed a fond compliment on his attire. There he smiled and thanked her.

As she earned his attention and temporary friendship, she dramatically opened her ware by way of suggestion,

"Think you might like to have a sugar?" she gently asked him. She was cautious; yet, hoping for a signal to commence a kiss or walk away.

He looked at her. And, he was equally friendly, cautious too. He shook his head, a cue that he would not buy her service.

"I've got a girl-friend. She'd be here any moment. I don't want her to kill me," he said to the black prostitute.

"Maybe, some other time, huh?" she suggested.

"No. Because she watches me closely. I don't do anything without telling her. Neither does she."

"O.K. Thanks anyhow."

"Thank you."

"See you."

"Hey, thanks for the offer. If I see some of my nice friends who might be interested, I shall refer them to you."

"I'd appreciate that. See ya."

"Good luck."

"Thanks." She walked away.

And, in one corner of the National Monument were some youthful American children. Boys and girls, whites, blacks, and Hispanics. They were doing their own thing: drugs. Not even the presence of the Chief Executive's wife and security outfits could deter them. They inhaled and exhaled, all with a great measure of kids-in-heaven type of pleasure.

The Chief Executive's wife looked, in their direction; then, she looked away. She knew how to deal with those troubled teenagers. Her husband was not here with her. He had other issues of national priority to attend. So, he did not join them for the pleasantly diplomatic walk. She knew how these hopeless children behaved: They behaved like rattlesnakes of the American wilderness. If you did not border them, they, in turn, would not border you either. But, if you did, they would pursue you and get you even if you tried to hide in your mother's womb.

And, some seven months earlier, the Chief Executive launched a massive campaign against drugs and drug-lords in Central and South America. It was a deft political move which earned him a double-digit score in political rating. Then, as ever, she was pretty proud of him, because he was the fair-minded leader of the free world. In an African village jungle, however, there was a living saying: 'A rodent, called 'ọkapi' is such a good healer in that it could heal every disease of the forest animals, except, of course, the awfully stinking sore of its protruding mouth.' But, America was a global policeman; therefore, the cop was always right.

As they walked away from the point of drug use, they met some native American Indians. And these were the products of concentration camps, ghettos, and contempt of capitalism. They lived in reservations, and their conditions were so tough, hard, and even helpless.

Along their devilish obstacle pathways, bedecked with variety of touches of tough attraction, pleasures and in jewelries, they

THE DEVIL'S LAND

found foot steps of prejudice carried out through the dawn of their living memories.

Also, they found, competing with those who pleasured in jewelries, drugs, the ancient profession of prostitution, were the street gamblers of America; they found foot steps of prejudice carried out through the dawn of memory. Also, they found, competing with those who viewed them as inferior human beings required a special place of courage, skill, cunning, and even cleverness. They knew that those who despised them hated them. And that to live in such a tough world was to navigate through the obstacles of human experience.

They held flowers in their hands, and they begged those who passed by to make some special contribution to the natives' education fund. They were mostly women, mothers and young girls dressed in the attires of their conquerors. Even so, they were proud people.

And, anyone who gave them some money, they rewarded the person by giving the person one of their flowers. They had their cherished pride; and, their native custom did not condone receiving without, at least, giving a token of something back in return. It was their custom, though ancient, but cherished. They were a country within a country. They were so poor; and, they were at the bottom of the totem-pole of a vulture-like, predatory capitalism.

"Would you please make some donation to the native Indian education fund?" A neatly dressed young native approached Mr. Pante Prute Datumbuku. They were just about the same age—the native girl and the African university student.

He reached down his pocket and brought out a dollar. "I don't have much. I'm a student. Please take this," he said as he gave her the money.

"Thank you," she thanked him. Then, she came closer to him and pinned one of her flowers to his breast-jacket. She touched him gently, and used her right-hand to brush off some imaginary dusts from his jacket. As she did that, he smiled and thanked her.

Then, an older native lady approached the 'First Lady,' equally neatly adorned in Western style. Before she could even get closer, a security service made haste and stood between the first lady and the native woman.

"What do you want?" the security personnel questioningly rebuked her.

"Oh, I just wanted to . . ."

"You're not allowed to get too close to the 'First Lady'; didn't you know that?" he rebuked her again. From there the woman withdrew to a safe distance.

"Oh dear," the 'First Lady' borrowed the word 'oh,' from the native woman, "that woman's great-great-grandfathers might have been an Indian Chief," the 'First Lady' remarked as she turned towards her guests.

"Those Chiefs were only good at ruling buffaloes, buffalo treehoppers and wildebeests, not human beings. That's why we had no choice but to bring them our European civilization. We're doing the same to Africa right now. But, Africans are much more receptive to the light than the goddam primitive Indians," said the man who had served as a 'missionary' in Africa.

The 'First Lady' did not particularly like the humorless and insensitive remarks. And, as she saw it, it was tactless. But, she had no choice. After all, she and her husband were among the beneficiaries who benefitted most by the European conquest of the natives. There, the 'First Lady' simply smiled at him, and kept on walking.

But, when he turned, to make face at the native woman, the native woman stared at him. The way she stared down at him made him quite uncomfortable. Her stare was telling. Telling in that she was very displeased with his lack of sensitivity.

With his remarks, really, he revamped a rage so deep, in the sleeping memory of the ancient native. She kept on staring down at him, like a fellow provoked without cause. As she stared, the

THE DEVIL'S LAND

guest of the Chief Executive could not take it anymore. Here was a man whose personal jungle of prejudice had made him quite and ably ignorant of all the people around him.

"Hey fellow, no offense," said the insolent man of God. But, the woman kept on staring down at him.

Then, he began to stare down at her too. After a while, she turned her back at him and walked away. And, as she walked away, she held her shoulders, even her head, proudly up high.

"Hey guys, don't let her just walk away. I wanna talk with her." The 'First Lady' came in to the rescue. Instantly, her two bodyguards gave the Indian woman a chase. They caught her and brought her back to the 'First Lady.'

"I wanna hear your story. What do you need, money?" the 'First Lady' asked the old Indian woman.

"No," the native lady asserted.

"I am the First Lady; I can help you. Tell me, what do you need?"

"No. I won't. Even if you were the first lady of heaven, I just won't tell you my needs," said the Indian lady.

"Why not?" challenged the 'first' American lady.

"It wouldn't be proper thing to do. Your people raped our land."

"A moment ago you were begging for help, now that someone is ready to help why not take it?" the First Lady probed her psyche.

"Yes, I know," answered the native American-Indian lady.

"Now can you open your mouth and tell me what you need?"

"I told you I won't. Have you forgotten what your people did to mine?" the Indian woman returned the rebuke of the first lady.

"That was something that happened hundreds of years ago. This is modern time. It's time to be pragmatic and let go of the past."

"Yes, that's excellent pragmatic statement," returned the Indian lady. "You said so because what you did to us did not happen to you."

"Looks like you're a tough one; I can't help those who can't help themselves," said the enraged First Lady, as she began to walk away.

"Better not. I won't take it," replied the Indian woman, now heading in a different direction.

*****
***
****

A year later, Dr. Jules and his family received another invitation to the Executive Mansion, known in America as the White House. They were invited to be honored as the 'most mission-minded family in the free world'. The honor was to be given on a special day. The day the nation honored her heroic sons and daughters, dead and living, who contributed, in different fields, to the American dream.

They were to be honored in the nation's Capital, all in the presence of foreign representatives and world leaders. They were to be presented as shining examples. The fine women, and great American men, who, in some special and remarkable ways, exemplified what living an American dream was all about. Movie-stars, and sports legends were invited. Industrial moguls, and the great and terrible CEOs, and even the very wheelers and shakers of American free enterprise system of Capitalism, were expected to be present, during the great event, in a good number.

Mr. Pante Prute Datumbuku was also invited. One morning, as he was getting ready to go to class, a man came to his dormitory room and told him that the school's President wanted to see him, right away. It was an urgent issue; he had no choice but to go with him. As he walked, with the man from the school's president's office, he feared for the worst. For example, he wondered if there were some bad news from his home. A flood of terrible images rushed through his terrified mind, for example, 'Is my dad dead?

Is my mother still alive? My wife? Did I do anything wrong? Are they going to kick me out from school? What's the matter? Is there any way I could know?' As all these thoughts rushed through his mind, he timidly walked behind the man who was leading him to the office of the powerful school's village chief. He was so terrified before he could even step into the school's president's office.

When he entered the school's president's office, he was greeted with an embrace and a wholehearted handshake. At first, however, he did not know what to make of it all.

"I've got something for you. I've been awake since the crack of dawn, hoping to meet you. How did you do it?" The exuberant school's president was so remarkably exuberant.

"Sir, I don't know. Can you tell me? I'm in the cloud," said the timid fellow who was scared to death on his way to the president's office.

"You still haven't understood what I'm trying to say?" asked the school's president to the bashful Pante Prute Datumbuku.

"No Sir," Mr. P. P. Datumbuku replied.

"The leader of our free world invited you to the Executive Mansion."

"Sir, I didn't understand. Who could that be? Do I know him? Does he know me? What does the fellow look like?" Pante Prute explored.

"You mean, you don't know the leader of our great American Society?" asked the president.

"Ohhhh! I see. I thought there was something terrible. I know the man very well. He is your Head of State, correct? I have been to his place before," Mr. Pante Prute Datumbuku replied to the president.

"You did?" the University president asked him.

"Yes, last year. We ate there. We talked, and his wife took us around; we visited Rose Garden, and Lincoln Memorial Monument."

"Really? So you did? Oh boy, aren't you going places?" The man became jealous.

"Yes, we saw inhabitants of lesbos, native Indians, teenage boys and girls and many other kinds of people around the national park."

"Wow," the leader of the college exclaimed.

"Yes, we saw everything, both good and bad."

"Man, I'm really jealous. I've been in this office for twenty one years, not even the Governor of my State could invite me to the State House. Here you are, barely two years in America, you'd had the opportunity to visit with the." The man was indeed even vocally jealous, but the youth on the receiving end of his jealousy rushed to rescue him.

"Sir, you are cordially invited," said the student, as if he were the owner of the Executive Mansion.

"What? Get the hell out of here," the proud president did not believe his student could pull through his invitation.

"Sir, I mean it," affirmed the student. He said it as if the nation's Chief Executive were his own father.

"No son, the leader of the free world invited you alone. There is no need for me to tag along."

"Sir, I shall write him a letter telling him that I will only come if he will allow me to come with the president of my school." Mr. Pante Prute Datumbuku promised his school's president.

"What?" He became friendlier to the younger man. "Can you do that for me?"

"Yes, of course," P. P. Datumbuku replied to him, so confident, in his ability to do it.

"How?" he asked P. P. Datumbuku, as if he did not hear the answer his student gave.

"It is easy."

"Smart kid. You go and draft the letter. When you've done, bring it to me so that I'd personally edit it for you. Don't show it to anyone. Understand?"

THE DEVIL'S LAND

"Yes Sir."

"Wait. I'll provide you with a pen and some pieces of paper."

"Sir, I have some in my room."

"It's alright; it's O.K. I'll give you mine," the school president looked around his office. His eyes caught the next desk in his huge office.

He walked briskly towards the desk. In his haste, to get there, he tripped over a telephone wire and fell. He stood up, so quickly, as if nothing had happened.

On the desk were three rims of papers. He tore open a rim, took out some loose sheets from the whole, and placed them neatly in the middle of the desk. Then, he took out a pen from the desk's drawer and placed it beside the neatly placed sheets of writing paper.

"Son, come over here," he ordered his helpful African student. The young man obeyed without complaint. "Sit down here and write. When you finish, bring it to my desk so I can edit it. O.K.?" he instructed.

"Yes Sir," Mr. Pante Prute Datumbuku went over. His school's president positioned the chair well for him. And he sat. Then, the president went back to his own seat. He began to write. While he was half-way through, his president walked over to see what literary progress he was thus far making.

"O.K, son, I think, I better take it up from here." He took over the half-finished letter, and deftly rewrote and added, to the entire missive, a professional and masterful touch.

He typed up the letter and asked the student to endorse it. The young man did. He typed up the envelope, addressed the letter to the Chief Executive of the American nation.

And, then, he accompanied the young man to the Post Office, to make sure that the letter would take off, and really fly off. After he had paid for the postage, express, he became more excited and generous with his purse. He gave Mr. Pante Prute Datumbuku two hundred dollars,

"Its for your lunch today, son," he said, as he gave away his money to the helpful foreign student.

"Thank you, Sir," the black student thanked the school's village chief.

"Son, you are greatly welcome. There's no way I could thank you for what you're doing for me, right now," replied the University president.

****
****
****

A week later, the school president invited Mr. Pante Prute Datumbuku to his office for the second time. Now they were friends, a fine connection for the president to attain some certain objectives, and a symbiosis in the making.

"Son, I noticed you're not yet in the Dean's List. But, it's not too late. I can help," said the school's president. And, without letting his student thank him for his offer, he went ahead to shower him with more blessings from the bosom of his gracious heart. "In recognition of your selfless service and willingness to contribute to uplift the high standard of excellence of this great institution of higher learning, I've therefore directed the School's Registrar to modify your grades to fit to the standard thus far set for the Dean's List," said the man at the top of the academic totem-pole.

"You mean I'm now . . ."

"Yes, son, if there is any other way I can help you succeed in our free country, I'll be delighted to help."

"Thank you sir," said the grateful student.

"Son, you know we're leaving tomorrow for D.C. Go to your room and have a good night's sleep," the leader of the school instructed.

"Yes, Sir."

THE DEVIL'S LAND

"Oh, I almost forgot. Come here," he ordered his African student. He was fully in control of this grand situation.

"Sir, here I am," the much younger fellow answered, and drew nearer to the older fellow.

"Here." He gave him another two hundred dollars. "For your lunch."

"I've not finished spending the one you gave me," he was somewhat reluctant to accept more gifts of money from his school's president.

"It's O.K. Take it. Spend it whenever you like," the President told him, and handed him the second set of two hundred dollars in just one week.

"Thank you very much, Sir."

"Oh, the entire pleasure is mine," responded the president.

*****

****

***

When the young man left, the University President began to prepare a special speech which he would make before the leader of the Free World. He knew quite well how the system worked; and, he was very prepared to capitalize for an upward gain.

He drew from his wealth of intellect, and wrote a superb speech. First, he lavishly praised the village chief of the American Village, as the greatest leader of the Free world, in his written introductory speech.

He praised his student, Mr. P. P. Datumbuku, as one of the smartest international students he had ever met. And, he had his favorite student's new transcript to prove his point to the Chief Executive.

Then, he began to praise himself. He praised himself, and outlined his dream to serve the Chief Executive of the free world in a better and more challenging capacity. He wrote down his

149

dream service; and, he expressed interest, a desire to be chosen as the Secretary of State of the free world.

He outlined how he would tackle, with zest, the issues of the day, serve the Chief Executive very faithfully, be a shining example, in that, when a new American history would be written, his name would be written in letters of gold, as the ablest Secretary of State to serve the best leader of the freest world.

He rehearsed his speech, several times. And, he memorized it from the first to the last word. He was ready to deliver, to quit his current post, and to jump into the Executive's Cabinet. He was so ready to quit the odd job as a mere 'school's president.' With a PhD, a wealth of experience, including a couple of briberies of four hundred dollars and an upgrade of a simple school's transcript, a great reward as 'a Secretary of State' was an offer even a fool would turn down.

****
******
****

When Dr. Jules and Mr. P. P. Datumbuku met again at the lobby of the nation's Executive Mansion, the man of God was quick to give him some thoughtful and sound advice.

"Prute" said Dr. Jules.

"Yes, Doctor."

"You must be careful."

"Yes, I always try to be."

"I know," agreed the 'missionary doctor' who raped his own daughter.

"Yes, Sir" the student agreed completely.

"You have to when dealing with black Americans. I'm not prejudiced. But, the way they behave made us to dislike them. They don't want to go to school. When they do, they won't stay

THE DEVIL'S LAND

in school; they drop out. They complain all the time that the white man is their problem. They can't learn. They won't get off from welfare. They smoke, drink, and kill . . . they do drugs. They rape white women. You saw what some of them were doing last time at the Lincoln Memorial Monument," the doctor told him in the way of advisement. And Mr. Pante Prute Datumbuku understood him quite alright. Also, he understood his visit in Texas, the incident with the very son of the same man of God, and even how well the man of God was training his own son; he remembered, and even recalled, his lack of prejudice before the native American Indian woman, even in front of the same very Lincoln Memorial Monument.

"Yes, I will" Mr. Pante Prute Datumbuku responded. And as he responded, he remembered too, and even understood the thoughts beneath the mind of the same man of God. He recalled there were more than black youths in a corner of the nation's Monument. He remembered there were also white and Hispanic youths who were waiting to inhale. "I shall put your advice in mind all the time. I shall always put it into consideration in whatever I do," said the student.

"You better, Prute, for your own good," added the man of God.

"There are many of them in my school," said Prute.

"You have to keep away from them," the man of God advised again.

"Yes, I will try," he responded; but, the way he responded was not quite convincing.

"Prute, you have to. I mean it. You are my friend. I wouldn't like to see you hurt," the nonconforming man of God insisted.

"I will." Now, Mr. P. P. Datumbuku fooled him with a show of enthusiasm.

"Good boy. I knew you would. You know where you came from. You'll always do something that would make your folks proud of you." He reached out and touched him, rather gently.

"You know, I sent your folks three magazines that showcased all our pictures with the president last time we were here. And, I'll send them more copies this time, too. They'll know you're doing well, representing them well in America," said the foolish racist.

"Thank you very much, doctor," the student responded to the foolish missionary.

"You are so welcome," he smiled impishly and he began to touch him on the forehead this time, as if he were a little boy. And, as he touched the head of the African, he began to rub his head as if he liked him.

CHAPTER TWENTY-ONE

There was a good devil in America, and the people knew it. The poor immigrants who obeyed the voice of the venerable idol, the gift of France, saw, in good measure, the handiworks of the wicked one.

The Prince of Prejudice was the Lord of the New World; and he ran the show with an iron fist. The poor immigrants who followed him without disobedience received the wealth of the promised-land.

Forever in floods, new and more immigrants came to the American shores. As they entered the promised land, they saw America the way the devil would have it. Of all the things they saw, nothing offended them more than the sight of robbers on the high altars of the Most-High, the Most Merciful God.

They saw the imps of the devil, advisors in human form, aliens on the American soil. They came to teach the teachers and to show the light of dis-salvation to the deceived people. They were fifty-two in number, plus one. Each of them was assigned to an American State.

There were other fifty-three aliens who came to America on a different mission. They came from God to counter the works of the wicked ones. They too were assigned to all the American States.

Hardly had they descended when they saw the damages done: They saw children armed with lack of trust and lack of obedience. They saw the elderly ones regarded with zenith of disregard. They saw broken families in abundance, fathers who left their families, and mothers who chased their men away from their lives.

They saw children without homes, homeless adults in urban degradation. They saw blood, mostly blood of the innocent ones shed by the hands of the criminals.

The angels saw the glorious kingdom, built by the devil, aimed to lure, and deceive the entire world.

It was a second kingdom, a replica of the one he used in testing Christ in the wilderness. They looked. They saw America from the sea to the other end of the shining sea. And they remembered—the pride of the devil was deeply rooted in eternal prejudice; there, the devil held his sway over his chosen land.

The monumental buildings were there. Glorious Crowns to charm men were supplied by the 'good American devil,' in good measure, for a complete and total cunning and even deceptive endowments. They were there as baits, traps, and even shining snares for those who were meant to be terribly led astray, in the wilderness of perfect lures and dynamic temptations.

"How far will a man go in trying to kill himself?" the leader among the angels pondered. He was there to supervise the activities of all the other angels. And, to send the feedback to God, the Most Merciful One of some imaginary heavens.

"The enemy is in their midst," another angel replied.

"Yes, I know."

"Arch, the holy servant, do you—think people in this sector of the battle are beyond redemption?"

"I would have loved to respond otherwise. Look, each man is heading toward his own charm and deceptive potion. He invents deadly guns, deadly camps, deadly poisons, and even deadly words. What do you make of it all?"

"Me think they are doomed."

"I second that observation; but, I don't blame them; there is devil in America," said the archangel.

"The Commodore Dragon is always snapping at his prey. We knew how he was in heaven. He never changed. Let's pray God would send Christ again for redemption of mankind," said another angel.

"Yes, that's true," answered the leader of the fifty-two angels.

"He works with his deadly poison which he ejects from his poisonous tongue. I remember the havoc he did with flames that erupted from his tongue in each of the battle zones in heaven. He might endeavor to destroy us soon after he learns that we're here in his chosen kingdom," replied the Fourth Angel.

"If he tries, he won't succeed because our good God has given us the wind of war. We can use it to speedy our transport back to heaven when the devil summons his demons," said the chief among the angels.

"It's a risky business."

"Yes, truth you said. And I firmly trust our wind of war cannot let us down. It did not when it was used in transporting the First Daughter of our God to the bosom of Her Father; it did not when our God brought Elijah and Jesus back to our Heaven's Paradise. It did not when it was time to bring back our friend, Enoch, back to heaven. So, it won't during our turn," the leader of the angels assured them.

While they searched the New World, they found things quite unique and interesting. They found there was always something to worry about under the sun, makers of sorrow down here at the headquarters of the devil.

It was either earthquake here or a tornado there. There were many a waterspout, windstorm, violent whirlwind and tornado-belt of sorrow in the great kingdom filled with dreams. It was either a murder at one moment, or a rape case at the other.

It was either a classic fraud in politics, or a monumental rip-off at a religious altar. Terrorists' bombings, and gangsters' shootouts were dancing to the music of terror, at every moment.

SUNDAY AHURONYEZE ABAKWUE

Fear and freedom were the clarion calls; and, money and sex, and even free sex were the very grease and engine that ran the virile shows. As such, in these things were the great freedom and the great wheels of the American entrapment.

Mass media and air waves were ubiquitous, ever ready to stay the glory of America. Of course they stayed glorious, the pride of the promised land.

Even as things stayed their course, the love between Dr. Jules and his wife was a tremor of earthquake: His love for her was as shaky as the breast of a woman; and her's was designed to weaken the essence of true love.

Theirs didn't last.

CHAPTER TWENTY-TWO

"Bob, Pilgrims can play God's advocates; but, America belongs to a good Satan," he remarked. His eyes were deep-red, stained with rage.

"Oh please, there is no such thing as a good Satan."

""Well, I'm a bit sarcastic about to whom the America belongs."

"Nothing could be so close to the truth. It's the land of thieves. The Pilgrims were pirates who pillaged the Indian buffaloes, robbed them of their land. Need I ask you who owned the land?"

"No, you needn't."

"Can we deny the facts of our nation's history?"

"No."

"Can we change it?"

"We can rewrite it to make sinners appear like saints; can't we?"

"Good. There is the root of our nation's false truths," she replied to her Bob. She was very short, indeed dwarfish. She wore that kind of shoes which people, in those days called 'high hill help my height.' And, she was invited by a man two feet taller, for a date. Though she was round-faced, and very pretty, she did not want to have an embarrassment, along the way, just on account of her own height.

"Do you think devil doesn't have a good heart?" asked Bob.

"You bet, he does," she responded.

"What then?"

"God and devil play politics with human conditions. It ain't fair."

"I think God's heaven isn't fair, either," he said.

"So too is God's earth," she observed.

"Earth belongs to devil, not God," he reminded her.

"To whomever, heaven and earth are bad places," she remarked.

"I know," he agreed. Then, he became quite thoughtful prior to remarking, "I don't know why Satan chose to have his headquarters in America. Do you?" he asked, rather as if he had no clue.

"Say, don't know why devil in America, huh?" she re-phrased his question.

"Yes."

"You know better than that, Bob. You can answer your question; why not give it a try?" she probed his mind for the answer to his own question. The answer, Bob was more than ready to give, the way he knew how.

"My two greatest disappointments in this America were God and Law. I trusted God too much without realizing the limitations of His love. I believed He loved me. I trusted that He could help me in moments of great need; boy, were I wrong."

"Yep."

"I was sad. I was terribly sad. Well, the Law in America was designed to protect the criminals. Whenever a criminal committed a crime against a fellow, then, the Law would restrain the offended and protect the culprit. To me, and, as far as God made me to believe, such was not fair."

"Yeah."

"Maybe, just, obviously may be, I should have become a star, a moon, or a non-entity. An entity without life, without any conscious force capable of trusting, or, even believing in anything. That would have been better than living and believing in an invisible God who lives up there on a heaven's mountain, devoid of desire to notice how much I believed and trusted him. Perhaps my believing was meant to be in vain."

THE DEVIL'S LAND

"Yes, I can understand."

"I trusted in the Bible and what the pastors said. There are things you tell friends; there are things you keep to yourself. I don't know why I'm telling you all these."

"Go on, Bob. I can understand," she encouraged him to 'go on'.

"Good. Now, let me express my regrets and resentments."

"Please, do."

"Don't tell me that God loves me. That's an entire mockery; now I know better."

"No, I won't; even if I were a pastor, I won't; please, go on."

"I'm so sure that our so-called God-Almighty does not care. He or She or It does not even give a damn about me."

"I agree with you."

"When I believed in him, her, or it, I trusted in whatever God was that I could have rendered my soul to be burnt to show the so-called God how much I loved him. Sorry I've been so disappointed that I do no longer give a fuck if he were still the damn creator or not; am so sorry, because I am so sorry I trusted in the first place."

"Go on. I don't even doubt you. Tell me more."

"God is no good. I have reasons for my conclusion."

"I do agree, go on."

"I am so sorry that I'd trusted in vain," said Bob.

"God has committed a lot of crimes."

"Please give me some good examples."

"Yes, he did. For example, in Zimbabwe, our whites shot, raped, hung, and tortured blacks, all in the name of God, just to snatch away the good land from the helpless blacks; today, when blacks want to get back what we stole from them, ironically, we are using our media to make the victims look like the real thieves; we use the Holy Books to make our victims look like the bad guys; we killed the native Americans, and took away their lands, then, we turned around and call them savages; please, who are really the savages: the victims, or those who victimized them? King David

159

killed the Palestinian people, on God's order, to grab away their land; now, the Palestinians want to get back their stolen land, we help Israel to label the victims terrorists; who then are the real terrorists? Who really are the true land grabbers? Please, tell me. Here again in America, the man whose picture is in every dollar bill fought the British red coats for freedom, liberty, and happiness; when he got his bloody freedom, liberty, and happiness, he went ahead and even refused to allow his so-called 'slaves' to be set free; he denied them the basic elements for happiness; and he even refused them their liberty; now, who really are we kidding here?"

"Hey, life is a game: You fuck me, then, excuse my language, I fuck you, too. You know what? The world is a crazy place. Everything is crazy. America is a crazy place. Everyone in America is crazy, including gods, and demons. There is no exception. The President is crazy; so is the poor man without home. A cop is crazy; so is his victim, and the crazy American law, which is nothing but a robust symbol of blind hypocrisy. The schools in America are crazy; so are the blind teachers who lead their blind student-followers. Food in America is a crazy-flower of advertisement. The exploited fellow, who mops the floors of the crazy food-chain is so blind in her crazy, blind allegiance to the hypocritical boss, who does nothing but exploit her. I'm talking about the illegal immigrant here, who's so used before she's admitted into the mainstream. But, hey, that's the system; that's the way things are; why should we care? What's all these recipes for overindulgence? I mean, what's the big deal? You're white; I'm white. The law and the God are on our side; why worry?"

"Yes; there is, big deal, big time. When a black man suffers, I do suffer too. When the natives suffer, I too do suffer; when the illegal fellow is used, and even cheated, I feel used and cheated too; it's not fair; let's face it. Really, when everyone, anywhere, does suffer, I too do feel the pain, because, I am a victim of all victims. I feel like I'm black inside, though I'm white, as you said."

"Oh brother."

THE DEVIL'S LAND

"In a white man's world a white is always innocent unless soundly proven guilty. But, in the same land, a black man is always guilty unless soundly, if ever, proven innocent," he said. "This is a land of great racism," he pressed on, "a land where the ocean shook hands with the desert, a land that belongs to the predatory eagle and the imperialist wolf."

"I do agree."

"Are we, as a nation, fair in all our dealings with other people?"

"No, we're not. But, you may wonder what the sum of your life represents; one thing is quite certain, though, we're white; they're black. God made it that way. I don't think God made a mistake. You can't question God, can you?"

"Yes, I can."

"Look, the situation is fine with me. The victims are free to resign themselves to their situation; we don't have to sympathize with them, really. I can't trade a place with them, if that's what you want me to do. If they can't take it, tough."

"Look, I can dump you if it comes to that." Her Bob was indeed very serious, and she could see it in his eyes.

"Well, we better talk about something else, rather than worse coming to worst," she co-opted for a creative diversion.

"So, you don't wanna lose me?"

"No."

"I'll tell you one thing, a secret that will blow your mind."

"What is it?"

"Are you ready?"

"Ready."

"Are you really sure?"

"Sure, of course."

"What if I told you that I'm half black, half white?"

"No way."

"Yes, my late mother was black. I was adopted by a white couple. I grew up in a white world."

"You mean it?"

"As you can see, you can be a witness that I don't look like mulatto, do I?"

"Not in a million years."

"Now you can see why I feel the way I do."

"If really you do, why not change?"

"Change what?"

"Your views."

"You might as well ask me to convert the fifty percent of my mother's blood to hundred percent white. You said it's God who made it that way. If God made it that way, it was also the same God who crossed the racial line. If God crossed the racial line, why can't you do so and stop burning the black Churches?" he asked her.

"Where is your wisdom, Bob?" she asked him.

"I should have asked you that. But, since you did, I'd like to answer. I left it in your kitchen."

"You are smart. Aren't you? If I told you that you trust too much. As such, I'd regard you as a fool."

"Well," he paused, "you can regard me as a fool for loving you. Tales of men who are more helplessly romantic than women abound in this world," he conjured up, "romantic love, you know, is the prelude to some tragic connubial enigmas."

"Thank you. But, you still need to wake up," she advised him.

"No, we two need to wake up; really, everyone needs to wake up."

"No, it's your problem, not mine."

"You sound as if you don't love me as much as I love you."

"That is true. I've learnt my lesson. I don't think I should ever love a man," said the young woman in her high-heels.

"Why?" he asked her, pointedly.

"Men are naughts. Whenever a woman falls for them."

"Yeah."

"Then, they become irresponsible brats."

"I don't think so."

THE DEVIL'S LAND

"You should. You are a man."

"Yes, I'm a man. I see you have a sharp tongue; but I'm not one of those kinds of men who'd disappointed you."

"How would I know?"

"You would only by trusting me."

"Oh yeah? So that you'd do the same as the other ones did?"

"No. So that you'd know that I'm rather different. Trust me. I'll, do anything to please you, only if."

"Get the hell out of here," she sharply cajoled him.

"I'm serious."

"Who has never heard that nonsense from men before?" she queried him.

"Who?"

"Yes, who?"

"Well?"

"Well what?"

"Well, its your court . . . call, whatever."

"So what? Hell, you think you'd fool me? Shoo, doggone it no way."

"You doggone it too. I can do anything for you."

"Oh yeah?" she jeered, "You'll do anything for me? Who are you kidding?"

"You don't believe me?"

"Hell, no."

CHAPTER TWENTY-THREE

They were kissing and coughing right in front of the cashier and other customers. They were a young white woman and a white-looking, bald-headed young man.

They were likely to be lovers, or a new girl-friend and a boyfriend; but not a husband and a wife. They'd met before; the young man gave her the real come on, she protested before she began to step carefully but willingly into his life. She was white; but he was a man of mixed blood. He could easily pass for a white, unless he revealed his true identity.

The cashier in front of them was a medical student; and she was a graphic artist. She and her new love came to buy groceries. The moment they saw each other, they fell heads over hill in love. She was dramatically ready to leave her new man for a newer one.

They began to look at each other. And they smiled at each other instantaneously. He asked her name. She told him; then her phone number; she smiled as she gave him her phone number. Her white-looking friend got jealous and frowned his face. But that did not perturb her.

"Can we leave now?" he barked at her.

"Leave me alone. Can't you see I'm talking with someone?" she barked back at him. Angered by what he was seeing, the whitelooking fellow stormed away from the store, and even from her life.

"Are you married?" the clerk then asked her.

"No," she answered.

165

"You have a boy-friend?"

"No."

"Can I call you and take you out?"

"You're so cute. I'll prefer a long term relationship," she intimated a broad green-light. "Hey, do you know a guy called Ala-Oma?"

"A lawyer, a Nigerian?"

"Yes, he's a lawyer."

"How did you know him?"

"I met him at Harvard when I was schooling there. He and I went out for a while before we broke up. And you, where did you know him?" she returned his question.

"I met him at the Executive Mansion, D. C. six years ago. He came there with his wife. We were all visiting your president," he replied to her. It was also the year his school's president became a member of the cabinet, due to his mutual help.

"Did you? How was he doing?"

"He was doing fine, pretty robust and his wife."

"That's my man. He and I were going strong when the other woman came in and stole him from me."

"I thought you said you broke up with him."

"Yes, because the other woman was richer. She flashed her wealth in front of him."

"That alone couldn't have turned a man away."

"Yes, beside, she was a law student. I was studying liberal arts. She was always in the same class with him. She'd hang out with him when I went out with other guys."

"So, you asked for it?"

"I guess so. I thought I could have it both ways. Anyway, let me go; other customers need you. Please call me."

"I will."

"See ya."

"Yes, bye for now."

THE DEVIL'S LAND

****

******

****

Their first date took place in the Pleasure-Side Department, Kansas State's Kansas City Ram-Day Inn. They were dressed for swimming, and they were enjoying it all the way.

The Pleasure-Side was divided into three luxurious compartments: the sauna, the hot-tub and the pool. There were many different kinds of people in the pool—mentally retarded, mentally competent, those bordering on the edge, healthy and the unhealthy ones—People of variable sexual orientations, people of different colors and detachments.

There were those who held different belief systems swimming in the pool. Also, at the place, were those who were physically handicapped, physically whole, sick and well.

It was an elaborate piece of facility with huge accommodative state of arrangement, for everyone. Those who were ill could do their own thing in the ill-section of the facility.

There was a notice 'THOSE WITH COMMUNICABLE DISEASES ARE NOT ALLOWED.' But, the idea, its fanciful ploy, was really a note to fulfil all measure of psychological righteousness. —namely, to really make the healthy people, who came to patronize for a good time, think that their health was always protected while and when they were in the facilities of the Ram-Day Inn. After all, the enterprise was a business. The owner of the enterprise needed the money. And, there was no sick money, that could come from either a sick or a healthy patron.

And, in a way, the notice served an added advantage:—It helped to keep the law of the land even at bay. And, that alone protected and covered the business owner from all forms of nuisance litigations.

Around the pool and hot-tub were so many love-seats. The owner knew American mind. And, as more couples sat on the love-seats, and, love-making, in the pleasant arena, knew no bound.

And, no one was ready to criticize, nor find faults with other people. After all, everyone was, in one way or the other, doing the same thing.

Some couples were doing it in the pool. There were some couples who were copulating right inside the sauna. Even the little ones, who came with their parents, were experts in doing it. It was all fun, the American way.

To Pante Prute Datumbuku it was a new thing and an awesome phenomenon. Here was the moment in time when he had really entered the real New World. It was indeed a worldly arena, a pleasant place to gratify all lustful craving in an Eden called Paradise. It was a new reality kind of a phenomenal world.

There were many other things which were happening in the Ram-Day Inn. Men who were married would sneak out down here and cheat on their wives. Some single women who loved it would too do the same. Some women who were married would too do the same. Newly married couples came here to spend their time, and to drink that honey from the moving moon.

Women's bodies were there for sale. And the women there were not ashamed to display their wares. After all, that was their profession, the way they earned their living, and their means to the American dream.

The rentable rooms, all in the suites of the pleasure Inn, were furnished and many. A man would simply ring a bell for service. And, all of a sudden, one or two of the 'sales girls,' would knock at his door, open his suite's door, like some fine professionals, and gingerly enter. They would approach him, ask him if he would like to buy. Then, it would be up to the man to embrace their bosoms, or postpone, or even cancel the enjoyment.

In one of the conference rooms were the members of 'World-Wide Missionary Inc.' holding a 'Mission Conference'. Dr. Jules was there. So was Rev. Jingle. They came because they were among 'the most distinguished missionaries' in America. And, their missionary zeals, even their gracious saving graces, were phenomenal, even phenomenally unbelievable, worldwide.

They had done so much for 'Christ' that even the American presidents knew their names. There was no doubt that 'Christ' himself would give them his own personal mansions in heaven, built by 'Christ's Father,' and a host of slave-like angels, without their natural hands.

Now, however, Dr. Jules came with his American girl-friend. His European wife who gave him two children, caught him. She found out what he was doing in the closet and confronted him. She caught him red-handed. And there was no denying the damages he'd done to their daughter.

And, as part of the pleasant divorce settlement, she took his house, his poultry farm, custody of the children and even his medical practice. His lawyer helped him settle with his wife this way, on the ground that she'd forever keep her mouth shut regarding what she saw her husband do with their daughter.

She was happy with the settlement; after all, she was now free, and rich, divorced Polish-American woman. She was now free to find man, preferably, a muscular black man to replace him. Twice already, she placed some long distance calls, from the Texas village, to Kansas, to renew some friendship with Pante Prute. She even intimated her interest in him, telling him, plainly, that she was now free to do as she chose.

She even ventured to the unpopular zone, calming the young man's fears that her son, Lamun, was now a much nicer child, than he was, some years ago.

SUNDAY AHURONYEZE ABAKWUE

****

Dr. Jules was a man who was always using his mouth in getting himself into troubles. Prior to his coming to this conference, he paid a visit to an African student who was studying at a University, a school near his village in Texas.

When he met the student, they greeted each other. They'd met before during an intercollegiate basketball match. He told the African his missionary exploits in Africa. That was months before his wife found out the greater lot, even portion of his mission work. During the match, though, the village college won, and the man of God, his wife, and their new African friend were hilarious with joy and excitement.

This time though, the man of God was on a mission of seriousness. He was not going to watch some tall black American boys play basket ball, rather, he was going to talk about God.

He was going to let all the other mission soldiers who had fought in the field know what a mission 'Field Marshal' he was. He saw it as an added duty to invite an African, just as he did when he visited the Chief Executive, in D.C, the nation's Capital.

The African, who he invited, had already agreed to go with him and his new woman. He drove by the school campus, to pick him up. He left his girlfriend at her house. Because she was fixing some stuff for them.

Now, however, he lived with her, as a live-in lover, hoping to raise some money, to get his own apartment, or, buy another house, since his ex-wife took his house as part of the 'amicable' divorce settlement.

When he arrived at the university campus, his new 'African friend' was already waiting for him, neatly dressed up.

They greeted each other; and he pressed a neat button, inside his car, and the car's door opened in its own accord. And, the African student jumped in and buckled up.

170

THE DEVIL'S LAND

"Son, we've invited you to this mission conference because we thought Africans are more refined than black Americans," said the venerable mission veteran, soon after the African student entered and buckled up in his car.

"Oh, Dr. Jules, I just forgot something in my dormitory. Can I just run and get it?" replied the African student, after a few seconds of Dr. Jules' tasteless remark.

"By all means," Dr. Jules replied.

His African friend carefully unbuckled, and opened the doctor's car door. He stepped out from his car. Carefully again, he closed the car door. He turned and said to the car owner.

"Sir, I'll be right back."

"Take your time," replied the fool, Dr. Jules.

Briskly, the young African student walked; then, he ran back to his school's dormitory. While inside, he did something. After which, he quickly slipped away through the back door and disappeared.

Dr. Jules waited for him for a half an hour; but, he did not come back. He got irritated, and, he got out from his car. He walked straight to the school's dormitory to search for him. He went straight to the African student's room.

When he got to the door, he saw a note, glued to the door, addressed to Dr. Jules:

Sir,

SOMETHING HAPPENED. SO, I WILL NO LONGER BE ABLE TO GO, THANK YOU.

SINCERELY,
SULAH AMINU.

"Foolish African," remarked Dr. Jules as he tore away the note from the door. "Those jungle fellows are quite irresponsible," he added. Then, he walked away.

171

****
*****
****

Dr. Jules was still the same—a popular and powerful man of God who was known by the Chief Executive, and the First Lady. He went back to his car; and, he drove back to his girl-friend's residence.

"Where is he?" his girl-friend asked him.

"Can you rely on an African?" he asked her in return. He was enraged. "The jungle fellow entered my car. Then, he told me that he forgot something in his dorm, I gave him permission to run back to the dorm and pick the hell up and come back. I waited for an hour, he was a no-show. I waited for a damn fucking hour, for that primitive fella, he was a no-show. I was concerned. I went to his dorm to find out what the hell was happening to that goddam fool, whether he was O.K. Guess what I saw at his door? This note." He tossed it to her.

"That's strange," she said as she glanced through it.

"That's how Africans are. Let's go. We've wasted enough time already."

They took off to the airport. They boarded a jet which brought them to the city where the mission conference was being held. Then, they took a limo to the Ram-Day Inn. During the conference, however, he exhorted the other parents; he advised them to be loyal to their families and even obedient to their children. He asked them to be humble servants of the Lord. Now, with a new woman in his life, he was even more vibrant, than ever. He talked louder during the conference. He made many an ugly face; and, he made fun of the places he had been to, on some 'mission works'. He talked about how primitive those places were, and how the only civilization those places knew were what came through the graces of 'American mission efforts'.

THE DEVIL'S LAND

He was applauded, time and again. He walked around and shook hands with would-be missionaries. And, as he did, he smiled, so impishly. There was a period of break during the conference. The people were going around, shaking hands, hugging and kissing those they knew.

"Hujambo mama," a black man who was a guest of a missionary greeted another African.

"Ah.Eh, Karibu."

"Eh. Asante sana," the woman he greeted greeted him back. They hugged and kissed, the American way, the American style, though they would ever be blacks, and black Africans.

"You African? I was a missionary there," Dr. Jules, with his new woman in tow, approached them and asked them. As usual, he was pretty comically impish in his smile.

"Yes we are," the black woman replied readily.

"Where were you doing the work of God?" the black man from Africa asked him. Now the white woman who stood beside him smiled as he gave an answer.

"In Lamuntall," he said with an American accent.

"Lamunta? I've been there."

"Oh, have you?" the mission doctor asked the man from Africa.

"Oh savai; habari gani?" he exclaimed.

"Yeah, asante sana. We thought your people how to live simple and spiritually while we were there." And, as he talked, the black man, before him, felt completely inferior. And, the young black lady noticed it and tactically walked away.

"I need to use the rest-room," she excused herself.

"Yeah, I'd talk to you later," replied the insensitive man of God.

About five minutes later, Dr. Jules approached the young African woman. He was happy again, ready to humiliate her with the selfish tales of his mission work.

173

"Those guys over there thought we were some kind of gods. I can't wait to raise more money to go there on another mission work," he said to her after a long tale of his exploits.

"It's amazing how some missionaries would travel millions of miles to bring God to the jungle monkeys when they cannot even stoop down and remove from themselves the rocks of prejudice which have already blinded them," she quickly rebuffed him. Then, she added so quickly "Mister, religious freedom is not freedom of insolence. You need to understand that. Thank you." And, then, she made an ugly face at him, and walked away. Dr. Jules was taken aback. He did not expect a black jungle woman to talk to him like that. Perhaps, she'd forgotten his status as a man of God. She should have thanked him for all the fantastic jobs he'd been doing for her in Africa. She should have been very grateful, even willing to be used by him in raising more money for his mission work. 'Why was she so ungrateful, even like the ungrateful African student who walked away from his car?,' he wondered. 'Perhaps, Africans are heading towards communism.' Then, his mission mind roamed, to grasp the psyche of the primitive woman,

'Did she not see the pretty white woman who stood beside him—as to be more sensitive, even sensible than that?'.

Why did she have to be so rude and arrogant when a man of God had told her his hidden agenda? The man of God was indeed disappointed in the ungrateful African woman. And, it showed in his impish face. His new woman looked and took some mental notes of the experience for some future reference.

****
******
****

It was the day the young man made up his mind to make the bold move. He had given the idea so many thoughtful considerations,

THE DEVIL'S LAND

so many a waking night on end. He had already written his ancient wife in Africa, asked her to remarry. But, she wrote back and protested, bitterly. But, her rival was so deliciously white. Now, more than ever, he was determined. And, indeed, he had already forsaken her, at least, in his distant mind. He had learnt enough in America to know how to ignore an abandoned wife.

'I know she will say yes,' his mind kept telling him. He loved her so much. And, the thoughts of her swept all his nightly dreams, to some sweet and pleasant things.

"How was your Christmas?" the young man asked the pretty artist to whom he had told 'I love you,' twice in the week.

"It was fine."

"Tell me. What did you do?" he pursued.

"I had a guest. We spent the Christmas weekend playing music together."

"A guy, or, a girl?" there was a subdued hesitation in his voice.

"A guy. He was my college sweetheart," she said, radiating like someone who had just captured a golden moon.

The man sank. He saw himself in a remarkable light: the king of all fools.

"I thought you said Ala-Ọma was your only friend?" Pante Prute asked so meekly; he was hurt, and he was about to cry.

"No. I went out with him for six months. But, this guy, I had him for one year. He got married; now he's divorced. Maybe, this is my chance to have him for good."

"Well, thank you. I'm going home."

"You look depressed."

"I am."

"Why?"

"I thought you knew by now. I'm going home."

"Africa?"

"No, not yet."

"Oh, I see. We can still be friends. The guy has already left."

175

"No, thank you. You talked me into asking my wife in Africa to leave. When you've succeeded, you turned around and found your old sweetheart. Thank you for it all. I think I am the most foolish person in the whole universe."

"So, you did that for me?" she asked him.

"Yes, I did." he stood up

"I'm so sorry."

"I know you are. But, I am a big fool. Therefore, I've lost both ways." He turned around, and walked away from her.

CHAPTER TWENTY-FOUR

Soon after Pante Prute forsook his wife, and was forsaken by his girlfriend, he turned to religion for deliverance. He became a member of Church of Serpents. It was an open church of a kind. It's members would meet every Sunday morning and worship Snakes.

Their missionaries traveled to several animal zoos in America, and got all kinds of exotic snakes. They bought snakes from Africa, South America, Australia, Europe, Antarctica, and even some snakes American Cosmonauts captured from the outer space. They wore the Egyptian symbol ankh, a cross-like symbol with a loop at its top, as symbol of their own faith.

They smoked Indian hemp, finely refined crack, and assorted brands of cigarettes. They punctuated smoking time with a lurid expression of free sex. There was no discrimination. The sex was free; free for all, married or single.

Most of the members of this very church were singles and professionals.

The homeless people were in there. So were the rich and upperclass. They were the disillusioned folks who had given up all hopes in all the redemptive promises the singularly moralistic system had held for ages.

They had seen the real church as the lair of the real vampire. Therefore, they decided to be the church of rebels and the members of the real thing. The founder of this Church of Serpents was a great white man. And, on the the first day he visited the church, he was baptized as a full member.

He smoked with them, ate with them, sexed with them, chanted with them and worshipped with them. And, everything, in the new church in America, was so special. For example, there was a period of "New-year resolution" right after the first phase of the worship. Then, one member after another came up and told them what he'd do during the new year. A member came out and vowed to kill ten people. Another fellow promised to rob a bank and to use a tenth of his loot to buy more Indian-hemps for the Church of Serpents. And, after him, another fellow came out and wowed the members of the Church of Serpents with his own pledge in a 'New Year Resolution'.

"My '96 resolution is to infect at least one new person a week with HIV. With all the guys—Mostly straight, looking for illicit sex in men's rooms, I'm ahead of schedule. Look for me in Kansas-City Hall, McDonalds, in City Square, etc." he pledged. There, the people in the church gave him a standing ovation.

The shape of the church's building, its design and all, and even the spots the church's very loud-speakers were placed, gave their roaring applause a quadrophonic sound. The fellow, whose pledge was wowed was a woman living in a man's body. He had lived this deceptive lifestyle for thirty years, all in a state of unhappiness. This time though, he decided it was time to convert himself into the true self.

He became a trans-sexual, a man who changed from a man to a woman. She promised the world what she would do. And she became a hooker and a call-girl.

CHAPTER TWENTY-FIVE

They were the formative years of the 'Party of The Black Dragons.' And, in step with the rule of racism, the 'White Serpents' had killed so many black people, and were willing to kill, even more.

Desire for revenge was raging. And, the blacks in America were determined to pay the whites, in good measure, in their own coin.

The atmosphere was tense. And the world stood. Tense. Horrified. Worried. And appalled. Quest for peace was zero. Apicad of racism was filled with shed blood of the victims of prejudice. Moral reprehension rang the hateful bell on top of the National Monument of Liberty. As the world watched, everyone in America stood on edge.

There were many faces of hypocrisies. Many black people, in those days, would virtually tell the whites what the whites wanted to hear. Even as the whites received the voices of blacks' hypocrisies, they were not fooled.

While the whites pretended to love blacks, the blacks who knew their hypocritical love, did not trust them. The atmosphere was a culture of pretense. Pretending became a virtual course for survival. Children, especially, the black children, were thoroughly and carefully drilled on how to pretend that they liked anyone of the 'other race,' especially when they were alone in the midst of the 'other race.'

SUNDAY AHURONYEZE ABAKWUE

And, the short lady, in her high-hills, was now without a man. Now, she wanted a man so bad, because she was a woman who could not survive without a boy-friend.

She picked up her telephone and began to call up all the men who were, one time or the other, in her life. She called Pante Prute; but, Pante Prute hung up on her. She called her divorced college sweetheart, he too hung up on her and warned her not to call again. He did not stop there; he went ahead and changed his phone number to prevent her from ever reaching him.

She called Mr. Ala-Ọma, but, Mr. Ala-Ọma reminded her that he was a married man, and would desire her no more. Indeed, she was frustrated in every call.

At last she called up the mulatto who looked like a white man. She succeeded in persuading him for a meeting for a cup of coffee. At first, however, he saw it as an innocent offer. But, she readily debased herself, with reversed applicable psychology, thus, making him see how innocuous her offer was.

"Look at you," she shouted, soon after he arrived at the coffee place.

"Yeah, how are you?" he replied.

"I'm fine," she said

"Oh, yeah?"

"Of course," she asserted.

"Cut it off; will you?" he admonished.

He was ready to resent her as the African woman resented the missionary who missed his mission. He knew her assertion was a put on, a disguise of a reptile.

"What do you mean?" her pretension took over. She switched like an able chameleon from a green environment to a yellow one. All her joyful disposition changed to the one of a facial surprise.

"I know you are not happy to see me; why pretend you are?" the man was the type that didn't mince words. He looked squarely at her face, and he could easily read her mind.

THE DEVIL'S LAND

"I don't know how you read this; but, I could concede I've got nothing against you," she tried to cover up.

"Don't patronize me. I don't respect pretenders. Why not act like a human being, and stop imitating a chameleon. You know, when some people act this way, they become imbricatious," he said.

"Are you?" she teased him.

"I said, are you no longer a human being?"

"Yes, I am," she agreed.

"Then, stop acting like a reptile."

"I do not," she denied.

"Yes, you do," he insisted.

"No, I don't," She began to show some rage.

"Please cut it off," he pleadingly cajoled. "Ever since I met you, you've been good at disguising yourself," he stated, then he added after a long pause, "As if you're hiding yourself from some predators."

"Well, maybe," she reasoned.

"Maybe what? Why not admit it?"

"You know, the world is full of beasts of prey," she reversed.

"And they'll prey upon you when you give them the impression that you're their meal," he replied.

"Perhaps so. But, how can I change the way I've been since childhood?" she asked him.

"It's good you've began to see yourself the way you truly are. You are the one who made yourself the way you are. You are also the one who will change yourself from the way you are," he answered.

"I guess, I'll need some help."

"I will be glad to help."

"Can you?"

"Yes, why not?"

"Thanks."

SUNDAY AHURONYEZE ABAKWUE

"My hearty pleasure. Hey, what else could one do for a fellow human being, is it not to help them change?"

"I think, it's more than that."

"You know better. What else?"

"Help them with."

"With what?"

"With the change. You said it right."

"Are you ready to change, then?" he asked her.

"Well, provided," she paused; then, she added, "are you ready to help me change?"

"I told you yes; do you want me to repeat it?"

"I'm ready to accept your help."

"I hope you are. Otherwise I would not want to help anyone who is not ready to help himself."

"Herself," she readily corrected him, "I am a woman; don't forget that."

"I know."

"Then, why did you say 'himself'?"

"I'm sorry."

"No, you're not; this male thing called chauvinism is your driving force; please, when are you gonna get rid of it?" she asked him.

"I know it's our invidious male-egotism."

"Yes, it is."

"Believe me; I'm not a chauvinist."

"Get outta here."

"No, I'm not."

"Is it because I'm here? All men are that way. We don't make a fuss about it."

"I'm not sure of . . ."

"Of what I just said, huh? I know. Remember you are helping me to evolve from my reptilian state of evolution. I hope my helping hand would not stick himself in the same evolutionary niche while helping me to evolve from it."

THE DEVIL'S LAND

"Why not stop those twists and turns of insults?" he rebuked her.

"Insults?" she appeared surprised.

"Yes, they are," he stood firm.

"You are the one who insulted me first. I accepted your egoridden, male-chauvinistic insults with feminine grace. You see, you could not even accept the bitter pills which you generously dish out to your patient female patient, doctor chauvinist"

"Ah, my proud patient, when are you going to heal yourself?"

"It will be when I stop swallowing your bitter pills."

"Then, stop swallowing them, if you are wise."

"Oh sure. I will. I shall stop any moment from now. I shall get rid of my great healer knowing that his prescriptions are based on his personal, ego-stuffed ignorance."

"I can't take this anymore."

"Yes, but you can give it to others forever," she replied.

He began to pace around, angrily, at every pace. His rage was furious.

"I've never laid my hand on a woman," he murmured. It was a diphthong murmuring. But, she understood him.

"Why not dare it?" she dared him. Then, he looked at her with a terrible glance. But, she was not even intimidated by his angry glance. Rather, she was emboldened. She readily double-dared him. "If you dare lay your hand on me, I will not only put handcuffs on them, I will make sure you will never again see the light of day," she promised him.

"You are not my wife."

"Even if I were," she smiled a bit, as if to compliment and cherish that thought. Then, she got serious, "I wouldn't allow you to do a shit."

"Don't fuck with me lady," he got seriously angry.

"What if I do, can you fuck me back?" she was even readier to take him at his word.

"I can screw your life to hell."

"You can't do a shit. I promise," she doubly promised him.

"Don't test my patience."

"I've already done that, fool. Why just don't you lay your hands on me? Why just don't you pretend that you own me, that I were your wife, and just lay your hands on me, and see what will happen to you?"

"I can't."

"Why not? Are you not a brave man?"

"I can. But I won't."

"Coward."

"No, I'm not."

"Yes you are. If you weren't. You would have slapped me."

"No, I won't."

"Why not?"

"I said I won't."

"There you go, a chameleon. Once you can; then you can't; now you won't, changing from one lie to another. You are the one that is a chameleon. You are the one that needs help. You are the one who is unstable."

"No, I'm not."

"Yes, you are. You should be ashamed of yourself. Look at you," she mocked. Then, she began to laugh at him deridingly, "If I were you, I would simply hang myself because a man like you is not fit to be a man," she told him.

Again the man began to look at her. As he looked, his angry look changed gradually. Her words sank and made their marks on him, all before her eyes. He seemed edgy, even unsure of himself. He looked at her face again; but her face was stern, emotionless and even powerful.

Her face looked like that of someone who was ready to rebuke again. Then, his glance fell. He was ready to cry.

Sorrow clouded his ex-angry face. Tears took over. And, he began to cry.

"Poor thing," she mocked him once again.

THE DEVIL'S LAND

"Please don't," he voiced out. But, she did not allow him to complete his sentence.

"You are pathetic."

"Am I?" he queried her like an unsure child.

"Yes, you are. Didn't you know that?"

"No, I didn't."

"Then know it now."

"Okay," he wept more, and tears rolled down from his tear ducts, like a rolling stream.

"So you've already accepted yourself the way you are?" she asked him.

"Yes ma'am." The watery stuff covered his eyes.

"Good."

"Thank you" he said.

"I knew," she looked at him condescendingly. "Pitiful brute," she added, jeeringly.

"Please, mercy me mama."

"I'm not your mother."

"Please, you know what I mean."

"No, I don't. I can't pretend to know what an S.O.B. like you thinks I should know," she said.

"Oh mama, I'm sorry."

"Please, get out of my face before I slap you," she ordered him.

Totally reduced, and so humiliated, he began to walk away.

CHAPTER TWENTY-SIX

There was a heart bleeding within a heart. It was a heart of the wounded-knee, a heart of the Indian Soul.

In Germany, however, was the same old call to hate the people of Jewish race, and those who were not of the German blood.

The quarters of immigrants were easy targets of racial hate. Burning and neck-lacing were the pleasures of neo-Nazis, the Super-Aryan race. Hundreds of immigrants were killed while the German police would stand by and cheer. In thousands the immigrants were thrown out from running speed trains.

The government gave its tacit support to the culture of hate because it did not invite the immigrants to the German land. Across the Ocean, the son of Nazi Colonel cheered and celebrated. He was happy because his eyes were seeing his father's dream come true. He was happy because the Spirit of Hitler would rejoice that he did not die in vain.

The so-called 'Japs,' who hated Jews, saw their big German brothers on a rampage. They were eager to send their kind to Jerusalem, on a suicide mission, even like the bomb-strapped Palestinians, who were fighting for a lost cause. They chained themselves with suicide bombs, and flew over like zealots of kamikazes.

The iron-minded, war-hardened, American war-lords were assembled in the war-room of the Octopus of Yankee Imperialism. The air warlords, land and sea were there, ironing out their creative war outfits.

They were watching, with razor-sharp interest, over what was happening in the world around them.

The war-lords of land, sea, and air were razor-sharp ready. They'd never been afraid to fight, to kill, to die, much less being killed. In fact, they loved it all.

They wouldn't mind putting a few explosives over Hiroshima and Nagasaki, if the elements of Kamikazes harassed State of Israel, too much. They knew too how to help the Kamikazes do their harakiri, if that also would help them speedy their way to their ancestors.

Even as America stood and watched, America would not hesitate to pressure Israel to give her God-given land to her hateful neighbors—an obedience which could easily spell an Israel's doom. Even as Israel refused to obey, America would not help but cherish its desire to be praised as the giant peace-maker of the Middle-East.

A land, too small to be divided, was surrounded by men, very hateful enemies. They were men whose thinking faculties were creative embodiments of all things that made for unrighteousness.

Even among those who hated were pleasant souls who were dragged into the arena of hatefulness. These were men of love who were turned into men of red, and embodiment of great hate.

Africa, the weak continent, was already poor and war-wary. Divisions in the continent were a major cause for concern. And, even the Hutus and Tutsis were on each other's throats; Liberia was already a war-zone. Zaire was not sure. South Africa was a battle ground of prejudice; North Africa was hated by those who saw it as a terrorist region.

Political instability had already ripped through the conscience of the giant of the continent. In south Africa, however, apartheid was an issue too slow to die easy. Ethiopia was the chosen land of famine. East Africa was ever the jungle safari of the Western World. The trees in Cameroon jungles were dying fast, fastly converted to fanciful furniture for the residents of France, Europe, and the Americas.

And the oil in Nigeria belonged to the foreign firms. The indigenes, who stood up, were crushed with the might of an iron will. Among those who perished were the thieves of the Igbo abandoned properties, the Igbophobes, the crafty pretenders, total agitators, and a cunning poet with a hidden dream to rule a small but rich, 'Oil Kingdom'.

The big firms were the vectors of environmental racism. They were doing to the third world what they would never do, nor, be allowed to do, in their homelands.

Europe was no good: the cows in Great Britain were agents of madness. Vectors of disintegration were tearing Yugoslavakia apart. And, the American bombs were falling on the people, like huge flakes of rain, in a rainy season.

Bosnia was a theatre of war criminals. Serbia was the paradise of warlords. Croatia bled with an unquestionable thirst for war-blood.

The old Soviet was quick to abandon her old ways. Now, more than ever, she found a new ally in her old enemy. Unstableness visited the ancient Kremlin. Even a civil war was raging in the land of the red bears. And, the Asian tigers were forced by the powerful eagle to forsake their old ways. As the devil looked and saw his world as he would have it, he shook his head in total approval.

There was an anger in the rage of angels. 'The Satanic Desires,' even in 'the devil's land, had provoked them. Street war-fares in 'the Devil's Capital,' gave Japanese visitors a main reason for patient alarm. Japanese students were mistaken for blacks and were shot at close range; indeed, they were sent home, to their ancestors, from the American shores of the global wilderness. And, those who shot them, were quick to give one excuse after another, and they were easily acquitted, as non-criminals, the American way.

The Court and law helped them, in one way after another, to cover up their hate crimes.

***

******

****

Japan was enraged, but could not fight those who had beaten her in a global war game. Her voting people were out to express an outrage; 'but, what could a small Japan do to a mighty America?'. Even as they lobbied to control guns in the New World, more and more black churches paid the price of diverted vengeance.

Crack and cocaine were available even to the unborn child. Some children killed their parents for the sake of rich inheritance. And when the law caught them, they came up with the beautiful idea that their dead parents molested and sexually abused them.

There was even a greater outrage in the promised land. The Church burners were crafty and cunning men. And, those who would not hesitate to burn down black churches were quick to neutralize the public opinions. And, the moment the world people were stunned as they watched, they turned around and began to burn down a few white churches—just to create the impression that it did not happen to black churches alone.

The global populace saw and they were doubly offended by the cover-ups of the cunning dragons.

"What do you make of them?" a Jamaican Diplomat asked his fellow Diplomat in the Office of the Jamaica House.

"Hypocrites. They can't fool the world all the time."

"Sure."

"They are hypocrites. You said it right."

"Mark my word: the case between white and black will end before the judgment seat of a righteous God."

"I think so. Whites will never leave blacks alone; blacks will no longer take white man's perpetual insolence. When things reach this level, only a third party of a higher personage can resolve it. In this case, it's only God"

THE DEVIL'S LAND

"Oh dear, the runaway children are growing daily, all in record number."

"Need you ask? The reasons are so obvious."

Parents who did not listen to Dr. Jules' Principles found themselves abandoned by their children. The power of liberty got the parents so hand-tied that "children honor thy father and thy mother" was found as an obsolete, dead law of some imaginary deity. Beside, the dead law was not meant for the offsprings of the New World.

In record numbers, mothers and fathers, who desired to use the Biblical rod to train their children, found themselves in prisons, even in jails, doing time. Probation officers constantly reviewed their cases, to find out if they were fit to obey their children. Some of those parents were confused as to who'd train the other—the child or the parent. And, in record number, the children, who were thus empowered to rear up their American parents, turned in their parents, to the authorities, for the appropriate discipline.

Modern slavery was done the hi-tech way. It was done between the New World on one side. Asian tigers and red China on the other side. The trade on human was done in the guise of child-adoption.

There was even a greater sodomy and abominable infamy, in the promised land. There were men who called themselves women on the world-wide web of the internet—men who did so to attract their fellow men as sexual partners. These were men who defied nature and enraged God with their sexual preference.

There were youths who were quick to copy the adults. These were teenage boys who showed no shame in displaying their true sexual preference in public places, public trains, public buses, and in public boats. They were free to do as they chose, even free to be super gangs, and super sex-predators in the promised land. These were young Americans who would sex chart on papers, and sex-chat online, and even have some oral sex, all through the awesome force of the information megahighways.

Priests in the land were not holy; altar boys were their special prey. A great land of fame and sodomies, there were some flakes of ironies in every practical demonstration of the laws in the holy book.

And, majority of the people, in the great land, were unique in some unique ways. For instance, there were some things quite peculiar, even unique, about them. They were mostly children of the Aryan race, the super-humans, and the offsprings of the fallen angels.

They were rebels, and even as rebellious as the deported angels. They wowed and terrorized the American people. They were everywhere. And, they were camera friendly.

They built the walls of hates; and, they presented them to Americans, as gifts. And, before the masses stood the irredeemable walls of abomination.

The over-educated American children, the super-achievers, in gun-use, the mathematicophobes of the New world, found a fine solace in the explosive devices: They were happy to be American citizens. They were happy to be free. And, they were free to arm themselves. They armed themselves with handguns. And they detonated their manure-bombs at the feet of street poles.

They harassed the elderly, the motorists and pedestrians alike. They shot and bombed. They caused the elements of the police force to increase unnecessarily, to work so much overtime that their average earnings were higher than those of Governors who hired them.

They enraged the law of the land, and, even of the universe; they enraged the law-makers; and, they enraged those who were obedient to the rules of the land. There were children, among them, who were better than super-terrorists. Some of them were, by far, much more advanced in handling bombs than third-world terrorists. Among them were the children of the deadly world, the

THE DEVIL'S LAND

offsprings of the deadly Satan, the devil's desires, and the fulfillers of the demonic wishes.

Gangs, and, gang-busters were on the rise, everyday. The former were the youths; the later, the members of the armed police force.

The youths were quick to adapt. They were violent, the explosive genes of their forebears. The violent teens grew quickly into super-predators. They held the society in perfect contempt, though they were equally proud of their nation.

They had no respect for their elders; yet, they held themselves as Supreme. Some Executive Aspirants saw what future held in store, and called their newborn babies nothing but mega-predators.

The youths were ready to respond to political insolence. They formed their own political party. The Terror Party of America, or T.T.P.A. for short. They formed alliance with the drug-users of the upper-class white neighborhoods. They received money from the drug-users, and helped them shift the raps of condemnation upon blacks who lived in ghettos, around the vast nation.

To them life was not easy; it was either death or repayment. In there was their quest for the supreme and ultimate truth. And, there was neither doubt, nor doubting Thomases about it.

The members of The Terror Party of America were uniquely terrible. Oftentimes, however, they'd capture some innocent walkers, mostly women. They'd tie up their victims, legs and hands. They'd gag them with cotton, and put tapes over their mouths, and even over their noses.

Then, they'd carry their half-dead victims to some isolated railroads. There they'd tie their victims unto the railroads. Then, they'd hide and wait for the next in-coming trains to finish off their dirty jobs. Many people died through this way before the Chief Executive could even learn about it.

Many school children, and so many helpless women died, in such many an horrible way, even before the Executive could set up a panel and a commission to look into the affairs of 'The Terror Party of America'.

And, more men and more women were recruited, into the armed police force, to fight the new menace to the great society. But, the crimes and damages were already done. They were the crimes that shocked and broke the peoples' hearts. Even so were additional crimes—white mothers who killed their children, including millions of their unborn babies.

And, many of such women, were quick to make up stories, even on how some 'black men kidnapped and murdered their unborn babies.' And, so many of them were found to be nothing but bags of liars, before the judges, in the courts of the great land.

And, with passage of time, more and more people began to see the hidden truths. And, as they saw the truths, they would no longer share interests in the excuses of false hood.

They began to insist on biased laws of the hearts be changed with the changing time. However, as they stood against the odds, the laws of prejudice persisted and long endured, even forever.

CHAPTER TWENTY-SEVEN

Africa, the home of Mr.Ala-Ọma and Mr. Sulah Aminu was scared. America, their home away from real home was not even safe. An undeclared war was going on, against the late comers, to the promised land.

The new comers came, all because the lady of liberty had reached them by way of an open invitation. They came. They arrived. They entered. And they saw the open space. They rejoiced. But the old comers to the promised land refused to welcome them. Rather, they made the sharing of American apple-pie nothing but a deadly game. They'd kill to save blood, shed blood to keep land. Bloodbath was everywhere.

The lady of liberty could not talk, all because it was nothing but an ancient idol, a myth whose time had passed away into an irredeemable memory. It was an idol. It had feet, but it could not walk; mouth, but it could not talk; hands, but it could not even use them. It was as good as the ancient Baal of the Semites; it was worse than the African idols; and, it was not even better than the human-shaped idol, worshipped by Nebuchadnezzar, the king of Babylon. And, those who worshipped the robust idol 'would not only be like it,' but, were to receive the fury of God, at the very end of their Babylonian time.

These, however, were not the days when God and Satan were having a cup of coffee over the fate of God's servant, Job. They were not the days God prided himself in Job. And they weren't the days Satan accepted God's pride, threw down the gauntlet, re-challenged God that Job was faithful only because he had all earthly riches at his beck and call.

Rather, they were the days the devil had successfully taken over the entire world of God, laughed God in the face, and stood firm as its new lord. They were the days God had tactically surrendered his beloved earth to the devil, and urged his followers to make peace with the devil, and fight on.

They were the days of spiritual warfares, and mortal physical aggressions. They were the days trusting became a prelude to downfall. And the new arrivals easily found themselves in a very tough shape. Those who took advantage of them preyed upon them, repeatedly, without desire for repentance. Sooner than later, the newcomers found out, the victims would always be blamed in the promised land.

The idol of liberty was a national symbol, for sure. But, a nation 'under God' could not adore unGodly symbol to the contrary. To do so, according to the same God, would be to provoke God to a fearful rage. But God, himself, knew the promised land. He knew that the devil was the lord of the New World; and that those who made peace with the devil had chosen to follow their new king. The lures of the devil were too much for their power of resistance.

Mr. and Mrs. Ala-Ọma were still in love. Married. Now with two sons. They'd visit Africa, twice a year. Pass by the nation's idol, as they went out and came back.

As they went outside the promised land, they saw new missionaries who condemned the idols in foreign lands, but would do anything to protect the very idol in their own land.

They saw them condemn those who practice elementary racism called apartheid, but would do everything to uphold advanced apartheid called racism in their own land. They saw the followers of Reverend Jingle in the mission field, the powerful dragons on a mission of a different cross.

They travelled to Lamunta, the home of Dr. Sulah Aminu. They met his father, an ancient farmer who preferred traditional worship to the imported culture of the white elephant. The old fellow was happy and sad. He was happy to see those who brought him good news about his son's good health in a foreign land. He was sad because those who brought in the culture of foreign elephant condemned him as an idol worshipper.

They told him how he'd burn in an eternal fire lit by their own better deity. They tried to scare him with the threat of an unquenchable fire, ridiculed him to give up his old ways.

"You know, you shouldn't even let their arrogant pride to bother you. Your son, my dear friend, I'm sure would give you the same sound advice. Yes, father, this is so. Those people who made fun of your ways are not even better. The only civilization they know is their culture of stereotype," said Mr. Ala-Oma to Mr.Aminu,the father of Sulah.

"Thank you my son. Your words of wisdom were nothing but an enlightenment. May the spirits of our forefathers guide you and protect you as you journey in that foreign place. Yes, my son, I was so worried and angry at them. I was even scared because of the things they said. Look at me, at my old age. How would I endure being put in an unquenchable fire, which was kindled by some angry god who made his home up in the Sky? Yes, their words gave me many sleepless nights," said the old man.

"No. You needed not be. They are simply ignorant. Many of them who visited you, believe me father, that was their first time ever to travel away from their biased land. Let me add here, for your own benefit, a wise guest is not supposed to bring untold worries to those who hosted him. Their seeds are the fruits of the tree where they belonged. As such, they are as much learned as their culture could provide," Mr. Ala-Oma consoled the old man.

"Oh, I'm very happy you are telling me all these things. As our people say, wisdom and knowledge belong to those who have enriched themselves with travels to distant lands."

"Even so, you are much more learned than those who came here to condemn you."

"I don't believe biased condemnation is the proper way to teach others to accept foreign views."

"Over there it's called bigotry. They think anything they do is the best."

"But that is wrong, son."

"I know. Even your son, Sulah, my dear friend, feels the same way."

"Have they?" the old man asked.

"Yes, father, several times. They've tried several times to talk him into believing the way they do."

"I know my son wouldn't yield to that phase of learned ignorance."

"Yes, indeed. And I know him. He never will."

"It's good you're open to the spell of perfect understanding," said the old man.

"Yes father. But, a spell of perfect wisdom can only work for those who are open to his working magic. The missionaries are set in their ways. They'd come here and tell you one thing. When they go back, where they came from, in the awful land of flaking snow, they burn down the black churches."

"What?" asked the old man.

"Yes, that is the fire of their god."

"So, if I were over there, if I had chosen to worship their own god; and after following in their own footsteps, they'd turn around and burn down my temple of worship?"

"Sulah, your own son will tell you in detail what the white people have been doing to the black people in the New World. You see, I am telling you these, though I am married to one of them. My wife here, though she is white, she is a woman with a different heart. When she sees wrong, she calls wrong, wrong. I've never seen her take side with evil. That's why I will always love her."

"Son, your wisdom will keep you. Your choice in marriage was a very wise one. The spirit of our fathers went before you. And our gods helped you make the right selection."

THE DEVIL'S LAND

"Thank you father."

"Yes, son, we hear there are so many women in white man's land. Also, we hear that some are good. Some are evil. As we offer our seasonal sacrifices to our ancestors, we ask them to protect you, guide you, and lead you in the right path."

"Thank you father for all the sacrifices. If they worked for none, I'm sure they worked for me," said Mr. Ala-Ọma through an interpreter.

"And you are one of the few who are open to it."

"I'm glad I'm. The spirits of our ancestors and all your sacrifices have always been the true light unto my path, the true guide in all my decision-making processes."

"And few are so," said the old man.

"Yes father, though as few are those who follow the true path, so few are those who benefit from the riches of our ancestors."

CHAPTER TWENTY-EIGHT

"I learnt this lesson either too early or too late in my life: the moment you reject me, I'm rejecting you too. Maybe I'm wrong; maybe I'm right about this philosophy. Whatever, I've adopted it. So does my God."

"Yes, you worship what you know; you worship your god because you were brought up to do so. We worship our ancestors because we were brought up to do so. You should not condemn what we worship because we've not desired to condemn yours."

"You are right on this score. But, a wise man cannot be wise forever. May be what you do not desire to condemn could even be the only wrong thing you've not known. Why not try to figure this out?"

"How can I know unless he who knows shows me the way?"

"Yes, how can he who knows teach he who does not know unless he who does not know is willing to learn from him who really knows?" artfully stated the smart man of God who was on the second leg of his missionary journey.

"What a brilliant soul. I am ready. Teach me," said the native doctor to Dr. Jules.

"Yes, as I told you during my last visit to Africa, you must destroy your idols. My God, the true God will only get mad when he sees you worship them because they are not the real gods."

"Son, if your god is mad, we don't need an insane god."

"No, I mean he will get angry."

201

SUNDAY AHURONYEZE ABAKWUE

"Aha! I see. So madness means anger in your own language?" the native doctor asked him.

"It means more than that."

"What else does it mean?"

"I'm talking about your false idols."

"Yes, I've heard what you said. I heard you say so a twenty and six moons ago. I've not forgotten. Now, my dear, if my gods are not real gods, why not just touch them and see what will happen to you?" the traditional worshipper, Mr. Aminu, challenged the zealful missionary, by the powers of his own gods.

"Do you want me to touch them?" Dr. Jules asked the native fellow.

"You've insulted them. They can kill you if you touch them. I'm not telling you to touch them. I'm telling you, if your god is stronger than my gods here, why don't you touch them and see if your god will prevent them from killing you?" the native doctor threw down the challenge, once again.

"My God is able to protect me. He will give his angels charge over me. I shall step on a scorpion, it will not sting me. I shall step on a viper, and it will not harm me," Dr. Jules boasted.

"Really? So your own god can do those things? I will like to see some of those spirits that run errands you mentioned."

"Angels are everywhere; my God is able."

"Well, if you can prove what you said concerning your god here and now, I will burn my gods, all the same, and forever worship yours." Mr. Aminu turned toward his two sons, "Go to the forest of the dead night and gather me some brown scorpions. Bring one or two vipers and a puffadder. A hognose snake does not spare. We shall use them to examine the magic of this foreign god this stranger has been talking about."

Away the two young men went. Two hours later they came back with all the deadly creatures their father had asked them to bring.

THE DEVIL'S LAND

"Otulendo," he called his second wife.

"Yes, my master," Madam Otulendo Aminu answered from her own mud house.

"Bring me the metal box," her husband ordered from his guest house.

"Is it the scorpion-box, my master?"

"That's the one. Do we use metal box for any other thing? Bring it here before I reach out and put your head in it," Mr. Aminu warned her.

"I'm coming. I was not lazy, my master."

"Who called you lazy?" Mr. Aminu corrected her.

"I didn't say you did, my good husband. I was only cooking the morning meal for you and for our visitor from the distant land." Then, she brought out the scorpion-box.

When everything was set and ready, the native doctor challenged the missionary to be brave and step on the deadly creatures.

"No, I won't do that."

"Why not?" asked Mr. Aminu.

"Because they're dangerous," Dr. Jules replied quite quickly.

"I heard you say you could do it."

"It wouldn't be a wise thing to do."

"I see. It would be a wise thing to say to convince some converts, but not a wise thing to do to build up their own faith. That's something. There is nothing my ears will not hear in this world." The old man cleared his throat, to grind his teeth.

"Why should I do it to please you?" Dr. Jules asked Mr. Aminu, the native fellow.

"Son, help me here, if my interpreter didn't interpret well," the old man re-directed. "But, I believe he does, because he studied in a distant land. He knows how to explicate your language, so very well. Now, did you not say your god will protect you from a scorpion and a viper if you stepped on them? I guess your god is not a fraud; is it?"

SUNDAY AHURONYEZE ABAKWUE

"No, it isn't," quickly replied Dr. Jules.

"Good. Neither are mine. Now, is it you who is afraid, or your god who cannot do what you said he could? Answer me," Mr. Aminu asked the man who came to him with an exotic faith.

"My God said, 'we should be as wise as serpent and as innocent as doves.'"

"Son, you sound like a man of great wisdom, and a man of many books. A man of immense learning recalls wise teachings as you do. We learn from the Oracles of our great gods. And, you learnt from the wisdom of great men inscribed in their ancient books. We hear about Holy Koran. We hear about Holy Bible. Even so, my son, here in Lamunta, a deity is just as good as what it says. If a god is good, so too must be its words."

"Yes, my God is good." Dr.Jules listened so intently, like a good student, before he made an answer.

"I and my household will believe you if you will, here and now, step your feet on these scorpions and on these hungry vipers. If they did not kill you, in an instant, we will burn our gods, shrines, and all our temples of worship, and begin to worship your own god. I believe in worshipping a strong god; so, when my enemies try to hurt me, my god will come to the rescue; don't you think so?"

"I wish I could take on your challenge."

"I wish too. Right now I believe your god is not better than mine. You should respect what we worship as much as we respect yours. When you came with arrogance of empty boast, you will always be humiliated wherever you go with your weak god. May be, your god is telling you to be humble, at all times. Maybe, it was the will of your god to humble you before our own gods. If your god can respect our gods, why can't you, a servant of a god, show the same respect to other gods?" Mr. Aminu lectured and questioned the missionary.

After the admonition, the man of God walked away.

CHAPTER TWENTY-NINE

The Kingdom of Lamunta had two sons in America, namely, Dr. Sulah Aminu, and Dr. Pante Prute Datumbuku. Both men could not go home permanently. They were now virtually Americanized, almost as civilized by the white man, as he did to the native Indians.

The civilized Indian remnants were forced to change their native names to English ones because white man's God could not pronounce the Indian names. But, not so with the men who came from the Kingdom of Lamunta. They could speak the white man's language with accent; they could not change their names to please the white man.

Dr. Sulah Aminu, soon after graduating from medical School, travelled to Atlanta for his residency. He found Atlanta to be nothing but a third-world city in America where people lived easy and died easy. He saw the abode of grander and curmudgeon; youths and elderly alike.

He saw Atlanta, the great city, a clear depiction of the whole nation. He saw the Peachtree Club, a landmark of prejudice—a towering cardinal point made of many tens and three stories high—On its East, the Stone Mountain, the place the son of Nazi Colonel briefed his followers regularly.

The South, the Sweet Auburn, where the greatest enemy of the yellow, two-legged dragons was born, raised and churched. He was a man who was ready to bury the abominable evil in its own grave. The Ebenezer Baptist marked him as the John the Baptist of his time.

Further South, the Auburn Avenue, the home where the oppressed showed off their opulence—the street where blacks business acumen thrived and flourished. Even below this street was a symbol of great harmony and unity, a herald of events to come.

He saw a city of colorful prostitutes, a rainbow of fornication, And each of the hookers got the legs, persona, congeniality, and even presence. Atlanta, a city of contrasts—a land where licensed prostitutes, from nationwide, vied to dance for the world-class Olympians—the same city that met the rage of Sherman. It all took place in the land where the unregistered prostitutes got confused, enraged, and even began to tell on the man who made their nation. But, Dr. P. P. Datumbuku became a changed man—a man who was burnt twice by women was too careful to take a third chance. He got deeper and deeper into the Church of Serpents. He gave up his medical career, and was given an ankh, a soul key of a living generation, a key which would unlock the next kingdom which had a gift of eternal life.

He was so devoted in that he did not want to miss out on the reward of his soul when his mortal flesh was gone. He was determined to die a faithful member of the Church of Serpents.

The founder of the Church of Serpents made him the Chief Among Missionaries, an arch-servant of a group who went out, periodically, in search of exotic snakes. He applied his knowledge of Biology to his new Faith. He treated the sick snakes, instead of sick people. He found peace in touching snakes, instead of touching women. And he preferred the cold-blooded reptiles to the women who sent a super-cold winter down the spine of his subconscious.

There were some female members of his Church who showed a genuine interest in him. But, he had been burnt twice by women. One, by a black; second, by a white woman.

And, he was not ready to venture for a third chance.

In his home, Lamunta, was a saying that came back often to his mind, a perfect memory recall which was able to endure, 'a wise man does not always listen to the voice of a woman. Neither does he always allow what a woman said determine his fate in future, nor his aspiration in life'. Such were the words of the elders. The elders who received the godly honour in Lamunta were men of wisdom whose words were treasures of ages. And Dr. P. P. Datumbuku was also brought up with these views. Now, more than ever, he found the validity of the aged wisdom in a foreign land.

He did no longer think about having another wife. For him, to have children was out of the question. Now he found no joy in female companionship, And the wise son of Lamunta forsook his home, his career, and even his wife. He found joy in the Church of Serpents, and he gave up hope of ever returning home. He made his co-worshippers, of the legless dragons, his new brothers and sisters.

***

*****

The devil's land was still the same world from which King William, the Conqueror, stole the wealth of all nations, and enriched his own Empire. It was the same old world the powerful sat as judge while the oppressed stood condemned.

It was the stage in time the nobles and lords stood as the epitomes of coy and righteousness, the stage in quest with blood of the weak was the key to high places. And, forever the legacy of the victors long endured. And the men of mission were enshrined in letters of gold.

The greatest mission success Dr. Jules made in Lamunta was the establishment of a foundation: American Organization For The Salvation Of African Beasts.

He secured some major grants from the U.S. government, and the support of the King of Lamunta.

SUNDAY AHURONYEZE ABAKWUE

He set up a zoological venture in the middle of a Lamunta forest. He told the villagers, the owners of the land, that his America would train them and teach them how to take care of their own animals. He told them that their young boys and girls would be sent to America to study how to take care of their African animals.

Then, he showed them a fine piece of paper on which all his fantastic promises were written in good faith. He called his fine piece of paper, 'an agreement.' And he talked the elders into agreeing to his written piece of agreement. And he asked the same village elders to thumb-print on his agreement. They did.

But, Mr. Aminu, a lone critic of the imported god, refused to give his consent. He'd learnt from the boasting of the mission man that the man from a foreign land was not genuine. If he were the sole owner of the forest, he would have equally refused to give it up. But, the words of the Communal elders prevailed over the dissent of a lone voice. In him Dr. Jules found a lone opponent of his just cause. And a tit for tat was a fine game he knew how to play so well.

Dr. Jules had many allies in the jungle-land. The elders of Lamunta loved him and his promises. The villagers rejoiced and believed him. They came out, en-mass, to lend their helping hands. They helped him clear the forest. The village men used their knives and machetes in cutting down the trees of the forest. The village women used their hoes in weeding the forest. The children helped too because they believed in Communal effort. They worked, every day, without pay. They worked very hard. And, they worked till the zoological venture was set up.

The young men helped him trap down the dangerous animals for the zoological enterprise. They captured live tigers, lions, cheetahs, gorillas, chimpanzees, giraffes, and even some wild elephants. Some of them died in their quest to capture the beasts of the forest.

THE DEVIL'S LAND

And the villagers willingly buried their dead and worked on. They worked hard because they believed in the future. They were willing to make more sacrifices because they believed their offsprings would go to America as the man of God had vowed before them. They saw Mr. Aminu as a selfish man, because his own son was in America, and he did not want any other child to cross over and learn more.

They brought Dr. Jules all their meagre contributions which they got by way of communal levying. They taxed themselves senselessly. And Dr. Jules was quite impressed when the village Chief handed him the Communal Contribution for the Zoological project.

They helped him construct cisterns for the animals, habitats for the wild creatures, and fences around them.

CHAPTER THIRTY

As time passed by, however, Dr. Jules got more money than he could spend. He forget his promises and he refused to remember his agreement, made in good faith. Many non-profit associations learnt about his drive to save all the endangered beasts in Africa; and, they were quite ready to praise him. They praised much more than his ex-wife had praised him before the nation's Chief Executive.

Many organizations in the promised land donated dollars in millions, all in support of his American Organization For The Salvation of African Beasts. He secured a tax-exempt status for this venture abroad. He took pictures of the rescued animals and sent them to America by way of Air-Express.

He told many nice stories about how well he treated the beasts, fabulous salaries and wages he paid those who served free, huge amount he paid to acquire the forest land. He wrote many newsletters, detailed descriptions of how he'd recruited some imaginary professors from some imaginary universities in the Kingdom of Lamunta—to teach the rural people about their wild animals.

He staged some natives who simply obeyed what he asked them to do without even knowing why he'd asked them to do so. He staged them receiving lectures from the staged professors. He staged them giving fine food to the wild animals. He staged them receiving salaries from him, which were later taken away from them.

He staged them smiling in front of the camera; and, he taught them how to smile and say 'cheese' when the photographer was ready to shoot them. He staged them smiling in front of the camera, appreciative of what he was doing in their midst.

He staged them following him wherever he went, as their second Jesus Christ, the Messiah of Lamunta. He staged them following him too, all in an effort to influence him to set up more zoological ventures in the kingdom of Lamunta.

He sent the pictures to America, to his sponsors and supporters. And, in return, more and more money poured in into the special account of his foundation.

Then, he learnt that someone was doing something similar in the Stateside. It was about the activities of the founder of the Church of Serpents. He was excited about it. Then, he wrote the founder of the Church of Serpents a letter of support and encouragement.

He praised the founder of the Church of the legless dragons for all the imaginary good works he'd been doing, in America, and even in the whole world. He pledged his support for him, and even gave him hope of eternal bliss, with the ankh, as the key to the eternal bliss.

Then, he told the founder of the Church of Serpents about his own mission in Africa. He hinted his true desire to supply him with new and exotic snakes. He encouraged him to found Church of Elephants, Church of Lions, Church of African Ants, and even Church of African Earthworms, or Church of Hermaphrodites.

He asserted that America was ripe for new and better spiritual enlightenment. He promised him success, followers, power, and huge bundles of money as the upcoming rewards.

The man who was once condemned as a devil, by the arch-pope of America, suddenly found a new ally in the Christian field. He did not hesitate to say yes to all that Dr. Jules suggested. He formed the Church of Elephants; and, he wrote Dr. Jules in Africa to provide the elephants. He formed the Church of Lions, three months later, and wrote his faithful ally to supply the animals.

By the end of one year, he'd founded all the animal churches, as his mentor in Lamunta suggested. There, business began to boom for the two men, both in Africa and in America.

Dr. Jules did not stop. He formed alliance with some rich American business tycoons who desired to protect their wealth from the heavy hammer of the tax-man. They made huge tax-deductible 'donations' to the ventures in Africa.

In return for his services, they promoted his missions in Africa through the media in America.

Again, the President remembered him as one of the greatest missionaries of the modern time.

****
****
****

The next phase of worship Dr. Jules explored was in the realm of idol worship. It was the religion of idols which perfectly captured his capitalistic greed, interest, and perfect desire.

He began to document different kinds of idol worship in the kingdom of Lamunta. He documented idol of the great forest, idol of the rivers, idol of the land, great thunders of the land, gods of rain, deities of the forgotten sun, gods of sand, and even gods of the living trees.

He envisioned a way to blend, the gods of idol with the Christian God, all in the realm of American dream. He dreamt that God would give a holy approval to his American dream. He dreamt that such would be a workable dream; after all, America was still the land of dreammakers and the home of divine opportunity. He was an American. He was born free. And, indeed, he was free to do whatever he liked; he was free to try them out; that, at least, for his own good and enlightenment.

He knew that he would succeed. He saw the longing in the spiritual stream of the American consciousness. He could fill the space and claim the right, and pocket the profit from the enterprises.

America was his home. He was free to travel anywhere in the world, and bring to America whatever he liked. He was not a black; he was not even a black preacher, nor a black Muslim cleric whose journey within or outside the country was always under constant surveillance.

He was a full-blooded Irish American, a pure breed of the ruling class. He was free to slap a black man around, free to make Hispanic, or Americans of Asian root know where they belonged. He was free in a free world. He called his friend, the founder of the American Churches of African animals. He told him about his new dream, and his imminent venture, and future profit.

And the man of Kansas was a ready game and a willing hand. They talked for hours; and he invited him over to Africa as a guest of his venture, a man on a mission work.

He wrote the Kingdom of Lamunta Embassy in Washington, D.C.; and he helped his friend in Stateside secure a multiple visa. Mr. Aaron Acuridol was ready to travel to Africa. And he travelled to Africa to meet his mentor and his friend.

They met at the airport of a neighbouring country, because the Kingdom of Lamunta was too poor to afford an airport. The little, and special wealth the Kingdom had belonged to the King as his eminent domain. Being a man who loved his own power, the King used the wealth in protecting his own palace, and in paying the warriors who protected him and his own palace.

"Why are we doing all these for them?" Mr. Aaron Acuridol asked his mentor, Dr. Jules, quite knowingly.

"Simple. Africans are so ignorant. They don't know what they can do with their wild animals. They need somebody like

Americans to show them the way. Look at their politicians, they can't manage themselves unless they travel to Washington to learn the rules of democracy." Dr. Jules was quick to lend his protege a new awareness.

"I see. I'm thankful for our free enterprise system." The protege, Mr. Aaron Acuridol, was easily accurate on the new rules of idol worship.

"You bet," his mentor, Dr. Jules affirmed. "Who wouldn't? If you teach them right, they'll beat you to the game. Why take the chance? We know how the system works. If you're smart, use the dumb to make yourself superrich," Dr. Jules revealed to him. The two crooks hugged themselves, and shook their own hands, quite warmly. Then, they sealed their crooked plot with a warm, high five, the American way, on African soil.

"I'm so glad for this day," said Mr. Acuridol.

"I'm gonna teach you how to do business in Africa. After all, we're Americans; and, we're white. You have some rich friends, State side, don't you?"

"Sure; but, any friend that's rich?"

"Being rich is being rich, it doesn't matter."

"O.K. I do. But their business is sheddy."

"Drugs?"

"You got it."

"Who cares? Business is business. They have other things to cover-up their tracks. Don't they?"

"That's for sure. Some of them run bubblegum and peanut businesses to protect the main thing."

"Great. Do they like paying taxes?"

"Who does? Uncle Sam is a big crook," said the partner in the crooked deal.

"I'm, glad you know that. They take from the rich and give to the poor. It's not fair."

"I know."

"The welfare system is not good for America. Those Hispanic women, black teens, even some of our own, they're just out there to make babies. They don't know the dignity of honest hard work. When you and I work so hard to make our money, all that Uncle Sam does is to collect millions from us and give it away to those lazy ones. We ought to be smarter than that. Well, since I discovered this business, I've never paid another dime to the tax-collectors. Instead, I receive more tax-breaks, even tax money than I'd ever spend. It's being smart, buddy. I'm gonna teach you how to do it right," said the mentoring crook.

"Why not? I'm ready to learn," replied the willing student of the crooked missionary.

"I'm sure you would. A sharp guy like you would use this opportunity to make himself super-rich, just like me. You've already demonstrated that you're capable. All it takes is ingenuity. And you have it. You set up a special church in the face of all odds. You didn't let what people were saying around you to deter you. You single-mindedly expanded your churches from coast to coast. Fire-brands, trail-blazers, that's the people we need in our free world."

"Thank you. I couldn't have done it without you. I'm sure you'll help me here too to do the same here in African jungle."

"Yes, I will. You're a fellow American," Dr. Jules reassured him.

"Thanks again."

"You are surely welcome. Let's go. Our driver is waiting, a black fellow who smiles like my dog."

"Funny."

"Yeah. The fellow will do anything to please me. He's poor. He needs his job, as my personal driver. He has two wives and six kids."

"How?"

"Africans marry many wives."

THE DEVIL'S LAND

"They live together, or he kicked one out before he got the other?" Mr. Aaron Acuridol got excited as he talked about having more than one wife.

"Not in Africa. They live together, in peace. I don't know how they do it, but it works for them. I was once married, where is that marriage right now? At any rate, their's is none of my business. I'm here to do my business, to make my own money, oh, I mean to convert them to Christ. You know what I mean. Don't you?" asked Dr. Jules to Mr. Acuridol.

"Sure. I'm here for the same stuff. We the Americans have always been keen in our free enterprise system. We beat the Germans during world war two. We took their rocket and space programs back to America. We can do the same with all the African animals. We've got enough spacious space for them. The only difference is that we won't have to fight to carry them away. As I can see, Africans are just ignorant."

"They're more than that. They can also kill you with kindness."

"Really?"

"Really. They're not dumb. But, they don't know the use of their beasts. Don't let them know. If you do, you ruin the entire business."

"Thanks for the tip. I won't. We know how to fight to protect our interest, that's why we Americans have the greatest army in the whole world, to respond or crush any threat to our American interest abroad."

"Yes, that is correct."

"Well, as we say, different folks different strokes. We beat the Japs to defend Alaska and our democracy."

"No. It was Hawaii, Pearl Harbor, remember?"

"Yes, you're right. I'm sorry I forget our American history."

"That's O. K."

"Thanks. Well, we beat the Japs quite alright."

"Yes. Here is Africa."

"That's right. To protect our business, the only way we'd beat the natives is to keep them ignorant."

"Yes. You can always see them as potential competitors, even adversaries. You must not let down your guard. From the bat called vampire I learned my lesson. When the bat is sucking your blood, he'd use his saliva to make you feel good about what he's doing to you. You'll only feel the effect when the beast had left and long gone," said the 'vampire' called 'missionary'.

"You figured it all out. I think that's the only way to do a jungle business and come out a winner," replied the man learning to become a 'jungle vampire' too.

"Here is Africa, my friend, the new frontier of American enterprise."

"One thing I'm worried about though. Aren't there some people from here who'd travelled overseas?"

"Sure, there are. Why?" asked Dr. Jules.

"When they come back, they might cause trouble for us," Mr. Aaron Acuridol expressed some concern.

"No way. Educated Africans are leaving their countries in record numbers. Those among them who travelled abroad 'for further studies' do not even desire to come back."

"Great."

"You see what I mean? All their William Pens aren't gonna return home. They're stuck."

"They're in America?"

"Yeah. In Europe too. They naturalize wherever they go. I know a couple of them from this jungle kingdom. I checked them out with the I.N.S. They're now American citizens. They're not coming back. You see. Africa is now ours," claimed the vampire, 'a doctor of a jungle mission work'.

CHAPTER THIRTY-ONE

Within a space of ten years, Dr. Jules and The Most Rev. Acuridol became the most influential Americans in the world. They added wealth to bout. And, their names made histories, and their good deeds took over the front pages of the elite magazines of the 'free world'.

The Executive and the King of Lamunta knew their deeds and praised them. The public of Lamunta admired them, and they forgot the promises, written on a leaf of paper. All and sundry, in the Kingdom of Lamunta, faithfully followed their teachings. They forgot their past, and pressed on with the future brought in by the two foreign men.

The words on a leaf of paper withered away from their memory. Now, all the people cared about was to do something which would please the two men from the foreign land. They knew that god of Acuridol and god of Dr. Jules were one and the same god. And they knew that same god with the power of written words was superior to all the gods in Lamunta. They feared, and they dared not criticize the two men.

And, even as they followed without question, there remained a few critics who saw the men and their mission in a different light. Mr. Aminu, the native doctor, had learnt to distrust the men from a foreign land. And, Mr. and Mrs Ala-Oma, though in a faraway land, also held their mission deeds with outspoken contempt. Dr. Aminu, the son of the native doctor, loved Christianity. But, he hated the way some missionaries used it in enriching their own private pockets. He hated racism too.

"It's only those who'd been blinded by the flash of racism that wouldn't see it as evil. But some of us who'd been mortally hurt by it, we'd always condemn it as an abomination before man and God," so said Dr. Aminu when a King of Klans' Dragons tried to teach him that slavery and racism were good for human progress. He saw fingerprints of prejudice everywhere.

He paid visits to the Southern Churches in Atlanta. While there, however, he saw those who loved to preach. He came face to face with them. He saw them praise themselves so much as to use self-praise to eradicate their own sins. He saw the spiritually weak laud the virtues of spiritual strength.

He saw idol worshippers pretend to serve God. He saw those who came for money preach money as the sole American god. He loved their vibrance, their enthusiasm, but feared their motive.

Also, he saw churches separated by colour. And he saw love, kindness, and human touch lacking in the places they were supposed to be in abundance. As he admired their tools of propaganda, their media as the element of self-praise, he feared for their souls, their souls' destiny, at the end of time.

He saw the element of the sixth pride, the devil in pretty gown. He dreaded the sight as he saw him. He saw the beast of prejudice in the midst of Holy Ones. Moreover, he saw some Holy Ghosts in the mission of prejudice. He saw some vibrant ghosts in blacks and minority churches. And he saw the silent ones in the whites churches.

He saw the gifts of the unseen spirits in manifest expressions. He wondered if God and Holy Ghosts had an issue in the whole thing. Then, he reasoned and wondered if their clash-of-will had been an issue that led to the segregation of the Southern Churches. And, he feared if God and Ghosts were the makers of segregation.

He saw some white angels as parts of the whole prejudice. He saw them serve in the black churches. And he saw some black

THE DEVIL'S LAND

angels serve in the white churches. And, he noticed too, those they served were blinded from seeing them. Then, he looked around. He saw the system in all its ugliness, a naked embodiment of crimes and perfect hypocrisies.

Then, he went home, to his own apartment. As he got home, he knelt down; then, he prostrated on his rugged floor and wept loud. He cried to God to forgive them. He wept to Christ to forgive them. He hallowed the Holy Ghost in supplication to forgive them. And, he adored the Great Prophet, Muhammed, all in a soul-searching plea, to forgive them.

He learnt, through first hand experience, that America was a hopeless society rich in material consolation.

He saw power as the embodiment of self-pride, and, even self-praise. He saw pride as the embodiment of self-praise. He saw luxury as the embodiment of self-praise. And, he saw blood-stained riches as the machine of it all.

He saw Atlanta, the home of future terrorists—men who'd kill foreign reporters who came to see them. There were men who'd pull the fast ones, their pipe-bombs to scare the entire world. The flamboyant cowards who showed off that they were the children of a stolen land, all simply by disrupting an Olympic world.

In that city, he saw, were great war giants, men who loved to shoot rather than read. Men who believed themselves as superiors, and would use the poisonous tails of the dragons, the hate-stained burning cross of arrogance, to justify their false claim.

He saw the ill-educated security dragons gain fame in an instant. He saw the terrorists terrorize the world and claim a global and worldly fame. They were men who'd stored some bomb-making materials as agents of terror of the great American society. He saw them, and they were there to enjoy their fame at the expense of human lives. Indeed, such were their many a piece of pie of their American pipe-dream.

They were men who woke up the Executive, in the middle of the night, while he slept with his wife, because of the terror they struck at the soul of the heartland. They were men who found sadistic joy in giving their nation's leader nothing but sleepless and thoughtful nights.

In there were men who did not care as they reined and showered terror during an Olympic show. And he saw Atlanta, it's terror-inspiring security outfits, mostly ill-educated, but all seeking the same thing:—cheap media fame.

They were selfish terrorists who called in their own crimes; cowards who talked from public phone-boots. They were cowards who were blinded by their desire to do evil, and commit nothing but terrible crimes.

Then, he saw the President do some thankless jobs for a selfish society. He saw the poor Executive do the same thing those who were before him had done. Right there, yes, right there

Dr. Aminu reckoned that America would surely honour it's dead Executive only on a piece of paper money—thus adding him in the list of its dead gods.

Now he saw those who smiled in front of the Executive as if they loved him—the camera happy hypocrites who were embodiments of maximum pretensions—same people who would tear him in pieces as critics behind him.

"Oh, America is so beautiful. Don't you agree?" was a question he received from a preacher—dragon.

"Yeah, I know. But, the beauty of American dream is media hype. All have seen it. We're not impressed," he answered.

Indeed, he saw beautiful women who were treated as if their beauty did not belong. He saw it. And he felt for the women. He was now in Atlanta, the third-world city in a civilized world. He saw people who felt threatened by simple acts of kindness. Also, he saw the pressure groups who were out to legalize laughter in a city, a small New England, where smiling was seen as an act of threat.

He saw some gorgeously plumb women. They were women so gorgeous that the size of their bodies alone, even how their

THE DEVIL'S LAND

undulating bodies swayed as they walked, could easily give men an eternally pleasant dream all night long.

Then, he saw those who were insecure in the things that made for real beauty. He saw those who had little knowledge of beauty—the ignorant fools with lack of appreciation—the arrogant racists who had no chance in beauty–He saw those who looked beautiful outside but extremely ugly inside—among them were those so jealous and so insecure—those who could not help but stereotype. They were the children of the father of all ugliness. They were the people who stereotype and degrade plumb and gorgeous women.

He saw them talk ill of those who were the most beautiful women in the world. He saw their arrogance and the deadly blood that fueled it. He lived in the city of prejudice, and was a witness to all manners of racial crimes.

He saw youths, blacks and whites, fed with the deadly milk. He saw them grow with it. Then, he saw them pollinate and bear fruits. And, the fruits were supergenes of criminal tendencies. By their fruits he understood their family trees. Now,—he understood why the two men in Lamunta were doing things the way they were doing them.

Now he could understand why they chose Africa as their base of the American dream. It was so obvious, because the resources of the new frontier were plenty, in the jungle. The beasts of Africa were there to be transferred to America.

The next regions of their mission enterprise were scheduled for Burma, Taiwan, and South America. From these places, however, they'd adopt the gifts of exotic magics and add them into the real money-making issues of free enterprise.

They'd build new kingdoms, and spread the gospel to the lost frontiers of the uncivilized world. They'd recruit more missionaries and train them for the harvest. They'd gotten enough wealth of experience and powerful connections to do as they pleased in their free world.

There was no going back. And, no one could now stand to rebuke or even correct them, because they were missionaries. And they knew how to do war: And, of course, they also knew how to use The Most Holy Reverend Jingle and the Southern judges to put the odd couple in a straight line.

They'd already set up a trap to get Mr. Aminu in his own land.

It was only a matter of time before their lone critic in Lamunta joined the dance of his ancestors.

They were smart men in a jungle land. They were not cowards of heart. And they had never been. They'd fight for theirs, even defend their right not to be criticized in a jungleland.

"They're leading a lie," the native fellow jeered, "If you call their way Christianity, I certainly don't think their Satan will ever get angry at their messenger spirits, nor at anyone who will ever think of worshipping their own god."

CHAPTER THIRTY-TWO

The two men, The Most Graceful Reverend Acuridol and Dr. Jules did not like the views of the primitive man. They had no room for a different truth and understanding. Because the primitive follow was really different.

Now was their time to clear the way, the time to separate a man from hardened men, the time for a tough and an unmistakable action. They were in their new frontier and, they would burn it to claim it. They were the fire in Africa. And they could burn it with passion. They had a date with destiny to deliver Africa; and they could equally do so with rage of destruction.

Mr. Aminu was too small a fish in their shallow pond; and, they were the kingfishers in their own pond. Mr. Aminu could get sick somehow, someday; and his sickness would surely require American medicine in this jungleland. And Dr. Jules could meet him in a nearby hospital, and get him right there. After all, he was the only certified medical doctor in the jungle-side of the Lamunta Kingdom. The transient issue could not be a set back to their mission in the African Kingdom. A perfect elimination was the solution. And no one would find out. Yes, he was the only authority who could state, confirm and certify what killed their native patient.

Dr. Jules alone was superior and arrogantly imperial. He was indeed a true American with no apologies attached to it. He was a man who could not stand to be criticized by a primitive man. He came to teach the beast the way, and not to be insulted.

And, he was able to get rid of the 'native beast' within a year, all by way of luck and special plan. In the course of time, however, Mr. Aminu, the native doctor, became sick; it was a stomach ulcer which gave rise to a whole lot of constant stomach pain. And, with pure passage of time, the chronic pain became the beginning of the end of the native fellow's insolence.

The rude native fellow travelled to the Kingdom's lone city, the Capital of Lamunta, and telephoned his son in America. He told his son about his constant stomach ache. And, his son, Dr. Aminu, was quick to respond. He advised the old man to return to the capital city for medical attention.

Mr. Aminu, the native doctor, obeyed his son; but, he added to his obedience a special touch of greed instinct. He changed the choice of his son's medical facility and went to the cheaper, village clinic. He was admitted to the very village clinic where his foreign enemy was ready, awaiting for him, to heal him in a special way.

Being the lone medical doctor who worked at the village clinic, Dr. Jules got his prime opportunity to get even, the American way. The chance he waited for was ripe, ready, and in his hand. With an ill-trained African nurse, who stood as his aide during surgery, he did what he had to do—the way the Puritans would have done to the rebellious Red Indians.

His nurse, a black girl dressed in white, could hardly speak good English; and, she was almost an illiterate as a trained nurse. Mr. Aminu passed away during surgery when the able doctor, Dr. Jules, was helping him to live. It was such an unfortunate incident, the first time ever a patient had died on him during surgery in Africa. Africa, as he saw it, was a different world. He could not make as much money, from his jungle clinic, as he would in a hospital setting 'back-in-state-side'. He was 'doing the primitive people a great American favor,' he said to himself. Really, he knew why he was there in African jungle. And, he knew his mission very well. Here, though a jungle, he was making more money, per day,

THE DEVIL'S LAND

than ten surgeons, per month, in America. He was a doctor; and, he had the license to heal, and even to kill.

He'd taken a few lives in the way of abortion, at his clinic, while in America. And, the life of an inferior doctor, an African for that matter, was too small to hurt his conscience. He did the job very carefully. For example, he cut off the main blood route to the native's head, thus, he deprived him the life-giving oxygen to his silly brain. He punctured his kidneys, several times, thus, he permanently destroyed the acid-base regulation, vital excretion, and even the regular concentration, plus the metabolic rates of the primitive doctor.

He damaged his liver with the knife which he was supposed to use in saving the lives of his patients; and, he killed the native doctor in the process. He smiled impishly, as usual, knowing the job was well done. He made his favorite ugly face at the dying man as the native fellow gave up the helpless ghost.

"He's dead," he announced to the 'primitive African nurse' who could hardly understand his foreign accent.

"Sir," she called back; and, she made haste to hand him the forceps and other surgical instruments.

"I said he's dead," Dr. Jules repeated, remorseless and nonchalant.

"Sir, you say football?" She looked outside and saw some naked African boys, who were playing soccer, with hope of becoming future Peles, in an adjacent football field. She ran off from the surgery room, to the soccer, or football field. She grabbed the football from the players, not even paying any attention to the displeasure of the young boys; then, she took the ball to the missionary surgeon, in the surgery room.

Then, Dr. Jules slapped her.

"He's dead, dummy," Dr. Jules shouted at her.

And, then, the primitive nurse began to shed tears.

CHAPTER THIRTY-THREE

Dr. Jules was a man under the influence of a different world. And he would spare nothing to rule the different 'world.

Mr. Aminu, the odd, primitive native was on the way; and he used what his lone enemy's son knew to eliminate him. It was advanced medicine, something superior to the healing effect of the native's practice. It was acceptable and noble medicine—something similar to the advanced abortion which enlightened women could use to eradicate such unwanted babies which happened to be in their wombs, even in their way.

Dr. Jules, the great physician, lived at number sixteen Ndi-Ọcha-Di-Njọ road, all by himself. Soon after eliminating his lone enemy, he proceeded to write a detailed report about how the chronically-ill patient died. He upgraded the stomach ulcer to 'raptured, and inoperable appendicitis'. He reported that his 'patient's condition was at a hopelessly advanced stage'. He mentioned that the six month old ulcer was indeed 'an appendicitis'; that 'it had been there for more than ten years'.

He intimated how negligence of personal health the diseased patient had been. He recorded how a 'rupture of the appendicitis' as 'the very straw that did him in'.

The report was so detailed that his academic dean in school of medicine would have recommended him for a 'Nobel Prize award'. And, he painted a glorious picture of his 'personal endeavours' in his 'fight to save the ignorant man'. And to sum, he blamed the dead for his own death.

He was extra-careful; and, he did not hesitate to go for the overdrive. He had his medical report translated, not just in Swahili, but also, in 'Niger-Kurdofarian,' as well.

He hired the best in these two lingua francae, who did a superb translating job for him. Then, he photocopied the natives' and English versions of his reports.

He sent the mimeographed copies of the three to the son of the dead man in America. He added a letter of condolence to his report.

***
*****
******

When Dr. Sulah Aminu read the report, it dawned on him that a classic case of criminal cover-up had taken place. He was so enraged that he vowed to kill the man who killed his own father.

The report contrasted with everything his father told him, regarding his ill-health. For example, merely four months after the old man noticed that something was wrong, he travelled to the nearby city, sixty miles away from his village. From here he called his son, call collect, and told him about his new health condition.

His son made haste and cabled him enough money to take care of the ulcer. His son advised him to go to the best hospital in the kingdom. He asked him not to delay the prompt medical attention.

Being a frugal man, he preferred to save some of that money by way of the nearest health-care services available. That was how he chose the very semi-clinic run by the very missionary who hated him.

He paid part of the money his son sent him; and lost his life too. The man who lived at '#16 Ndi-Ọcha-Di-Njọ' road, lived up to the true meaning of his street's name.

THE DEVIL'S LAND

Dr. Aminu was mortally enraged at so many inconsistencies between what his father told him, and what Dr. Jules wrote in the medical report.

It became self-evident to him that something monstrous, something so fishy, something so nocuous had taken place in his absence—a medical malpractice so deviously calculated, and so unpardonable.

He would have been quite willing to endure, to take it, had the man of God been brave enough to inform him—that the whole thing was nothing but a professional accident. With that, he would have been very accommodating and even understanding. But here, he saw a pure crap and criminal concoction. Here too, he saw a medical crime, in cold blood.

In Lamunta, for sure, false-accusation was regarded as an abomination. But, a deliberate act of deception was unheard of in the whole kingdom. And, in fact, Dr. Sulah Aminu could not recall if there were any word for such deed in his native language.

He was enraged to the bottom of his heart; and, he was psychologically wounded. And, the wound he now sustained became a burning pain in his mind, and in his soul. He took out his pen and wrote back.

"Those cowards who killed my father should be brave enough to confess," he replied to Dr. Jules. But the man he was about to fight had greater power even in his own home.

***

*****

****

Dr. Jules did not waste time in getting the King of Lamunta to believe his own version of the great truth. He convinced the king to write the son of the native doctor that his father died, otherwise a natural death. That he should not fight those who were otherwise helping his father to stay alive. And that to do otherwise would be irresponsible and a mark of foolishness.

Rather, he advised him not to come home, but, to get himself the services of some grief experts, in America, who would help him clear and cope with his grief, in a mature manner.

Then, Dr. Aminu turned to the Board of Medical Practitioners in America. But, the man who killed his father had already fortified his case, and closed in to kill off any evidence to the contrary.

Now Dr. Aminu found himself and his case rejected at home and abroad—His case was a dead case, a word of the dead against a written report of living physician. And there was no way a dead evidence could stand against a living testimony.

Now, he could not fight anymore, though his father appeared to him in his dreams and urged him to fight on. Now he could not fight those who conspired and killed the man who brought him into the world. He found the power of the white men to be too much for the black race. He had seen it in Atlanta, the home of the indomitable dragons.

Now he'd live to dread the terror of the men who hurt him, humiliated him, and scared him to submission.

Dr. Jules was not a man to be trifled with, especially, by the son of a primitive man. He launched his own counter-offensive against the man who tried to stain his professional reputation. He sued Dr. Sulah Aminu in the United States of America's Supreme Court, and won his case, with relative ease. As part of damage compensation, Dr. Aminu's medical license was permanently revoked. Now, and forever, he could no longer practice medicine in America, nor anywhere else in the free world.

Now, also, he was not even fit to fill in as a nurse, nor as a health-aide. His medical career was over; and, all the years he spent studying medicine flushed down the drain. He became the living testament that prejudice could ruin the career of a brilliant man.

THE DEVIL'S LAND

He found himself despised and hated. In his drive to cope with the dual blow, he fell in love with funky music. He used the remaining savings he had, after all the legal battles, to form a funky band.

He began to sing from one black bar in Atlanta to another. He sang from his heart, and even from his soul. He sang the songs of slavery with the new voice of an archangel.

He sang love songs, and songs filled with perfect sadness. He sang about his father, Africa, and about his people, the natives of the Kingdom of Lamunta. In his dreams, however, his father appeared to him, and urged him to sing on. He kept on singing, and his fans grew in number.

His mother wrote him and urged him to "take heart and sing on." He obeyed those who brought him into the world, and sang on. He sang to the joy of the mountains, even to the sorrows of the great African hills. He drew the attention of the music producers, and struck a deal for an album.

Again, his father appeared to him in a dream, and taught him a new song. Mr. Sulah Aminu became a very popular funky musician.

Since he could not fight those who killed his father, therefore, he began to sing about them. He sang about the two crooks, the two guests in the ravaged continent. He sang about America as a stolen land. He sang about Africa as an ignorant continent.

He sang songs of praise in honour of African leaders who were hated by those who ravaged and raped the continent. He praised Idi Amin in his new song. He praised Moamar El-Gadhafi in his new song. He praised Kwame Nkrumah as a Messiah of the Black Continent; and, he praised Dr. Azikiwe as the God and even Christ of the black race.

His first album became an instant hit. The lyrics were clear and direct to the hidden point. They were clear expression of what happened to him, though in a foreign land.

He sang the solo; and, his backup singers sang the harmony. His back-up singers were ten in number, each from each human race of the globe called earth; and, all his backups were women.

They sang the African way, long and from their own hearts. He amplified his tenor with the help of a musical instrument. He sang with the soul of a mountain, joy of a hill, and even with the sadness of a denuded valley. His voice reached the souls of the audience; and, those who listened, mourned and rejoiced with him, in every song.

His first song, taught him by the spirit of his father, became the first song in his first album. The music's rhythm, tune and melody, had each of the unique qualities of reggae, highlife, pop, jazz, and classical. Even rap was in there. Rhythms of interior soukous were in there.

But, before he released the first record, he did an intensive research on the man who killed his father—and the research yielded wealth of information which were nothing but an open book. There he saw that the dead knew what the living had done, but denied, for so long.

He versed them in stanzas. He arranged the songs in rhymes, schemes, verses, and some in rhyme-royal minus one. And the first song was just thus:

1. "Mixsionaries na thief thief oh (solo)
   Mixsionaries na thief thief (harmony)
   Mixsionaries na murderer oh" (solo)
   Mixsionaries na thief thief (harmony)
   Mixsionaries dem de bad my brother oh' (solo)
   Mixsionaries na thief thief (harmony)
2. Mixsionaries no be good oh' (solo)
   Mixsionaries na thief thief (harmony)
   Mixsionaries molest dem pikin oh (solo)
   Mixsionaries na thief thief (harmony)

THE DEVIL'S LAND

Mixsionaries de divorce oh' (solo)
Mixsionaries na thief thief (harmony)
3. Mixsionaries no like God oh' (solo)
Mixsionaries na thief thief (harmony)
Mixsionaries hate Jesus oh (solo)
Mixsionaries na thief thief (harmony)
Mixsionaries de deceive oh' (solo)
Mixsionaries na thief thief (harmony)
4. Mixsionaries na idolaters oh (solo)
Mixsionaries na thief thief (harmony)
Mixsionaries no de sam sam oh' (solo)
Mixsionaries na thief thief (harmony)
Mixsionaries de bokwu bokwu oh (solo)
Mixsionaries na thief thief (harmony)
5. Mixsionaries na palaver oh (solo)
Mixsionaries na thief thief (harmony)
Mixsionaries na wahala oh' (solo)
Mixsionaries na thief thief (harmony)
Mixsionaries no de holy oh' (solo)
Mixsionaries na thief thief (harmony)
6. Mixsionaries na wayo oh' (solo)
Mixsionaries na thief thief (harmony)
Mixsionaries dem be robber oh' (solo)
Mixsionaries na thief thief (harmony)
Mixsionaries de tell lie oh' (solo)
Mixsionaries na thief thief (harmony)
7. Mixsionaries no be work oh' (solo)
Mixsionaries na thief thief (harmony)
Mixsionaries crook kpata kpata oh' (solo)
Mixsionaries na thief thief (harmony)
Mixsionaries na blind guide oh (solo)
Mixsionaries na thief thief (harmony)
8. My brother keep away oh (solo)
Mixsionaries na thief thief (harmony)

My sister keep away oh (solo)
Mixsionaries na thief thief (harmony)
My people keep away oh (solo)
Mixsionaries na thief thief-f-ff (harmony)"

At the end of the song, he began a solo talk: "Where is my hope, Oh God? I came to America, in search of dream. But, America has already reduced my dream to zero potential.

Oh, how I was lied to, and deceived by the missionaries' men, and yes, and women who came to us and told me and my people so many good things about love.

Soon after I arrived at their shore, they simply, easily rolled out the crushing rocks of racism on me. They came on top of me. They tried to use them to crush my resolve to survive. But, they failed. They tried to use them to crush my dream. They knew what my dream was—to better myself as a free human being.

I saw them show intense hatred towards me—I saw them display their racist instinct with terrible Ku Klux Klan's exactitude.

I saw them in their true colors—blue, white, and red—I saw the deadly blue color of the devil in their eyes. I saw their pretense in their color-assumption. They were yellow-. True, they were yellow as yellow fever. They were not white; neither would they be as white as snow. But, they pretended to be.

I saw red in their hands, even on their heads. They were the red color of all the blood they had shed. They were the blood of the innocents, and the guilty burdens on their heads.

They hated me, intensely. They told me they'd never seen an African who had brain enough to become a medical doctor. But, events proved them wrong.

I noticed why they told me that—just to discourage me. Some of them tried to force me to change my academic major—just to have their racist way. I was offended by their high degree of racist assaults, and many an insolence.

THE DEVIL'S LAND

Oh, how I was betrayed by my best of friends. Oh, how they taught us love, but here I found out the love they had in mind was practical hatred.

Oh, I saw the meaning of the nation's flag. Yes, they're many stars of stolen land, spangles of torture, and stripes of blood and even wickedness.

I've seen the land-lords put in the abandoned caves of their forefathers. I saw pirates rule the blessed land. I saw the true owners deprived, like a hated dog, hanged with an ugly name.

Oh, I've seen the Devil in his own home. What I saw my African God will never love. I've seen the dance of the Devil with the music of angels."

******

It was the beginning of a new election in the great land. Some naturalized immigrants were chosen as speech makers, to stump for the Chief Executive, during his campaign stop, in Atlanta, Georgia. Mr. Sulah Aminu was one of the chosen few.

He was chosen because he was seen as once a poor immigrant who had realized so much in his American dream—a man who was nothing before he came to America.—A man who studied quite hard, using all the God-given opportunities in America, he became a medical doctor.—A man though through some personal misfortunes, lost his medical license. He did not count it as loss, did not give up.

He worked hard, using more American opportunities; he became a funky musician; he hit it big. A man who symbolized toughness of mind, rag-to-riches drive of the American way.

During the thing, however, he was introduced to the audience by a powerful white woman—a gorgeous woman who had made so much money as an actress, in real estate, as a wife, and as a campaign chairperson: She was a woman so peculiar. She had some certain internal triggers which made her bi-polar insecure:

You show interest in her, she became insecure about it. You show no interest in her, she felt insecure about it too.

She was a pathetic case in that though she was rich and known, she was raped at a tender age. Due to her ordeal when she was so impressionable, she became quite uncomfortable whenever she saw a male fellow near her presence.

Mr. Sulah Aminu was quite unaware, though, that the nation's political sensitivities were more important than following the footprints of the laws of the nation's God.

He began to remark on the things he'd seen since he came to the New World—things so terrible for any form of political advantage. He saw the Executives who hid notorious keys to deadly bombs and weapons in birthday cakes. Also, he saw same Executives publicly deny their secret crimes. He saw the Executives who went to church services in public, but secretly consulted the oracles of the demons.

Even as he kept on talking, the political blue dogs were ready to bark and bite those they were not used to, especially those who tried to rub them wrong. These were the people who had done wonders in the promised land; these were folks who shook and paved the paths of realities—when they went forth to steal the Indian lands, they called it the 'hand of destiny, and even of civilization'. Thus, they knew how to make their evil deeds the acts of righteousness.

He saw crooks on a national scene; and, he talked about them. There he saw the almighty dogs of war. There, too, he saw politicians and makers of deadly angels who paid an overwhelming support to the moves to shed the blood of the innocent children of Babylon.

CHAPTER THIRTY-FOUR

It was the era some insane blacks were pushing the helpless Asian immigrants into the running trains. The Big Apple which could no longer hold those in mental institutions simply set them free, left to their own devices.

Some of them would go around, and harass people, at random. There were those among them who took pleasure in killing the weak fellows, members of the free society, who crossed their paths.

The insane whites were dishing out pills of insolence to anyone who passed across their way. They'd call you all sorts of foul names, ask you if you'd be disrespectful to the white people around you. And when you get angry at them, they'd be quick to apologize as if they were normal human beings. Some of them would pose as doctors. But, when they talked, the smell of their mouth would exude more foul odor than the odor coming from the grave of some dead demons.

The way they'd shake your hands, many times within a minute, would show you that they were indeed insane.

In those days however, God was on the shoulders of men; and men did not know it. The medical Board knew about Africa, and about the case; but, they did not know about the right things. The yamangoro man had given them the American version of the truth, truth told slant. And they believed him. He and his partner were able to fool others too.

Dr. Jules became a voice of the nation, at home and abroad, and an envy of the medical professionals. Many a time he'd be invited as the honourable key-note speaker at medical conferences.

His second, The Most Gracious Reverend Aaron Acuridol paid visits to one religious revival after another.

Even so, the crooks on a waka-about still had their reasonable critics.

"God is jealous. Satan is proud. Which of the two is better than the other?" a man asked Mr. Aminu after a music concert.

"I don't know. But, Dr. Jules, the missionary, is a product of the two," answered the funky musician.

"Yes indeed. He cannot be otherwise," agreed the man who happened to share Mr. Aminu's view.

The men on a mission made an assessibility journey to the Asian tigers. They were fascinated by the fires of earthquakes coming from the lands of the Pacific Rim, Malaysia and the Rings of Fire, even the Rings of Archipelago.

They visited the lakes of fire in the lands where lands and water were claimed as parts of their national boundaries.

They were inspired by the rings, and terrified by the awful nature of the lake of fire to come.

Even as they admired the golden rings of fire, they remembered their crimes, a crush of guilt in that they were crooks with the blood of the innocents in their hands. They could not repent because they were missionaries; and they would not confess, because they were proud Americans—the elite genes, the enviable phenotypes of the superior race.

They gazed at the fire; then, they looked at each other. They remembered their crimes; and they could not forget that they were guilty men. Their guide, a poor Asian fellow, stood at a respectful distance and watched them. They remembered all the gbagbati they caused in Africa, and even all their yamangoro which they did the kpata-kpata way. They understood who they really were—the

THE DEVIL'S LAND

big time Oloshi, even Ori-Odaa—the super-foxes who could not be out-foxed by anyone.

Their quest in Asian nations was marked by a rapid success. Many converts followed their footsteps to God. They built churches, medical clinics in the middle of Asian jungles. They made friends with native magicians who taught them their own trades. They befriended the leaders of the Asian tigers who became their mission allies. Even as their mission works progressed, they dreamt some better dreams.

With their dream of global conquest, through the venue of mission work, came an eternal fear that the beasts in sheep's clothing would somehow be revealed. Same fear made them quite cautious, and even super suspicious.

They hardly trusted anyone, apart from themselves. They viewed their most faithful followers with hidden, ultra-suspicion. They distanced their minds, always in constant guard, constantly guarding their tongues, lest they say the hidden things to the wrong people.

And, even as they behaved the way they did, their reclusive aloofism turned them into a magnetic legend; and the more they dared to trust less, the more their followers dared to trust them.

In Asia they dined and wined with the popular and powerful. They rubbed shoulders with Emperors, and paid visits to the temples of foreign gods. They consoled the smaller gods who were once ridiculed, condemned, and despised as no gods by their own Superior God.

They made the lesser gods feel important before the messengers of the greater God. They made the lesser deities feel great, even superior to their once Superior God. They asked the Asian gods to forgive God, and to join hands with the African gods with them as their points of contact.

They bribed the Asian gods with thanksgiving offerings and sacrifices of praise.

They followed the footsteps of the temple priests, and worshipped the idols as if they were true gods.

They pledged their allegiance, with greater hearts of pledge, than they did to their national flag, the cloth of their nation.

And, they turned their backs, though on a mission work, in a foreign land. They stayed in Asia for three months. Then, they travelled to the land of the Aborigines, named Australia by the white man. There they saw sharks, crocodiles and some white men swimming together in the waters taken from the natives. And they liked what they saw. It reminded them the teachings of the elements of Jehovah's Witnessess—their coming paradise where lambs and lions would live and walk side-by-side in peace. Then, they saw a shark kill and eat a white man. They saw whites use blacks to set traps that wiped out the sharks in their natural habitat.

They saw white women who loved the crocs so much as to lead a move to protect them. They saw some foreign vacationers whose lives were taken by the armored reptiles. They saw exotic animals, worthy of worship, with short hands, in the land of kangaroos. As they watched the kangaroos, they remembered the Kangaroo Courts in their own land.

Then, they left the kingdom of Jungle, the Kangaroo Kingdom to Sidney, the City of Brides. They saw women who were always looking for men to marry them. They met women who proposed to them. They had fun with them; slept with them; broke their hearts; and rejected them. They visited the natives, and learnt about their herbs, their potencies, even many their medical use. They documented their herbs, promised the natives of some imaginary royalties. Then, they took samples of the herbs to the United States for patent ownership.

They became the owners of new drugs; and those they helped shelter their drug money from tax hammers helped them build drug empires, and distributed their new drugs worldwide.

THE DEVIL'S LAND

The Executive learnt about their new conquests and praised them. Again they paid more visits to the White House, to the Congress, to Capitol Hill, and even to the Senate. They loved the setting of the ancient Shrine of Jupiter.

They rubbed more shoulders with the most powerful men of the New World.

They became the regular guests of the daytime operas, and late-night talk-shows of the media services.

The newspapers and radio stations took cues and gained greater ratings just by basking on the luminaries of their presence. Nothing now, as ever, could dare bespatter with mire their shining reputation. They were Americans. They were men who dreamt for big things. And they got them in a big way. They were the shining apostles of free enterprise Capitalism. They were men beyond reproach, the reproachless two who had stumped for America, and American God worldwide.

Now they could dare claim empery over the repsold with money, even by paying the brilliant ones at the NASA emporium. There was no turning back. America was now solidly behind them. All the bad publicity Rev. Aaron Acuridol gained were remembered no more. And, all the lyrics of ex-doctor Sulah Aminu's funky band were seen as the hateful noise of some disgruntled lunatics.

The American men were always the winners wherever they went. The losers who did not join them would always find themselves left behind. They were men destined to visit the moon, the sun, even a triumphant landing on the far-flung and farthermost planet from the American Jupiter.

The world, the planets, even the universe belonged to the offsprings of the fallen angels. Their God had already willed it. And, that alone settled it. And every issue in the conquest was nothing but secondary.

SUNDAY AHURONYEZE ABAKWUE

Their God gave it all to the brave heart, the lions of the American prairies. The wilderness was theirs to conquer. And when their ship at Plymouth Rock landed, it landed on the natives with doom eternal.

CHAPTER THIRTY-FIVE

The native's prophet saw the vision of doom before dawn. He warned his people in advance, but the divided tribes did not heed his warning calls.

He told them about the black moon which was swimming over across the great waters. He told them the black moon would bring the dark days such unheard of upon all the Indian tribes; but his words were dismissed as the words of a drunkard. At the appointed time the Chief of Wachussets saw the glory of the tall ship at the Plymouth Rock. He made haste to welcome her crew with open arms and unbounded love. He gave them boiled corns and roasted turkey. They ate together, as friends, though the first time they had ever met.

He took them under his wings, and catered for them through the cold days. He killed the buffaloes, and used their hides and skins to clothe them. He fed them. And he sheltered them. He taught them how to plant the crops of the New World. He told them the time to plant and the time to harvest them.

All the while he played the role of a good host. And, with passage of time the crew of the black moon set up a dinner table and thanked him. Right after this dinner, the guests began to act like guests who had received some kolanuts from their hosts. They began to show their hosts the contents of their visitation.

Some of their contents were bizarre; some zeroed in on the indescribably snide. Some of them were sensible; and some were outright rejection of everything the hosts held dear.

From this point, however, the chief of Wachussets found his own personal error in prophetic disobedience. He went to the prophet's village to seek for his advice, only to find out that the rejected prophet had been killed, many moons ago, by the same guests he prophesied about.

It all happened so many moons before the rumble of bubonic plague pushed the Old World to the verge of extinction. Yes, even before the King of England expelled the crooks and criminals from his land in England.

And, that was even before the New World Moses was even born, who later emerged to lead his gang against the British Crown.

***
****
*****

They came because they saw the need to come. They came because they could not help but come. As they came, they were welcomed, though uninvited.

They came, though they were not invited, but because they had to come. They came because they were once a burden on the Old Europe.

They came because they were chased away by bubonic plague. They came because they were on the run from the rat disease. They came because they had no choice.

Among them were the political prisoners of the British Crown; the heretics of the Crown's religion; the half-breeds of the Aryan race, rejected by the pure breed.

They were men, women, and children on the bidding of a different God. They came to condemn the Great Spirit and to proclaim the same spirit with a new name.

They came, the confused masses, with little dreams, but astounded by the wealth of abundance.

THE DEVIL'S LAND

They came, the sick, weak, and women of the Street of the Old World. They came, the old residents of the Old World; they arrived, the new citizens of the New World. Among them were the lunatics of the old breed. They were men, women, even children who talked to themselves while they walked on the streets of gold. They were the mentally handicapped, many a social charge of the old Europe. As they walked the streets of gold, they shouted as if they were shouting at somebody.

Even as they shouted, thus displaying their individual lunacies, certain blessings tracked their steps as nothing but flashes of brilliance. They invented messengers of death in art form. They designed those that flew in the naked sky. They invented deaths which swam in the great waters. And they came up with vectors of death which killed like the bubonic plague. They became proud of their inventions; and, they were ready to test them.

They tested their brilliance on their hosts who welcomed them. And their tests sparked off a war of attrition. They used their messengers to kill off the Indians and their buffaloes. As they killed them, however, they put to shame the burial sites of their ancestors. They took pride in humiliating them.

Now, those who were once on the run from the bubonic plague suddenly found themselves on the chase to grab riches and fertile land. There, they saw the hand of their God and His promise—they saw the Manifest Destiny written on the Indian soil. They saw the hand of God lead them. They saw the Almighty take the Indian land and give it to them as their new inheritance. They heard the voice of God tell them to take over the Indian land by the powers of their brilliance. And, they hastened to follow every dictate of the Great Spirit in His new name.

They reined down like monks with fire of hell to burn the natives. They descended like angels of death with no love to rescue. They killed them without mercy; they killed them like the rats that brought them the bubonic-plague.

247

CHAPTER THIRTY-SIX

The emergence of the Pilgrim's Philosophy became the beacon of the Indian doom. The land which was once an Indian land was not, by right, supposed to belong to the Indians.

It was the land of God; and, God had the supreme right to hand it over to whosoever he pleased.

God did not want the meek to inherit His land; therefore, he called the braves, the people with lion-heart, to fight for its control. He sent down some angels to show the new land. But, when the angels landed, they saw the land firmly in the hands of the Evil One. The angels were few; so, they could not fight in the devil's land.

They began to spy the new land of the dreadful angel. They saw the dark days of the prophecy, the prophecy of the dark moon. They saw tears of God, falling like rain, on the Indian rain. They saw the devil dance in the tears of God.

They saw God weep for the fallen prophet. They saw the lamentation of God in Indian summer, Indian Winter, and even during the season of Indian Fall. They saw God shed tears for the fallen prophet who was not listened to by the Indian Chief.

They saw God in human form. They saw Him shed more tears as the Pilgrims shed more Indian blood in His own name. They saw the offspring of the fallen angels raging with insatiable greed, greed so overhead, and so terrible and horrible.

Then, they began to forget that they were spy-angels. They began to shed off all their earthly disguises, and to assume their true forms. They visited the idol of liberty; and there they saw the Devil on his high throne. They greeted the Devil with the salutation which the Devil enjoyed when he was the Fourth Power among the Powerful Lords of the Heavenly Paradise.

There, the Devil recognized them. He had anticipated that God would do this—but, he did not anticipate the visit to be when he was sitting on his earthly throne. He anticipated a legion of angels come down on a holy war; but, here he saw a few angels smiling before him.

He returned their greetings, as he used to, true angels of the Heavenly City. He asked them about God. He was amazed how beautiful they looked after all their journey from the City on High.

Then, he began to feel ashamed of himself. He remembered his former throne, the Fourth Majestic Throne, of the Paradise of God.

He felt ashamed of his earthly place and all the earthly decadence therewith. He wondered if God would somehow forgive him. As he wondered his guests read his mind. Then, his old pride took over. His total repentance gave way to proud obstinance

He asked them what they had learnt since they came down. They told him their knowledge of Indian language called Osage—which they knew even before they came down. Then, they greeted him again and left him.

The angels on Godly mission were not prone to disobedience. They did not come down for battle, but to see the land, as God asked them to. They saw a filthy world with bloodshed and decadence. They saw the filthy conscience and dirty deeds of noble men. They saw the rage of the Devil on the weak and lowly. They saw variety of insanities on the highways.

And, they saw trials of sadness and rivers of sorrow in a condemned world. And, as they saw they raged with bitterness, and a longing, for God to come down.

THE DEVIL'S LAND

And, as they saw, however, they began to pray. They prayed that God would come down and fight the great evils under a bleeding sun. They prayed that God would fight with rage of hell, which was there as God's last resort, in the mortal war.

They saw the damages the angel of rebellion had done to the world which God once blessed and called beautiful. They watched the proud angel, ever arrogant, ever righteous in his own sight.

They knew that the Devil would never receive a perfect repentance. Therefore, they knew that his eternal fate was sealed.

They saw the Devil build Auschwitzes in the New World, and the Nagasakis in inner cities. They saw religious fanatics bombed in their many an Auschwitz, and many blacks perfectly eliminated in the Hiroshimas of the New World. They saw incinerators built for blacks, for natives, and for aliens who had no legal status.

They continued to search. They saw the debris of death, the ashes of those who had no voice in the Devil's World. There, they remembered what God had told them: If you get too close to the Devil, you get pain of the promised land. They saw those who were pained in so doing.

$$*** $$
$$**** $$
$$***** $$

The messengers of the Devil worked overtime, everyday. Then, the Devil began to build some super-structures in the presence of the spy-angels. It was his desire to impress them—that though he was cast down, after all he was equally determined to reclaim his grand, though lost heritage.

He wanted to impress them, and to show them that he was ready to fight God. He sent out his messengers to all corners of the world to recruit them to serve him. He offered them money, luxuries, and pleasures of the New World in abundance. And, they came, the most brilliant men and women of every nation under the sun.

They came, child-prodigies, and intellectual genii of all races and professions. They came, the super-brains who could dream and invent. They came, the bloody intellectuals, military tacticians of the genius caliber. They came, men of means whose wealth could buy a Prince and his Crown.

They flooded through the idol of liberty, waving the cloth of the new nation. And, as they passed below the Devil who sat on top of the great idol, the King of the great land rejoiced over them.

He asked his messengers to give them their non-sans papiers' status, so that they would be eligible to work in his kingdom.

He gave them living quarters, huge financial benefits, and an added passport to visit and enjoy the centers of attraction. They were generously induced to perform in every way.

Those who were single among them were given gorgeous mates to service them. Luxurious means of getting around were at their very beck and call. They were told to ask for anything. And, everything they asked for received its provision in abundance. And all their needs were so sufficiently supplied, even met in a way far beyond their mortal dreams. And, their joys were filled with satisfaction.

More and more people came to the New World—men and women who had always had a special longing to be in the Kingdom of Saint Satan—these were men and women who believed that true baptism did not depend on wearing some special religious clothes. Also, they came, and they passed through. They came, those who'd not been fully appreciated in their own lands. They came, the brave hearts, and those who were able to dare.

They came, the mad jinni of the Muslim world, the wise men of the Orients, the philosophers of the ancient Greece, the Chinese of noble intellectual heritage. Even the arrogant radicals of the forsaken lands braved through and came in.

THE DEVIL'S LAND

They came, insane geniuses of variable intellects, and intents. They came, the weak, but trail-brazing walkers of the hostile deserts. And, as they came they began to work, so hard, all by the prodding spirit of the American free enterprise. And, as they worked hard, they were rewarded in many ways. Those who could invent the angels of death found their glory in greater dimension.

The best brains of the world began to build some greater super-structures, many a new wonder of modern time. They built highways, and paved alleys. They built certain underground machines which could transport mortals to eternity. They built elements which were wolf-like coffins that swam throughout the waters of the world.

They built wonders in the sky, wonders on the land, and even wonders in the waters. They used certain wonders and birds of death to send their kind to the moon to search for the answer to immortality.

They sent missions to the hot solar planets in search of the answers to the problems and earthly diseases which they caused and created. They went deeper into the deep space, all in search of certain deities called gods; but, they found none. Instead of gods, they found rocks; instead of answers, they found new questions; and instead of key to immortality, they got the rays to eradicate lives.

They boasted of their drives and their achievements; and, they wrote about them. From the moon they proclaimed: One True God. Soon after they came down, they worshipped their false gods. There were some biospheres made by the assembled brains of the New World.

In their biospheres they studied the creatures and mushrooms they stole from the moon. They studied the pieces of rock which they took from the higher planets.

They felt that the distant creatures would give them clues to life eternity. Yet, they received none. They racked, raked, and stormed their individual brains in search of answers to their own questions. They were able to create new plants with earthly and space ones.

They perfected men who could bear children without women. They perfected women who could have sex without men. They made sex the centerpiece of the American dream.

They created cyber-optic sex. They created windy sex, sex of sunshine, harmful sex, pleasure sex, erotic sex, visual sex, oral sex, swim-suit sex, flying sex, political sex, Hollywood sex, movie sex, film sex, indoor sex, outdoor sex, photographic sex, bimodular sex, cellular sex, and even molecular sex. They became a sex-tribe.

When they looked at all the sex apparitions they had created, they found transient pleasures and an eternal flame. And, like God, they admired all their handiworks and called them pretty. And, they held them that way. Dr. Jules had a stinct with the sexual institution. He went back to school for his post-doctorate. He re-married, divorced again, and married a third wife.

They began to build the Kingdom of sex, and set up a secretariat to look after its activities. The homongous project claimed a homongous tax dollar of homongous proportion.

They set on operation and began to manufacture sex agents. They invented sexstimulators and their opposites. They manufactured sex awareness without reproductive potentials; and they called this enlightenment, condom. They did more research on it; and they manufactured a variety of sizes and forms of this product. They manufactured variety of this thing for humans and for animals.

They manufactured things which could work like human beings; and they called them robotics. Dr. P. P. Datumbuku became a special tool in the hands of the demon to advance the ideals of the dream world. The African doctor who joined The Church of Serpents came up with sex therapy for serpents. He invented variety of condoms for the unholy, yet spiritual serpents.

He studied and developed how to fix his inventions in the male serpents' sticks of malehood. He became an expert in this area. He was richly rewarded. And his success began to make him a

THE DEVIL'S LAND

virtual and real prisoner of his own research brilliance. He could no longer travel outside the great New World without some special agents going with him.

There developed a fear in the government circle, a man with such special talent could easily sell out and betray his new nation—that he could reveal his research results to other nations, especially, to Cuba and to the communist countries—thus, reduce the strength of the great nation.

To prevent these things from happening, the secret agents were on a secret order to eliminate him, should they find a genuine reason, or even an effort, on his part, to betray the great trust.

They were regularly assigned to travel with him, whenever he travelled outside the Great Kingdom.

CHAPTER THIRTY-SEVEN

They built cities which could fly in the open sky—They built towns and villages, armed with death angels. They organized tribes of fighters, clans of warriors and their warlords. They sent them to roam around the world, all in search of new wars.

Then, they built city-like structures which could swim in any water. They armed these floating cities with deadly angels of mass-destruction. They told their trained tribes of fighters to go around the world in the floating cities. They taught them how to kill, how to be arrogant, and how to stand tall. And they went out, proud, superior, even arrogant.

They waved the triple-coloured cloth of the New World, wherever they went. They chose a war-lord to lead each floating city in the water.And, they would do anything to maintain order in their deadly mission.

They worshipped each of their war-lords like a demi-god; and they obeyed each demigod as the sole source of their lives and deaths.

Their lives were based on hierarchies of relative priorities. They went ahead and reduced the ability of Nebuchadnezzar to make wars. They saw to it that King of Persia would have no voice in modem colour, and among the Arabinas.

They went around suppressing every smaller nation which desired to be like theirs. They flogged Babylon with an iron rod. They whipped Medea and Persia with whip of a crazy horse.

They caused the ancient Cyrene to bow to her knees; and they brought famine and a new disease to the Land of Emperors. And, they broke the knees of the Asian tigers; and, they made their helpless victims to beg them for mercy.

They made peace with the First Empire with which they fought for their new room, and breathing space.

They made Israel an heir and a Chosen Son. And they would fight to defend him.

They loved to be praised as great, all the time. They'd easily act as global policeman when there's something that touched their interests. And, when they're doing that, they'd fool the world into believing that they're doing so to protect the freedom of everyone.

And, they lived fast, and died so fast. Even as they did, they wondered why there was no redemptive value in the operations, and even in the promised-land.

They manufactured death-angels who could fly without feathered wings. They came up with rounded inventions which could explode and kill.

Their brains gave birth to motile instrumentations which could kill without mercy. The mad prodigies in the new land saw their mentors in a new way a high gear of progress—a high gear of inventive recognition.

Then, they were challenged to surpass their heroes. They began to challenge themselves with the inventions of super-death angels. They manufactured things which could readily mix with common air and kill. They gave their new angels some new names.

Then, the Devil, the King of the Land, recognized them. They rejoiced because they were glorified in the presence of the masses who adored them.

The nobles of the great land paid them regular, glorious visits. They rubbed shoulders with the great and powerful.

THE DEVIL'S LAND

Such men as Dr. Jules and Most Righteous Reverend Acuridol became their regulars in the arena of friendship. The gold-hunters of the promised-land began to look for a way to rob them. They came to them in the guise of love-seekers and friendship.

They came as spouses, lovers, and new friends. They dressed provocatively sexy as to evoke lust and deadly passion. They came as admirers and true fans. They graced them with love letters as pen-pals.

They called them up by telephone, and asked for dates. They told them how much they loved them with weeping hearts.

When they'd secured their baits they ruined them without mercy. Then, King Devil saw the need to prevent the weaklings of other lands from coming in. He asked his angels to establish lois pasqua through the congress. Then, tough immigration laws began to descend upon the Great Kingdom. The sans papiers saw themselves easily cornered, and even deported.

There was another devilish wisdom in the able grand scheme of things. Child pornographies and licensed prostitution became trades of the nation. These were beautifully written in the articles of trade, the touch-light of free enterprise. The leaders of business talked to their representatives. Their representatives, in turn, passed a bill to preach against them abroad, and to defend same at home. It worked so beautifully well in that if you want to practise the trade, you have to come to the promised land.

Once in every session, he modified the old laws with clauses of new additions. He researched the old ways to build his empire on a grand scale. He had engineers trained with global conquest as the ulterior motive. He mobilized his trained soldiers with aim to new glory.

They worked for him on a grand scale. 'Produce, perform or get fired' became his work slogan and a scare tactics. Those who performed, he paid them bonuses as gracious additions.

There was something inherently adhesive in the whole program—an allegiance to the Devil through the cloth of the Kingdom. It was an idea worth dying for—a pledge of blood to ever see the Old Glory fly higher and higher in its dazzling red, white, and blue colours. No nation under the moon could be so proud of their nation's flag as the Americans.

CHAPTER THIRTY-EIGHT

Dr. Jules saw the voice of wisdom in the idol of liberty. He became a regular guest at the altar of liberty. Here he would pray, and show some intrinsic gestures for the public to see. He'd pray and thank the main idol of the nation for all his blessings.

The Great Devil on top of the idol would smile at him, and remained gracious to him. He would send out his angels to guide him, as he went out to spread the gospel, voracious lion in the cloth of a meek lamb. He recognized his craving for approval, and desire to be praised by the nobles of the Great Land.

The King of Hell was ever ready to supply all his desires in a way far beyond his finest dream. His second, Most Righteous Reverend Acuridol, was a man dear to the Devil's heart. The Devil loved him because of his eccentricities. He was a vital tool in that he'd made millions of people worship the Devil's first incarnate, a serpent, at various churches of serpents.

The Devil loved him; and he loved the Devil too, through serpents. The Devil made him a prophet of the mission. And he prospered in his demonic calling, a drum-major prophet of all the Churches of Serpents. And, through prophetic vision, though, the Devil, in guise of God, revealed himself to him; then, messenger of hell made him and his partner a faithful promise of riches and fame, of faithful followers who would honour their footprints forever.

Reverend Acuridol told his partner the vision of the prophecy, which was already in progress; and, Dr. Jules believed him.

Reverend Acuridol was endowed with a sound addition to his prophetic talent—a spiritual gestaltism that confounded the minds of the new converts. He became a chorus man of the Devil in a field filled with grains—a charlatan in the arena of true God.

The Devil gave The Prophet a prophetic bonus—It was a gift of tongue in that he could speak perfectly foreign languages and quite understand them. He used his vision of prophecy to twist the minds of the new converts. And, he did it all in the name of God, through obedience to the Old Serpent.

He was honoured often, and glorified as the spirit of the Devil told him in the prophecy. He prophesied, all the enemies of the great nation must fall to their knees. With passage of time, that came to be. He prophesied the Great Kingdom would rise above every nation under the sun. That, too, was fulfilled in his lifetime.

He foresaw the nuclear age—the age in time birds of death would force the nation's wishes upon those foes who wished the nation no good.

He saw the era of terrorism in prophecy; he saw the means to transform it. He saw tigers of terror in the nation's dens.

And, he saw how the Great Kingdom would use them to fight their enemies to submission.

He foresaw the ordered and orderly succession of the Kingdom's dynasties—in that violent overthrows of governments were not known in the Chosen Land. The Prophet was honoured because all his words of prophecies were true, sound to the masses. He saw other nations copy the Great Kingdom. He saw the nation use this copying to export prostitution as civilization. He saw the Great Kingdom export decadence too to the nations that copied her.

He saw the profits that poured in into the Great Kingdom. And, he saw the Devil in Godly gown rationalize the exchange as fitting, proper, and even righteous. As he saw them, he bowed down his head, in his cataleptic prophetic trance, and worshipped.

THE DEVIL'S LAND

***
****

The Great Devil was up again. He ordered the world to dream a sound dream—to dream of living in his kingdom forever more. He used the media of every magnitude to spread the news. His voice was heard loud and clear. He made lust for riches the clarion call. He made eternal dream the beacon of the lustful dream.

He sent out his envoy, chosen from every tribe and color, who had scored big in the American dream. He used them to spread the news to the lost, but distant lands. He gave them hope in their midst of hopelessness. He showed them the light of liberty without the cords of its substance.

He pulled the strings through the influence of those who he made to score big. He made them believe in the dream; he showed proof thereof. And, they could not help but believe him.

The messengers of the Devil were witnesses that the dream was true. They showed off their riches that the land was full of promise. They told them their tales of sufferings in their Old Worlds. They were tales of hardship, tales of lack, tales of penury, and tales of economic nightmares.

They told them how they came to the land of opportunity, poor and wretched. Then, they told them how, with little dream and little work, they were able to amass wealth and opulence, for themselves and for their children.

The Devil saw his mission in a higher gear. He saw the world dream of coming to America. He saw them forget their old dreams. He saw them work hard to cross over to the New World. He saw the tricked masses scramble in quest of an elusive dream, even an elusive world. He saw them think that the only heaven to be known was the paradise of the New world.

He deceived them; and he confused their deception so that they would never find out. He made them think, those who'd endeavor to tell them the truth were only endeavoring to discourage them from entering the promised-land.

He made them think that such discouragers were nothing but selfish. He obliged their hopes with anticipation. He obliged their senses with sensations of glamors which could only be obtained by going there. He used his High Priests,—the proteges of Dr. Jules, the great man, Dr. P. P. Datumbuku, and Supreme Prophet, Reverend Acuridol, to honor his presence.

The Devil, the Supreme Lord of America, was the lord in every way. He knew his tricks, at home and even abroad. He began to use more of his tricks at home to influence events abroad. Since he'd made them believe in America, he made them feel the land was free of racism.

He made them think there was no prejudice in the promised land. He hallucinated them with dreams of gold everywhere.

He did not tell them, that so many churches of the black worshippers were burnt down through the powers of prejudice. He avoided telling them the number of blacks, Chicanos, and even Orientals in many an Auschwitz, called jails.

He carefully refused to reveal the truths to them. Among the unrevealed truths were the nature, and segments of homelessness in the promised land. They were not told about the beggars in the streets of the chosen land.

And, they were not informed that there were numerous drug users, pushers, and drug addicts in the blessed land. The joy of prejudice was beautifully twisted for Devil's advantage.

All the sorrows in the land were painted with many an opposite paint. Each strand of sorrow was painted as a string of joy. Suffering was painted as pleasure. Those who were serving time were painted as movie stars.

There was something concrete, even extra in the whole painting—the media were there to paint the Devil's dream, Devil's deception, Devil's aim, Devil's objective in the Devil's ways. And the Devil was able to triumph.

CHAPTER THIRTY-NINE

"Remember this: if he's not willing to bless you, you can't force him," he said to the convert who could not travel to the New World. "To those he'd chosen he called; those he justified through blood, he redeemed."

"Does that mean I've served him in vain?" asked the convert.

"It could be your heart is not right with God. There must be something wrong with you. Maybe, your heart is not right, or pure before God. Maybe God does not want you to go to the promised land. Maybe God wants you to repent, and serve him here as a preacher in this God-forsaken jungle. Think about it, beloved; maybe our God will forgive all your sins and redeem you from your spiritual bondage," said the missionary.

"I am not sure of all these. It could be that God does not love me," the convert reasoned.

"Away from baseless idea and foolishness. Haven't I told you before that God is love? You have no right to believe otherwise. If God did not choose you, I cannot ask him to do otherwise."

"But you are a missionary, a God's agent here. If God wouldn't listen to you when you ask him in prayers."

"You must stop all these foolish talks. I've told you God's grand design for your life. You have no choice but to obey the voice of God."

"Sir, I will have to decline. You are not God. I don't think God can speak through you if you're only out here to discourage those who're willing to better themselves so as to serve God even better."

"Well, well, well smart monkey, huh? I can't help you. Even if I could, with this type of attitude, I won't."

"Yes, please don't," said the black convert "My God can help me with or without you. It would only be in your best interest to help me so that same God would be glorified through you."

"You're an idiot; I won't help you."

"Yes, I'm an idiot because I've told you the truth. If I had."

"Shut up right now; or else I'll."

"You can't beat me up. This is Africa. I've read many things about black panthers and racism in your own country. Is it not true that your people burn down black churches so as to discourage them from worshipping God?"

"Smart aleck. I knew you're. The so-called black churches were centers for social dependency."

"What do you mean by that?"

"They were welfare recipient centers."

"Even so, even if they were, did you have a God-given right to burn down their buildings?"

"We have the right to discourage social dependency."

"And what?"

"You've read too much. It's people like you who cause a lot of trouble in America."

"You're a liar; I know. If I may not insult you with the truth, it's people like you who killed Malcolm and Dr. King."

"Oh my God, you knew about those monsters?"

"They were not monsters. They were righteous men like Christ and Muhammed. But, you betrayed them the way the ancient priests delivered Jesus into the hands of sinners. We know why you do what you do and the way you do them. Listen, our eyes are open. For you to cheat those who look up to you as an agent of

God is demeaning to the very essence of Christianity. I think and believe you can do better than that."

"That's why we want to save you."

"You can't save me from your own sins. You can't save me when you have the blood of the saviors in your two hands."

"I wasn't the one that killed them."

"But your words support the killing; therefore, you are a party to the unpardonable crime."

"If you were a woman, I'd have called you a hag," the man of God tried to divert the topic with creative insolence.

"You can call me that, too. Haven't you called me a monkey already?"

"Me? That's a lie," the man on a mission denied it.

"I know a white man will always deny the truth whenever he's caught in name-calling."

"You're a pathological liar."

"Fine. Thanks for that. If I'm a liar, the pathology of that lie is you."

"Well, well, well here comes a black devil."

"Thanks again. You know how to give blacks the dark names. As the saying goes, 'you give a good dog a bad name so that you could have a reason to hang him.'"

"I've had it. If I were you, I'd consider the fact that my career were on the line. You were approved for a Green Card lottery, I don't think you should ever have it. Now, I think you want to go to America."

"So?"

"Which school do you plan to attend?" the man of God roared. The way he roared those words, it was self-evident that he'd keep on standing on the way of the young black man.

"Destroy my career if you have to; bear in mind you are what you act. You cannot preach Christ with Bible and destroy his followers with acts of prejudice," said the black man.

SUNDAY AHURONYEZE ABAKWUE

"We'll see," said Rev. Acuridol.

"Yes, we'll see. I'll either see you in heaven, if you do the righteous deeds, or watch you from heaven if you continue to follow the footprints of prejudice," said the black convert.

Reverend Acuridol was angry, and greatly baffled by the creative insolence of the young black convert who wanted to go to America for academic enlightenment. He'd been to the dark continent, six times; and, this was his second visit to this Isle of Madagascar, where he met this young black, who dared to insult him.

CHAPTER FORTY

It was the detour of the Devil with racist prejudice. It was made in America, a land that belonged to neither whites nor blacks, but to the native Indians.

The black man of Madagascar, who was once offered admission to an American University, suddenly, received a letter of rejection. He knew the brain behind it, all by instinct. He knew the missionary, The Most Righteous Reverend Acuridol, had given him a dirty deal. He couldn't have insulted a white man and gotten away with it. He was dealing with an American, a powerful Reverend Righteous, not a bloody, native African who could easily forgive an insolent youth.

Here was an implacable man of God who had no room for forgiving path of his primitive converts. He believed in the tough American way: You give me a Holocaust; I'll give you a Hiroshima plus extra. Moses of the Bible couldn't have been more proud of him.

Stephanotis Madang, the unfortunate African, was taught to settle a displeasure through an argument. That was what he knew. And, that was how he grew up. He had no idea that one's hidden enemy could ruin one's distant dream, so as to even up a seemingly resolved score.

He wrote back the school, and told the school's president how his admission committee had no right to annul his admission. The infuriated school's head honcho wrote back, casting him as an unfit, rude, and barbaric, and even idiotic fellow. The letter went as far to hint what a disgrace he must have been to dispute the decision of those who were wise, even good enough, to reject him. The head of the school pointed out, for his primitive benefit, that those who rejected him were good enough to create him.

And, as far as the school's Big Kahoonah was concerned, the decision was final. And, there was nothing the primitive follow could do about it. Mr. Stephanotis Madang saw his dream to go to America ruined. He could not fight them through legal battle. Even if he could, he could not even pass through the American Embassy, to fly over, to meet those who rejected him.

The man who told him, "I think you want to go to America; which school do you want to attend?" was a man, tough and superior, in his own way. He was a god, in his own right; and, he had the godly right to ruin the dream of any primitive man who dared to challenge his authority.

He had no room for some primitive insolence of a young fellow who he truly regarded as less than a human being. All things put on the table, there was a clear line of demarcation—the native had to respect it.

The man on a mission missioned his faithful promise, pretty well. He made sure Mr. Stephanotis Madang's name was added to the 'black book' of all American Embassies, in Africa.

And, to seal his revenge deal, he made sure, beside Mr. S. Madang's name were these words "Potential terrorist, unfit and inadmissible." Mr. S. Madang had no idea how far Reverend Acuridol would go to ruin his overseas dream and ambition. He did not know who he was dealing with. He was just a tough and robust cow ready to pick a playful fight with a teethly armored hungry crocodile.

Reverend Acuridol learnt the trick from his friend—you have to be deadly tough with the natives—every native—whether Indians or these Africans. There, he began to behave like 'the proverbial African rooster who saw someone pluck out the tail feathers of his favorite hen that went into an incurable rage'. He was not

THE DEVIL'S LAND

supposed to be challenged by a black convert, talk less face him with an argument. The black convert should have known the clear line: black-white racial demarcation.

"I've seen a few primitive people, none has dared stump his nose at me," the man of God remarked, during the fateful argument.

"We might as well talk about racism which is a living sin in America," rebutted the young black man who loved to insult him.

The Reverend drew closer and regarded him with an angry gaze. "I doubt if you're gonna get away with all these."

"Sir, with all honor due you, let's face some simple and nothing but simple facts; white people killed the son of their own God. It was your people that did it. Jesus did not die for us. We know that. We chose to believe that because we know that God is universal. Yes, your people killed his only son because he disagreed with you."

"As I said, pal, you just won't get away with."

"Yes, as far as I'm concerned, we know the truth, and the truth shall set us all free."

"We do everything for you, all we get back from you folks are all these insults."

"What have you done for us?"

"We feed the world. We give them Green Cards to work in America."

"Oh Yes, we understand how you do so. You bully the world; that's number one. How can you feed the world when your homeless ones are dying in the streets of America? Your so-called Green Card? Are you no longer a missionary? Don't you know what a Green Card means? If you don't, please re-study your Bible, the prophecies, for sure. Your so-called Green Card is six six six, the mark of the Devil, the beast. Those who don't have it do not have a chance in making it in the kingdom of Satan."

"Let's change this topic before somebody get's hurt," the man of God redirected and smiled a terse smile. And Mr. Madong returned his apt graciousness with his own abrupt smile. "Now, answer me," the Reverend continued, "how would you define a politician?"

"A politician is someone who will criticize an opponent to get his job; but, the moment he got the job, he turns around and begins to do the same things he criticized before he got the job," the black Madagascan answered and stood his ground.

"Good answer. Bold and courageous. What is your view about our America Christianity, and the role we're playing to save the world?"

"America, as the world knows, serves her own interests. Christianity is very close to Socialism. If you doubt, read the story of Pentecost, very well. They shared and distributed among themselves in that there was neither needy nor homeless among them."

"So?"

"So, you cannot integrate Americanism and Christianity, as much as you cannot mix pieces of rock and water and drink both at the same time. For you will either filter out one and drink the other. Yes, for you will either serve one master and neglect the other, or be devoted to one at the expense of the other."

"Good answer; but erroneous," said Reverend Righteous A. Acuridol.

"No Sir," Mr. Madang was quick to disagree, "I do not see any error in the simple truth."

CHAPTER FORTY-ONE

Mr. Stephanotis Madang felt perfectly rejected when he read the rebuttal from the school's president. He did not know all his plans and preparations could so evaporate when they were so young. He didn't know whether to cry or disappear from the universe.

He didn't know whether to fight or to complain. He didn't know whether to start all over, or to give up the entire idea as the school's president demanded. He saw himself, a person whose dream of paradise turned into a lake of burning hell.

Then, he began to blame himself. He felt he should not have entered into that argument with a man he hardly knew.

He intently and intensely blamed himself for his failure, pride and arrogance. "I've frustrated my own career," he cried "Oh, how could I be so foolish? Oh, how could I be so foolish?" He jumped around, and threw himself from one place to another. And, as he did, he bitterly and self-reproachfully pinched his own body, like a Zulu warrior, who had truly offended his personal god.

He began to feel that he'd be an indigent forever, an insufferable prospect for a young man, with Zulu blood, like himself. That would be unthinkable. Should he tell his parents about it? He wondered. How would his teachers react to such an awful news?

He was not known as a troublemaker in school. To be sure, some of his Secondary School teachers gave him a world of good recommendations. But, Africans, as he learnt through books, were equally regarded, at best, as crooks, by the white Americans. And, a world of African recommendations were not as valid, even as honest as the word of an upstanding American missionary, as that of The Most Reverend Acuridol. And, a man like Reverend Acuridol was there in Africa to teach the natives how to tell the truth, to repent from their sins, and to become as civilized and as righteous as Americans.

The men who gave the 'potential terrorist' fine recommendations must have been bribed, or, they had not even felt the redeeming grace of the gospel of Reverend Acuridol. The school's president and the admissions' committee knew that. They knew how Africans were—crooks who could easily breed dictators—dictators who would in turn murder their own people like nothing but cannibals.

They knew all these brutal facts. The media, being American media, were always right. They knew how much Europe had done for Africa—just to civilize the primitive dogs, without luck. Colonization, the height of Western civilization, was so graciously given to Africa. Trade and commerce were brought in there. Slave trade was given to Africa, in golden plates. But, Africans would hardly listen.

Mineral exploration was undertaken; yet, the brutes remained uncivilized. University of Timbuktu was taken away from them, so that they could travel abroad to learn; yet, the black race could not see the light. Even when their folks were dumped in the Atlantic, in millions, to improve the size of Ocean sharks, the stupid black race could not see the beauty in the white man. How then, in the great white world, could the blacks be civilized, unless the whites continued to teach them the way of civilization?

Millions of them were brought to the New World and put in the cotton-farms to work. Instead of them to do a fine job, to work like their closest cousin, an obedient horse, they became nothing but ungrateful agitators, always complaining against the graciously good white man. They gave the graciously good man hard time. The ungrateful beasts, they complained daily, against the good man who graciously bought and brought them out of the jungle, and out of the dark hole, and deadly continent, and into a fantastic light of Western civilization.

What more? What else could Europe do for the uncivilizables? They took the learned men of Tuareg and made them indentured teachers of Europe, yet, the stupid Africans could not learn. They took away the institution, the global center of learning, yet, the dark people allowed the darkness to envelope their continent. It was foolhardy in that the people who were so helped could be so ignorant.

****

There was a deadly red mission in the wind. It was a red anger of revenge. It was a ragged arena of falling blues.

It was an earthquake of the soul, an ugly stuff for an unforgiving heart. The man on a mission was about to dive into the Ocean of true regrets, for his rush to reprisal. He was a man conversant with the thought, that suffering alone was the closest step to eternal damnation. And, he did not desire such a hell, for himself, as a reward for all his mission's unforgiving heart.

He waited as if the red eyes of a black God were about to consume him, because he was an unforgiving man on a mission work. He was a man who could inflict, but pretty afraid to receive pain of retribution.

He waited, nervously, like one about to face the rage of a black God. He was about, but unwilling to drink the bad taste of his own brew. He was no longer in America where he could keep on ruining careers of young blacks, and kept on getting away with it. Here, his home's dictatorial democracy could no longer apply to boost all his racial prejudice.

The Yankee Gringo was dancing his honky-tonk in the white man's grave. He did not know what mosquitoes did to his people who came before him. If he had known, he would have decided against coming. For he was a man who had an irrational fear of a clear death.

Suddenly, he was summoned to the Prime Minister's office for questioning. The man who ruled Madagascar was a distant cousin of the fellow whose career he was bent on ruining. And, the Prime Minister was enraged when he got the news, from some relatives.

He called the school's admissions office. And, when they tried to give him a runaround, he demanded a word with the school's president. His arrogant persistence paid off. He demanded the school president to tell him why his nephew's admission was suddenly annulled. He threatened to expel all Americans in his country, if he were not given a satisfactory explanation.

Then, Dr. David Petticoat saw that a major pot of trouble was brewing. He took the letter which Reverend Acuridol wrote him, and faxed it directly to the Prime Minister.

Reverend Acuridol did not know why he was so urgently needed at the Prime Minister's Office. He made haste and dressed up, because there were four armed police escorts, who came to pick him up.

Soon after he arrived, a General in the Madagascar army took him to a small office. There he was shown the letter he wrote. And, he was given twenty-four hours to leave the country.

Reverend Acuridol left Madagascar to Ghana. When he got there, he began to hear the news. He learnt that certain villages in Africa were a 'no-go' for the white man. He heard about how mosquitoes beheaded the most daring of the Europeans who were bent on taking over the continent. He learnt that yellow fever discriminated against those who did not have the black skin. Also, he learnt, tsetse flies, brought in by the white man, did not find reason to be an ally of the black race.

He decided to do to the blacks what the African mosquitoes did members of his own race. He was good at what he was about to do. He contacted his friend, Dr. Jules, and told him about his new

THE DEVIL'S LAND

dream. He needed an expert on how to breed European tsetse flies in a tropical environment. And, Dr. Jules knew how to it.

They united in their mission and got new grants from their home government. They told the world that they were conducting a research on the vectors of tropical diseases. Some communist scientists ventured to join them. But, they flatly turned them down.

They bred millions of harmful tsetse flies, every month. They took their new breeds to the jungle villages, and released them. They did so, one month after another.

One year later, the two men of God began to have a taste of their own brew. They caught the disease, trypanosomiasis, borne by some tsetse flies. They left their village mission station, to Accra, for treatment, in a major hospital.

While in the hospital, they saw many other people, who were going back to their ancestors, all because of the disease they increased in their village laboratory. They saw blacks; also, they saw whites.

They saw the fruits of their labor; and, they were scared. They did not want to die; therefore, they resolved to leave Africa for the Stateside. They flew black to America for better medical treatment.

Soon after they arrived, they died. Their bodies were put in some maroon-colored, 'executive type coffins' made by some good, old American coffin makers. And, their coffins were draped with, each, a piece of the triple-colored Old Glory.

Their bodies were laid to rest in the Arlington National Cemetery—a place for the noble and great heroes of the great nation.

It was an honorable burial for each of the Prince of Crooks. The nation's Executive was there, during the monumental burial. So were a few of the past, living Executives.

Many other nations sent their words of consolation, through their Embassies, in the nation's Capital. The King of Lamunta

SUNDAY AHURONYEZE ABAKWUE

came in person, to honor his friends departed, who did so much good for Africa.

A person, after another, sang their eulogy. A black poet, with nobel prize under her belt, read a specially prepared poem, all in praise of the two phenomenal crooks.

A choir, made up of all tribes of America, sang, when their hopeless bodies were lowered into their graves. Some glowing words of praise were artfully inscribed on each of their gold-plated, diamond trimmed, useless tombstones:

"TO OUR GLORIOUS DEAD—HE DIED OF SLEEPING SICKNESS IN HIS HEROIC BATTLE TO SAVE THE WORLD. MAY HIS NOBLE EXAMPLE CAUSE US NOT TO FORGET THAT FREEDOM IS NOT FREE."

CHAPTER FORTY-TWO

The death of the two mission crooks marked a new beginning in the promised land. And, the new immigrants, in the great land had, for so long, seen the begging desire for a phenomenal change; but, the King of the land was too powerful and solidly wise. The men who served him were faithful; and, the article of service and the code of conduct were finely written in the kingdom's constitution. And, Dr. Jules and Reverend Acuridol did not disapprove, by any means, the articles of the nation, till they left for eternity.

Mr. Lamun Jules, the son of the departed, was present when the nation paid his great father the last respect. In fact, he was not a great admirer of his father, because of the things his mother told him. But, seeing kings and nobles pay such tributes to his late father, he, invariably, changed his mind about all the foolishness that went between his father and his mother.

Now he was determined to be like his father, especially, in the field of mission work. Now he was determined to follow the footsteps of his father. Now, there was nothing to hinder him. Now, it was just a year before his finishing of his studies in a medical school—a course he took, just to spite his father, and to help his mother run his mother's medical clinic.

He was now determined to go to Africa, as a missionary, to ably continue the research program that was in progress. He knew that his father had some radical detractors, the ancient Sulah Aminu, and his hippie-like, rag-tag singers. He was now smart enough not to let them bother him.

Beside, he knew some waspy Klansmen of German, English, and even of French extraction. Just a few telephone calls would take care of that.

He knew how they worked, how they defended the interests of the superior race. He knew who they were—they were the rough-neck romantics, fanatics of upperclass ideologies; they were tough and ready blue blood, the old money Americanism at the fatal and crucial best.

They were the real men, the adventurers of the calling wilderness. They would dream fat dreams; they'd dream on how to help the poor countries; when it came to helping, they'd rob the poor ones stark blind. 'The poor,' they'd say, 'the world would always have'. And, they'd make the poor even poorer without regrets. Lamun could also use them to make himself fabulously richer than his late father. They had connections in the media, in the governments, in businesses, and even in many other nations and distant kingdoms. Their hands were in the purest of righteous deeds, and even in the worst of horrible crimes. Either way, Lamun would only stand to gain.

He was well placed, an heir of a legacy, a family tradition so deep, so vast, and so profound. No one would ask for a better inheritance.

He knew too, there was no one who would challenge his position. His lone sister was already married to a British merchant who preferred living in his British Castle, in United Kingdom, to the land of promise. And, her husband was a man who remarked time and again that America, being a mental society, was unfit for a British lord like him to live and raise his family.

He and his wife would come for a visit, a few days, twice a year, and back they went to the gentler land of many rains.

Lamun was the only son, a lone tree in an Ocean of fertile soil. He knew America, and Americans, how they respect the special place of a well-placed Anglo-Germanic American. He was white and waspy, a man of blue-blood with the old money. He'd already

THE DEVIL'S LAND

gotten a few picture opportunities with many money makers, even with the Pope, and with the Chief Executive of the great land.

He'd started to build his own portfolio without even knowing it. After all, the whole thing ran in the family—he was the son of his father—a powerful pediatrician whose steps and progress were an eternal envy of the most prominent medical greats in the whole world—kings and heads of states paid him their homage.

They rubbed shoulders with him when he was but a young man. The Chief Executive felt honored, time and again, to dine and wine with him. An African King stood by his grave and wept. What more could he ask for in a father of such a noble repute?

CHAPTER FORTY-THREE

The Spirit of a true God descended upon a Child-Priestess in the Chinese village of Kwan-do, saying, "Thou art a holy child; in thee I am well pleased."

She was in a Temple of Sun when the Spirit of true God came down upon her.

"Who are you?" the Child-Priestess screamed in terror.

"I am the God of all Gods. With me there is no God," said the God, who identified himself as the 'True God'.

"What do you want from me? I am only a child," the child returned.

"Yes, you are. You are a chosen child. Go to The Devil's Land and prophesy saying, 'You must never again allow your missionaries to disgrace you in the presence of the world. For I am Jehovah, who made you. Otherwise, I shall visit you with signs and wonders. Your plights will replace your joy.

Your sins have crowded my Table of Mercy. I shall have them no more. Repent, or you will likewise perish. The blood of heathen nations cry forth from their graves against thee. Innocent ones lament on account of your wickedness. Repent, or the day of your visitation draws near.

The blood of the native land are angry with earthquakes everyday. Thy sins go out with tornadoes to hunt thee. Repent, or else they will find thee.'".

When the child came out from the Temple of Sun, she was pretty terrified. She did not know exactly how to begin. Neither did she know the meaning of 'The Devil's Land' which I, the God of all Gods, was talking about.

But, the Spirit of the true God was not through with her. "Go to the Kwando river and stand guard; stand there, for there I will show you vision of my mission," the voice told her in front of the temple of sun.

She ran to the river, as the Spirit told her to do. There it was revealed to her, in moment of time, her prophetic destination. She saw the nation and her people:

She saw random and senseless killings ravage the streets of America. She saw the killings go on at an unprecedented rate—thousands of homeless 'John Does,' and 'Jane Does' killed in the streets of City of Angels, Los Angeles. They were numberless faces whose names were forgotten, even unknown to the greater society.

Also, she saw other beings quite distinct from human beings. They were some unknown beings which began to pay unscheduled visits to the nation at an alarming rate. They'd come down in their vehicles, and land on the highways, farmlands, urban squares, thus evoking a grand scare and many a stampede.

At times, however, they'd throw down some rock-like stones on the urban dwellers, thus, causing deaths and even many a great damage.

Their weapons of destruction would even burn like an inferno. Whatever their stone-like rocks touched, on their path, would quickly burn, for so many hours, before quenching.

The religious lords of the nation began to preach louder than ever for the people to repent. She saw them tell the masses that the rage of God was upon the nation.

They'd stand on the streets and ring their bells of repentance. They began to avoid television stations, because houses with televisions became the hostile targets of the alien invaders who descended from above.

Then, she saw the Devil in his High Throne above the idol of liberty. She saw the fallen angels who were at the Devil's service.

"So, America is the place?" she asked God, in her language.

"Yes, my child. Bring out your tongue," the voice of the Great Almighty God asked her. She obeyed. And God touched her tongue with His second finger. Speedily, a flame and some smoke came out from her tongue "Put back your tongue and close your mouth," God said to her.

And, she obeyed too. "Look, I've purified your tongue. A new tongue have I given you. Go home and have a dinner, for your long journey is so near."

****
******
****

Away, in the distant land, the second time, in a obscure, primitive village of Kwan-do, China. God Almighty visited the young girl, His chosen prophetess.

The Spirit of God descended upon her, and the glory of the Almighty overshadowed her. She was eating some rice with a pair of chop-sticks when the Power From Above came down.

From that moment, however, the ten-year old girl, who could hardly pronounce letters of English Alphabets, began to speak in perfect American English Language, even with perfect Anglo-Saxon, American accent. It was really a clear, and an amazing miracle. The people, who were with her, mostly her parents and relatives, thought that their young one was going crazy. They tried to grab her; but, she took off and ran away. They gave her a clear chase; but, she ran faster than they could; and, she did so towards the great Ocean.

By the Ocean, however, was an American warship, which was making a port-of-call at the Chinese shore. The girl ran straight towards the warship. And, her parents hotly pursued her. She jumped unto the stairs of the ship and kept on towards the main ship.

"Don't let them hurt me," the girl pleaded with the navy boys as she passed through them. Her American English accent made the naval crew think that she was an American girl. They had no choice but to protect her.

"What are you doing with those people?" the ship's Captain asked the young girl.

"Just take me back to America; I'm on a mission," the girl responded.

"Oh boy, they almost got you. Did your parent leave you?"

"Sir, please take me back to U.S. When I'm there, I know how to take care of myself." the girl responded, to the second question.

"Well, young woman, welcome aboard. First, I must tell you you're going to have a long ride with us."

"I really don't care," the Chinese girl, chosen of God, with American accent, speedily replied to the ship's Captain.

All the while, her parents tried to get into the war ship. But, the American boys quickly shoved them away from the warship. A few of the navy boys began to use other methods to scare them away—two of them grabbed their machine-guns and pointed them at the intruders. One of them fired in the air; and the girl's relatives froze. Then, they began to turn back.

Fifteen minutes later, the entire Kwan-do village men, armed with knives, bamboo rifles, and den-guns, came. They came to retrieve their own. Their intent was obvious: They came to fight to rescue their crazy daughter.

They were men who had fought inter-village wars. They were not afraid to lose blood, take blood, and sacrifice to have what was theirs. They drew closer, closing in on the warship. Their intent was dangerous; and, they were hell-bent for the danger and for their objective.

THE DEVIL'S LAND

The Captain of the warship was a wise man. He'd seen much more blood, even enough blood in that he did not want to provoke a war between his country and the most populated Communist country in the whole world. Therefore, he gave an order for the ship to take off to the high sea. And, in an instant, the warship took off, with the girl on-board.

That was how Lin Don Wu left her village, Kwan-do, to the United States.

CHAPTER FORTY-FOUR

When the Prophetess arrived, she went straight to the White House. And, as soon as she entered, the Spirit of the Great God descended upon her. She began to prophesy:

"Hark, thou house of this nation, come and reason with me," she shouted on top of her voice.

"Young lady, how did you get in here?" A couple of security agents rushed to her and questioned her.

"I'm here on a Divine mission. I demand to speak with the president," she answered.

"You have an appointment?" said number one security agent.

"I said, I demand to speak with the president," she returned.

"You'll have to leave these premises," the second agent said.

"I'm here on God's appointment. I'm not leaving until I speak with your president," she dared the security agents with her own resolve.

While the girl and the security agents were exchanging words, the First Lady watched them from inside. And, when the two men began to drag her away, the First Lady came out for a prompt intervention.

"Let her go," she ordered the two men.

They obeyed. Then, she turned to the young prophetess, who now embraced her and said:

"What can I do for you?"

"I demand to speak with the president."

"Of course, you got your demand," the First Lady responded.

"Ma'am, she doesn't have a clearance," one of the two security agents protested.

"That wouldn't be necessary," the First Lady responded.

"Yes ma'am, she could be a terrorist; why don't we search her; just in case?" said the other security service.

"Oh please, a young child will not kill my husband," the First Lady chided the extra cautious agents.

After that, however, she took the young girl in.

"Hmm, I don't mean to be; but, how did you know it's voice of God you'll be bringing to the president?" the First Lady of America asked her.

"Look out your window," shouted the young Prophetess. "Behold the rage of Almighty. For thy doubt, thou wife of the most exalted noble, I AM will strike thy mainland with tornadoes, and thy Island with earthquake. The red fire of the angry God will show you that it's I AM who sent me."

"Wait a minute," the First Lady tried to humor the shouting girl.

"Unless there's a genuine manner of repentance, I AM will strike thy nation with ten scores of deadly plagues. For the power of I AM is strong. What He says, He will surely do. I AM is not a politician that He should tell one thing and do another." Then, she disappeared in an instant. And, the nation's First Lady was bewildered.

CHAPTER FORTY-FIVE

When the Prophetess came back, a band of news-media were waiting for her. The entire nation, the people, were amazed when the First Lady went on the air, before the nation, and told them what she saw, and how the words of the young girl were fulfilled within a moment's notice. She pleaded with the nation to repent, and keep the nation's fingers crossed.

She told the nation that she had the innate feeling, the young girl who disappeared on her, would reappear for greater opening of her prophecy. She reassured the nation, urged the nation to pray, and draw closer to God, that everything would be alright.

She talked like a mother; she consoled like a wild African hen, calling to protect her young ones from the predatory claws of a hovering hawk. She glanced around; she gestured in front of the one-eyed machine and pleaded, and even cajoled.

She begged them to turn around. She pleaded for repentance. She threatened with reprisal; and she looked around as if the anger of God was about to explode on her American children.

There was a genuine concern in her voice. Her mood was somber and clear. She looked before the camera like a sailor who had seen the eye of the storm, yet, determined to evade its havoc. There, before the nation, for the first time in her life, she called herself a sinner before God.

All her pride, as the First Lady disappeared. Her pride disappeared from her, just the same way the prophetess from Kwan-do disappeared on her. She was now resolved to do good with her new her, even her new self. There, before the nation, she pledged to help the nation turn a new leaf.

She became so transparent as to be vulnerable. Virtually, she became as transparent as transparence itself. And, there was no guile.

The First Lady of the nation made appeal to her nation, to her world, and to her own conscience. She pledged her commitment to the noble cause. She promised the nation to be the light of her repentance. She bared her heart; and her heart was clear.

Just soon after the First Lady made the public appeal, the news-media, at home and abroad, began to make fun of her. They ridiculed her. The News-Net of the Old Empire called her "THE WEEPING MOTHER OF THE NEW WORLD." At home she was depicted as a woman who wanted to turn herself into a goddess, but could not fool America.

Some of the News Media went far beyond the call of duty to attack her. They said that she was unfit for her station. Some asked her to shut up her mouth and say no more. Some pleaded with her husband to sack her; some went as far as to call her a national disgrace. There were caricatures of her all over the nation. And her new repute became a street joke.

To convince the nation that the prophecy was true became a tough mountain to climb. The political adversaries of her husband saw their grand opportunity to reduce her husband's rating before the people. The Devil, the King of the Kingdom, took notice and helped them with daring strategies. They came in waves on the onslaught. They took advantage of the whole situation, of the grand opportunity to reduce him.

Within a few hours, the man whose rating was in high gear of double-digit was in lower grid of single digit. There was an added impetus, a grand design for him to lose the next election. Surely, a grand political opponent was quite positioned to be the next Executive of the Kingdom of Satan.

THE DEVIL'S LAND

The Great Chief Executive became a very unhappy man. He thought about revamping his sliding grip on public pole; but his friends who would have helped, such as the two princes of 'mission work,' had already left for eternity. His other friends who ate and drank with him had either jumped wagon, or simply, not as popular for the real job.

He found himself alone and left out. He asked his wife to retract her speech before the nation; and, soon after he made the request, she began to pour out tears of heartfelt lamentation, rolling down from her two eyes. She became uncontrollable in her vexation. Her husband who thought she would be quite understanding found himself feeding from two full-plates of different troubles. There, the man felt that his entire world was falling apart.

"Honey, why are you doing this to me?" he asked her.

"Aha! That's exactly what I should have asked you. I told you what I saw. You believe the public more than you believe your own wife," her tears became more unconventional. They poured heavier than a rainy day.

Her husband felt like a man suspended between a deep Ocean and a firmament of burning fire. The first twenty-four hours of this day became the greatest ordeal of the man's life. He dreaded it, every moment, and every minute of it.

****

******

****

On the second day, the media went on, on their onslaught. They came to the White House to ask the First Lady if her imaginary prophetess had played her mind a second trick. The poor woman saw what damage the media could do to a victim of their onslaught. She refused to come out; and, the men with cameras refused to go home.

She sent out some security agents to ask them to go home. But, the media sent them back that they were there on behalf of the American people. They pitched their tents, and resolved to stay till the First Lady gave them more words of sensation.

The woman and her husband were cornered and holed in. They could no longer come out from the White House, for some fresh air, because the media surrounded their residence.

The Executive resolved to wait it out. He knew, to call in the army to chase away the media would only compound his troubles in the promised land. He was a wise captain in a sinking ship.

He was an apostle of Dalai Lama, of Jesus, and even of the great, and Venerable Mahatma of the Universe, even in the arena of patience. He stayed with his wife, and consoled her. They resolved to fast till the day of their deliverance.

On the seventh day, when the night was fast spent, they fell asleep. All of a sudden, an unusual light, rainbow of multiple colors, overshadowed their bedroom. Same moment, the cock of the nation crew, four times.

"Honey, it's four O'clock. What is happening here?" the startled Chief Executive asked his wife who was equally awake.

"Honey, it's the girl. Look, she's there at the corner, surrounded by that beautiful rainbow of many colors. I knew she'd come through."

"You," the young Prophetess pointed at the Executive.

"Yes, what do you want?"

"Yes, I said the same twice when I AM came to me in my village, Kwando, China; first in the Temple of Sun. Second, when I was eating dinner with my parents with our traditional chopsticks," said the Prophetess.

"You're kidding. What are you talking about?" the Executive replied to the young Prophetess.

"I do not kid. Stand up and follow me," the Prophetess ordered the man and his wife.

They stood up and followed her.

THE DEVIL'S LAND

When the media saw the Executive and his wife follow a young girl from the White House, they too followed her. They walked towards the pool of Lincoln Monument. When they got there, the young girl walked around the oblong-shaped pool, seven times. Then, she shouted with a loud voice, "Behold, the vision of the nation."

Suddenly, the pool, filled with water, crystal clear, turned into blood. Then, the blood turned into yellow. Then, the yellow water turned into blue. Then, the blue water changed into green. After this, the green-colored water turned, and became orange in coloration.

Soon after, it changed into the color, known as indigo. The indigo became violet. The violet became, again as red as pure blood.

Soon after, all the seven colors of the rainbow became evident in the national pool. Then, the rainbow colors changed, gradually, into a royal purple.

"Behold, the sins of the nation," shouted the Prophetess before the people. Then, gradually, now the royal, purple-colored water changed into a giant screen. Some rays of light from heaven came down upon the screen of the national pool.

Sins of the ancient of days appeared on the screen, like things on a movie screen. The people drew closer and looked and they saw:

They saw the sins of slavery and slave trade. They saw the swords of slave-dealers in their deadly hands. They saw the slave ships in the Ocean. They saw the trade which lasted for four hundred and eighty years.

Then, they saw the slave lords treat their weak slaves as waste goods. They saw the dealers shoot the pregnant slaves with their den guns. Also, they saw the slave-owners stab the children who became sea-sick during their voyage.

Then, they witnessed how the slave lords used their own swords in cutting to pieces the helpless bodies of those they'd killed during the voyage. They saw how the slavemasters used the bodies of pregnant women in feeding the voracious sharks of the Atlantic Ocean.

They saw the flesh of slain slaves which became the salted food of the Masters of the sea, and even in the New World. Also, they became the visible witnesses on how the slave dealers used the sick children in fattening the sizes of the Ocean Monsters.

They saw the color differences between those who fed the sharks, and those who became the meals of the Ocean, human-eating organisms.

They saw the barbaric civilization of the Western World. They saw the true barbarians, and the real jungles of the human minds. They saw the true spirits of civilization, of colonization, and of barbarization. They saw the three as one.

They saw the victims of severe deal. They saw the deal as rotten, and as it was unpardonable. They watched as the movie from heaven shift it's focus: Crimes and righteousness became evident. There, other crimes against humanity made their presence known. They saw how the Indians welcomed them. They saw how they thanked the Indians during a ceremony of thanksgiving. Then, they saw how a new deal began—they saw how they poisoned the Indian livestock, and shot those who protested.

They saw the Indian rage, the rage between the Pilgrims and the warriors of the Indian natives. They saw how the Pilgrims gained an upper hand, and rolled the symbol of welcome, the Plymouth Rock, over the defeated natives. They saw the Pilgrims and ministers of the gospel hunt Indians for money. They received a reward on each head; and they cut off the ears of Indian warriors as sign of their conquest.

They saw the era of name-calling. They saw the continent called jungle, and landlords called barbarians. They saw the winners tell the stories, and losers called nothing but ugly names.

Many other sins of the nation came down from heaven and stood before the nation's pool. They saw the concealed sins of

THE DEVIL'S LAND

the missionaries and even of the noble men. They saw the native doctor who was slain by a missionary.

They saw many other hidden truths, including the truth hidden in the funky song, the hidden truth of the deprived man, the hidden truth that missionaries were nothing good, but, 'na thief thief.' They saw the need to make amend of the past crimes. Also, they saw the deftness of the two crooks, and the adroitness of each of the Prince of Crimes.

They saw them the way they truly were. Here too, their rage as being deceived, doubly deceived, knew no bound. They saw the rage of the native son. And they saw the nation's eagle fly with lone, but a broken wing.

The warning and the nature of punishment came down on the national pool. Fear and desire for repentance gripped the nation.

They saw the crimes of passion, crimes of greed, crimes of negligence, horrible street crimes, good-neighbor crimes, and pride of the kingdom as the embodiment of all crimes. Then, they saw The Great King of Pride pump fluid of pride into the fabric of the society. They recognized this King, who sat on an Invisible Throne, on top of The Great Idol of Liberty. And, they saw The Great King of the Kingdom, look at them, all with a terrible manner, and even with contempt. There, for the first time, they saw the significance of the idol of liberty, and the true meaning of Green Card.

They saw the grand design of global deception which came from the King of Eternal Hell. When they'd seen it all, the young Prophetess told them to go home for repentance.

CHAPTER FORTY-SIX

The Devil saw the first major challenge to his earthly throne. And, he was ready to deal with the agent of God, the Prophetess. He knew how God expelled him from the place on high. And, here, on earth, he would not give in without a major bloodshed.

He knew how to fight God then; now, he was better prepared to fight back. He sent out a wave of tornadoes to wipe out those who'd seen the vision of the past sins. The tornadoes struck; they killed a quarter of the people by the national pool.

Some of the people were critically injured. About half of them escaped unharmed. Among them were the First Lady and her husband. The Spirit of the Lord which followed the young girl from China sheltered her, the first couple, and some of the cameramen.

Most of the cameras were damaged beyond repair. The deadly rage swept through with intent to perfect annihilation. But the Devil who came through forgot that God's Power was even near. He looked; and, he saw the survivors. He was deadly enraged. He summoned more deadly tornadoes and an earthquake for a second strike. This time,—the powerful forces of nature were scared to obey him.

Soon after, the Devil turned red. He came closer to find out why the natural forces refused to obey. As he drew nearer, he began to assess the damages he'd done. There, he saw God pointing an accusing finger at him. And he hastily withdrew from the presence of an angry God.

When the Devil left the scene to a comfortable zone, he began to plot and to scheme. He knew that he'd got a new apostle in the person of Dr. Lamun Jules; and, he'd use him to wage an unholy war. He rushed to him a spirit of greater ambition. And, he injected in him a spirit of desire to be the next Chief Executive of the Deadly Kingdom.

Dr. Lamun Jules was excited. And the spirit spoke to him, with him, and even assured him of success. Now, he was so sure of victory that he rose up and was ready to go.

The young man had all the things needed by the Devil—he was tall, white, and of Aryan heritage. He had the impish smiles of his father, a true link to the Devil who'd sponsor him. He was rich and well-connected. He was smart, the American way. Beside, America loved him, because he was a rising star.

He was quite educated, an MD, a crowning glory of his academic excellence. He could easily appeal to, and impress the young women and sugar-mums, alike, because of his youthfulness, and charming and noble mien—a hell on wheel of enthusiasm, and he'd find it quite easy to campaign for public votes.

There was no dream for a would-be valiant effort to meet no desirable objective, for the Devil, after, was the grand Master-Planner of the aim, the lofty end in view, and the desirable objective. The Devil, now, wanted to put the current Executive, who listened, in a dark political hole, because he listened to the prophetess, and found the truths about the Kingdom. It was going to be a war all the way.

The Devil was ready to shed blood for his dear Throne. He was now exposed in his hidden corner, cornered to a corner of no retreat.

His rage against God was about to be taken out on God's chosen prophetess. The young girl, chosen of God, would become a deadly target of the demons, the servants of Satan.

The Devil knew how to howl and harass those who faulted his calling in his kingdom. Hard-hearted, and a conscience made of

THE DEVIL'S LAND

stone, he'd show no pity in the process. The young girl from a distant land was not about to have an easy time in the land of demons.

***
****
*****

The Devil made Dr. Lamun Jules see the Prophetess in his own way—a danger to the prime purpose of the American ideal. In her he saw a coming danger from the Orient—a deadly red which brought about expulsion of the holy man, Reverend Acuridol, from Africa.

He saw the link, a Sino-Madagascar connection which could ruin everything American. He felt the heat of the future wave. And, he resolved to fight back the red flag of the communists. He'd rather die than see the Old Glory bow down to the communist flag. He was a patriot with a blue blood. His life, his dream, and his destiny were dedicated to the ideal worth dying for—thus, he'd become a national hero, a worthy servant of the Kingdom more honorable than his late father.

He knew, America would remember. He knew, America would honor him. The Devil made up his mind for him. His zeal for the nation became a passion. Hell-bent, and goal-bound, he began to make the moves to campaign against the Executive.

He dived into the calling of dangerous campaign advertisements. He painted the Executive as a puppet of the Communists. He painted the prophetess as a leader of foreign cult—that she came to destroy everything American.

He accused the Executive of a sell out, of being a traitor of Americanism, an apostle of foreign thought and ideal on a grand scale. He pointed out, a man who could sell his soul to a foreign ideal was unfit to be an American president.

The era of campaign mud-slinging found its own corner of quantum leap. And, within a few weeks, Dr. Lamun Jules became the greatest political mud-springer ever to appear on the kingdom's political scene.

He'd paint himself as good, paint his opponent as bad. He'd paint himself as fit, paint his opponent as unfit. He'd show himself as able, show the Executive as inept. He'd praise himself as great, and caricature the President as not.

He had a way with mockery; and, indeed, the American people had fun with the way he degraded their Executive.

Dr. Lamun Jules began to encourage the political voyeurs to stand up and help out. He began to define America in his own terms, as the Devil gave him utterance. He came up with unique statements which became his political slogan:

'WE CANNOT STAND A WORLD WITHOUT RACISM. LET'S BE REALISTIC, PEOPLE. THAT WILL BE A GRAND ILLUSION. THAT WILL BE UN-AMERICAN.'

Dr. Lamun Jules made this motto his campaign slogan. He portrayed perfect integration as a red flag of the communists. He became a new wave and a new advocate. He advocated, Communists should learn from Americans, never Americans from the Communists.

He urged Africans to return home. He urged Asian-Americans to return to the land of their ancestors. He asked the remnants of native Indians to be grateful for their conquest, for being colonized, and to see the presence of the white man as the best thing that had happened to them.

He urged them to bow down, like worshippers, whenever they're in the presence of a person with a white skin. He asked them to see the white man as their new god.

He became the new advocate of the Aryan race. He came up with new ideas and new sensations. He changed the minds of many people who were on the verge of repentance. And, many of those who felt that a savior was in the wind began to forget everything about the Communist Prophetess.

THE DEVIL'S LAND

Her ideas were, indeed, un-American. America had its own way, and its own God. And, God who dwelt on top of the lady of liberty was the only American God. And America could not serve any other God. That's American. And that settled it.

America had no room for a puppet who'd feed American people with deceptive milk of Communism. America was uniquely qualified to change the world. And, no one outside America had any right, or savior-faire, to teach Americans things which were un-American.

He energized America with his rhetoric. The Southern whites who'd always believed in separation of races, to a man, formed a bloc behind him. They'd seen their man.

At last, though they lost the war, they'd seen their new savior in Nazi form.

They began to campaign for him. They worked for him with aim to elect him. They'd seen the hand of the clock, it had the joy of racial prejudice. And, they were ready to drink the juice of prejudice till eternity.

They'd dance the dixie, and sing to the glory of forgotten confederates. There was joy in the wind—the pleasure of prejudice—a time to roll back the tide and bring back the slave days.

CHAPTER FORTY-SEVEN

The new man on the political scene was seen as an anathema by the new immigrants. Blacks, in particular, hated him. The natives who'd been wronged since the coming of Pilgrims, staged days of marching protest.

Asian-Americans formed their own bloc, and staged their marching band. The liberal whites, who'd desired integration with caution, found room to distance themselves from the man who became the embodiment of neo-Nazism.

Gangs, who loved to ride the waves of turmoil, found a fertile ground to germinate their violent seeds. America, once again, became the land of turmoil. The Chief Executive found a need to restore calm. But the Devil who ruled the land was against him. When the Devil made up his mind to fight a mortal, it was only the hand of God that could prevent that.

The fight was staged, and the war had just begun. The Devil vowed to replace the Executive. God vowed to retain him. Caught in the middle, the Executive found himself praised by one political party, and reviled by the opposing political bloc, loved by the integrationists, hated by the segregationists, admired by God, and despised by Satan.

The natives began to rebuild their pyramids of dead magicians. Desire to restore their lost pride became a new wave in the Indian reservations. Pride in themselves, rather than pride in their conquerors, were stressed by the native scholars. A new rebirth, and a rebirth of confidence began to gain momentum and ascendancy.

SUNDAY AHURONYEZE ABAKWUE

Some Indians began to dream about recovering their stolen land. But, their scholars who ignited the dream advised them to live in peace with their conquerors.

It was the year of an Executive election. Waves of politics, and political noise-makers were in the air. It was time for the self-righteous, Christian political bloc, to make loud noises, around the Kingdom. They'd talk against abortion in the public, and murder their unborn babies, in the private.

They'd dress to kill, and appear on the national television, as if they were on their way to heaven. There were the despised Muslims in America, who lived a far better, and clean life, than the self-righteous Christians who despised them. They showed no interest in all the political foolishness, which the white man, enjoyed even at the price of Arab blood.

'Integration Reform Party,' or I.R P. and 'Segregation Party of America,' or S.P.A. were the two political parties in the nation. Dr. Lamun Jules was chosen by the Segregation Party of America as its presidential candidate. While President C. C. McTimothy retained his nomination as the leader of I.R.P.

"THE DEVIL IS EXPOSED. THERE'S NOTHING YOU CAN DO" became slogan of President C. C. McTimothy, leader of or the very flag bearer of I.R.P.

Dr. Lamun Jules began to enter one political hot soup after another—a political stertorous without its cardiovascular pulmonary resuscitation. His haydays were passing by. New political maydays were rolling in. Once, a notable political mud-slinger, his opponent had dug up enough of his dirts to push him around with them.

America loved sensation. And, the Chief Executive, President C. C. McTimothy, was dishing out the onslaught. He took on his mother's case, and it was a political bomb-blast. His mother's, for one, would reduce his rating before the American people, as a loose woman.

She was a woman who loved to have lovers. At sixty, she chased young men like a teenaged prostitute. Since she divorced

THE DEVIL'S LAND

her husband on account of molesting her baby, she'd taken a delight in her choice of nothing but a black love.

Twice, her son, Dr. Lamun Jules, got rid of her black boy friends by planned accidents. But, she mourned for each of her lost love, and quickly replaced her dead love with a younger black love.

Her son, Dr. Lamun Jules, hated the idea that his mother would shun all eligible white men, and gave her bosom, to the 'male niggers of inferior race'. Now that he was a politician, at a crossroad, he hated it, even more.

He'd given her a soul to soul, heart to heart talk. But, she was adamant. He'd tried threat; but, that didn't work, either.

He killed two of her black boy friends, without letting her know about it; the accidents didn't change her. She'd pick up a young black man, usually, the foreign black university student, as a new love. She'd impress him with her riches and her chain of luxury cars. She'd entice him into her bed, and make love to him.

She'd hold him so tight, as if by holding him that would transfer his youthful energy into her aging spine. She'd tell him that she's a woman who loved to have sex. Again, she'd remind him her desire to help him get a Green Card, the ironic 'sign of the great beast'. She'd tell him she'd love him till her bones returned to the dust of eternity—that it was only death that could separate her love from him. And, she'd appear so genuine in so doing.

Then, she'd go ahead and tell him how cruel she'd be should he leave her for another woman.

And, she'd begin to pour the young man with caressing affection, with love notes, and romantic cards. She'd buy these cards from love section, greeting card department, of a convenience store. And she'd send one love card, every day, to her new love. It was a pattern she'd not break.

A very creative woman, she knew how to capture a man. But, she never knew how to keep him for so long. Kissing was her passion. Holding a man's hand was her lifeline. Making love was

SUNDAY AHURONYEZE ABAKWUE

her eternal dream come true. And thinking about men was all her prayers come true.

Daily, she'd dream about all the men in her life. Daily, she'd send each a love-reminding card that she was still faithful and devoted. There was this insatiable thing, in her bosom, which craved for every young black, a black so dark as to be foreign-born.

She'd draw pictures of a black man holding hand with a white woman. She'd label them, give them names, and kiss them. She'd collect some black and white chicken feathers from her poultry farm, and mail a white feather and a black one, together, to each of her black love.

She'd do so as a token, her symbol, and her way of telling him there was a special union between a black man and a white woman. She'd compose some poetic songs, even some letters for the young men, telling them how she cried because she missed them.

She was white. But her soul belonged to the black race. She'd hold hand with the young love when she's cruising with him in one of her flashy, sports cars. She'd trade kisses and smiles along the way. She'd call her love, 'honey,' 'sweetie,' 'cutie,' 'dear,' 'darling,' and all that good names.

Then, she'd steal glances at, and from, for mutual reassurance. All the while, her son, Dr. Lamun Jules, learnt about the doings of his love-sick mother. Thoughts of her rendezvous and liaisons got him worried everyday.

He got angry, daily, over the whole thing. He could cajole; but, he could neither force nor beat her up, because she was his mother and she was also independent.

She could have gone to Africa, to get herself an African husband, the way many young American women were doing. But, she preferred to stay home, to enjoy the black lovers, who were available, at home, especially, in most of the citadels of knowledge.

Her son, Dr. Lamun Jules, could not win. His hidden crimes, as a murderer, became a national obsession. The nation's Board of

THE DEVIL'S LAND

Crime Bank began to investigate him. He killed two Africans, Mr. Anamanwuanwu and Mr. Agamanwurugi, were foreign students in Texas. The two young men were, each, a live-in lover of his mother, before he died.

His accomplice, a partner in the hidden crimes, told a news-reporter about the whole show; and, he got a few thousand bucks, and Presidential Pardon, for his service.

CHAPTER FORTY-EIGHT

Soon after the crimes were made public, Dr. Lamun Jules, became a wanted man. The sins of his mother, even the crimes of his late father began to haunt him. Now, he could see himself as the real Devil, exposed before the American public.

He began to hate himself with a passion so deep, so bitter, and so deadly. The media, the mural of the savvy king were there for the overkill. The munjacs of the kingdom became quite belligerent, even as belligerent as the nation's badgers. The badger-State turned on their war-hawks, rough riders, and cowboys for the offensive. They had all his chambers, his turn-arounds, and even his hide-aways perfectly covered through the powers of the electronic lens. All the ex-layers of his own world lost their powers of protection. Such were indeed the subtle distinctions of his pleasant past from his present condition.

His reputation as a mud-slinger waned in an instant. Those who loved him began to hate, and to despise him to distraction. They could not have a murderer as their president. The man who was easily sought-after for campaign rallies began to run away from the law, a first-class fugitive of Nazi-blood.

His mother could not hide him from the law. Because she had already denounced him as a deadly son. Beside, the law which once protected him had set up a web of investigators around his mother's place of abode, to apprehend him.

A connection of international police was alerted. In Madagascar, for example, a security outfit was beefed up, all in search of the man who had disgraced his calling.

The black-stars of Ashanti-hene summoned all the powers of the Golden Throne. They were equally ready for the son of the devil who killed thousands of Ghanaian people with his disease of trypanosomiasis. Their quo-amino was obvious—to pay his father back: As his father sowed, so would his offspring reap.

The King of Lamunta was appalled to know the truths about his dead friend and his dear son.

"THAT IS HORRIBLE. THAT IS HORRIBLE. GOD FORBID," the king spat out in disgust. But God did not forbid his dead friend from committing the deadly crimes.

He became sorrowful, even sorry that he travelled abroad to lavish homage at the graves of common criminals. He felt fooled, and taken for granted. He felt stupid, and taken for a ride.

He felt bad that he refused to listen to the words of Dr. Sulah Aminu, an enlightened young man, and his subject. The cumulative ironies in the whole games were self-evident, even obvious in everything. How pure inseparability of contradictions were apt to endure—the ying and yang and the worlds of opposites—truth and a lie, facts and deceptions, mission work and slave trade, words of God and deeds of the demons, all working together to create a New World—depriving Africa, Europe, Asia Minor, Asia Major, the Kangarooland, the land of everlasting cold, and even the Red Indians in the process.

The King began to question everything he held so dear. It was a terrible blow and psychological reversal. He began to doubt the mission friendship which he held so dear. His thoughts were terrible, the thoughts of being taken for a fool even in the presence of the Devil.

Then, he saw the opposite side of the Devil's coin. And, then, it dawned on him an aura of surprising enlightenment.

"Does white man have conscience?" he asked himself regarding what white man was doing to the blacks and the entire world. Dissatisfied. He wondered "Do blacks and the entire world have souls of understanding to comprehend the sins against them?" He was baffled. He was sad. And, he was enraged—And he regretted the letter he wrote to Dr. Sulah Aminu to seek 'grief-experts' in a foreign land, when he should have urged him to come home to take care of business.

He shifted his mind from mission work to the code of conduct. He focused. He began to think about the issue and the code of 419. As he thought, his mind began to dwell in the aura of understanding, and even of a special enlightenment. He began to think about the meaning of the code, the genesis of the number, the home and the anatomy of the same, and even the phenotype of 419.

And, as he thought, he was opened to a better aura of enlightenment. He saw the origin of the deadly code. And he understood it. He saw the meaning as the code of crooks, by the dogs of loots.

He saw the techniques of the crime—the advance fee sleaze. And he saw a new dimension and the psyche of the few, but able fraudsters. He studied it in detail. And he understood that most of those who became victims were Americans. He understood that those who sleazed and fleeced them were superbly intelligent blacks who were on a special mission of economic vengeance.

He saw many people from many other parts of Africa. He saw people from Liberia. He saw those from Ghana. He saw, even men and women who came from South Africa, East Africa, Central Africa, North Africa, Kenya, and even Uganda. He saw them take part in the mission of 419. He saw them, black and white, pose as the citizens of the African giant, men and women who were apt to benefit from the crimes of their big brother.

Then, he studied their minds, their hearts, and their souls, and he came up with the tearful answer—they were offended sons and daughters of Africa who had seen the crimes of the rapers of the continent; and they were particularly indignant at the oil giants. They saw for every billion dollars of oil royalty the oil giants paid to the African giant, more than four billion dollars worth of crude oil had invariably left the continent, quite unaccounted for.

They saw the rip-off on a grand scale. They saw the thievery economics, and the balance of stolen payment. And, they were mortally enraged.

Then, they began a mission of payback on a small scale, a tokenism of imperialist proportion. They knew they'd never pay the oil thieves in equal proportion. Therefore, they decided to scratch them and their compatriots in their own far-away homelands.

They knew that a carnivorous fish would always fish for a smaller fish. Therefore, they thought and schemed, the way the oil giants had obviously thought and schemed. They baited the hungry carnivores with tempting prey. They wrote them and promised them an opportunity to steal better from the oil wells. In their letters they told them how to steal from the African coffins and continental chests. They gave them clues on how to do it. They pledged to be their partners in the deal to rob the oil revenue even more.

They painted the picture of the sleaze deal in a way the beasts couldn't resist, a way that totally captured their greed and predatory instincts. And the plot, and ploy, and even the decoy were nothing but a winner. It was an opportunity to steal. And the beasts rushed for the baits. They fought for the prey, and they had the baits, each beast with its own catch.

They began to swallow the prey and its hook, and even its sinker. They swallowed hard and in a rush. The fishermen on a mission caught them, and as fast, pulled them out from their mighty water of residence. They secured them in their boats and lofty canoes. They paddled them away to their hideouts and rendezvouses. And, they sleazed the beasts real good. They sleazed them in a way they had never been sleazed in their home before. They sleazed them in a way that the oil giants could not defend them. They sleazed them in a way that the oil giants saw them as potential competitor, and even parasites who were not careful enough while in their drive to exploit their angry hosts.

Then, they went back to America, to Europe, or Asia to report their individual ordeals to their own people, Europe heard them, and told the world the new wave from the hearts of darkness. Asia too saw the tricks of the dirty continent. Then, came America with airwaves, and a mission of sanctions. As they did, the Senate and Congress began the crusade of name-bashing. They called the Giant of Africa a nation of crooks.

They stereotyped every person from that Giant as nothing but a crook. They found a fertile reason to give a free rein to their racist prejudice. And they began to victimize many innocent Nigerians in their own land.

And, as they went for the overkill, many white women, who knew better, began their own crusade of correction. They went to the senate and congress to correct them. They told them, for every rotten Nigerian, there were, at least, one hundred thousand Nigerians who were upright, honest, diligent, and even righteous. They charged the Congress to desist from their campaign of stereotype. They urged the Senate to suspend their laws based on prejudice. And they asked the victims of sleaze deal to curtail their appetites for stolen wealth.

And, events began to show that deeply-rooted racist views could not die so easily. And no matter how and what the one hundred thousand people did, the sin of the rotten one would always stand as their lone judge. And they knew, a rotten apple in a basket filled with other good ones, would always be known as a basket with rotten apple.

And, they knew too, if a clean finger touched some palm-oil, all the other fingers would always share the same reputation. That was it, a legacy of racism, and its way with stereotype.

The one hundred thousand knew themselves very well, despite the verdict of their judge who condemned them with the sin of a lone apple.

And the lone apple knew itself very well, as a rotten element that shared the views of the oil thieves.

Then, the King began to think about the Capital of Nazi philosophy. He zeroed in on the great cities of the sound empire of great Europe.

He detailed the great nation that produced such mawkish maverick, a first-class racist, champion of the Third Reich, the legacy of Nazism. He remembered the name of the mawkist as Adolf Hitler.

He understood the gene that drove him: a quest for Jewish eradication.

He reviewed the theory that even Adolf Hitler had some Jewish blood through his family tree. Then, he wondered what was wrong with the 'white race'.

Then, he wondered, and was saddened that someone with certain blood of the Patriarch, father Abraham, could turn around and unleash a mission of culpable annihilation against his own people. It was a patrimonious picric of a distrustful proportion.

He remembered German contributions to modem civilization. He remembered German benz, German racism, pure race, and German prostitution.

He began to think about the beautiful city of Homburg, the humbug of German civilization. He remembered the beautiful city as a city of serious prostitution. Then, he diverted for a moment, and thought about the ancient polyandrists of the native Indians.

He remembered how they married more than one husband at a time, because there were fewer women. He thought about the polymorphous perverse of the heroes of conquest. Then, he thought about Africa, the Africans, and their matrimonial lifestyles. He thought about Utah, an African brother.

THE DEVIL'S LAND

He fixated on monogamy, then on polygamy, and on how the men ruled their clan-like family-kingdoms with their ferocious iron-hands. He saw the West as the embodiment of woman's society, and Africa as man's society. He saw Japan as African brother.

Then, he went back to the main issue which claimed the embodiment of his thinking enlightenment. He dwelt, for a while, in thoughts about the misogynists of the German Empire. He remembered the United Kingdoms of Austria, Hungary, East and Western Germanies. He remembered how they formed the powerful Third Reich, an offshoot of Roman first and second Reichs, the pure breed of Nazi Empire, the epitome of the pure race.

Also, he remembered the misogynists, their gospel and their demagogues. He began to review the philanderers of the great German Empire. And, as he did, he remembered Bonn, Berlin, and the beautiful Homburg, the cities of German civilization. He recalled the humbugs of the last city and the prostitutes having sex with German shepherds—mere dogs, so openly, even for guests' money, and for the visitors' and even for the public entertainment.

He figured out why many Germans behaved the way they did. He understood there were German-o-philes, and even German-o-phobes.

He began to think about the spirit of superior race as the philosophy of German civilization. He recalled, once more, how the rich callipygians had sex, in open view, with highly-trained male-dogs, known as German-shepherds. He thought about how the consuming public paid to watch the show. He saw the difference between primitive race and the pure race. He summed up the whole thing; and, it was a sure thing.

It was a sure belief, a sure thing and a sure philosophy in their blood. He saw how it held them together. And, he noted how their hearts were on the ground; and, they could not believe otherwise, as Germans of superior race.

**
****
*****

When Dr. Lamun Jules was arrested at the Chicago airport, he was disguised as a beggar. When they searched him, the security agents found in him a fake passport, a fake I.D. and a different name.

He was about to flee from the kingdom, to an unknown destination. He had, in his possession, a cool two million dollars, all in hundred dollar bills. He packed them, neatly, in a bag, which resembled that of a homeless dude.

His face was covered with nothing but artificial beard, which became the epitome of his creative disguisation. He looked uncouth; and, the airport security did not even recognize him, till, suddenly, he betrayed himself. He did so when the Barbados-bound jet was about to take off. He stood up, walked straight to a female airjet attendant and asked her to vote for him. When the lady asked him who he was.

"I'm Dr. Lamun Jules; didn't you recognize me?" he said. Indeed, it was him, all in perfect disguise, a fugitive longing to rule a nation.

"Yes, I do," she replied. She excused herself. And, she went to the jet's co-pilot, who alerted the security.

The jet taxied to a stop. Armed police men, and their leader, a woman, boarded the jet plane. They arrested the man who was in beggar's outfit.

They led him away from the jet; and, they searched him. They found all the money he had, money he intended to use, and live with, in a relative comfort. They seized all his money, and charged him with multiple crimes. They told him about the black blood in his hand, act of money-laundering, and act of running away from the law.

THE DEVIL'S LAND

Each charge was heavy; and, each crime was punishable by law. Now, there was no escape. He would have to face the prosecutors, face the jury, beg his defense attorneys, face the judge, and do a very long time. He'd face the media, the sick mural of the society. And, every thing he'd say would be used against him.

He'd live with other deadly criminals, and be numbered among them. He'd eat with them, talk with them, and face them in some mortal combats.

Those who dreaded his political mud-slinging would only live to laugh at him, and talk about him and his destiny. They'd shake their heads in disbelief, how a man so powerful and so popular could have committed so horrible some heinous crimes. From his fate, they'd learn some lessons about the deadly thoughts of some ambitious men.

The Security Police took the defunct leader of the Segregation Party of America to jail for safe-keeping. They chained him, hands, feet, neck, and waist, to prevent him from escaping.

They brought some Military Police, as guards, to watch over him. These were the elite Delta Force MPs whose security know-hows were the best in the Kingdom.

They were trained. And, they were smart men. They were able. And, the kingdom could count on them to get the job done. A look on their faces could easily inspire a world of heavenly confidence. They were Americans, all at it's special best.

CHAPTER FORTY-NINE

A wave of massive repentance began to sweep across the Kingdom of United States of America. The two devils who once held the kingdom for ransom found themselves in a tough corner, booed by the angry masses, all the time. Blood and thunder of the kingdom's media reached a new high. And, the once invisible demon who held the kingdom at its throes became a known scoundrel worthy of public despisation. And, his apostle who held the nation through the powers of his charm, and persuasion, became another joke of the nation.

There was no doubt that the masses had identified the ills of the society. And, they were prepared not to go back to the old rule.

The old enemy who ruled them for so long, and the invisible power of his presence, could no longer hold sway the thinkings of the political leaders of the Great Kingdom.

There was something even peculiar with the people who were rebelling against the king of demons. Reputed as rebellious, it was not the first time. They were free to discard any great leader who held them, and, who did not let them make up their own minds.

God began to send down more angels to the earth. The spy-angels who did the dirty job were asked to go back to heaven, to reveal the victory to their brethren, over the king of demons.

They went. They invited their kind to come down to the kingdom which was once a domain of Satan. And, within a passing wave of moment, the people who were once obedient slaves of the Devil turned away from their unrighteousness, and away from all their satanic stupidities.

***
******
***

It was a mighty war that was brewing in the mind of Satan. His kingdom was invaded, and his capital was under siege.

There were some talks within the political circles to bring down the idol which harbored the Throne of the king of demons. He didn't like it. And, he was mortally enraged in the new zeal to humiliate him.

He began to mop up his plans to wage a perfect war on the universe. And, there was a call, by the Devil, for a war on all the earthly zones. He had the floating cities, birds of war, and his imps as commanders of his deadly weapons. He knew how faithful they were, devoted and obedient souls in the face of Divine rage.

They'd fought in heaven before. They were ready to fight again, here on earth, to defend their last place of abode. They had practised their war-games since they came to earth, and pow-wowed regularly; and, they had sharpened their skills to a new and terrible high. Indeed, they were ready. And, they had been ready for a very long period of one, even eon of one.

For sure, they had wondered why God had been so slow in coming down, in view of the fact that they had made a mess of God's world. In the past, they'd taunted God to come down and fight them. They knew how God kicked them out from heaven; and, they did no longer care if God would repeat the heavenly thing.

Their lives were devoted to the Devil, their Master, who they loved and adored to distraction.

They were ready to die for the Devil, as a perfect expression of contempt toward God who created them.

CHAPTER FIFTY

On the day the Lady of Liberty came down, the Devil declared 'the war of all wars on the four corners of the entire world'. There was a perfect touch-down of the Devil's ball in the village of Kwan-do. And, all the villagers were obliterated.

In Madagascar, the Devil rained down his balls of tornadoes, far beyond the universal proportion. The Ashanti Empire witnessed the raids of the Devil with his deadly birds.

Asia, and Africa became quite uninhabitable due to the flying balls of the floating cities. Most of the true, and faithful Muslim Arabs were wiped out. The Holy City of Jerusalem became a war zone. And, even New York, and Moscow became the centres of Armageddon.

Some false Christians, who had served the Devil so faithfully, were spared for the doom's day; and, a greater doom awaited them.

Soon after the war began, God began a 'Wage of Deliverance.' This was a method, a system, and an action. He sent out His 'spy-angels,' to the four corners of the world, to redeem the righteous.

The angels went and gathered the righteous, who had not found within themselves, any reason, to either honor the Devil, with acts of obedience, or to touch the deceptive mark, known as six six six.

The spy-angels transported the redeemed to heaven by a measure of the Wind of Deliverance. And, when they got to heaven, they were set at rest in their mansions above. They were greeted by the righteous prophets who went before them. For example, Jesus greeted them. Muhammed greeted them. Enoch greet them. Elijah greeted them. Mahatma Gandhi greeted them. Confucius greeted them. Dalai Lama greeted them. And, Methuselah greeted them. And, the three wise men who visited Christ, cradled in a manger, came to them and worshipped them.

Then, the spy-angels went down to the earth, again, for more deliverance. They visited one nation after another. They saved the righteous in Kingdom of Lamunta, in Kwando village, in Jerusalem, and, even as far away as the most remote places in the Pacific Rim.

They saved the nobles of the land, including the First Couple, who were redeemed as righteous. They visited the Oceans, and delivered the living righteous of the Oceans.

They went out on a rampage of deliverance. They visited the deadly dens of armaments, and delivered the righteous among them. They went to the camps of assassins, the centers where future rebels and dictators were trained, armed, and sent out to destabilize their own countries for the Devil's interests.

These young warriors were recruited from foreign lands, and indoctrinated in the Satanic ways and philosophies. They were taught to kill for the devil. They were taught to place a perfect allegiance to the kingdom of Satan.

They were taught how to sabotage their own land so as to be rewarded by the Devil. They were told to overthrow their home governments with promise of being elevated to the position of leadership.

They were taught how to rape and ruin. The Kingdom's Board of Secrecy showed them how to exploit the very poor of their own lands. They demonstrated their teaching by infusing deadly drugs in Hispanics, Blacks, and Asian neighborhoods of the inner cities. They formed an ally with the inner-city drug lords. They exploited the very poor of these neighborhoods. In turn, however, they made millions in the process.

THE DEVIL'S LAND

Indeed, they transferred their millions of dollars, the great wealth of sin, the drug money, to the foreign accounts of rebels they were sponsoring.

They asked their trainees from foreign lands to emulate them. With tacts and razorsharp wits, they twisted all the impressionable minds, and molded them in a way it would perfectly serve the Devil's grand objective.

There were, however, some young men who came with aim to learn from the Devil, and to use their learnings to better defeat the satanic objective. But, sooner had they joined the satanic band than they were rooted out.

They came to play games with a master whose grand designs were to build the great empire, destabilize all the other nations, thus, make the Devil's Empire an envy of the entire world. But, the young men who came with a dream contrary to the Devil's dream found themselves soundly defeated. And, they did not succeed.

***
******
***

The spy-angels saw the damages, and doctrines of the demons used in sealing the fate of so many for the Devil's cause. They went and began to unbind those whose fate were sealed by the deadly seal of six six six. The imps of the Devil saw them do so; and they received the redeeming spy-angels with deadly balls of tornadoes. A fight began. Reprisal and counter reprisal rose without limit.

The angels of deliverance saved some of the trained warriors; and they were unable to deliver the others from the deadly bondage. The Devil was alerted, and he ordered his imps to hide the untouched warriors from the next assault of the redeeming angels. Bewitched, and with twisted minds, the hidden warriors from foreign lands could no longer make up their own minds.

They were placed in a limbo, deprived of psychological choices, they became nothing but zombi-like slaves of the Devil's war.

Satan had them. Satan owned them. And, Satan saw them as his personal properties. He put them in the place he had always wanted, co-secured for eternal damnation.

These were men whose predecessors had ravaged their own nations with aim to rule by any means necessary—warriors who became multi-millionaires—the predecessors who had given the Devil something to be proud of—blood of many shed without cause. They gave him wars; they looted; they pillaged the treasuries; they plundered; and they carted away their booties to foreign bank accounts in Switzerland.

They showed the Devil how much they loved him by being cruel to so many. They demonstrated their allegiance to the satanic flag by setting one nation against another, selling drugs to finance wars, and by selling deadly armaments to warring zones.

The news of the war between the Devil and God reached everywhere. Those who served the Devil so faithfully had their names decorated, so proudly engraved in the Devil's Wall of Gold.

Now, the King of Lamunta could understand. The men who killed thousands of his fellow Africans with trypanosomiasis were not his friends, really. He could see their tsetse flies, daily. He could remember them, daily. And, he would regret honoring them by self-pinching.

All his love for them became a perfect hatred so deep for word. And, he got confused in hatred in that he did no longer want to believe anything, including the views of the well-meaning men with a foreign skin. He began to act like a child stung by the small black ant named AGBISI, who became phobic of all ants, including the harmless ones. And, the passionate love he once had for foreign Christianity became a hateful obsession.

"You, put a stop to that. When you are trying to protect racism in the guise of spiritual superiority, the entire world can see

THE DEVIL'S LAND

through that. It's so transparent. We have no room for transigience. Go home, and preach to your own people," the King of Lamunta cajoled him. The young man, a missionary, who paid a mission visit to his palace, was promptly deported. Clueless, the young man he cajoled was such a novice. He did not know the damages which his duo-predecessors had done to the nations of Black Continent.

CHAPTER FIFTY-ONE

In the society, however, the concepts of rights and foolishness were the conscripts of the individual's mind. When God did something, for sure, some of the people would say "that was not right." And, when the Devil did his, the masses would say "that was a foolish act."

There was no regrets in every individual's act. Rather, the masses would prefer to shift their blames to other people. For example, thieves in the kingdom would blame their victims for their evil deeds. They would blame them for allowing them the opportunity to take from them.

The teenage murderers would blame their deeds on drugs; black sinners would blame whites; white criminals would blame their crimes on the blacks of their society. The demon-busters of their crimes were always on the run, never stopping, and never to be found. It was not fun.

The tremor of political earthquake was raging. Devil and God were at war. Heaven was boiling; and, earth was in chaos. There was no peace for mankind. Children would regret being born into a world of violence. Adults would gnash their teeth in testimony.

Women who had children in their wombs would testify that the days were full of evil. And, the young men, brave of heart, were scared to death. There were troubles on earth below the sky. And, heaven knew that sunshine of doom had cast its darkest rays on a terrible world.

Heaven knew the violence the earth was going through, for the heaven had been a witness to the deadly show. Satan, the king of earthly jungle, was the leader of the earthly rebels, the zombi-like warriors who pledged their blood, to die for the Satan's grand design.

There was terror in the midst, fear in every land. The Devil, the King of Terror, knew quite well what havoc this tool could do to the hearts of fearful men. He capitalized on it, like a grand master of Capitalism. He wowed his followers, and terrorized the living faithfuls who had not reached the saving hands of the angels of redemption. He doubled his efforts, and amplified his zeal of vengeance.

He hated those who called on the name of God. And, he vowed to torture them to destruction. He magnified his terror tactics. And, he made some of the faithful feel hopeless.

He showed them the dead bodies of their dead faithfuls. And he promised them he'd lead them down the same valley. He played deadly games with their minds. And, he tormented the minds of those who resisted him. He made some of the believers to know that he was totally in charge, And, he dared them to call on their God to come to their rescue, if at all their God had ever delighted in them.

He showed them some of the spy-angels his imps were able to capture in battle, all in chains. And, he told them, there was no one else who could deliver them.

He set up a mock hell, and he cast his captive angels in the mock lake of fire. And, he told the tortured faithfuls that he captured this lake from their leader, the so-called God.

He repeated these tricks till their will to hope began to fade away. He mocked them; and he flogged their souls with painful words of terror. He cursed them; and he clouded their world with his own measure of darkness.

THE DEVIL'S LAND

He taunted them for believing in a God who had the power to disappoint them when they needed Him. And he spat on them for being so deluded with the gospel of Christ. The liquid content of his mouth made its mark on their bodies, as those who had been spat on by the eternal King of Terror.

CHAPTER FIFTY-TWO

The war between the two worlds saw a new level and a new high. God on His High Temple issued a new edict, a new infusion to the war zones.

God was angry. It was a passionate hatred towards the angel who was so dear to His heart. Nothing pleased the Devil much more than challenging God.

They had quarrelled often. And, they had been at each other's throat several times. Heaven, and all the planets were aware that God and the Devil were mad and hateful of each other.

The war of nerves intensified. Deep, down his heart, Satan knew that God had greater power to subdue and ruin him. But, the pride in him was too great to bow in obedience. It was contrary to his nature, since the war in heaven—the very war which he lost, and was exiled from the home on high to the miserable earth to dwell.

There was no way Satan could, again, honor God through the grace of self-volition. They were now mortal enemies, so mortal that the thought of each other re-kindled the ancient animosity that would never die. Sin of Satan was not a venial aggression. Rather, it was a flagrant violation, a brutal rebellion against the Holy of Hollies on high.

The imps were on the Devil's order to ruin the cause of God. Some angels were on God's command to redeem the lost from the hands of Devil and his faithful followers. There was cloud in the air, cloud of sorrow at four corners of the world. Bright sunshine

SUNDAY AHURONYEZE ABAKWUE

of God's love overshadowed some of those who were delivered from the deadly hands of the Devil. Their fate was sealed in that they were redeemed by His perfect wings of protection.

Some thunderous balls of eternal doom would fly from one corner of the earth and land on the other side of it. They would come in waves, roaring with awe-inspiring sound, across the smoky sky.

They were released by imps from cannons so huge, from one end of the earth's hemisphere, to land on the other end of the shaky hemisphere.

Satan had vowed by his Throne to make the world uninhabitable for God, for angels, and for God's children. He pledged his word with the power of destruction. And, he was bent on fulfilling his faithful promise. For he knew, it was quite a reprehensible phenomenon for a self-proclaimed deity to fail to fulfill a pledge and a vow he made before his own Throne. He saw God make a pledge to bring him down; and God did bring him down during the ancient war in heaven. He recognized that as a characteristic of a powerful deity, a deity who had enough power to lord over those he claimed as his own. Since then, he'd not failed to do anything he said while on his Throne, atop the idol of liberty.

And, his followers, his ever-faithful imps, were smart enough to observe, and to help him to follow through. They knew his ways, his idiosyncrasies, and even his mood swings. They knew his happy moments, and his moments of outrage. They studied and understood him the way a smart student would a teacher who had a way with quality teaching.

They called him their master, and they followed his orders and footsteps. Upon the Devil's command, the imps went into the world and possessed the minds of many. Those who became homes to the demons went out on a rampage. They burnt down the dwelling places of the faithfuls, of those who faithfully believed in One True God.

THE DEVIL'S LAND

They demolished their churches, Temples, Mosques and Ashrams. They pillaged; they maimed; and they killed. It was a mayhem on a mayday. They were on a mission of outrage; and, they unleashed wave after wave of destruction. Ruins of the demons turned the angels in heaven into a raging swing.

God, on His High Throne, looked and saw the dirty deeds of the unclean angels. He was offended; but, the unclean angels did not care. They wallowed, like dirty pigs, in the agony of the righteous. They were unpleasant in all their deeds towards God, and towards those who were faithful for the Almighty God.

They made the beautiful world unpleasant, even uninhabitable, just to fulfil the pledge of the Devil. There was sorrow written on every face of every creature called a human being. And, the Plymouth Mountain, Plymouth River, Valley and Solid Rock,

and The Rock of Ages saw a sound reason to pledge for reconciliation.

The former were the rocks of oppression; and, the latter, rock of deliverance; they pledged to take no sides in the bad blood between Lords of heaven and the lords of a ruined earth.

They pledged neutrality in the whole show. In the past, though, they had seen so much bloodshed. They had seen humanity in their worsts of creative ideation. They had witnessed sorrow, suffering, and grand scale of abominable injuries. They had saved the unsavables, and comforted those whose souls were not made for the seeds of comfort.

There was something wrong with humanity, they were able to conclude, who allowed the Devil to rule them. Indeed, they were the present witnesses of the flagship of the Devil, and the redflag of his angry mood.

In the waters, the Devil created some monstrous sharks with a mission to harass, and kill those who believed in One God. He gave them teeth of steel, and skin of iron. He gave them a body size, ten times, the size of the blue whales crated by God.

He armed them with saliva, the mouth-liquid, which could eject like a volcanic outburst, and cause some deadly damages to some distant ships, a few miles away from them.

He had enough power to reduce an Ocean to a sea, a sea to a river, and even a river to a lake, and a lake to a pond. He turned the five Oceans into Arctic pond, Pacific pond, Atlantic pond, Antarctic pond, and the Indian pond. Then, he asked God to reverse them.

He did so to show his followers that he had enough power to influence God to obey him. But, God did not. Rather, God ordered him with a thunderous voice to reverse his enchantment. And, the Devil cowered and caved in. Because, he could neither stand the power of God, nor the rebuke thereof.

He knew what God could do. And, there was a limit to his deceit, and self-pride.

*****
****

God and Devil began to intensify their war of nerves. God ordered a legion of angels to come down from heaven. When they began to come down, Devil ordered his birds of war, and floating cities to shoot them down from the open skies. About one-half of the angelic legion lost their lives in the process.

Enraged God vomited a burning fire from His mouth; and, He ordered this fire to hunt down the demons who killed His angels. And, the fire from God went forth and hunted down all the demons, and consumed them. The Devil tried to mimic his maker, but, his fire did not do a considerable damage to the host of angels.

He and God fought again. They tested their wits. They tested their resolves. They pledged the blood, and the lives of their followers to ensure victory on their individual sides. They fought in all corners of the universe.

THE DEVIL'S LAND

Rage was true on both sides. They vowed by their Thrones to fight till the end. Their eyes turned red in their quest for victory, and for the blood of their mortal foes.

They wanted to exact revenge on each other so bad that they forgot that love was nurtured with the seeds of forgiveness. The world, indeed, became an unsafe place, a war zone between the forces on high and the powers below

-It was true, as the Devil vowed he would have it. But the price he was paying to have it was too much. There was so much destruction. The Devil, God, imps, and the living angels were on a rampage. It was a state of war, the grand of which, humanity had never been a witness.

Mortified living beings went to the rivers, and begged the rivers to drown them up. But, the rivers, in turn, showed them their own sorrows in good measure—Then, as the living beings tried to plunge themselves into the flowing waters, the rivers took to flight and disappeared right before their sight. Then, many of them left the new dry land and travelled to the Oceans, and some to the seas adjacent to the Oceans.

They pleaded with the huge bodies of water to help them end their agonies. But, the sinful waters wept before them. They wept because their own burden of sins had already overwhelmed them.

They were no longer in the mood to take away lives. They began to tell their guests their own stories. They told them the number of slaves who were dumped in them, as gifts, sacrificial offerings, during the slave days. They showed the living how tempting it was to dance to the tune of the slave dealers, how good it was to drink the blood of the black slaves.

They showed the living the sword of John Newton and his Amazing Grace. They showed them how the man used his slaves in feeding the sharks on the high waves. They showed them the legacy, and the terrors of the slave trade.

SUNDAY AHURONYEZE ABAKWUE

They told the living how the notorious slave dealer was struck by God, like Saul of Tarsus, who became Paul the evangelist. They told the living creatures, humans, birds and beasts, how sins of men had ruined their chance of salvation before God.

And, then, the living pleaded with them to have mercy. There, the waters called upon the vultures to be their witnesses. The vultures came and began to plead before the seas and Oceans for forgiveness. They begged the waters to forgive them because they feasted on human flesh, the carcasses of those who were drowned, killed, and jettisoned by the slave dealers in the Oceans of outrage.

They pleaded with the Oceans as if the Oceans were the God who created them. As they pleaded in tears, the Oceans opened up their own bags of sorrow before them. The living and the vultures saw their hope of deliverance even in a worse shape. They looked at each other, and there was a mutual agreement between them.

And, without word, they agreed to outwit the waters, so as to end their own agonies. And, as they tried to plunge into the waters, the Oceans took to their heels, and disappeared right before their sight. Again, they were disappointed.

They turned to the Plymouth Rock, Plymouth Mountain, Plymouth River, Plymouth Esteemed Valley, and Solid Rock and The Rock of Ages. They told these rocks how good they were in helping humanity in times of need.

They reminded the Plymouth Rock how it rolled over and crushed some slaves, and killed most of the native Indians, how it was used in serving the cause of civilization.

Then, they told the Rock of Ages how it protected the Pilgrims in times of danger, and in times of war. They praised the rock for all the countless victories that came about because it was there for them.

And, as they talked, the two rocks asked them to close their mouths, to shut up and listen. It was first time the offsprings of the Pilgrims had heard a rock speak. Right there, each of the rocks refused to yield.

Each rock told them that it was in a worse shape than they. That it was terrified to face the burning rage of hell, because it was willing, in the first place, to harken to the whims and dictates of the sinful men. And, when the people tried to use it to end their own agonies, the rock began to protest in a loud voice.

And, then, the people began to use their metal levers to pry the rock to roll over many of their own folks. But, the rock noticed. Suddenly, there was a rocky metamorphosis. Each of the two rocks developed a pair of wings. And, with their wings, they flew away from the living.

CHAPTER FIFTY-THREE

Again, the global war gained in momentum. The ponds in the kingdom were turned into a lake of fire. The fire-fighters who had done a fine job in the past, were no more. Now, every man was in search of a way of his own deliverance. Now, greed of capitalism, coupled with its selfishness, gave themselves a new meaning.

Soon after God raided the Churches of Serpent, the Devil sent out his imps on a mission of reprisal. They began to touch all the churches where the name of God Almighty was honored.

They travelled to China, and touched all the Churches, Temples, Mosques, and Ashrams in there. They went to Africa and brought down their demonic fire with them. They ruined Alaska, Madagascar, and Ghana all alike. They demolished, not just the places of honor, they made all the places of abode in these places desolates of havoc.

Their terror made the ruins and aurae of Hiroshima and Nagasaki look like nothing but a child's play. They ruined Europe, Middle East, and Australia. They sent down balls of doom on the tombs of the patriarch, Confucius, and of the first Emperor of Japan.

They demolished the Mosque of Mohammed, ruined the spot where Jesus took flight to heaven. They raided the sepulchers of Babylon, and they made a mockery of the tomb of King Nebuchadnezzar. They visited all the holy places of India; and, they turned all these holy places into mere mockery arenas.

SUNDAY AHURONYEZE ABAKWUE

And, then, they revisited Africa with a view to greater era of demonic darkness. And, it was so. Africa saw a demonic grandeur, a darkness far greater than the five centuries of slave days.

God, in His bloody rage, could not let the Devil go scot-free. He summoned His army of angels and sent them on a mission of counter-reprisal. They were clothed with the armor of steel. Their eyes were filled with tongues of fire.

The living were terrified to see the deadly breaks of these days. Those who had gone before, the very ones who died in the Devil, dreaded the terrible rage of an offended God. All the gates of portal, where they were, were jammed and locked; and a four-headed beast was stationed at each gate of the unpardonable dead. These ugly-looking beasts had the order of God to vomit eternal fire on those who would venture to escape from the land of eternal skulls.

It was the greater beginning of a turn around of the global show. The crafty God Almighty was out to outwit the Devil in every way. In his divine candor, God proudly showed the Devil His superior wisdom, like a brilliant teacher who was only out to objurgate an obstreperous child.

He ordered His half-legion of the living angels to visit all the Churches of Serpent in the Devil's Kingdom. They went. They captured all the living members of these churches while they were worshipping the Devil through his first incarnate.

Upon God's order, they turned all the living members of the Churches of Serpent into nothing but serpents. Thus, the word of the prophets came to pass—those who worshipped them will be like them.

And, then, they visited all the Churches of Elephants, Churches of Dragons, Churches of Hermaphrodites, Churches of Commodore and their commodious, and able communards. Also, they swiftly made themselves the unwanted guests, even the lamentable ones so, in all the Churches of Ants in the Devil's Land.

THE DEVIL'S LAND

They converted all the members into the likeness of each of their objects of worship. And their mission spread far and wide, to every nook and cranny in the kingdom.

Those who had pledged allegiance to the tall idol and the triple-colored cloth of the nation were mortally terrified.

They feared for their state, their lives. Terrified in that they did not want to be turned into either an ancient idol, with a burning torch in it's hand, or into a piece of cloth, that was nothing but a piece of junk. The idol had nose, but it could not breathe; legs, but they could not walk; head, that had no brain; eyes, but they could not see. Everything about the idol was an embodiment of uselessness.

They saw how foolish they had been in following the dictates of foolish men. They lamented against the days they became American citizens. They pinched their hearts, the way the King of Lamunta pinched his own body, as a perfect expression of total self-reproach.

They could not turn to the ancient founding fathers, nor to the ancient King of the British Empire, because the men who laid the foundation, through the help of Satan, were burning in eternal rage. Sharing a like fate was the vindictive pope who ordered the carnage of the infidels. There was no hope. They had no hope, because their own world was hopeless.

And, every moment of their hopeless state was a groom in search of a disastrous bride. It was a retinue, even a house of lamentation. God was angry; the sinful world knew it. The Power on High had descended. The Devil who made fun of Him was fighting a losing war.

His mock hell had died down; and, his followers had seen him as a deceiver, a traitor, a rebel, and the father of all liars. They were now so disappointed in him as to crown their hatred of him in perfect abhorrence. They would no longer sing, nor bow before him. But, their repentance was too late. For they were rebels too.

They did not listen to the voice of the Chinese prophetess who revealed to them the nature of the beast before the nation's pool, right beside the monument of the kingdom. There was no room for them on the other side. All the days of grace were gone. They were lost, perfectly lost in the bosom of doom.

All their belated repentance, a self-reproach so late, could no longer help.

All their measure of sorrow, their penance, and heartfelt quest to be with God, were turned down. God did no longer desire them. Christ rejected them. And, the Great Prophet Mohammed, now, did no longer plead their case before God.

All the eternal seals were sealed. And, God had vowed before His own Throne never to unseal the sealed seals.

God, in His glorious rage had delivered the righteous from the terror to come. He locked up all His acts of mercy in the deepest pit of eternal doom. He resolved never to retrieve them.

The gate of the doom was sealed with a special covenant, a pact such that God Himself would die should He ever retrieve the keys of His benevolence. And, from the moment the pact was sealed, God resolved to visit the sinners with a full measure of His justice.

He visited all the dens of the Devil, done through the mission of more hosts of angels. They landed, upon God's order, to carry out the commands of their maker, the True God.

There was anger in the heart of God. It was a burning rage against the Devil, and his imps.

The fire of God went forth from every corner of the earth, all in search of the rebels, the sinners, and all the people, outside the kingdom, who had worshipped the unpardonable Beast, and his incarnates.

The Beast was damned by God, the second time. He was wounded in the battle, and his left hand of wickedness was bleeding quite profusely. With the bleeding came forth the smoke

THE DEVIL'S LAND

of confusion, combined, and ejecting from his wounds quite simultaneously.

There, in his hand were the eternal marks, each a curse and a mark of the Beast. The curse was a signature of God that the Devil was an unredeemable reject. The mark was a sign that his fate was perfectly sealed, the first heir of eternal damnation.

CHAPTER FIFTY-FOUR

The fall of the idol brought about a change of venue of the Devil's Throne. It was transferred to a more central location, a unique and more symbolic location with view to offend God even more.

The world body, in New York City was central to global peace. United Nations was its name. On top of this building was a new place for the Throne of the Prince of Demons.

He chose here to spite God, to show God that America alone was not big enough, but the entire world was under his dominion. The spiteful Demon was out to slight his creator on a higher plane, and even on a greater scale. He launched an all-out assault on everything deemed holy by God. The King of Doom did not have to yield. Proud and determined, he sharpened his unyielding spirit to fight ahead. Ahead he launched dreadfully deadly assaults, one blow after another, on the warrior-angels who were fighting on God's side.

The land which once harbored the most of the earthly commerce was visited by ruins so huge for mortals to describe them. The balls of the Devil blasted all the solid bunkers, built by the Kingdom, during its hay days. All the underground safety nets, the underground cities built for the Chief Executive and his henchmen, military lords and nobles of the great land, became death-traps for those who ran into them for safekeeping. And, they were demolished by the acts of the Satan's imps.

SUNDAY AHURONYEZE ABAKWUE

Satan brought to the land a cloud of terror, and a rain of burning fire. His terror consumed many trees and livestock. It devastated the sub-temperate bushland, the grand prairies, Everglades, and American forests. It turned the modern cities of New York, Chicago, San Francisco, and even the Holly Wood, all into some untouchable deserts. It sparked an earthquake in every city. And the earthquakes poured their red, molten lava on the dwelling places.

They charred the roads, fields, and lawns with ashes of the deadly eruptions. The overflowing lava of the consuming volcanic rock poured on and spread over the courts where athletic stars once came of age.

They poured over the rivers, and the aquatic organisms lost every hope of surviving in their natural habitats.

When God busted the second home of Satan's Throne, the Devil began to fly and perch, like the proud African bird, which the lgbos call 'ebelebe'; he flew and perched from one tree to another, making fun of the child-hunter, who was out to hunt him down.

Like the bird, ebelebe, first, the Devil left the ruins of the United Nations and flew to the Great Wall of China. He settled there for a while before God sent a ball of thunder to demolish the third place of the Devil's Throne.

And, then, the Devil left the Great Wall and travelled to the Kremlin in Old Russia for settlement. God saw him settle down. He waited till his Demonic Throne was put in place. Then, God sent out seven balls of heavenly thunder to do their destructive job.

Off the seven balls of God went. On the top of the Kremlin they landed. They destroyed the Kremlin, the Demonic guards, and the Devil's Throne.

Satan was slightly wounded in his waist. He bled; and his blood was mingled with the smoke of eternal rage. Then, the Devil made haste in packing up, and in moving from Russia to India.

He settled on top of the Singing Tower of India. He thought that God would not be able to find him here. He camouflaged his

Throne with the idols, and the Hidden Cities of the Great Land. There were many tourists too. These people, to him, and for his Throne, became a new addition of camouflage. He was ready, and he used them in protecting his dear Throne even more.

Ebelebe, The Devil, the jovial bird of unsettledness, was once again on the move. The kid-hunter, God, found him and pursued him. He moved from the Singing Tower to Africa in search of Tower of Babel, the Root of Perfect Confusion. But, the tower was no more. In his confusion, he left Africa to Europe, and found a transient settlement in the Land of Kangaroos.

He made the City of Brides his new home. But, sooner had he settled down when the hunter found him. He was cornered, and wounded. And, he was not ready to run again. He faced his fighter with new attitude. He began to fight like a badger. Fierce and ferocious, he faced the child-hunter like a badger fighting off a wolf that wanted to steal away his prairie dog prey from him.

He launched an assault on the weapon of an angry God. He ordered his imps to use his floating cities, angel-blasters, blaster-missiles, and birds of war to counter the onslaught. They did. And they engaged God. It was a deadly battle in Kangarooland.

As the battle raged, some of the imps changed themselves into kangaroos, and fought the angels. As they changed, however, some of the angels were confused; and they could no longer identify which were which.

In the midst of confusion, an archangel sent out an angel to the Devil's Land, to ask God for assistance. While the angel was on the way, a battalion of imps, who laid wait in ambush, took him a captive. They chained and tortured him. They injected in him the white, sinful blood of the Devil, the blood which was sealed with mortal hatred of everything eternal. And, they stamped a seal of the Devil in the tongue of the angel. They cursed him with the Devil's curse. And, then, they adjured him to curse God with his new tongue. But the angel was adamant in his refusal to do so. Then, they lit up a mock hell and cast him in there.

Satan was working overtime. It was high time God stood up to him in a way that would put an end to all his satanic foolishness. But, that was not meant to be, especially, at that time. He had, in his left hand of unrighteousness, a magnificent symbol comprising of the white color of sin, the blue color of rebellion, and the red color of damnation. The battle, which began in Kangarooland, was transported, with speed, to the Devil's Land. And, as the Devil made many a victorious again, so did he gain in confidence. He captured many angels; and, he tortured them, his own way. He humiliated his captives, and he cast them in the mock lake of eternal doom.

They were in a radical moment. And the radical moment needed some radical thoughts of imps, and even of angels. The imps unleashed a wave of onslaught on the angels.

They brought the war home to recapture their conquered home. From four corners of the Kingdom, the floating cities unleashed thunderous waves of attrition, bombarding from the air with supporting columns of birds of war. God was tangled. So were His angels. He made haste and summoned His Winds of Deliverance from His home on high.

His Winds came in waves and transported Him and His remaining angels, back to heaven. The Devil was glorious in recapturing his own land.

"This is our land," the Devil boasted, after the victory, "We can't allow coward invaders to take it away from us. God is a coward. He knew that before he came down. If he comes again, we'll chase him back to heaven. Brave warriors, isn't that so?" he billowed in his shrill satanic voice before a crowd of warrior imps.

"Yeah, we can do that," the imps billowed back.

"They came here, those cowards, to take away our land from us. This is our Kingdom.

We'll never surrender an inch of it to anybody," said the Devil, in a more billowed shrill voice.

THE DEVIL'S LAND

"Yeah, we won't," the imps billowed back.

"We're gonna rebuild. We're gonna make it stronger. We're gonna build more powerful weapons. In the place of birds of war, we'll build fighting cities. In the place of floating cities, we'll build nations on the high seas. Nothing ever will again challenge our supremacy. We'll create an order of pure race. We'll erase all the nations which fought against us during the holy war. We'll cover their land and fields with salts of retribution. We'll snow on them the greatest rage ever known to mankind. I've spoken. So shall you help me do.

We shall rebuild my Throne from the ashes of our hard-won victory. I swore by my future Throne, the entire world will be my Throne forever."

"Yeah-h-h," the imps roared in jubilation.

CHAPTER FIFTY-FIVE

There were some faithfuls left behind in the promised land. Even as the Devil reasserted his maximum control, the faithfuls prayed and worshipped in secrecy. They prayed that God should visit the world, a second time. They prayed that His own Kingdom in heaven be brought down to the earth. They prayed for themselves, the remnants who were left behind, seemingly abandoned, yet, unforgotten and unforsaken in a world ruled by the hands of the Devil.

They prayed that God would speedy the day Satan would be arrested, and jailed in the eternal doom. They fasted in secrecy, and pledged a perfect allegiance to their lone God in a far-away land.

While the few faithfuls prayed for the second coming of God, the Devil began to build a greater nation, an America that would trade the truth for patriotism. He began to build new air-roads, air-buses, air villages, air towns, and even air cities which could fly from one grand sky to the shining sky.

He built open cities which floated in the great waters of the world. He built many a metropolis, states and nations, armed with weapons of mass destruction, which floated in the open seas. He armed them with many a hidden device, which could cause them to self-destruct, if in the wrong or enemy hands.

He built new bunkers, and safety nets across his Empire. He gave every weapon a new name, an honorary name of a brave imp during the great war. And, he ordered an imp as commander of each and every new weapon.

The Devil began to dream, a day would come when he would go up to heaven, and do to God's what God had done to his kingdom. He dreamt that his second victory would be so sudden, and so unexpected. He dreamt that he would take over the Throne of God.

And, then, he began to think about how he would make heaven a second seat of his great government. He dreamt that such would happen in a twinkle of an eye. He saw himself rule both heaven and earth in his own dream. And, as he dreamt, he began to share his thoughts and aspirations with some of his hench-imps who craved to return to heaven.

He was a cautious fallen angel. He did not desire a repeat of just-ended incident. He dreamt a measure of prevention would be the ideal proposition. Therefore, he began to give room to his preventive instinct, a cautious impulse for prevention. He stationed some flying cities in the bright open skies, to watch out for next descent of angels.

Tough measures demanded tough reprisals. He armed the flying cities with enough weapons to wipe out a thousand legions of angelic army from the open skies.

Such was his measure, an enormous preparedness for a from-heaven potential eventuality. He knew, as far as he had claimed the God's world as his own, he had also contracted a date with a certain war. God would not let him steal an entire planet without him paying a price for so doing.

The demons of the Devil were trained imps. They patrolled the open skies in squads of military formation. They pointed the barrels of their weapons towards the corridors of heaven. They had their Satan's command to shoot at any movement in the skies. They were armed. They were dangerous. And, they were ready to shoot to kill.

THE DEVIL'S LAND

***

*****

****

The very task of rebuilding the Devil's Kingdom was not an easy task. He summoned fresh blood of elite intellectuals from all parts of the ruined world. He began to rebuild the demolished idol, and armed her with a larger touch.

He armed the magnificent idol with electronic gadgets to make it walk and speak like a caring woman. He recreated the idol so that it looked so beautiful, giant mermaid—a lady with a human head, hands, dancing breasts, but the tail of an Ocean shark.

He made it look like a pretty bride, the very type of most beautiful bride, who awaited to be received by a charming prince. And, the super-robust idol began to act like a human being; indeed, it became a human being, and, she began to walk like an Oriental goddess; she spoke like a royal Queen, and even with the sweet voice of a singing Zulu.

She had a tube of eternal fragrance attached to her tail fin. And, the French cologne magnets vowed to supply her with the nice-smelling liquid till eternity. And, they did.

Her hair, blond, and curly. Wavy, each strand of her hair shone like a gleaming armor, even like the long, brilliantly dark hair of a Japanese Empress. Yes, her hair were more lustrous than the filaments of a Beauty Queen, and even more gorgeous than that of a Priestess of a Shinto Temple.

Her porous tail emitted, at each passing moment, the pleasant fragrance of the French's best. And, her body shone like the plump body of the most beautiful Calabar woman who had just graduated from a one year grooming in a beauty home.

And, she was set, in her new place, with pomp and festivities. And, as soon as the Idol Of Freedom was installed, in a better, Inland Island, the 'great' new King of Britain could not help but sneer at the terrible exercise in stupidity. Indeed, it was a rocky ado without substance; this was so, because there was nothing he could now do about the lost colonies.

For one thing, really, never could he ever rule the land which Satan, in his majestic wisdom, was able to snatch away from his great-great grand-parents. For a good dose of an eminent reason, the true leader of the vast land, vowed to bring his great-great grand-parents to their knees. He did so, especially, to his arrogant great-great grant-father, with aim to spite him. He made all his distant, semi-Kingdoms, once under his great-great grand-father's iron grip, not only to reject, and even rebel against his draconian dominion. And, the devil helped them gain their independence. And, the devil used his great-great grant-parents' angry neighbors to totally bring them down, even on their knees. And, he made the 'Great King,' who trusted in God, to bow, not only before his serving slaves, but even before his former colonies.

And, the devil turned a few more events around, totally to spite the once 'Great King of English Empire.' And, now however, as time went by, all that the great-great-grand-son of the ancient king could do would only be to either complain, and whine about the whole loss; nothing else.

And, for a blessed sanity of his own mind, a pure reflection, on how things were, instead of on how things could have been, would do him a great good in a fast-changing world.

The devil began to breed a different specie of human race whose views, lifestyles, and even philosophies, and sexual orientations were farfetched from what former earth and its human beings had ever known. And, God, in his defeated state, was hard-pressed to

THE DEVIL'S LAND

believe that his former slave, Satan, could have come up with such a high degree of sexual sacrilege.

But, the devil recreated humanity in a way that would only serve his demonic tastes, and even his diabolic objectives. And, among the outcomes were new women who enjoyed having sex with only their pet dogs; men who enjoyed sexual intercourse with only their horses; and, even children who took preference in sex, only with their home-grown chicken.

And, the imps of the devil were able to make sure that these verses of sexual perversions were carried out to the fullest. And, the new ways became the new norms of the great land.

And, the new glory of the 'Newer World' became a bleeding culture turned upside-down. And, forced upon the new people, and even enforced with the shining armors of terrible threats to the lives of the new people, with either great rewards, or even some terrible punishments, the NEWER AMERICAN WAY began to spread to the entire world. And, the old African adage, that 'EVIL RUNS FASTER THAN GOOD THINGS' became so true in the newer world.

Rebuilding the Empire was a major task in the table of Satan. He began to follow his instincts and past experiences. He summoned, more often, his most-trusted arch-imps for a brainstorm.

They planned and plotted. They tasked their individual brains on how to rebuild the world in a way that it would look better than the home of God.

Now that they had secured their air-defense on high, they were no longer afraid of any raid which would come from the army of God.

They divided themselves into several units. Among them were talents in the fields of engineering, geophysics, musicologies, architectural designs, medicine, law, oral miracles, verbal beauties, and so on. They knew what to do with their talents. And, they were ready to do so.

They went out from their House of Conference; and, they travelled to all corners of the war-ruined world.

They were on a mission of new talent search, talent recruitment, and of course, on a mission to reward the willing-to-work talents. They visited all the Temples of Asian Tigers; and, they made pacts with the Imperial gods. They visited the Land of Singing Zulus, and brought them to America to sing their songs of entertainment. They travelled to Kangarooland, and brought in the black Aborigines, as the wave of new slaves.

The Nazis of German blood were brought in, in good measure, to further the quest for a pure race. To the Land of Palestine the imps went, and they came back with Jews to the American shores. As they brought in the Jews, the Jews had in their luggages the ancient blessings of Abraham, the moneymaking brains of the Jewish race.

To Japan and India the demons went, and brought back with them the electronic and computer wizards.

Also, they travelled to Tibet and China, and induced the wise men of the Orients to come to America. They went to the main land of Europe, and found the origin of the bubonic plague, and the cure for the mother of trypanosomiasis. They travelled to Africa, the forests, jungles, and white men's graves, all in quest of the origin of the deadly mosquitoes that fought for blacks during the colonial days. They spoke with the mother of all mosquitoes in Ghana, Guinea, Dahomey, and in Madagascar. She travelled with them from one African Kingdom to another. But, she kept the secret to herself.

She told the imps from America that her pledge of silence was made before God, even before the Throne of Almighty.

THE DEVIL'S LAND

The imps tried to impress her with all their victories. They told her that God had been defeated. They told her that God could no longer do anything even if she revealed the secret.

They vowed to give her all the blood of the people in all the African kingdoms, if she'd just tell them the secret. When she refused, they added, in good measure, all the people of the Kingdoms of Europe. They tried to induce her with the Crown of the British King. Yet, she kept on saying no to all their ploys and briberies. Then, they cursed her and left her.

And, before they left, they promised to kill her offspring with sprays, should they ever visit the Promised Land.

They took off back to Europe. France offered them the chance to be grateful for the first idol of liberty. They saw the way the French women kissed; they loved it.

They decided to bring in many French people to the NEWER WORLD. And, as they came in, these French men and women began to teach the Americans how to be more sexually expressive. They showed them how to kiss in public, hug from head to toe while making love, openly, in the process.

The Polish people came in with Polish condoms to zap up the new sexual revolution. Then, the French polished them with the drugs of abortion.

The aristocrats of the British land came in. They brought to the American hand their bakeries, pastries, and their lifestyles. They built their castles in Hollywood, and suburbs of the Newer World.

Then, came in the Irish. They came with their new wines. They planted the land with wine-producing crops. They built pubs, bars and grocery stores for the new wines. They sold; they drank; and they drove under the influence. They sang to the old days; and, they gossiped about each other; and they talked ill of the British when they calmed down.

The Soviets came in perfect disintegration. They came as Russians. They came as Georgians. They came as Armenians; and they 'came as war-torn refugees. Their women in the old land advertised themselves to the American boys. They did so as to get out of the old land.

There were those who came as Soviet Jews. They barely spoke good English-language; but, they were determined to leave their social Leninism far behind them. Among them were medical doctors who could not work in American hospitals, lawyers who could find jobs as janitors; Their dons of great academia could only find jobs as sweepers of the streets of the promised land. They came in; united, they rebuilt the Mighty Empire on a grander scale.

Even as they rebuilt the American Kingdom, all in luxuries and great grandeur, the Devil did not forget the noble missionaries who served him faithfully. He remembered his faithful servant, Dr. Jules. He remembered his chosen prophet, the man who brought his incarnate to a higher glory, the Righteous Reverend Aaron Acuridol.

He remembered the son of Dr. Jules, Dr. Lamun Jules, who died in jail serving him. He commissioned a living edifice in commemoration of the past missionaries whose souls were burning in eternal hell. He carved out their names in golden ink; and, he caused the edifice to be fixed at the left hand of the kingdom's idol, the Mermaid of Freedom, of the Great Land.

Wherever the mermaid went, the people who saw her read the names of the three great missionaries who embodied the essence of the American dream.

Also, he honored all the Christian brethren who destroyed the holy reputation of a Christian God. He inscribed their names on a second national edifice.

He knew the ways of the Christian world, their faith in God and their loyalty in same. Through certain victorious experiences, the Devil found out, if God were to die, certain Christians would not even weep for Him. They'd given up God for a wholesale. They'd served God as hypocrites. In their midst were those who called themselves Christians, but their hidden dreams and aspirations

THE DEVIL'S LAND

were different. Dubious at heart, indeed a good number of them realized their dubious dreams by dubious means.

***

******

****

When the angels were gone, the Devil rejoiced. He began to set up a new system, a grand institution known as sex-society.

He set up a foundation that would promote oral sex, spiritual sex, and a variety of other sexual enlightenments. He commissioned his imps and human merchants of dream to build a SEX PARADISE in the Newer World. The homo-sapiens who had longed to pervert themselves sexually lent themselves to a variety of deadly sexual indulgence.

He set up the Mermaid of Freedom as the grand sex symbol of the sex-starved Newer World. He used her grand appeal to lure the world to enter in.

The merchants of dream, the new waves of immigrants passed through, between the expanded legs of the walking idol of liberty. As they passed through, she poured on them the rich aroma of her everlasting fragrance. Her fragrance was a sign, a clue that the land of the Devil was full of promise.

Again, in millions the people came from all over the world. The war which claimed millions of lives in the kingdom was over. And, indeed, the Devil was victorious. Now, the king of victory needed the people to repopulate and rebuild his kingdom. He offered the new arrivals, the J-J.Cs or Johnny Just Comers, an unlimited open space—a spacious room to roam, a spacious room to apply their talented imaginations in building a better American dream.

With the help of the special imps, they began to build some mega-structures of the Great Kingdom. They built submersible bridges, flying roads, and mansions which could jump from one location to another.

They built space-boats which could kill the powerful forces of gravity. They built underground cities where the rich, brilliant minds of the aristocrats would set their daytime worries at ease. In these cities were libraries made of diamond-glass, pubs made of gold, and swimming pools floored with onyx, plated with filaments of precious metals.

The libraries were filled with talking books which could read themselves to those who came to read them. The golden pubs had their human-like idols which were at the very best of service of the pubs' patrons. And the pools had devices which could undress the patrons, massage their bodies, and gently lift them into the warm and roomy pools. Even as they landed softly into the warm water, they were greeted with soothing sound.

And, as they were welcomed, they heard a gentle sound of a lovely music. The sound, so soothing and so beautiful. It was the music that touched and melted the hearts of those it touched.

The music drove all the earthly headaches away, even to the land of portals. It made one feel at home with oneself. "Yes, sweet yes. Love me, love. My dear, God is good. But, to hell I swear—Betcha, your life on it. Satan, our king is better," the sweet voice in the music repeated to the swimmers' many a subconscious, over, and, over again.

***

THE END